Crimson

Nights

The Crimson Series

Book 8

Georgiana Fields

ISBN:	978-1-7364600-9-2
Editor:	Mary Marvella
Cover Design:	Gina Dyer
Photography:	Gina Dyer
	Sean Pavone, Shutterstock
	StockPhotosLV, Shutterstock
	hedgehog 94, Shutterstock
	DenisProductions.com, Shutterstock
	Zwiebackesser, Shutterstock

Dedication

For everyone who has followed their dreams and never given up.

Chapter One

Cordelia drew in a deep, shuddering breath. Her face ached, and she knew she'd sport a black eye in the morning. At least she was alive. "As I said, Officer, they didn't speak. I didn't see their faces. They wore black, zipped-up hoodies, skeleton masks, and gloves. I couldn't tell if they were male, female, white, black, or green with purple polka-dots. I can tell you one had a Glock similar to the one in my nightstand. That is why we're here talking, and whoever those people were, have my car and purse."

"But not your phone?"

"No, I'd just ended a call with my ex and pocketed my phone because it was easier than sliding it into my bag with my keys in hand. My attackers must have been crouching next to my front tire because I always check for feet. I learned to do it in a self-defense class. Before I had a chance to run, one grabbed me and hit me in the face while the other snatched my purse. I was on the ground, and the next thing I knew, my car was speeding away. Neither of my attackers uttered a word."

The officer eyed Cordelia, his lips pulled into a thin slash across his face. "Ms. Parsons, please reconsider having the paramedics take you to the hospital."

"I'll be fine." She waved them off, meeting their concerned gazes. "I'm officially declining the offer of taking me to the hospital. I promise I will call my physician in the morning." When she had time. Right after she meets with Margo. Maybe.

The paramedic nodded as he picked up his gear and headed for the exit.

"I really wish you'd gone with them," the officer reprimanded.

What was his name again? She glanced at his badge. "I'll be fine, Officer Marks. This isn't my first concussion," she muttered that last part. "I could walk home. I don't live far, but I'll call a rideshare. I'll be fine. Honestly." She smiled, the action making the left side of her face ache.

"Okay. I'll file this report." The longer he perused her face, the thinner his lips grew. "You can visit the website in three to five days and print off a copy of the report." Marks held out a card to her. "You'll be notified once your car has been located."

"I activated the tracking on my vehicle. They're the ones who notified you." She didn't know why she told him, but she did. Maybe she was more rattled than she'd thought.

"Those systems make our jobs easier. Someone will notify you as soon as we locate your vehicle. Are you sure you're going to be all right?"

"I'll be fine. Thank you." Cordelia smiled through the pain for him, hoping he realized she wasn't as bad off as he thought.

He nodded, then left.

All she wanted was to get home. She opened the app one of her students had downloaded for her for the rideshare. While waiting for her ride, she made a few calls, the first to her bank. Next, she called the insurance company, giving them her information.

Today had started out fine. Well, fine-ish. She'd planned to relax all day, then enjoy a nice dinner at Francine's with Edna. But, thanks to Snot, all her plans went down the flippin' drain. She despised her ex.

Scott was a cancer that devoured everything good. It'd been almost fifteen years since their divorce, since Scott had murdered what was most precious to her and taken everything she'd owned, leaving her nearly lifeless and penniless. Now he was back, making her life a living hell. His presence stoked the hate in her to the point of destroying her very soul. If she allowed it, he would win.

Lord, she hoped this wasn't a sign of how the rest of her year would go. *Happy sucky birthday to me.*

Cordelia's phone dinged. She glanced at the screen, wishing she'd never taught her great aunt how to text.

Where r you? Said you'd be home early.

I'll be home when I'm home, Edna. Something came up. Send.

There was no way Cordelia would worry her aunt by telling her what had happened. Edna would find out when Delia made it home.

Cordelia's phone dinged again. She read Edna's text.

Is the something tall, dark, and sexy? Edna included a *GIF* of a male stripper.

No. Send.

The device rang, and she glanced at the ID, groaning. Great. Simply great. Today was just getting better and better. Her finger hovered over the reject button. If she didn't take his call, he'd just keep calling. "What, Scott?"

"Heard you had a little trouble. Just thought I'd let you know I can't come get you."

"Don't worry. I have a friend." She disconnected. "How the flippin' hell had he known?"

Her phone dinged once more. Almost too afraid to see who'd texted, Cordelia tapped on the message. It was from her bank, confirming they'd frozen her credit cards. At least something was going in her favor. The little assholes who carjacked her got her car and wallet, but they wouldn't have access to her money. Tomorrow she'd start ordering new bank cards, driver's license, and insurance card. Blast it. What else did she have in her wallet? The keys to her art studio. Well, crap. She'd just installed that lock. Damn it! Why was the universe screwing with her?

A small Honda pulled up along the curb, and the passenger side window lowered. The driver didn't look old enough to drive. "Ms. Parsons?"

"Yes." She glanced at the picture from the rideshare. At least the face matched.

"I'm James, here to pick you up."

Please, God, don't let this be a mistake. Cordelia opened the back door, slid in, and fastened the seatbelt. "Thank you for getting here so quick."

Atlanta rush hour traffic sucked, which was why she loved working from home. A horn blared, and she gripped the door handle as James weaved in between cars. He cut across three lanes of traffic to make her exit.

"Sorry, it slipped up on me." He flashed her a grin in the rearview. "If you need me to pick you up tomorrow, you can request me on the app."

"Oh, thank you." No way ever would she get in the car with him again. She wouldn't tempt fate a second time.

James pulled to a stop in front of her home. The simple two-story brick house had never looked better.

"Thank you," Cordelia replied. Even speaking made her face hurt. The rest of her muscles protested as she unfolded from the tiny car. Why had she dressed up today? Because it was her flippin' birthday, and she wanted *Snot* to see how well she was doing without his sorry, abusive ass.

Blast it! Wasn't it the truth? Since her freedom, her creativity had exploded to the point her sculptures were in several galleries. Edna had been right all along. Scott was an incubus. It was bad enough he'd siphoned off her savings, but he'd also drained Cordelia's creativity, leaving her an empty, unmotivated shell. Within three months of leaving him, Cordelia regained her desire to live and create. Within a year, she had her own art studio and submerged herself in sculpting. Granted, her studio was the small free-standing garage the previous homeowners had built in the backyard. She wished it had windows, but it had electricity.

Every step Cordelia took in her heels seemed like miles. Perhaps she could make it inside before one of her neighbors spotted her. Their small neighborhood was old, but her neighbors were friendly. Too friendly sometimes. Several blinds and curtains fluttered as she inched toward the front door. She noticed a man's dark silhouette peering from the house beside hers. The house had sold. The new owner, maybe? The only good thing about nosy neighbors, they helped deter crime.

A dark red Bentley caught her eye as it slowly came down the street. Someone had money. If Snot saw her driving his dream car, he'd die. Hmmm, wonder how much it would cost to rent one?

Cordelia exhaled the moment she stepped inside the sanctuary of her home. A hot bath, then bed. No. A hot shower. As battered as she felt, she might not have the strength to crawl out of the tub. She shut the door and leaned against it. Dang, she wasn't looking forward to facing her aunt.

"About time you made it home," Edna shouted from the kitchen. "The party you went to must have been a doozie."

"It wasn't a party." Cordelia opened her eyes and pushed from the door. The subtle movement shot pain through her.

"Happy birth—Hell's bloody bells!" Edna hurried across the room. "Did that bleeding bastard do this to you?"

"No, Scott didn't. Someone carjacked me."

"Humph. He probably hired the bastards, just like he did the knobs who broke into your studio."

"I'm thankful whoever broke in didn't steal or damage anything." Delia massaged her temples, wanting to go to bed.

"What did snot-face want *this* time?"

"Same old song and dance. Now, he's saying I plagiarized his sculpture, *Phoenix Rising* with my *Flight of the Peacock*."

"Isn't it the one the Baldwins commissioned and gave you the photograph?"

"Yep. Patsy and Luke shut him down by pointing out every difference between the two pieces. The only similarity the two statues have is the long tails, which are different. But Snot insisted the two were twin pieces and demanded fifty percent of my commission. Luke shrugged and told him we'd see him in court. Scott and his lawyer got up and stormed out. I just know he has something else up his sleeve. The man's an absolute douche bag. The interesting thing he knew was I'd purchased a new kiln."

"Proving he'd seen the inside of your studio. Well, let your lawyers handle him. I think putting Snot-face in his place gives them the jollies." Edna glanced at the wall clock and cringed.

"You've best not have planned a party with the neighbors." All Delia needed was for them to see her with two black eyes. She'd be the talk of the cul-de-sac.

"The neighbors think I'm crazy." Edna slid her withered hand to the small of Cordelia's back. "Come on with you. Let's go into the kitchen where the light's better so I can have a better look at your face."

The doorbell rang, and Edna shouted, "Who is it?"

"Birthday," a male's voice cracked. "Special-Gram."

"What have you done?" All Cordelia wanted was to go to bed.

"Don't be cross." Edna flung the door wide, revealing a man dressed in a cheesy police uniform. "*Hiya*, you're a looker. After the day Delia's had, you'll do nicely. Just don't stare at her face, love."

"Edna?" Cordelia would wring her aunt's neck.

Her conniving aunt covered her mouth and giggled like a schoolgirl. "I ordered him for your birthday, Dilly." Edna flicked her hand at the man—boy. "You can start stripping."

"Oh, heaven's no!" Delia glared at the man. His October-sky-blue eyes had her wishing she were twenty-five again. "You keep your clothes on. I don't need to see your jiggly parts. Matter-of-fact, leave."

"Delia, I don't think any part of him jiggles. I bet he's all nice and hard."

"Edna!" Her aunt was right. Cordelia could make out the man's hard muscular body through the cheap costume.

"What?" Edna flicked her hand at him. "Just look at him, Delia. I bet…What's your name, son?"

"Glen."

"I bet Glen has a multi-pack under his shirt. Go ahead, Glen. Take your shirt off and show her."

"Edna, please?" Cordelia huffed. "It's bad enough I turned double nickels, but with everything else that's happened today— I don't need this." She thrust her finger at him or where he'd been standing. Where the heck did he go?

He'd slid around her and Edna, heading toward the kitchen.

"But I paid good money."

"Edna! My head is throbbing enough without dealing with your antics." Cordelia marched into the kitchen, her head pounding with every step.

She found her unwanted guest rummaging around in her freezer. "What the flipping heck do you think you're doing?"

"Getting you an ice pack." His deep Scottish brogue weakened her knees. Either that or she was about to faint. "Your wound is bleeding." He wrapped the freezer pack in a dishtowel, then handed it to her. As he perused her face, he slid out one of the kitchen chairs. "Sit."

"I don't need a boy scout, but thank you. You can leave now, and don't worry, I'll give you an excellent review."

He stared down at her. "What happened?"

She tilted up her chin, staring right back at him. His eyes were so blue she could get lost in their depths. Dang, ink-black hair and sky-blue-eyes, could he be any cuter? "None of your business."

Edna flopped down into one of the other kitchen chairs. "Someone carjacked her. They nicked her purse and bopped her in the noggin. Delia, stubborn as always, refused to go to hospital."

"Would you like to tell him my height and weight, too, Edna?"

"There's no need to be cross."

The boy scout's lips thinned, and under the harsh kitchen light, his eyes seemed to glow with a hint of red. "You realize the robbers have your license, giving them your address?"

"Really? I didn't know, Captain Obvious." She shouldn't be snarky to the boy. He probably meant well, which meant his momma raised him right.

Her aunt gave her *the look* before smiling at the boy. "Scotland?"

"Aye. Are you over here visiting?"

"Oh, no. I came here after The Second World War." Edna twisted the ring on her finger and sighed with the same faraway look she always got when speaking of England. "You look so much like a young man I knew. His name was Glen, too."

Cordelia cleared her throat. She'd always meant to take Edna back for a visit, but life seemed to impede her plans. One of these days. "Yes, well, *this* Glen is leaving. Now."

"Stop being ugly, Delia."

Her unwanted guest glanced around the kitchen. Glen's attention lingered on the windows and back door. The action unnerved her. "They have your keys. You should have your locks changed tonight or no later than in the morning. You should also reset your garage opener. It wouldn't take me long to do everything for you tonight."

"Not your problem, boy scout." He was right, though. If the person or people were brazen enough to mug her in front of a busy law office, what's to say they wouldn't invade her home?

Glen reached behind him and groaned. "I've left my mobile in the car, along with my clothes. Before I leave, is there a place I might change?"

"Yes, at *your* home," Cordelia replied. She hadn't meant to sound so sharp, but she just wanted him gone so she could have a hot shower and break down.

He chuckled and nodded. "Happy birthday, Cordelia." As he turned, the Velcro gave at his hip, revealing the thin strap of a black thong and a very muscular butt cheek. He caught her looking and winked as he pulled the seams together.

Dang. Busted.

Her aunt's eyes widened with her grin. "You can change here. In the kitchen."

"Oh, for Pete's sakes, Edna. We're both old enough to have changed his diaper." Cordelia tried not to laugh. Glen probably had hoped to perform in front of a bunch of twenty-somethings. Instead, he got two crotchety old women, one of who was acting like a nymphomaniac. "You can change in the bathroom under the steps."

"Thank you. Let me grab my things." He hurried toward the front door while holding the costume seams together. It was tempting to lock the poor boy out.

"But I paid for him to strip." Her aunt crossed her arms over her chest. "I wanted the full Monty."

"Edna, please."

The moment the front door closed behind Glen, Edna's eyes crinkled with her grin as she fanned herself. "He is a looker. Isn't he?"

"Yes, he is. But what I need is a hot shower and sleep."

"Are you sure you don't want me to have him strip? I mean," Edna sighed. "I don't think you feel up to going out for your birthday dinner, not with the goose egg rising over your left eye."

"I'm positive. As for dinner, we can go out later in the week." She gently touched the welt. "Dang, that stings. Maybe this will be gone by then."

A quick knock on the door had Edna out of her seat. "His mum raised him right." She hurried from the kitchen. "Please don't think poorly of Delia."

"Never."

Great. Cordelia sighed. Now the kid pitied her.

The bathroom door clicked closed, and Edna strolled over to the stove.

"I think I'll put the kettle on for tea. You look like you could use some."

"I could use something stronger."

She jumped when her phone rang. "Now what?" The last thing Cordelia needed was to deal with another issue or a nosy neighbor.

"I've got it." Edna snatched up the annoying device. "Hello. No, you cannot, Snot. She's busy, and I will not interrupt her. Goodnight." Edna powered off the phone. "That put his knickers in a wad."

"Did Scott say what he wanted?" Cordelia was almost afraid to ask.

"He wanted to speak to you." Edna sighed. "I wished you hadn't put the kibosh on Glen stripping. I paid good money, and I think it would have put a smile on your face." She pulled the familiar pink and white Harney and Sons tea tin from the cabinet.

"You'll get over it." Cordelia chuckled. She wondered if Glen was built as nicely as she'd imagined. What was she thinking? She was old enough to be his mother. She shook her head and focused on Edna's chipped ruby Wedgwood teacup and glued-together saucer sitting on the lone shelf. They were the only items she had of her family. The gold edging on the cup still gleamed after all these years. The battered cup and saucer reminded Delia so much of her life.

"You *dinna* have to worry about it."

Cordelia jumped at the sound of Glen's voice.

Glen strode into the kitchen, looking ever so handsome. His tight jeans and black t-shirt left nothing to her imagination. His biceps were as thick as her thighs, and some sort of tattoo peeked from under his short sleeves. She could make out every chiseled line of his rectus abdominis muscles through his shirt. The man didn't have an ounce of fat on him. What Cordelia wouldn't give to sculpt him. Better yet, what she wouldn't give to be twenty years younger.

When he caught her checking him out, heat rushed to her face.

"I'll make sure you're reimbursed, Edna." Glen had the audacity to wink.

Her aunt giggled. "Would you care for some tea, Glen? The water should be ready in a few minutes. And we have Bakers lemon biscuits." She pulled the red phone box cookie jar towards her.

"No, thank you."

"Oh." Crestfallen, Edna slid the cookie jar back. She did love her sweets. "You never told us your last name."

"Edna," Cordelia warned. If she didn't keep an eye on her aunt, the woman would have the man over for dinner every night. *What would be wrong with that? No, no, and heck no.*

"It's MacPhee—"

"MacPhee. Glen MacPhee," Edna whispered, twisting the ring on her finger. "How…peculiar. I knew a Glen MacPhee once. He was one of my boys. What do you do for a living other than taking off your clothes?"

"Edna!" Dear God, sometimes Cordelia couldn't believe what came from her aunt's mouth.

"I run a security company."

"I see. Perhaps in time it will be profitable, and you wouldn't need to moonlight as a birthday-gram stripper—"

"Edna!"

"What?" Her aunt gasped. "Why else would he be doing this?"

Glen's rich, deep laugh filled her kitchen and did things to Cordelia's insides. Her attention flickered to his face. Ah, crud, the man even had dimples. She'd bet he had a million girls falling over him, or with her luck, he was gay. Or married, but no ring. She cared? Why?

"Ms. Parsons," Glen's deep voice washed over her. "a word of advice. When making a bet with family, ensure you know the terms of the bet before agreeing."

His blue eyes, rich brogue, and sexy-as-hell grin had her so flustered she could hardly think straight. She was a mature woman, not some hormonal teen who wanted to run her fingers through his black hair. "It's Delia, and I'll keep that in mind." She scooted her chair back and stood. "I'll see you to the door." At least she'd have something to dream about for a long time.

"He can't leave, Delia," Edna huffed. "He has to change our locks."

Cordelia dropped her chin to her chest and drew in a deep breath. There were days—Lord knew there were days. "I'll have a locksmith come by tomorrow."

Edna planted her hands on her rounded hips and stomped her foot. "What if someone uses your keys tonight and ravishes me?"

"Edna, please." Cordelia glanced at Glen, noting the twitch of his lips. At least he had the good grace not to laugh in her aunt's face. Now, if she could just get him out the door.

"This is my home, too. I'll even pay for it." Edna reached into her pants pocket, pulling out a wadded-up bill. She waved it at Glen like a stripper's tip. "We have three doors, four counting Delia's art studio. I want the best locks. Here's twenty dollars. This should be sufficient to cover the cost, and you can keep the change."

"Edna, will you please stop?" Cordelia snapped. "I just want to go to bed. We'll get the frigging locks changed later." She didn't wait for her sexy boy scout to follow as she stormed toward the front door. Her face hurt. Heck, her whole body hurt, which added to her anger.

Cordelia's fingers scarcely brushed the doorknob when some idiot leaned on the doorbell. The shrilled sound drove an ice pick through her brain. She yanked open the door and groaned. "What, Scott?"

"The crone said you were busy." He loomed over her, trying to intimidate her but failing miserably. Those days were long gone.

"I am." Cordelia slammed the door. What had she ever seen in him? More importantly, why had she stayed married to the ass for as long as she had?

The door flew open, nearly striking her.

"Don't ever slam the door on me again, Cordy," her ex shouted, raising his hand.

One second Cordelia stared at Scott. The next, Glen's back blocked her view.

Chapter Two

This male is a threat to what is ours. We should kill him.

For once, Glen agreed with the daemon who shared his soul, but agreeing with the creature and doing as he said were two different things. There were rules to follow. Besides, killing Cordelia's ex in front of her and Eddie would not win them brownie points.

Not a problem. We kill him when they're not looking.

This is why I'm in control, and you're bloody aren't. Glen reminded his pain in the arse daemon.

Do you think Eddie recognizes us?

Doubtful. "Glen MacPhee." He held out his hand to the *nyaff* in front of him as he sized up the intruder. Glen knew all he needed about the self-serving narcissist in less time to draw a breath. "Daemon Securities." He didn't hold back the creature's growl from his voice.

"Daemon Securities?" The prick arched his perfectly manicured eyebrows and stepped to the side.

Glen mirrored the movement, blocking the ass from entering. Had Cordelia wanted the man in her home, she wouldn't have slammed the door in his face.

Cordelia eased beside and slightly behind Glen. "Go away, Scott."

"Seriously, Cordy? It's bad enough you throw good money away on a kiln. Now, you hire the most expensive security company because your car was stolen, but you refuse to pay me my due?"

"*Your* due? You're due nothing."

Eddie marched toward the arse, only to have her path blocked by Cordelia. "How do you know Delia purchased a kiln unless you were the one who broke into her studio?"

"Edna," Cordelia warned.

Scott cut his cold brown eyes toward Glen. "I thought Daemon Securities only provided bodyguards."

"Among other things." Glen stared the man down, committing his image to memory. He didn't have a hint of gray in his professionally dyed brown hair, and from the tightness of his forehead and around his mouth and eyes, he'd had some serious plastic surgery. Though he had upper arm and chest muscles, the rest of him had gone soft, major dad bod.

Glen couldn't see the arse doing his own dirty work. He'd hire someone to do it for him. The daemon just might get his wish, after all. Especially if he was the one behind her attack and break-in. "The lady asked you to leave."

"Oh, I'm leaving," Scott sneered. "And heading right back to my lawyers to inform them who Cordy has hired. I just might get another zero added to my demands."

"Precisely what you're getting, a big fat zero." Edna darted around Glen. "Delia didn't hire him," she jabbed her bony finger into Scott's chest. "I did. Now, bugger off, you gormless, cockwomble."

"You? I didn't realize Social Security paid that much." Scott backed from the door.

Glen watched him stroll down the street toward an older model black Mercedes. A few seconds later, he squealed tires, peeling away from the curb and nearly sideswiping Cade and Paul as they parked.

"Thank you, but you didn't need to get involved." A sad expression formed on Cordelia's beautiful face. "Scott's a yapping dog whose bark is worse than his bite."

"You should put more ice on your wound."

She lifted her fingers, lightly touching the swelling over her left eye. "Is it oozing again?"

"No, but it would help the swelling." A few drops of his blood would ensure her healing, but he kept that information to himself.

Glen rolled his eyes, staring at Paul and Cade as they strolled toward the house, carrying more equipment than needed. From the looks, they'd cleaned out the supply room.

"Oh, good grief. I don't need any more visitors," Cordelia muttered. "If y'all are coming here, you can keep moseying along," she shouted.

Glen motioned to Cade and Paul. "They work for me. I sent them a text while I was changing. Once they replace your locks, we'll be gone." He may have overstepped *just* a bit. However, after witnessing Cordelia's ex's threat, there was no way Glen would leave his mate unprotected. Mate! By the saints, he had a mate, a gorgeous, dark-haired siren. Her exotic looks had him drooling.

Cade and Paul were laughing and joking with each other as they approached. This was Glen's lucky day. He'd finally found his eternal mate, and his two problematic employees weren't trying to kill each other. Bloody hell, he might spend a pound and buy a lottery ticket—not that he needed the money.

Cordelia squared her shoulders, glaring at him. He'd guess she stood about five foot seven in bare feet. Perfect. But then everything about her was perfect. "I told you no."

He didn't miss the silken thread of warning in Cordelia's voice or the ire burning in her dark brown eyes. The last thing Glen wanted was to make Cordelia's day worse for her. He had to think fast.

"I told him yes," Edna replied. She shoved her hand into the front pocket of his jeans. "If you don't want the money," she grinned at Glen as she slowly withdrew her withered hand. "You can give it to them to split."

His daemon shook off the feeling of being accosted by Eddie. The ole girl had given them an in with their mate, so he couldn't be too upset by her actions.

"Fine," Cordelia snapped. "But we're not paying a penny more than what Edna has already given you."

"Oh, my." Edna fanned herself. "Are all of your employees so devilishly handsome? It's enough to make an old woman drool."

"Oh, for heaven's sakes! Edna Cooper, act your age."

Glen watched the sway of Cordelia's hips as she stormed off toward the kitchen. The power suit she wore accentuated her perfect body. Cordelia had curves in all the right places. He couldn't wait to strip her and feel the weight of her breasts in his hands. The only thing he didn't like about her was how she wore her hair. The severe bun she wore looked painfully tight. *Wonder what she does for a living? From her clothing, she probably works in an office.*

"Oh, bollocks! Go about your business, and I'll tend to Delia. I think I've mucked up a bit." Edna hurried toward the kitchen.

Paul chuckled. "The older one's a hoot. The other one is a—"

"Mine," Glen growled.

"Wonderful, beautiful, lady."

Cade's eyes widened, nearly as big as the grin splitting his face. "Congratulations." He pounded Glen's back.

"Ah, we brought the locks you asked for, but," Paul lowered his voice to a whisper. "Do you think the older one can remember a five-digit code, or should we also activate the biometric system?"

"We'll use both the passcode and the biometric." Edna had been one of the best damn female soldiers Glen knew during World War II. He stared at the shadowbox hanging over the fireplace. Memories of a war he wished he could forget flooded his mind. He stared at the tattered Union Jack, Auxiliary Territorial Service cap badge, rank insignia, Royal Artillery's white braided lanyard, and grenade collar badge. Mementos that were carefully preserved. Glen mentally shook himself. Bloody hell, he'd like to know what had happened to Edna. She'd just disappeared one day. Glen couldn't ask tonight without leaving himself open for questions he wasn't ready to answer. "As for Edna, let's find out if she can remember a passcode."

Glen grabbed the tool bag and headed toward the kitchen. He found Cordelia sitting at the small table, her mobile held to her ear.

"Thank you. I understand. No, it's fine. I'll figure something out." She ended the call, dropping the device on the table. "Flippin' darnation! Can this day get any worse?"

"More bad news?" Glen placed the bag on the floor, wanting to pull Cordelia into his arms. He would. Soon. Very soon.

"Good and bad." Cordelia rubbed her fingers against her temples. "My car's been located. Unfortunately, the carjackers torched it. The good news is my insurance company deemed it totaled, and according to the representative I just spoke with, it's worth more than I thought. Bad news, they won't send a loaner because the only card not locked is the reloadable one I used to pay the rideshare, and the rental company can't use it."

"Not the birthday I'd planned for you, Dilly." Edna set a toasted crumpet in front of Cordelia. "Let me get the kettle. The water should be hot enough."

"I'll get it," Glen offered. He couldn't erase today's events, but he bloody well could ease his mate's pain. "Real quick question. These are the locks I'd like to install." He pulled one from the duffle, setting the box in front of Cordelia. "They're keyless, so we'll need to set a passcode for you. We can use one, or you both could have your own codes. These locks also have a biometric system, but if you have on gloves—"

"Thumbprints wouldn't work." Cordelia glanced up at him, meeting his gaze. "I've been researching these particular locks. They're a tad more than what Edna gave you."

He shrugged. "A wee bit."

Edna slid the box toward her. "They'll look nice on the house, and I know precisely what my code will be."

"You like them. Good. Cade, Paul, set up their passcodes and prints." Glen picked up the tea tin. "Is this the tea you want?"

"It is." Cordelia nodded. "Edna's already filled the strainer and warmed the pot."

While Paul and Cade had the women's attention, Glen shifted the nail on his index finger, pricking his thumb. Several drops of his blood fell onto the tea leaves. The small amount of blood wouldn't heal Cordelia completely, but it would ease her pain and speed her recovery. He poured the hot water over the leaves, then placed the lid on the small teapot before carrying it to her. "Let it steep for a few minutes."

Paul and Cade grabbed the tools they needed. Paul headed toward the living room while Cade worked on the kitchen door.

It didn't take Cade long to drill out the box and replace the lock. "Who wants to be the first to try it out?"

"Oh, let me." Edna followed Cade outside.

Cordelia wrapped her hands around the teacup. "Thank you for doing this. Please send me the bill. Like I said, I know how expensive those locks are."

The kitchen door creaked open. "Delia, this is brilliant! Come see if your fingerprint works."

"Later." She lifted the cup to her lips.

Glen didn't like how drained Cordelia appeared, but at least the knot over her eye was shrinking. "Actually, we need to ensure all the locks work for both of you. Come on. The sooner we ensure everything is functioning properly, the sooner we'll be out of your hair."

"Since you put it like that."

The second Cordelia took his hand, Glen's daemon roared in his mind. Lightning shot up his arm. Over the years, he'd teased his sisters miserably about the romance novels they read. Bloody hell, if those damn books didn't have it right.

"Are we going to check the locks?" Cordelia asked, staring up at him. "Or are we just going to hold hands?"

Heat rushed through Glen's body. "Just making sure you were steady on your feet."

"I installed my locks," Paul announced, dropping his tools into the duffle. "I'll go give Cade a hand."

"Right." Cordelia pulled her hand from Glen's and followed Paul out the door, shutting it behind her.

Edna peered at Glen. "You fancy my niece, do you?"

He'd never deny it. "Aye. I do."

"Slight age difference." She laughed.

He shrugged. If you consider over three hundred years as slight, but he wasn't counting.

The kitchen door opened, and Cordelia stepped inside. "Works like a charm. Come along, Edna. Let's see about the other two doors so these men can leave."

"What about your studio?" Edna followed Cordelia down the hall.

"If these work, I'm sure it will as well."

Glen would leave, but he'd be back. Soon.

He pulled out his business card and dropped it on the table before searching out his mate. He found Cordelia and Edna testing the front door. "Everything working all right?" He hoped it wasn't but knew otherwise.

"Like a charm." Cordelia held the door open. He could take the subtle hint. *Cade, Paul, what's the hold-up?*

We're coming in now. Cade's voice echoed in Glen's mind as the back door closed. A second later, both joined him. "Everything's packed."

"All right." Glen's daemon roared, pacing in the back of his mind, demanding they stay the night. Glen had to come up with an excuse to return, and fast.

"Miss Parsons." Cade cleared his throat. "Did you paint the wolf in your studio? It's beautiful."

"Thank you. I dabble a little with oils."

"I wouldn't call that dabbling," Paul added. "I could almost see the wolf breathing. You're good."

"Thank you." Cordelia's cheeks pinked.

Edna gasped. "You don't have a car. What are you going to do about your meeting with Margo Sinclair? You're to meet her at the gallery tomorrow to discuss your exhibit."

"I'll work something out, Edna. Goodnight, gentlemen."

"Good night," Paul and Cade spoke in unison as they exited.

Glen paused. His luck couldn't be this great. "Ivy and Rose Art Gallery?"

"Yes." Cordelia's forced smile clearly warned he treaded on thin ice.

"I have to go by there tomorrow, as well. What time is your appointment?"

Edna's face lit. "She has to be there at ten."

This was bloody brilliant. "Perfect. I'll pick you up at nine." He bent down, pressing a quick kiss to Cordelia's cheek. "Happy Birthday." The second he was over the threshold, Cordelia slammed the door. He might have overstepped it there.

Dinna look back. Keep moving. He urged his daemon forward.

We should go back. Our mate's not pleased with us.

If we go back, she definitely won't be pleased. Glen started his car. He glanced back at her home, noticing a solitary light flick off at the house beside Cordelia's, piquing his curiosity.

Glen had already put his foot in it. If Cordelia peered out her window and saw him sitting here, he'd be up to his neck. He pulled away from the curb and headed home. With luck, he'd have some fascinating dreams about his mate tonight.

"I have a mate! I have a beautiful, feisty mate," he shouted. It'd been two years since he moved to Atlanta. After living most of his life in Europe, he thought he'd miss it. He didn't. The only thing he missed was his family. But he wasn't alone. He had Fiona, Percy's sister, who was just as conniving. Conniving, underhanded, and a bloody pain in his arse. Earlier tonight, he wanted to rip her heart out through her nose! Now he'd give her a raise.

It was Fiona's fault Glen was put in a sticky wicket. "Oi," he pitched his voice high, mimicking hers. "it's just a flutter. A teensy wager. What will it hurt?"

Him! That's who. Had he known he'd be finding his mate tonight…Shite! Cordelia's first impression of him was in a tacky Velcro police costume. She must think him a nutter. Who said God didn't have a sense of humor?

Glen's mobile rang, and Royce's name flashed on the information panel. "You're up late," Glen greeted his cousin.

"Name, age, occupation, and when are you bloody mating her?"

"Hell's bloody bells! How?"

Royce chuckled. "Cade texted Chase. Chase told his mate, and the rest is well…you know."

"Yeah, I know. Stacy told Jenny who told you."

"Actually, Chase told Stacey and Caitlin first, and Stacey rang Brat."

"Bloody hell. Knowing my sister, she's told Mum." So much for his good luck.

"Which is why the women nominated me to interrogate you, since the only thing Cade said was you'd found your mate."

"Her name is Cordelia Parsons. She's beautiful, sexy, has big brown doe eyes, and comes up to my shoulders." He didn't know what else to say. Delia was perfect.

"And," Royce prompted.

In for a penny. In for a pound. "I found Eddie."

"Piss off! What happened to her?"

"I *dinna* know, but she's still wearing Whitaker's ring and using her maiden name. Cordelia's her great-niece."

"Her great-niece?"

Glen lived too far away to read Royce's mind, but the tone of those three little words said so much. "Cordelia's fifty-five. Beautiful, sexy, strong, intelligent, and perfect."

"And likely not able to give you a child."

"Royce." Glen didn't want to have this discussion.

"Quaid is wrong. We removed the fragments, and you healed," Royce repeated his mantra as if his words had magical powers.

The knife twisted deeper into Glen's chest. War was hell and shrapnel was the devil's blades. The metal shards have long been removed, his scars faded, but the damage was done. "You know as well as I do that I should have died that day. We lost so many on that cursed beach. Eighteen of us died at Normandy. Aileen and David lost their son, William."

"You don't have to remind me. I still see their faces and hear their screams as they crumbled to dust." Royce's voice hitched before he cleared his throat. "Did Quaid recheck you after Jenny healed your vision?"

Jacking off into a test tube wasn't Glen's idea of fun. "Not all of us get second chances. I've accepted my fate and thanked God and *Yeva* for blessing me with such a perfect mate. If we are blessed with a *bairn*, I'm sure it will be a child like Michael or Hope, a child who needs a loving home."

"Look, I'm not pissing on your news. I know how you are with the kids. I've seen the longing in your eyes. Glen, it gutted me when Jenny lost our child. It guts me every bloody time she loses a baby to the point—to the point I called Quaid asking him…By the grace of Yeva, we have Michael."

"You lecture me about what I have no control over, yet you've given up yourself." Had Glen uttered those words to Royce's face, he'd be holding Glen's heart in his hand.

"It's not giving up." The pain lacing Royce's voice had Glen wishing to call back his words. "It's caring for my mate."

"Jenny's stronger than you give her credit for being. Much stronger."

"When do we get to meet your mate?"

"Saints, Royce, I just met her tonight."

"Brilliant! We'll see you in a couple of weeks."

"Oh, piss off." Glen ended the call.

Shite Royce ripped the plaster off and rubbed salt in the wound. Glen shifted gears and took his exit. He pulled into his condo's complex. A car with its light off sped through the gate before it closed behind him. *Let's see if the rabbit chases the fox.* Glen circled the parking deck twice before heading to his section. No ID-ing the driver, as he wore a hoodie with a skeleton mask. No one dressed for Halloween in April for any legitimate reason.

Glen parked and got out of his car, locking it. The mystery car rolled slowly toward him. Glen had only seen a driver but heard two heartbeats. Unless the guy behind the wheel was pregnant, someone in the car didn't want to be seen.

Not looking back, he continued toward the elevator bank. The subtle click of a car door opening and soft footfalls rushing up behind him had his daemon itching for a fight. *Oh, tonight keeps getting better.*

Glen took two steps before a pistol pressed firmly to the center of his back.

"Keys," a young male demanded.

Fear permeated the air. The bloody knob was petrified.

In a smooth motion, Glen turned. Before the kid knew what happened, Glen had the boy pinned with the pistol pressed to his temple. From the trembling kid's build, he couldn't be over fourteen. "You picked the wrong bloke to rob. I used to be paid to kill people. Now I do it for shits and giggles. Ah, the sweet, pungent smell of piss. Bloody good thing you didn't get none on my boots."

The driver threw the car in reverse, squealing tires and hitting several cars as he sped toward the exit.

"*Dinna* worry, kid. Your friend isn't going far. While I was circling, I rang the cops. Told them they'd best get here fast if they didn't want to involve the coroner."

The words no sooner left his mouth than a police cruiser came into sight. The officer hit the siren and flashed his lights, as if Glen couldn't see the bloody black and white. He pulled the barrel from the kid's head but held him firm. "If I let go of this little bitch, you're chasing his ass down Peachtree."

"MacPhee, you're a crazy mother." Thomas Marks exited the patrol car. "This crew's been busy today." He pulled his cuffs from his belt as he approached. "They carjacked a woman around four. Pistol-whipped her. We found her car torched."

Amber Jones silently followed in Marks' wake, eyeing the pistol dangling from Glen's finger. He liked her. She was an excellent officer who observed everything.

Had we known these were the same punks who'd harmed our mate...we would have dealt with them. His daemon snarled.

We dinna harm children, even ones who threaten ours. Glen reminded the creature.

The disadvantages of being a good guy.

"Your weapon?" Marks asked, handcuffing the kid.

"Please. *Dinna* insult me. It belongs to Skeleton boy." Glen handed Jones the pistol.

She secured it before placing it in an evidence box. "It's not the weapon used on the first victim. The VIC said that was a Glock."

"Yeah, well, everything can't be easy," Marks replied. "Maybe Davis will have better luck with the driver. Let's see who we have here." He pulled the mask down from the kid's face. "Luka, Luka, Luka, following in your older brother's footsteps."

"My father's gonna have your badges." He jerked from Marks' grip and whirled on Glen. "You're a dead man."

Glen dipped his gaze to Luka's urine-soaked jeans. "Brave words for someone who's pissed himself."

"Come on, Luka. You know the drill." Jones led the kid toward the car. "You have the right to remain silent—"

Marks perused Glen. "Been meaning to ask. What did you do before moving to the States?"

"Law enforcement like you. Scotland Yard."

"And before Scotland Yard?" Marks' face remained expressionless, but his pulse quickened.

"Classified." Glen had plans to make. The last thing he wanted to do was tearin' the tartan with Marks.

"Classified by who?"

"The Crown, your government, and a few others. What's the deal with the kid?"

"Luka Petrov, his parents have more money than common sense or parenting skills. Come on, let me get your statement."

Chapter Three

Cordelia gasped as her body spasmed with release. Her fingers dug into Glen's rock-hard shoulders as she stared into his ice-blue eyes.

"Damn, ye' beautiful." His rich brogue caressed her.

Her body peaked again, and she cried out. She woke with a start. Her heart pounded, and she tried to steady her breathing. Wow! May all of her dreams be so...orgasmic. Was that even a word? During her entire marriage to Scott, she never had an orgasm so intense, and the ones she'd just enjoyed were from a dream. Good grief! If wet dreams were a part of menopause, she wouldn't dread it anymore.

Cordelia sat up and stretched, glancing at the space beside her. The Glen in her dreams had just the right amount of hair dusting his chest. She wasn't a fan of tattoos, but the Celtic knot design, circling his biceps, was downright sexy. Good heavens, she couldn't believe she'd nipped the inked clan badge he had over his heart. She wondered if the real Glen had the rampant proper Demi lion encircled with the motto *pro rege*. Perhaps she'd been too quick last night in her insistence he'd not strip. "What am I thinking? I sound like Edna."

She tossed back the covers and made her way into the bathroom. Cordelia flipped on the light and flinched, closing her eyes to the brightness. She turned toward the mirror, dreading what she'd see. Cordelia slowly peeked at her reflection. Hmm, not too bad. She leaned closer to the mirror. The knot over her eye wasn't as swollen as last night, and the gash wasn't as bad either. In fact, it looked almost healed. She still had a purplish bruise running from her eye to her cheek, but concealer and a little makeup should take care of it.

After a quick shower, Cordelia pulled on her favorite pair of jeans and tunic that reminded her of a Monet painting. There was no need to put on a power suit. She wasn't going into battle like yesterday. Besides, she and Margo were friends. Today's meeting was simply to finalize plans for the show. It was a pity *The Guardians of the Isle* wouldn't be part of it. But dang…it sold, and the customer didn't bat an eye at the price, according to Margo. She also said he was drop-dead gorgeous.

Mouth-watering aromas teased Cordelia's nose and made her stomach growl. Skipping dinner last night had her starving. She headed downstairs, anticipating the sausage she smelled.

Edna sat at the table staring at an old photo album, not bothering to look up as Cordelia entered. "Breakfast is in the microwave."

"You didn't have to go to all this trouble." Cordelia retrieved the toasted crumpet, topped with a fried egg and a sausage patty. "But thank you. I'm starved." While she ate, she watched Edna flip through photos of the war. It wasn't like her to be so quiet. "What are you looking at?"

"Oh, sorry, dear. Just going down memory lane." Edna glanced up, beaming. "Your face looks so much better. You're not bruised at all."

"I'm bruised, but some concealer and a tad bit of makeup did wonders."

Edna turned another yellowed album page. She tenderly ran her finger over the old black-and-white photo with a remarkably familiar face. "I can't believe they look so much alike." She slid the album around for Cordelia. "Of course, your Glen has longer hair."

"He *isn't* my Glen." If Cordelia hadn't known better, she'd swear the photo was of the same man she met last night. He even had a faint scar over his right eye. "Now, who was this guy, Glen's twin? They look identical except for the hair color."

"This handsome devil was his lordship," Edna tittered. "Lord Royce Alan Lucard. He and Glen were cousins and two peas in a pod, always getting into a mess. When I first met them, I thought they were brothers." She turned several pages. "Here's a photo of all of my boys. Royce, Glen, and the tall bloke is Vaughn Madoc."

"He doesn't look happy."

"Vaughn always looked like that. I think because something happened to his wife, but I never found out for sure. Poor man."

Cordelia flipped through the album, stopping at a large photo of her aunt and four men. She studied the face of the man with his arm around Edna's waist. Her Whitty was a handsome man. Every night, Edna kissed the photo she kept next to the bed. "Let's go this summer."

"Goodness, look at the time." Edna shut the album and stood, tucking the book under her arm. "Beth should be here soon for our Silver Sneakers class."

Cordelia could never imagine the pain of losing her one true love. The price of war. "Do you think Beth could drop me off at Margo's?"

"Don't be silly. Glen said he'd pick you up." Edna hurried from the room.

Cordelia wouldn't hold her breath. It looked like she'd be riding MARTA—but no, she wouldn't. Her Breeze card was in her wallet—something else she had to replace.

The doorbell rang, causing butterflies in Cordelia's stomach. It was probably Beth.

"I got it," Edna shouted. "Oh, don't you look dapper?"

Cordelia placed her plate in the dishwasher.

"Delia, look who's here! You didn't think he would show."

No man should look so good in jeans and a polo. Cordelia plastered a smile on her lips. "Glen, what a surprise."

Images of her dream flashed through her mind, and her face flushed. Blast it. She was acting like a hormonal teen.

"Are you feeling all right, Delia?" Edna frowned. "Your face is turning awful red. Are you having a hot flash? I was in my sixties when I started going through the *Change.*"

Oh, good grief, would the floor just open up already? "I'm fine, Edna."

"Have you had breakfast?" Glen's eyes shimmered, and the faint sound of amusement rang in his voice.

"I just finished. What about you? Have you eaten?"

"I did." His smile grew, showing off his blasted dimples and revealing perfect white teeth.

"Are you sure you're okay, Delia?" Edna's withered hand gently gripped Delia's wrist. "You're not feverish. But I heard you moaning last night."

Dear Lord, could her aunt make things any more awkward? Yes, she could. "I just couldn't get comfortable last night."

Glen cleared his throat and motioned toward the door. "Shall we be off, ladies?"

"Oh, I'm not going with you and Delia," Edna replied. "I'm going off with the girls. We're having a late lunch. There's so much we have to catch up on. You know Sally's granddaughter is dating Karen's niece's son?"

"No, I didn't, Aunt Edna. You have a wonderful time with your friends." Cordelia slid her phone into her jeans pocket and headed to the door before she chickened out or had Edna regale them with any more of the latest gossip.

"Don't forget your purse, Dilly," her aunt called. "Oh, I forgot. Your purse was stolen."

Cordelia blew Edna a kiss, then stepped outside and squinted against the bright morning sunlight. It felt odd not carrying her heavy bag. It almost felt like she wasn't fully dressed. There was no need to have one. What would she put in it? Her phone and a tube of lip gloss.

"Something wrong?" Glen asked.

"No, just feels odd not having my shoulder bag."

"I *dinna* understand why women need so much stuff."

"Spoken like a true man," Cordelia teased. "In my defense, I carry a drawing pad, pencils, and often a water bottle along with my wallet, phone, and sunglasses."

Sunglasses. Well, at least they were a cheap pair. When Cordelia's vision cleared, an odd twinge of disappointment coursed through her at seeing a massive black SUV in her drive. She was going off with a man she didn't know, but hadn't she done that yesterday when she took the rideshare? At fifty-five, she was doing things she'd never done before. "I was hoping to ride in your sports car."

Glen slipped on dark sunglasses, shielding his baby blues from her. "I thought Edna was coming with us and didn't want to put her in the boot." He beamed approvingly at Cordelia and opened the door, offering his hand. "Mind your head."

"Thank you." She hopped up on her own into the vehicle. "Trust me, there have been times I want to put her in the trunk, usually once a day."

Laughing, Glen shut her door.

Delia flipped the visor down and drew in a deep breath. The wonderful smell of Chai teased her nose, and she glanced around for the source. Two coffee cups sat in the center console. They even had the little green plug sticks stuck in the sip openings.

"I swung by the coffee shop," Glen said, sliding behind the wheel. "I hope you like vanilla Chai."

"You didn't have to do this, but thank you." She took a cup, removed the plug, and took a sip. "Mmm. So good."

"I'm glad you like it. Since Edna isn't coming with us." He pulled the plug on the other cup. "No need in this going to waste."

Glen backed from her drive. Stopped and waited as a moving van pulled into her neighbor's drive. "Looks like you're getting new neighbors."

"Yeah." She leaned forward, squinting. No, no, no. It couldn't be. "For the love of Pete!" She had her seat belt off and reached for the door handle, only to have Glen grab her arm.

"*Dinna.* You'll be playing into your ex's hands. Take a sip of your drink and do not look at him." Glen lifted the lid on the console, removing a pair of Ray-Ban Wayfarer sunglasses and handing them to her. "These may help." He put the vehicle in gear, driving forward.

"Thank you, again." She slipped on the glasses, which were way too big for her. "I can't believe Scott's moving in. Why can't he leave me alone?"

Glen reached over as they drove past, taking her hand in his. The gesture and the warmth of his hand calmed her.

"Security cameras may deter him."

Cordelia pulled her hand from Glen's. "Sounds like a sales pitch. Sorry…It's…I've put up with his crap for fifteen years."

"It's none of my business, but how did a vibrant woman like yourself end up with such a douche bag?" Glen took the on-ramp to 85 and stopped. *Gotta love Atlanta traffic.*

"We only have to go two exits." Cordelia stared at the sea of red taillights ahead of them as she finished her drink.

Glen was right. It was none of his business, and yet… "When I graduated high school, I wanted to attend Stanford because of their Cantor Center for Visual Arts. I love Auguste Rodin's works, which have one of the largest collections in the world. Anyway, after I graduated, I worked at the center. Fast forward a few years, I took a sculpting class hoping to improve my skills."

"You met your ex in the class."

"Scott was the instructor." She lifted the empty cup to her lips. Why had she gulped it?

"Here." Glen handed her his cup.

"Thank you." They inched forward, and she glanced at the clock on the dash.

"Relax, we have plenty of time." Glen flipped on his turn signal, easing into the right lane. "I'm taking this exit."

"Hmm, the long way might be quicker today." Cordelia stared out the windshield. When had her life gone so wrong?

"Before I knew it, Scott and I were married. He controlled my life like he did clay."

"Did he ever hit you?" Glen's words sounded like a growl.

Cordelia peered at him from the corner of her eye. "Slapped me once, and it was the best flippin' thing he could have done. It knocked some sense into me."

"He still touched you in anger." Glen took the exit, coming out onto a tree-lined two-lane road along with a million other drivers wanting to get around the traffic jam.

"I'm confused." Glen turned down the street Ivy and Rose Art Galley was located. "If he lived in California, how did the *nyaff* end up in Georgia?"

"The who?"

"Sorry, *nyaff* is an irritating person. He's also a *lavvy heid.*" Glen winked. The humor in his eyes had her smiling back.

"Toilet head. Edna uses the phrase a lot." Delia laughed. "Don't worry about cussing. I won't be offended."

He glanced at her. His lips twitched before he burst out laughing. "My sisters still blame me for my nieces' and nephews' more colorful phrases."

What was it about Glen? Just being in his company soothed her soul and sent her spirit soaring, making her want to explain more to him. "Scott's a sore loser. Five years ago, he moved here, saying he wanted the inspiration the East Coast offered. Whenever he has a failed showing or is between women, he makes my life a nightmare. He also has an uncanny ability to show up at the most inopportune moments."

"I see."

Somehow, the traffic thinned between one second and the next, and they drove in silence. Cordelia glanced over at Glen as she finished the second cup of Chai. The muscles in his jaw twitched, but his hands remained relaxed on the wheel. Guess her vomiting the highlights of her life were too much for the boy. *More's the pity.*

Glen pulled into the gallery's parking lot, finding a space near the front door. He killed the engine and turned toward her. "What I'm going to say, Cordelia, I *dinna* want you to think I'm another *mon* trying to control your life."

"Hmm, just one sounding a little ominous."

"When we leave here, I'd like to swing by my work and pick up a few cameras—"

"Glen—"

"Hear me out. In my line of work, I've dealt with men like your ex. You. Left. Him. You bruised *his* pride. Last night, I witnessed him raising his hand to you."

"He shoved his finger in my face."

"If I hadn't been there? Delia, the *nyaff* has moved in or is helping a friend of his move next door to you. Please, let me at least put up a few cameras. They may deter him or make him think twice before trying something."

She couldn't argue with Glen's logic. She could, but she had been thinking of installing some kind of security system. Scott was just forcing her to do it sooner than later. Over the past few years, he'd become more confrontational and demanding. For some bizarre reason, she wouldn't put it past him to break into her art studio and destroy everything. "Okay, but I'm paying for them."

"Deal." Glen grinned. Before she had her seatbelt unlocked, Glen was at her side, opening the door for her.

Instinctively, she reached for her purse. "Dang, hard habit to break." Cordelia took Glen's offered hand this time and slid from the vehicle. "Thank you."

"By the way, you look nice."

Why was this thirty-something flirting with her? Probably because he pitied her, or she reminded him of his mother. *Why couldn't I be a little younger and Glen a tad older?*

Glen held the door for her as she entered the art gallery. Margo and her husband had worked hard converting the turn-of-the-century warehouse into a premier gallery with elements highlighting the displayed art.

Cordelia scanned the empty room. Strange, someone was always at the desk. "Margo should be here."

"Good morning," Margo greeted, rushing from a backroom. "Did you two arrive together?"

"We did." Cordelia hugged Margo. "Since Glen had business with you also, he offered to give me a lift."

"Okay. This makes everything easy." Margo glanced at Cordelia. "Let me speak with him first, before we get started."

"Margo, you look wonderful this morning." Glen bent down, kissing her cheek.

Something flared in Cordelia, and she turned her back.

"You haven't boxed up the piece yet?" Glen's sharp tone had Cordelia turning back to them.

"About that," Margo said. "I was going to call you—"

"The artist hasn't changed his mind?" Glen arched his black eyebrow, and the muscles in his jaw twitched.

"Oh, no, nothing like that," Margo rushed out. "This was my idea. I'd like to keep *The Guardians* on display through the show."

Wait a minute. Had Cordelia heard right? Glen was the one who purchased her piece. Was this the reason he was acting so amazing? What was he up to?

"As much as I want it, I *dinna* have a problem with it being on display." He crossed his arms, and a shrewd grin curved his lips. "However, I have one thing to ask. I'd like the artist's contact information. I'd like to speak with him about commissioning a piece."

Him? Cordelia crossed her arms. Then the answer to her question would be no. Glen didn't know she was the artist. This had to be serendipity. Either that or the cosmos has decided it was mess with Cordelia week.

Margo glanced between Cordelia and Glen. "How long have you two known each other?"

"We just met last night," Delia replied, trying to keep the humor from her voice, but failing. She just hoped Glen thought it as amusing.

"Why?" he asked. As the word left his mouth, Glen's eyes widened. "You!" He pointed at her. "Saints!" His rich laugh echoed throughout the gallery. "I thought you painted."

"I said I dabbled."

Margo rolled her eyes. "You do more than dabble, Delia. In fact, I think it would be wonderful to add some of your oils to the show."

"Maybe." What did she have to lose? The only person who hated her paintings was Scott. "On second thought, Margo. I think you're right. I have a few paintings in my shop, we could add."

"Good." She hooked her arm with Cordelia. "Now, let me tell you my vision and see if you agree. We have plenty of time to change anything you don't like."

"You ladies, take as much time as you need. I'm going to check your security system." Glen strolled toward a door behind the desk.

Despite the numerous times Cordelia accompanied Scott to his shows, she never realized how much planning went into one. It was nearly as complicated as organizing a wedding reception. Cordelia's head throbbed once they finished going over the details. This exhibit was as important for Margo as it was for Cordelia. If the event was successful, it could mean more business for the gallery. Margo had invested a good deal of resources in advertising. She even purchased space on several billboards. An image of Cordelia's sculpture, *Crying Woman Falls,* was over the 85/75 split. When Cordelia saw the billboard for the first time, she nearly rear-ended the police car in front of her, which was how she met Officer Marks. Bless his heart. He'd only given her a warning before congratulating her.

Cordelia stared at the figures on the paper. How often had she heard the adage 'You have to spend money to make money'? This also explained the phrase, starving artist.

Her phone dinged, drawing her from her woolgathering. A quick glance at the text knotted her stomach, and she pocketed her phone.

"Delia, I have seen the same dazed and confused look many times before. Trust me, everything will go off without a hitch. All you have to do is show up an hour before and smile. Your sculptures and paintings will sell themselves."

"I couldn't agree more." Glen strolled toward them. "Delia, your artwork is amazing. Trust me when I tell you I've seen some amazing pieces in my lifetime, and yours are phenomenal."

"You're biased," she informed him. Her cheeks burned from Glen's praise. Scott had always told her she was mediocre. Blast him. He'd really whittled away at her confidence.

Glen shrugged. "Margo, everything checks out, and I'll have a team here the night of the exhibit."

She was Cordelia Parsons, not Rodin. "Margo, you didn't mention a security team. Why do we need one?"

Glen rested his hand on Cordelia's back, and she leaned into the warmth. "Your art exhibit will have some of Atlanta's wealthiest people waltzing through those doors. We always provide security for these events."

Margo clasped Delia's hands. "Stop worrying. It will be fine. As soon as it's over, you'll want to plan another show."

"Then I'll need to get busy creating."

Margo grinned and clapped her hands. "That's what I like to hear. Since you don't have a car, do you want me to send the van to pick up your paintings? Are they already crated?"

"They are, and that would be wonderful. I do have one that isn't in a crate."

"Since I have to take Delia home, I can load up the artwork and bring it by later today," Glen offered.

"I'm going to tell you like you told my husband. Leave it to the professionals." Margo fluttered her lashes at Glen as she pulled up a calendar on her tablet. "I can have the guys at your place around ten tomorrow morning. Would that work for you?"

"That's perfect." Cordelia slid from the stool. This was going to happen! Her first exhibit of her own. No Scott, no other artist, just her.

Margo's phone rang, and she frowned. "I have to take this. Call me if you have questions."

"I will." Cordelia waved bye as she headed toward the door.

"Nervous?" Glen rested his hand on the small of her back as they left. Her skin tingled wherever he touched her.

"I didn't know it showed."

"Just a wee bit." He opened the car door for her. "Mind your head."

"This is my first exhibit. Well, my first solo. All others I shared with Scott." *Who made sure I never outshone him.*

"How about we grab something to eat?" Glen shut the door before she could answer.

She appreciated everything he'd done for her, but she questioned his motives. Why was Glen so nice? Did she remind him of his mother, or did he have a different angle?

Glen climbed into the driver's seat. "We need to celebrate, and besides, I want to talk to you about the piece I'd like to commission. Lunch is on me."

"Okay." She hoped he didn't expect her to create something in a week.

"Great. Let me call the office." Glen pressed a button on the steering wheel. "Fiona."

Cordelia's phone dinged, and she glanced at the text. It was tempting to block Scott, but her lawyers urged against it. She slipped her phone back into her pocket.

"Oi, 'bout time you rang in," a female's voice came through the speaker.

"I have Cordelia Parsons with me," Glen informed the woman.

"I'll keep it professional then, boss."

He chuckled. "Have Cade or Paul grab some cameras. I want them installed outside Miss Parsons' home, front, back, and around her art studio."

"I'll send them straight away. You should also come by the office. Payroll needs your signature, and there is a matter needing your attention."

"Anything else?"

"No."

"Then I'm going to lunch." Glen ended the call.

"What do you have in mind for the piece?" Cordelia asked, curious what he wanted.

"Good question." He pursed his lips.

Glen turned into Cordelia's favorite place to eat. Francine's was a New Orleans-style café and always busy. In fact, it was where she and Edna had planned to come last night to celebrate. *Hmmm, wonder if I can still get my complimentary birthday Bananas Foster?*

"With the detail you put in your pieces, I realize it takes time to create a sculpture." Glen parked, killed the engine, then faced her. "My parents have a significant wedding anniversary coming up. April 25, of next year. I'd like to give them something special."

Okay, so he wasn't expecting her to whip up a sculpture, and it was doable with him needing the piece a year from now. "Depending on the size, it could take me a couple weeks to several years."

"I realize this. As for what I have in mind, I have several ideas floating around in my head." Glen climbed out of the vehicle.

The moment Cordelia stepped from the SUV, she wanted to tap her foot to the sounds of jazz filling the air. She already knew what she wanted to eat. But looking at the line of people waiting outside with buzzers, disappointment set in. She doubted they would eat here. Bye-bye, Bananas Foster. *Hasta la vista* chicken and waffles.

"Come on." Glen slipped his arm around her waist, leading her up the steps.

"Hour and a half wait." The hostess didn't look up as she spoke.

Glen slid his sunglasses into his shirt pocket and cleared his throat.

The young woman glanced up. Her eyes widened, and a bright smile curved her lips. "Mr. MacPhee, your table's this way. Follow me, please." She snatched up two menus. More than one person grumbled as the hostess led them to a table for four, tucked away in a nook by the window.

Glen pulled a chair out for Cordelia, giving her the window view as he took the seat across from her.

"Do you eat here so much you have a private table, or did you make reservations?"

"If I tell you I made reservations while going over Margo's system, will you get mad?" The corner of Glen's lips twitched, and his eyes held a hint of mischief.

"No, since this is one of my favorite places to eat." Her phone dinged for the umpteenth time. Instead of checking the message, Cordelia flipped open the menu. Why couldn't Scott take the hint? She'd turn her phone off, except Edna might need to contact her. "So you took a lucky guess I'd like to eat here, or are you stalking me?"

"I figured this was one of your favorite places since you had their carry-out menu on your refrigerator."

"Very observant. I guess you have to be in your line of work."

Glen eyed her. "I also know that's the third time your ex has texted you."

She flushed, but held her tongue. The message she received from Scott at the gallery was disconcerting. How in the blazes had he known where she was? She didn't tell him and knew neither Margo nor Edna said anything to him.

"Why haven't you blocked him?" Glen's tone was gentle, and his expression beseeching, not condescending.

"My lawyers urged against it. They…They want to give Scott enough rope to hang himself. As for shutting it off, I'm afraid Edna will need to reach me."

"Makes sense. Delia, forget about everything and enjoy the moment." Glen reached across the table, slipping the menu from her fingers. He greeted the server approaching their table. "Two Banana's Foster. We're having dessert first."

"Yes, sir." The young man regarded them with amusement. "And to drink?"

"I'll have unsweet tea," she informed him.

"Make it two." Glen shuddered. "I love the South, just not how they serve tea."

Cordelia brought her hand up, stifling her giggles. She needed this with everything that had happened in the last twenty-four hours. Glen had elevated himself from boy scout to knight in shining armor, and he didn't even know it. Why, oh why, couldn't she be younger or him older? Better yet, why couldn't they've met before she knew Scott? Blast it! Maybe one of these days, the universe would smile on her.

Chapter Four

Eating dessert first may not have been Glen's brightest idea, but at least Cordelia was smiling. If she ever found out he'd eased into her mind, she wouldn't be. At least he knew what was bothering her and what her favorite dessert was.

He couldn't wait to taste her sweet lips. If his excellent luck held out, he might get a chance today. His thoughts had him half hard. He needed to get his mind off her lips.

Delia turned her head. The sunlight from the window caught the strands of silver streaking through her tresses, making them shimmer. It pleased him she wore her thick, dark auburn hair loose, allowing it to brush her shoulders. He preferred it this way over the severe bun she wore yesterday.

Bloody hell, she was beautiful. Her oval face was a balance of grace and strength. When Cordelia smiled, faint lines appeared at the corner of her eyes. He hoped to keep her smiling all of their life together.

"You're staring at me." Amusement flickered in her eyes, mesmerizing him. "Tell me about this piece you want me to create." Her face paled, and the humor in her eyes suddenly vanished. *Oh, God! How did he find me?*

Cordelia's thoughts echoed in Glen's mind, and he wondered the same thing. He noticed her ex brushing past the hostess, heading for their table. Scott was either following them, or he'd somehow downloaded spyware onto her phone. *So much for my good luck.*

"I don't want a confrontation with him." Cordelia sat stiffly, eyeing her plate.

"There won't be one," Glen assured her. He'd hunt Scott down later if he caused a scene.

Scott grabbed the back of the chair beside Cordelia. His hazel eyes turned colder as he glared at her. "Cordy, is something wrong with your phone?"

Glen hooked his foot around the chair leg, sliding it back under the table.

A satanic sneer spread across Scott's thin lips. "Since this place is so packed," He turned his attention to Cordelia. "You don't mind if I join you, do you, Cordy?"

Glen placed his elbows on the table and steepled his fingers. "We're having a private conversation." He eyed Cordelia, and she exhaled, nodding. "So, *we* do mind."

"Cordy?" Scott loomed over her. "You've been here for over an hour. Surely you've discussed everything by now."

We haven't discussed how to kill him. Glen's daemon snarled.

Don't worry. If the ass keeps this up, we'll be calling the cleaners.

Cordelia's lips curved into a placid smile as if she didn't have a care in the world. "Scott, leave. Stop calling and texting me. You and I don't have anything to discuss."

"The hell we don't, Cordy."

"Tell it to my lawyer."

His face turned an ugly shade of purple, and his eyes bulged. "No wonder you're getting fat, eating shit like this." He stormed off, shouting, "My lawyers will hear about this."

Cordelia exhaled. "I'm so sorry."

"You have nothing to apologize for." Glen watched Scott push his way through the crowd. "May I see your mobile, please?"

"Why?"

"I have a thought."

She pulled the device from her pocket. "What are you looking for?"

"Spyware. I'm turning off your GPS and phone. Some apps allow *anyone* to track a mobile simply by entering the number.

Other spyware allows someone to access your camera and microphone, allowing them to hear and see what you're doing."

"Is that legal?" She gasped.

"It's in a gray area." He handed her back the device, then caught their server's attention. "It would also answer how Scott knew how long we've been here."

"And also that someone carjacked me," she whispered. "He called my cellphone two minutes after the officer left."

"Sir?"

Glen handed the kid the money. "Keep the change."

"Yes, sir." He grinned. "Thank you."

"Generous tip," Cordelia whispered. A genuine, relaxed smile curved her lips.

Glen would make bloody well sure that expression or one of pure joy stayed on her face forever.

"Restaurant workers aren't paid much, and this kid works his arse off besides going to college full time." Glen rested his hand on the small of Delia's back. As long as she didn't protest, he planned on touching her every chance he had.

Once outside, she eased away.

Instead of crying like a two-year-old, Glen slipped on his shades. "Do you have any other place you need or want to go?" It was bloody hard not to reach over and touch her.

"Nope." Cordelia graced him with another soul-searing smile. "I'm all yours—I mean, I don't have anything planned. Thank you again for everything you've done for me."

Maybe his luck was holding out. "Brilliant. Would you mind if we stopped by my office?"

"Not at all. I'd like to see where you work."

"To make sure I'm legit?" He teased. "Or did you Google me last night?" Delia blushed—She Googled him, which had him grinning like a nutter and feeling like an idiot. She'd researched him, and he hadn't known his mate had created the statue he'd purchased. What did it say about his *detective* skills?

"Glen?" The panic in Delia's voice had him following her gaze.

The SUV's tires were flat, as in all four. Glen had a sound mind to turn Angus loose on the ass, leaning against the vehicle and using a knife to pick his fingernails. But if he did, it would set Angus's therapy back a few months. So, Glen would deal with this roaster himself. Calmly. There were too many people around for anything else.

Glen eased Delia behind him. "Stay behind me," he whispered, stopping several feet away.

His daemon bristled for a fight as they sized up their opponent. The expensive cut of the bloke's suit and casual attitude spoke of someone with connections. His buzz cut, how he carried his weapon, and his stance said military training. But which government? "You know they make nail clippers."

The man shrugged, closing the knife and pocketing it. He pushed away from the vehicle and strolled toward them, bumping against Glen's shoulder. "A warning from Mr. Petrov." Russian, and from the guy's vowel reduction, he hailed from the Southern region. "Perhaps you will think twice before pulling a gun on a child."

"Tell your boss, perhaps his *ребенка* shouldn't play with guns."

The man laughed, clasping Glen's shoulder. "You know a word or two. Good for you." The guy stepped back. His gaze shifted to Delia. "Your friend likes to pick on children. You should know."

"Only children wearing skull masks who carjack and pistol-whip women."

Delia gasped.

"Your words against Luka's." The man smirked.

"My words and the footage from the security cameras, which are uploaded every 2 minutes and kept for ten years." That wiped the grin from the man's face.

"Rent-a-cop," He poked Glen's chest. "You do not know who you are playing with."

"Messenger boy, your boss doesn't know who *he's* playing with."

Luka pulled up, driving a green Lamborghini Aventador. Guess the kid was old enough to drive. Or not.

Messenger boy backed away, then folded himself into the passenger seat. They pulled out of the carpark, followed by four other cars.

Glen slipped his arm around Delia's waist, pulling her against his side. "Are you all right?"

She sagged against him. "What was that all about, and *did you* pull a gun on a child?"

He fished out his mobile. "After I left your place last night, Luka, the kid behind the wheel of the Lamborghini, tried to carjack me. I simply relieved him of his weapon, then waited for the police." As he spoke, Glen sent a text to Angus. "He and the get-away car driver were wearing hoodies and skull masks, hiding their faces."

"The people who carjacked me wore similar clothes. Do you think it's the same gang, crew, or whatever they call themselves?" Delia asked, leaning more into him.

"I can't say for certain, but my gut says it was." Glen scanned the area for any of Luka's lingering associates.

"I can understand them trying to steal your Bentley, but what would they want with my ten-year-old Honda?"

"Nondescript vehicle for a get-a-way." Glen glanced down at Delia. She still clung to him, and it had his daemon preening. It also had the bloody creature on edge.

At least Glen and his baser side agreed. He needed to get Delia to safety, and the quickest way was to walk across the street to the office. Not the safest means, but the fastest.

No, we should wait for the tow truck. Glen's daemon argued. *There are too many places for a sniper to hide.*

This was a warning. They wouldn't risk an attack with so many witnesses.

Delia eyed him. "I don't imagine you have four spares."

"Nope, and even if I did, I'd want it checked out first. Who knows if they did anything else to it? My question is, do you want to walk to my office or go back inside and wait?"

Delia eased from him, tilting her head back, eyeing him. "Walk? How far are we talking?"

He pointed to the old two-story brick building across the street. "Over there. The building has a history. In the 1920s, it was a flower shop with a speakeasy in the basement, complete with a secret entrance which has come in handy."

"Seriously? I've driven by that building many times, wondering what it was. You need signage."

"Nope. The best part of security is hiding in plain sight. Besides, most of our clients prefer to meet here at Francine's or their residences."

"No wonder you know so much about the waitstaff." She took off toward the crosswalk.

"Wait a second." Glen slipped his arm around her waist, tugging her out of the way of the flatbed tow truck pulling into the carpark. "I need to speak with Angus, then we'll head over."

"You have your own tow truck?"

"It comes in handy."

Angus climbed down from the cab. The lanky kid strolled around the SUV twice, shaking his head and visibly sniffing the air. The bloke had a nose, but most of the shifters did. Angus was special. He could scent any explosive from a kilometer. Like all of Dorjan's refugees, Angus had a dark side. Something told Glen the kid was getting the scent of the person who violated the vehicle.

Delia covered her mouth and whispered, "Is he smelling the car?" Angus could still hear her, not that the bloke minded.

"Aye," Glen replied. "Angus is a tad odd, but the best mechanic there is. He names all the machinery and talks to it like it has feelings."

"They *do* have feelings." Angus strolled toward them, lowering his eyes. One of these days, Glen would get the kid to look him in the eyes. "The only thing wrong with Modan is he needs new tires."

In other words, Angus didn't scent any explosives. Glen figured there wouldn't be, but when Delia's safety was in question, he wouldn't rely strictly on his gut. "Good. One thing, Angus, there may be a clear set of prints on the fenders."

Angus arched his dark eyebrows, and a feral grin curved his lips. "I'll take care of it."

"We'll leave Modan in your capable hands, then."

"Fiona will be happy for your return."

"Fiona?" Delia's eyebrows rose a fraction. "The one you called earlier?"

"My office manager and personal assistant." He pressed the button for the crosswalk.

Angus snorted. "Fancy name for a cold-hearted banshee who makes Grendel's mother look like a saint." He flipped the switch, pulling the SUV slowly up onto the flatbed. "By the way," he shouted over the clanking noise. "The spawn of Satan is roaming the building."

Glen paused, looking back at Angus. "Why?"

"Apparently, the husband's been called out on an assignment."

"That explains her mood." Glen took Delia's hand as he waited for the light to change. "Fiona's husband works for the FBI and splits his time between Washington and here. Fiona would prefer he work for me."

"I can understand. I take it Angus and Fiona don't get along."

"Not since she scratched the paint on a vehicle. I told Angus what had happened to your car. He lit a candle for it."

Delia glanced up at him, laughing. "You're not serious."

"I am. Angus is a good kid. Different, but a good kid." The light finally changed, and they crossed the street.

Glen was proud of the renovations he'd made to the building. For all appearances, it looked like any other office building. Only it had more security than most government buildings. The bullet-resistant glass doors slid open, and Glen ushered Delia inside.

"Wow." She looked around the lobby. "This is nice. It's so open, and the natural lighting is amazing."

"Thank you. You can move your studio here." Silly as it sounded, her praise meant a lot.

"I'm sure your clientele would appreciate watching me wedging clay."

He knew he would. Glen grinned and took in the lobby, trying to see it through Delia's eyes and noticing the unattended reception desk. "Sue?"

"Sorry, boss." Mitch stepped from the supply room. "I was helping Fiona." He perused Delia. "Ma'am."

"Delia, this is Mitch. He's one of my best men." The bloke smiled, or as much as one as Glen had ever seen. The corners of Mitch's mouth twitched. "Is Sue at lunch?"

"She called me last night, seeing I'm between assignments. She said she'd speak to you later."

"All right, then. I'll wait for her call." Glen slipped his hand to the small of Delia's back, guiding her to the broad flight of steps leading up to the offices. "My office is straight ahead."

"I bet you can see everything going on down there."

"Even without the cameras."

"Hmm, you have cameras everywhere?"

"Not in the bathrooms."

"Good to know." Delia laughed. She stumbled, clutching his arm. "What was—Oh my, what a gorgeous Siamese."

"She's a sweet kitty," Fiona said, stepping from her office. "Aren't you, Miss Moneypenny?"

"Named after M's secretary in Ian Fleming's James Bond series of novels," Delia replied. "I used to have first editions of them all."

Glen wagered she'd left them behind when she left her ex.

"Let me guess," Delia said. "She's named because of your husband's job."

Fiona tapped the end of her nose. "Even if he isn't British or working for MI6."

Both women laughed.

Glen relished the knowledge Cordelia and Fiona got along. He cleared his throat. "Fiona, I'd like you to meet Cordelia Parsons, the artist who sculpted the piece I purchased. Delia, Fiona O'Brian."

"It's a pleasure to meet you." Fiona extended her hand. "Perhaps we can add some of your art to our lobby. I particularly like your *Untitled*, your nod to Agatha Christy."

Delia's eyes lit, and the brightest smile curved her lips. "Thank you. Few people get it."

Glen glanced from Delia to Fiona, then back to Delia. "I'm trying to figure out which piece."

Fiona tsked. "The old typewriter with the ABC blocks beside it and the magnifying glass resting on the typebars."

"I thought it was about writing, not Agatha Christy." He still didn't get the connection.

"The ABC blocks are the hint," Fiona replied. "Am I correct?"

"Very astute, Mrs. O'Brian." Delia winked. "I wanted something subtle, so I figured the blocks would hint to her *The ABC Murders*."

He still didn't see it, but he wasn't much of an Agatha Christy reader. Give him Koontz, Poe, or Lovecraft, and he'd be happy.

Loud purring filled the room. Glen glanced down at the four-legged menace rubbing against Delia's leg. His heart faltered as she squatted and reached a hand toward the purring terror. He grabbed Delia's wrist. "*Dinna* touch the cat. She's deadlier than a Bengal Tiger." Glen glared at the nine-pound predator as he helped Delia to stand.

Fiona scoffed, "She's only mean to you…Cade, Mitch, Paul."

"I'm sensing a pattern here." Delia's tinkling laughter filled the room. He loved the sound.

She shifted her attention to something behind him and frowned. "Excuse me." Delia strode toward Fiona's bookshelf. She pointed to Whitaker's photo of him in his War World II Royal Air Force uniform. "Who is he?"

"My dad." Fiona eyed Delia before glancing at Glen and mouthing, sorry.

Bloody hell, Glen hadn't thought Delia would have seen any photos of Whitaker.

"Your dad? Did he have a twin?" Delia picked up the photo and examined it before gently returning it to the shelf.

"No. Dad's an only child."

Glen stared at the second picture on the shelf and cringed. It was one of him, Royce, Vaughn, and Whitaker.

Delia's hand hovered over the second picture. "Who are they?"

"Dad's chums." Fiona picked up the picture. "What's that saying? Six degrees of separation or something? Who would have thought Glen and I would work together years later? Fate? Huh?"

"I can't believe the strong similarities between the two," Delia motioned between him and the photo of him. "Even to the scar over the eye."

"They say everyone has a doppelgänger." Fiona set the photo back on the shelf. "Why did you ask about my dad's photo?"

"Your father? Sorry. It's…you look younger than me. That was rude of me. Sorry."

"It's all right. I appreciate the compliment. Why are you curious about this photo?"

Delia exhaled, her lips pulled thin. "This will sound weird, but my Aunt Edna has the same picture on her nightstand. She kisses it every night."

Fiona's mouth gaped. "You're right. It is strange."

"According to the family story, Edna and Whitty," Delia motioned to the photo. "They were engaged, but on January 15, 1946, she was informed his plane went down, killing him."

"Oh, bloody hell," Glen exclaimed.

Fiona clasped Delia's hand in hers. "My father's plane went down. He had engine problems but didn't die. Edna was gone by the time they found him, and he was returned to England." Fiona shook her head. "Father searched everywhere for her. She'd simply vanished, and no one knew what had happened to her. Father even came here to America, searching for her, knowing her sister was married to a Yank. But there was no record of her ever arriving in the States."

Delia nodded. "The person who'd processed the paperwork for Edna listed her as a minor sibling, Parsons, using my grandmother's married name. When Edna applied for citizenship, she changed her name back to Cooper."

Glen wanted to bang his head. The mystery of why Edna had fled England and why he and Whittaker couldn't find her was finally solved. "I think you should tell her."

Delia shook her head. "I couldn't. He's married, and it would—no. You don't understand. Edna has mourned him every day of her life."

"My father isn't married anymore. Mum died shortly after I was born." A sad expression crept into Fiona's eyes. "I feel in my soul, Father and Edna need to know the truth. Let me speak with my brother and see what he thinks, but I believe Percy will agree. I'll ring you tomorrow if that's fine."

"It is. It will give me time to figure out how to tell Edna. If I tell her."

Glen didn't need the blood connection to know Delia wanted to leave. She hadn't been in his life 24 hours, and it seemed fate forced him to take three steps back for every step forward he made. "Well, Fiona, we'll let you get back to work."

"Before you leave, you need to sign payroll," Fiona reminded him.

"I knew there was a valid reason for coming in." He winked. "Do me a favor."

"Only one?" She eyed him.

"Bring me a new mobile. I'll swap the SD cards."

"Excuse me, Fiona," Delia addressed. "Where's the ladies' room?"

"You can use mine." Glen pointed to the door to his right.

"Thanks."

As soon as Delia closed the door, he eyed Fiona. "What?"

Fiona typed Delia's name into Google. "Look at this. I've already asked Percy to deal with it."

"Hell's bloody bells!" Someone had broadcasted Cordelia's personal information across social media, including her home address, phone number, social security number, and even some medical information, including that she'd lost a child. He bet that someone had the name of Scott Haynes. "I'll tell her."

Delia returned, eyeing him curiously. "Tell me what?"

He turned the monitor so she could see and waited for the waterworks. Her reaction wasn't what he'd expected.

She shrugged. "I know. I've been dealing with it for over a year. Right after I posted pictures of a few of my sculptures on the internet. My lawyers have sent letters to every social media and search engine to remove the information. But my info is out there, so not much I can do except keep a watchful eye on my credit and bank accounts." She shrugged. "It sucks."

"Yes, well, Delia. We have someone on it who will correct the issue. I can assure you of that." Fiona left only to return with a new mobile, handing it to Delia. "The first step is this, along with a new number."

Glen finished the payroll, leaned back in his chair, and watched Delia scroll through the new device. It surprised him she didn't argue too much when Fiona handed it to her. Perhaps Scott had worn Delia down with his excessive texting, or she suspected him to be the root of her problems. Glen had wished she would have allowed him to set up a new number for her. Baby steps, he reminded himself. At least Scott won't be able to download spyware onto this phone. "Are you getting the hang of it?"

"It's like mine, just four versions newer, and it has a far better camera. I'm kinda afraid to know the bill."

"Dinner with me and agreeing to do the sculpture."

"We just had lunch," Delia replied, keeping her features deceptively composed as she perused his office. She'd make a brilliant poker player. "As for the sculpture. I'm still cogitating on it."

He didn't know what he'd do if Delia turned him down. Glen wished he knew what she was thinking. Easing into her mind seemed wrong. He should have known it wouldn't be easy to get a date with his mate or have her agree to do the piece for him. As his mum said a million times, you appreciate things you work for.

Glen was thankful the only family photos he had were recent. He was already in a sticky wicket, trying to figure out how to tell Delia about his other side. He signed off on his computer and stood. "Ready?"

"That was quick."

"If you'd like, I can log back on and finish my chess game," he teased.

"You're funny. Do you think Angus has repaired your tires?"

"Probably, but I figured we'd take my car. It's such a nice day. We can even put the top down.

Typical Atlanta traffic had them creeping along. For once, Glen didn't mind. He glanced over at Delia. Her eyes were closed, and she rubbed her temples. "Is my driving that terrible?"

"No," she sighed. "Just trying to process today's events. The love of Edna's life alive, my ex-husband stalking me—maybe. To top it off, I have my first solo show in two weeks." She opened her eyes. "It's not even five, yet."

"Can I ask a question?" He took her exit.

"Sure?"

"Why is this your first? You're great."

"Thank you. To answer your question, it was all about Scott when I was married. After the divorce, it took me a while to find my muse again. I finally got my nerve up and spoke with Margo. Then it took me a while to create enough pieces for an exhibit. Speaking of which, how big of a piece are you thinking about? Monumental or study size, or somewhere in-between?"

"I'd like it to be of my parents. Something like the photo I showed you and large enough to go in their garden."

"The one with your dad in the kilt and your mom in the *earasaid*? Did I say it right?"

"You did." He turned onto her street. "Will the tartan be an issue?"

"The plaid pattern won't be a problem. Tedious, but not a problem. However, if you want it finished within a year, I can't guarantee anything larger than four feet, at the most, and depending on the detail, even that time frame could be pushing it. Also, I will need several photos of your parents to get a 360 of them. Usually, I do several sketches, but I have worked off photographs."

Glen glanced over as they passed her ex's home. The moving van was gone. Neither Delia nor Edna would spend another night here if Glen had his way.

"I have several photos taken of my parents at various Highland Games. You are more than welcome to go through them." 40s jazz greeted them as Glen pulled into Delia's driveway. "So, you'll do it?"

"Yes—Oh, good grief." Delia pointed at Cade and Edna dancing.

Edna spotted them and squealed. "Dilly, Cade, and Paul know how to do the Lindy Hop!"

Delia was out of the car before he finished putting the top up. An idea hit him as he killed the engine. A brilliant idea to solve most of his problems. "Delia, wait a second."

"What?" She glanced over her shoulder at him.

"Can you drive a manual?"

"Yes. Why?"

"Good." Glen took her hand, dropping the key in her palm. "Paul, have you and Cade finished installing the cameras?"

Delia dangled the key out to him. "I can't accept these."

"Is there a car in your garage you can drive?"

"No."

"Then it's settled." He grinned. "Unless you want me to be your personal chauffeur. Which, I *dinna* have a problem with."

She stared at him blankly with her mouth agape for a second. "What if it gets stolen? Or I wreck it? Do you know how much that car's worth?"

"Maybe," he said, chuckling.

Amusement shimmered in her eyes. "Of course you do."

He tapped the end of her nose with his finger. "That's what insurance is for."

Glen turned his attention to Paul and spotted Delia's ex glaring at them. "What needs to be done?"

"Nothing. We were finishing up when Edna returned home." Paul smiled sheepishly. For a wolf, that was something. "Eddie insisted we install a few outside the studio, just in case someone broke in. She also insisted we install some cameras inside the house, in the kitchen, living room, and heading up the steps, but none on the upper floor.

"Don't want you seeing me in my knickers," Edna snickered.

Paul cringed a little and pointed to the camera above the door. "As for the outside, anyone creeping around will trigger the cameras."

"Good." Glen motioned to Delia's pocket. "With the new phone, you tap the icon I showed you, and you'll see who's outside." He'd know and be on his way, but Glen wasn't about to divulge that bit of info to her...yet.

Edna grinned, clapping her hands. "Then we can dry Snot up for good."

"That's a good one, Eddie." Cade flung his arm around her shoulders.

Delia pinched the bridge of her nose. "Don't encourage her, please."

"You said yourself, Dilly, you didn't trust Snot." Edna rolled her eyes. "Speak of the devil."

Glen tore his attention from Delia in time to watch her ex storming toward them.

"What is going on over here?" He demanded, jabbing his finger in the air.

"None of your bleeding business, Snot." Edna planted her hands on her hips. "Get the bloody hell off my property."

Cade tapped his phone, switching the music from jazz to AC/DC's *Dirty Deeds, Done Dirt Cheap*.

Glen met Cade's eyes. *Subtle. Real subtle.*

I thought so. The cat's laughter echoed in Glen's mind. *Can we kill him now?*

Don't tempt me. Glen flexed his hands. One of these days, he would snap the *nyaff's* finger off, then shove it up his nose.

Scott glared at Edna. "I have the right mind to call the police on you for disturbing the peace."

Delia's eyes turned cold as a stony mask slipped over her face. "Is that the reason you purchased the house next door?" Her tone held an ominous ring. "To make my life a living nightmare.

Is that why you've been stalking me, Scott? Is it? Because here's an FYI. I have a new phone with a lot more security features. Try spying on me now."

The man recoiled, his eyes nearly bulged out of his head, and the ass turned an unnatural shade of purple. "You think everything is about you, Cordy? It's not." He met Glen's eyes. "Watch your back with her. She manipulates situations, so *she* appears the victim."

"Yet, you purchased the house next door," Glen replied.

"I didn't buy the house. I'm helping a friend move in."

"Right next to where your ex-wife lives. I find it *very* suspicious."

"I didn't know the house Britney brought was next to Cordy's." Scott turned his cold, hard eyes toward Delia. "Which is why I've been trying to speak with you." He thrust his finger at Delia once more. "Brit is a gentle soul, unlike you. Leave her the fuck alone and keep your demented hag away from her." Scott turned on his heels.

"Scott." Glen struggled to restrain his daemon. The creature's rage singed the mental chains binding him. "The next time you disrespect either of these ladies, you will deal with me. If you ever shove your bloody finger in Delia's or Edna's face again, I will remove the digit from your hand."

Scott paled. "Are you threatening me?" he stammered.

"Not a threat."

"Glen." Delia gently laid her hand on his forearm. "He's not worth your breath."

"You do not know who you're threatening. I'm *the* Scott Haynes," he shouted as he headed back across the lawn.

Delia dropped her chin to her chest. "Glen, please. Send me the bill. Take your keys and go."

Chapter Five

Men! Delia had had her fill. She didn't need anyone controlling her life. She was a grown woman and could make her own blasted decisions. She didn't need a boy scout telling her what to do. She had a good mind to rip the darn cameras down, flush his flippin' phone, and have his car towed.

Right on time, the phone rang. Delia sipped her tea, not bothering to answer it. One thing she could say about Glen, he was punctual. Punctual and persistent. Then again, so was Scott. Only he was punctual and controlling.

Good grief, what was Glen thinking? "I'll rip the digit from your hand," she lowered her voice, imitating his brogue.

"Still miffed, I see." Edna strolled into the kitchen, wearing purple leggings and a cherry red sweatshirt two sizes too big for her. "It's been four days. Are you ever going to answer his calls?"

"When I'm ready."

"I see," Edna tsked.

"I'm done with men controlling my life."

Edna poured her tea. "I didn't realize installing locks to ensure our safety was controlling. I guess loaning a car until you can purchase one yourself is also controlling. Is giving you a phone your ex can't use to track your every move controlling, as well?"

Delia snatched up the phone. "Glen could use this to track me."

"Then get a new one. It's not like you can't afford it."

"As for these cameras." Delia pointed to the one aimed at her—or rather at the front door. "He could be watching everything we do. Heck, for all I know, he could be listening to every word we say." She flipped off the camera.

Edna yanked open the drawer next to the stove, snatched the roll of aluminum foil from it, then slammed it down on the table in front of Delia.

"What's this for?"

"For you to make yourself one of those funky little hats." Edna wiggled her fingers at her head. "We wouldn't want aliens or *The Man* controlling your mind."

"I'm not crazy. You don't understand."

"Then explain it to me." Edna eased down onto the other kitchen chair and covered Delia's hand with hers. "I've not seen you so flustered since your divorce."

"The other night after he left, he called to apologize for overstepping and asked me to go out with him."

"Scott?"

"No. Glen."

"Oh, thank God. For a moment there, I thought you really were off your rocker. What did you tell him?"

"I hung up."

"You haven't answered the poor man's calls since." Edna tsked. "He asked you out to dinner, not to bang uglies."

"Edna!"

"What? What's wrong with going out with him?"

"I'm too old to be going out with a child."

Edna's lips thinned, and she sat up straight. The stern mask of authority replaced the concerned, loving look that had graced her face only seconds before. "Cordelia."

Cordelia? She met Edna's piercing green eyes, shimmering with unshed tears.

"You haven't gone on a date since your divorce."

"I don't need to date. I'm too old for that crap."

"Delia, you're too young to be alone. You need to jump back into the dating pool."

"There's floating turds in that pool."

A single tear snaked down Edna's withered cheek. "I may have had my Whitty for a short time, but I know what it's like to be loved. I know what it feels like to have someone look at me as if I'd hung the moon. Ida knew the feeling, as did your mom and dad."

Cordelia bit her tongue. She still hadn't told Edna about Whitty, and she might never tell her from how things looked. "Not everybody is as lucky."

"Luck has nothing to do with it. It's called taking a chance. You can't find true love if you don't open yourself up to it."

"You think I'll find it with Glen?"

"I don't know. What I know is you'll never find love hiding from life. Don't be like me. I go to bed and dream about a man long gone. Ida and Charlie tried to fix me up with a few of Charlie's friends. I refused to go out with any of them because I didn't want to betray Whitty's memory. Look what it got me, a cold bed and a life full of regrets. Life is lonely when you're by yourself."

Delia shuddered inwardly at Edna's revelation. "You have me."

"Yes, I do. I thank God every day for your company and love. But who will you have when I'm dead?"

Delia's guilt was so acute it was a physical pain stabbing her heart. But how could she tell her aunt the love of her life was still alive? How could she not? "I understand what you're saying. But Glen's thirty-five if he's that old, and I'm…I'm fifty-five."

"Good, then you'll both die about the same time."

"Edna!"

"What? Everyone knows women outlive men. Besides, does age really matter? Do you enjoy his company? Does his age really matter if he breathes life back into you?"

"Maybe not today or tomorrow, but it will matter when I'm seventy-five. Besides, what makes you think I'm attracted to him?" She wasn't. Delia couldn't believe she and Edna were having this conversation.

A knowing grin spread across Edna's lips. "You can't deny it, Dilly. You're attracted to him. From the first time he walked through the door, you've beamed. You never, *never* looked at Snot the way you look at Glen. Even on your wedding day."

Edna was right. Delia's pulse had never pounded with Scott. She often wondered if she ever loved him. "I think I'm going out to the shop." Delia carried her cup and plate, placed them in the dishwasher, then headed outside.

"Hi!"

Plastering on a smile, Delia paused and turned toward the sound of the all too cheerful woman. *Yup, the universe is having a field day with my life.* "Good morning," she greeted the smiling, blond, bright-eyed, twenty-something.

"I'm Britney, your new neighbor." She trotted across the lawn with her hand stuck out like a knight's lance.

"Cordelia Parsons." She strode to the fence and shook Britney's hand. "Scott's ex, for a reason."

Britney flushed, but her smile remained. "I want you to know I didn't know you were his ex when I was house hunting. I found out the other day when he stormed across the yard. When he returned, he loudly explained what had happened. I'm sorry."

"It's not your responsibility to apologize for him."

She shrugged. "Yeah, but as you know, Scott can be intense. I hope there are no hard feelings."

Then keep him on your side of the fence. "There aren't any. Excuse me, I have a project I need to work on."

"Really?" Britney's eyes widened. "Scott said you were a sculptor. I paint and just recently started sculpting. Scott was teaching my class."

A leopard never changes his spots. Delia shook her head. "I'd like to chit-chat, but I really need to get to work."

"Scott said you have a show coming up soon. Are you working on a piece for it?"

"No." Delia turned and headed toward her studio. Blast it. She hated to be rude, but the child was clueless. Who wanted to talk about their ex, especially to his new conquest? The last thing Delia needed was another screaming match with Scott.

Thank goodness she hadn't seen him since the other night, and he hadn't texted her. Maybe having Glen's car parked in her drive had kept Scott at bay. Yeah—Not. This was Scott, after all. Why couldn't Glen come and get his car? She told him she wouldn't drive it. Hell, she'd broken out in a cold sweat just pulling it into the garage.

***

Glen pulled into Delia's drive and shut off the engine. He was bloody tired of her avoiding him. If she wasn't going to take his calls, she'd at least hear what he had to say. He picked up the package left by the door, then pressed the doorbell. Almost instantly, it opened. Instead of Delia, Edna beamed up at him.

"I need to speak with Delia."

"Oh, Glen, what a pleasant surprise. Won't you come in?" Edna stepped aside, motioning for him to enter.

"Is Delia here?"

"Won't you have some tea? I have just taken the kettle off."

"I need to speak with Delia."

Edna grabbed his wrist. "You need a cup of tea."

He gently covered her boney fingers with his hand. "I need—"

"Sit your bloody arse down and have a cup of tea before I drag my Sten gun from the closet." She batted her lashes at him. "Your blood can do amazing things, my boy. I'm living proof." Edna turned and strolled toward the kitchen. Glancing over her shoulder, she asked, "Are you coming?"

Dumbfounded, he followed, finding Edna pouring two cups of Earl Grey. He couldn't kill her. He dared not alter her mind because heaven only knew how much brain matter she had left. His best option was to humor her. "Now, Edna."

"Stow it, Blue-eyes. I don't have dementia. My hearing is perfect. I don't have arthritis, my eyesight is better than 20/20, and I don't have any ailments. Pretty remarkable for a woman my age, wouldn't you say?" She placed a plate of blueberry scones on the table, then sat. "The only thing that sucks was your blood didn't prevent wrinkles."

Glen sank down on a chair. Shit just got real.

She pushed the sugar bowl toward him. "When I woke in hospital, I could hear voices in my head and thought I was going bonkers." A somber look descended over Edna's face. "You need not worry. I kept my mouth shut. I didn't want to be institutionalized for being a nutter. How fast I healed was something I noticed. My hands used to be ugly, with cuts and bruises from working with the artillery. Not anymore." She turned her hands over. "Only a few age spots. But enough about that. The most remarkable thing I had was a sense of when you, Vaughn, or Royce were near. Never had the sensation again after I left England until the other night. I take it, you each gave me blood. I know *you* did. Your face was the last I saw before the darkness took me."

"Edna..."

"I saw things the night they attacked us, Glen. I saw Vaughn take flight. You and Royce became gargoyles. Protectors. You ripped those Nazis to bits. Literally. Now, close your mouth."

He swallowed. "Why didn't you say anything to us?"

"I figured you all took a significant risk in saving my life. I owed you the security of keeping your secret." She folded her hands and stared at him. "I know you and the rest of my boys are good men. I heard your thoughts. I witnessed your compassion. My question is, what are *your* intentions toward my niece?"

***

Delia propped open the double doors to her studio, providing more light. The overhead bulb just wasn't cutting it. One of these days, she'd get around to installing windows. Heck, if she made enough money, she'd have a new one built with windows and skylights. Maybe.

She turned on the radio, then sat at her workbench. It wasn't fancy, but it would support a lot of weight. When she'd built it, she ensured it was the proper height to wedge clay without bunching her shoulders or giving her a backache.

She looked around the tiny room. Maybe it wasn't a traditional art studio, but it was hers. Against the far wall, she had her kiln. It wasn't big enough for monumental pieces, but it was big enough for most of her work. She had shelves with various clays, scales, tools, and countless drawing pads to her right. This was her sanctuary.

As the radio softly played, Delia stared at the paper as blank as her mind. She hadn't been able to concentrate since the other night. To make matters worse, every time she closed her eyes, she saw bright sky-blue eyes smiling at her. It didn't help her favorite song by Alejandro Botela played in the background. The haunting melody made her think of things she shouldn't.

Why not? What was wrong with going out with a younger man? Heck, after one date, she and Glen could end up as friends and nothing more. The worst thing that could happen was, he'd avoid her at all costs.

"Oh, blast it!" Delia grabbed the phone. If she were lucky, it'd go to voice mail.

"Hey," Glen answered on the first ring.

Now what? What was she going to say? An uncomfortable silence stretched out as she tried and failed to quell the panic rising in her chest. She could hang up, claiming a butt dial—no need to be childish.

"Delia, is everything all right?"

"I'm fine. It's just…when are you coming to get your car?"

"Do you have transportation?"

"Not yet, but I'm not driving your Bentley. I'm terrified of dinging it and don't give me a ration of bull about having insurance. Come get it. We need to talk."

"We're talking now."

A dull foreboding ache spread through her. She wanted to see Glen, but it appeared he didn't want to see her. "I know, but I'd like to talk face-to-face with you."

"Is there a chance of you going out with me?"

She didn't miss the hope laced in his words. "Maybe."

"Then *maybe* you should turn around."

"What?" Delia spun on the chair so fast she nearly toppled over as she came face to face with Glen. "What are you doing here?"

"Edna called me. By the way, I got your Amazon package from the front step." He stood in the doorway, staring at her as he reached into his pocket and withdrew the key fob for his Bentley. Blast it. How could a man make a pair of jeans and a polo look sexy?

"Thank you." Every time their eyes met, her heart turned over in response. She'd only known him a week, and it frightened the crap out of her about how he made her feel. How being with him made her desire things she shouldn't. "You scare me."

"Why? Because I asked you out?" He strode toward her, making her feel like prey.

"Yes. Why do you want to go out with me? I'm fifty-five, and you're thirty-five."

The teasing smile she'd grown addicted to pulled at his lips. "I'm a wee older."

"Okay, thirty-seven. Still…why me?"

"Why not you?" Glen reached over and took her hand in his. Warmth eased up her arm and made her heart tremble. "You're intelligent, artistic, witty. I enjoy being around you and want to get to know you better."

"Look at me." Delia motioned to her face with her free hand. "This is me. This is what I look like most of the time. No make-up and my hair pulled up in a messy ponytail. The only difference is I usually have clay under my nails and smeared on my face. My wrinkles, they're not going anywhere. I refuse to be nipped and tucked any more. I do what I can to stay healthy, not be someone's trophy. Been there, done that. At my age, what you see is what you get."

Glen squinted, leaning closer to her. His warm breath teased her cheek. "Hmm, I see fine lines—not wrinkles. As far as how you look right now." Slowly and seductively, he perused her. "You look just fine."

"Says the man who looks like he came from a cover shoot."

Glen leaned closer and whispered against her ear, "Says the *mon* who can look pretty beastly." He pressed a kiss to her cheek, and her lady bits throbbed with longing.

Delia cleared her throat and leaned away, pretending she wasn't affected.

The heat and desire burning in Glen's eyes made her flush even more. "Fine. I'll go out with you. But we need to talk."

"We can talk tonight when I pick you up at seven."

"Tonight? Darn, you move fast." Delia wished she could call her words back the second they fell from her mouth.

Amusement flickered in his eyes. "Do I hear a challenge?"

"Maybe."

"Maybe, huh?" Glen laughed and reached into his pocket. He withdrew another key fob and held it out to her. "Here. I think you'll feel better driving this."

"No."

"You've already said you don't have transportation. Besides, I can't drive two vehicles at the same time."

"What is it? A Bugatti?"

His deep, rich laugh warmed her. "Afraid not. But it is the safest compact SUV on the road. It also has a few blemishes. No need for you fretting about scratching it. Angus checked it over when Sue dropped it off. He's thorough. It won't break down on you. Come on, take a look."

There went every argument she had about not accepting the vehicle. "Fine." Delia slid from her chair. It wasn't like she was in the middle of mind-blowing inspiration.

As they stepped into the bright sunlight, she noticed Scott standing on Britney's deck, glaring at them. Would he ever get a life? Better yet, would he ever leave her alone? She had a good mind to grab Glen and lay a kiss on him.

In a smooth move, Glen slipped on his Ray-Bans and draped his arm around Delia's shoulder. "Might as well give him something to stare at." He bussed her temple. "Do you like The Abby?"

She knew it was once an old church that was converted and refurbished into a restaurant in the 1960s. "I've never eaten there, but I've heard it's nice."

"Then the Abby it is. After dinner, we can head over to The Joint if you'd like?"

"Sounds like I'm in for a fun night. I'd best find my dancing shoes."

"Do me a favor, no laughing at my moves." Glen chuckled, slipping his hand to her waist. The man was smooth, but she wouldn't call him on it. Oddly, it felt right having his arm around her.

She opened the gate, leading him along the garage instead of walking through the house. She loved her aunt. She really did. But there were times.

"Well, what do you think?" Glen motioned toward a small black SUV with window tinting so dark it was barely legal. The SUV wasn't flashy like his Bentley parked behind it. Edna must have opened the garage for him. "Will you feel more comfortable driving this?"

She hated to admit it, but…. "Yes." It was the car she was considering. As she drew closer, she noticed several small holes in the driver's door. "Are those bullet holes?"

"Sue didn't elaborate on what type of projectile made them, but my guess would be yes."

"Some guys bring flowers. You bring me a car used in a drive-by."

"Not used in, just caught in the crossfire. Would you have preferred flowers?"

"Flowers wilt and can't get me to the grocery store." Delia opened the car door, noticing the bullet holes didn't penetrate the interior. "You don't have to do this." She ran her hand over the leather seat. She'd bet it had every bell and whistle the dealer offered, along with a few more.

"I want to. Let's get it set up for you." He went around to the passenger side, then climbed in. "The back mirror—"

"The what?" She asked. "Oh, you mean the rearview mirror?"

Glen shrugged. He talked her through setting up her driver's profile instead of doing it himself. Delia ran her hand over the steering wheel. This was a nicer vehicle than she'd ever owned. Maybe once the insurance company sent her the check, she'd get one for herself.

Delia stared at Glen. It was now or never. "I have to ask. Do I remind you of your mother?"

He threw his head back, laughing. "Saints, no. Is this what you wanted to talk to me about?"

"No, but…"

Glen cupped her face in his hand. His thumb gently caressed her cheek, sending chills through her. "What do I have to do to convince you I'm attracted to you? Delia, I *dinna* give a doolally about your age."

Staring into his eyes, she saw the heart-rending honesty of his words. "If you're honest about wanting to see where this goes, be patient with me."

"I'm a patient man." He leaned forward and kissed her. The gentle caress of his lips sent the pit of her stomach into a wild spiral. "I'll see you at seven." His lips brushed against hers once more before he opened the door and slipped out, leaving her suddenly wanting more from him.

Delia climbed from the vehicle and shut the door. Standing on wobbly legs, she waved as Glen drove away. She continued standing there until she couldn't see his car anymore. "I'm acting like a hormonal teen."

"Getting a little friendly with the help, don't you think?" Scott shouted from the deck.

Instead of replying, she turned on her heels and calmly strode back into the house. She had to get ready for a date.

Chapter Six

Delia checked herself in the mirror for the hundredth time. Should she change into a pantsuit? No! She didn't want to look like Glen's mother, but she didn't want to look like a desperate woman trying to hold on to her youth. What was she doing? She should just call Glen and cancel. No, she wouldn't. She needed to speak to him about Edna. Delia glanced in the mirror again, seeing her aunt standing behind her. "Is this dress too short?"

"You're good. I don't see your tonsils." Edna frowned and sat on the edge of the bed. "What's the matter?"

"I'm fifty-five, yet I feel like a teen going out on her first unchaperoned date. I think I'm losing my mind. Part of me doesn't give a hoot what Glen thinks, and yet there's this tiny bit that does." She smoothed her hands down the simple light purple dress she wore.

"If you're worried about first impressions, don't. The first time he laid eyes on you, you looked like you went three rounds with Joe Louis. As for Glen, your first impression of him was in a tacky Velcro police costume."

"Since you put it that way, Edna." Cordelia straightened her shoulders. "Which necklace should I wear?"

"The beaded one and earrings you purchased from the art gallery in Monroe. You can also wear your do-me heels."

"My what?" Cordelia stared at Edna in the mirror. Some things that came out of her mouth had Cordelia questioning Edna's sanity.

"You know." Edna gave Cordelia *the look*, saying she was the one who'd lost her marbles. "Those heels you purchased at the consignment shop. The ones with the red soles. You said you would wear them the first time you went out with a man and not give a bloody darn if you saw the top of his bald head. Don't think you have to worry about that with Glen. He's a good head taller than you and has a thick mane of black as ink hair. I can't believe that sawed-off knob next door forbade you to wear heels, but considering his vanity, I can see it."

"You know, you're right. I've been dying to wear those shoes. I was going to save them for the exhibit, but they'd be perfect with this dress and the little bag I got."

"That's my girl!" Edna sighed, and the familiar far-away gleam entered her eyes. "Whitty and I would go to the canteen and dance for hours."

The doorbell chimed, causing a million butterflies to take flight in Cordelia's stomach. "It's Glen."

"I'll get the door." Edna scooted from her perch. "It could be Snot."

"No. It's Glen. I don't know why, but I know it's him." She slipped on her shoes and headed down the steps.

Delia slowed her pace once she reached the landing. No need for him to think she was eager. She drew in a deep breath and opened the door. Darn, he was handsome in his slacks and dress shirt. "Come on in," she forced the words out.

Glen smiled as his gaze slowly traveled down her body before moving back to her eyes. He swallowed, causing his Adam's apple to bob. "You're beautiful."

Her cheeks warmed, and she dropped her eyes. "Thank you. For a second there, I thought you were having second thoughts."

"Not hardly. Just stunned by your beauty."

"I thought the Blarney Stone was an Irish thing." Grinning like a foolish schoolgirl, she stepped back, allowing him to enter.

Glen chuckled. "It's no blarney, love. You're gorgeous. And I love that color on you. It reminds me of a field of thistles."

Delia blushed even more. She hadn't thought about the color, as this was one of her favorite dresses. "Let me get my bag." She retrieved her beige shoulder bag, the color matching her shoes perfectly. She also grabbed a scarf, seeing Glen had the top down on the convertible. "Edna, we're gone."

"Delia, a word, please." Edna headed down the steps toward them. "Please."

"Let me see what Edna wants," Delia whispered as she strode forward. "What is it?"

Edna clasped Delia's hand, slipping a few dollars into it. "Here's some mad money. Just in case…you know."

"Thank you." Delia folded her hand around Edna's, trying to give it back. "But I don't think I'll need it."

"You're right, but take it anyway. Every woman needs a little mad money." Edna went up on her tiptoes, pressing a kiss to Delia's cheek. "Doesn't he look sharp?"

"The man makes everything he wears look good," she whispered near Edna's ear. "Don't wait up for me."

"So, he's a man now and not a boy?" Edna winked. "Enjoy your night. I'll leave the light on for you." She winked at Glen before plodding toward the kitchen.

"Good night, Edna," He called, opening the door. "Shall we?"

"Yep." Delia stepped out as Glen closed the door behind them. Delia peered up at him as he checked to ensure he'd locked it. His lips pulled in a knowing grin. "You heard Edna, didn't you?"

"She didn't exactly whisper." Glen slipped his arm around her waist and leaned down. "Neither did you." His warm breath brushed her cheek.

"You look quite handsome tonight."

"Thank you." He opened the car door. "I can put the top up if you'd like."

"Keep it down. I grabbed a scarf to tie around my hair." She slipped into the seat and noticed Scott watching them. Well, she hoped he got an eyeful.

Glen shut her door, and the sunlight made his eyes appear dark red for a brief second. He glared in Scott's direction as he strode to the driver's side.

"Thank you," she whispered when Glen slipped behind the wheel.

"For?" he asked, backing from her driveway.

"Not flipping Scott off. I sensed you wanted to." Heck, she wanted to. Dang, it! She would not allow Scott to ruin tonight for her. Therefore, she was putting him out of her mind.

"You're welcome," Glen replied matter-of-factly as he drove toward the interstate.

"You're not going to deny it?"

"Denying it would be dishonest," Glen merged into traffic. "And I'll never lie to you."

"Really?" Delia turned in her seat, grinning. She'd have to put this to the test. "I can ask you anything, and you'll tell me?"

"Does that go for me as well?" He glanced at her. "Tell me one secret no one knows about you?"

"You're cute, but according to Benjamin, three people can keep a secret if two are dead."

Glen winked at her and flipped on his turn signal. "Well, my bonnie lass, there are some things I will not answer tonight, but if everything goes the way I hope, you'll know everything about me within a year."

A year? Did he hope their relationship would grow? Warmth spread through her. "Fair enough." Delia leaned back, closing her eyes and enjoying the sun on her face. "I could get used to riding in a convertible."

"Says the woman who wouldn't drive it," he teased.

"I said ride in it. I didn't say a thing about driving it."

"Point taken." Glen laughed. "What were you working on this morning when I stopped by?"

"Hmm. Believe it or not, the piece for you." She opened her eyes and exhaled. "I hate to say it, but I don't think the picture you showed me will do. I can use it, but I don't think it captures what you want."

"What do you mean?"

"From what I gather, you want it to celebrate your parents' love. The photo you showed me looks like any other photo of two people dressed up at some festival. It doesn't capture their love."

"Oh. So, you can't do the piece."

"No, I can, and I will, but I usually like getting to know an individual before sculpting them. This way, I can see a glimpse of the real person and their personality. For instance, I did a large piece of four children for a family, two sets of twins. Anyway, the photos their mother gave me were of four perfect angels. The piece I created showed the children's individual personalities. Are your parents planning on coming over for a visit anytime in the next few months?"

"Doubtful. They were just here for the birth of my nephew."

"Well, poo."

He pulled into The Abby's parking lot. "Meeting my parents would make the project easier for you."

"It would, but I'm not planning to fly to Scotland soon."

"What if the person is no longer alive?" Glen put the car in park and pressed the button, raising the ragtop.

"Then I do research. Videos are beneficial." Delia unfastened her seatbelt as the valet opened her door. "Thank you," she told the young man.

Glen stepped from the car. "Take care of it."

"Yes, sir." A kid who looked too young to drive slid behind the wheel. He killed the engine, trying to get it into gear.

Delia cringed at the sound. "You may need a new clutch."

"Then Angus will have something to do tomorrow, but I may have to park my car." Glen casually strode back to the valet station.

She couldn't believe he wasn't fazed by the grinding gears. Scott would scream at this point, threatening to sue everyone.

Another valet rushed past her. "Sorry, sir," he apologized to Glen and yanked the car door open, motioning for the other guy to get out. The new driver drove Glen's car off with no problems.

"Problem solved." Glen returned and slipped his arm around her waist.

"Ah, sir! Sir," the first valet called, running up to them. "I'm sorry…I didn't think it would be a problem." He rubbed the back of his neck. "I just learned how to drive a stick."

Glen eyed him. "No harm. With time, you'll be a pro."

"Thank you." The valet turned and hurried off.

Delia exhaled. "I promised myself not to mention my ex, but Scott would have blasted the poor kid instead of encouraging him."

"It's best to keep the head. Getting upset would ruin his night and have you thinking I'm a jerk, which would ruin my night. Besides, the kid was genuinely upset. No need to heap more grief on his shoulders."

"You amaze me, Glen MacPhee."

He chuckled. "Hopefully, in a good way."

"I assure you I wouldn't be here if it wasn't."

"Brilliant, because you had me worried when you said we needed to talk. I know the phrase, having several sisters, and the word *fine* means trouble."

"Well, we still need to talk. I need your advice."

"Then you will have it." He turned his attention to the host. "MacPhee. Party of two."

Their table was under one of the stained-glass windows. The last rays of sunlight through the colorful glass bathed their table in an abstract rainbow.

Soft music from the harpist in the choir loft filled the air.

Glen opened his menu. "I have to give Vaughn kudos for recommending this place. Of course, he could be biased since he brought his wife here on their first date."

Vaughn, the name sounded familiar. "Is he a friend?" Delia leafed through the menu and tried not to pay too much attention to the prices.

"He's my brother. Have you decided what you'd like?"

"So many choices, but I think I've narrowed it down to the grilled salmon with roasted vegetables." She peered over the menu at him. "What about you? Do you see something you'd like?"

"Most definitely." Glen's teasing expression didn't disguise the sensual look burning in his eyes. "Would you like some wine? Perhaps, a rosé?"

"Yes, please." Delia's heart pounded, and her pulse jolted. She squeezed her thighs together, trying to throttle the dizzying current racing through her.

Once they placed their order, Glen leaned back in his seat. "What advice do you need?" There was almost an imperceptible note of pleading in his eyes. With each passing second, Glen's smile slipped a bit more. "This advice, does it concern your ex?"

"No. Fiona called me yesterday." Delia's throat tightened, thinking about the grief and loneliness Edna had suffered all these years. "I can't believe all the years Edna and Whitaker were apart...."

"Was a tragic misunderstanding," Glen finished her statement as he reached across the table and clasped her hand.

Just his touch lifted the burden and gave her strength. "Yes. I've hesitated, telling Edna because I don't know how she'll handle it. She loved her Whitty so much. Is still in love with him, or rather, his memory."

"Would you like me there when you tell her?"

The waiter brought their food, giving her time to mull over Glen's offer. She could use the support, but... "Part of me does, but part of me doesn't. This is personal for her."

"I understand, but you should tell her soon. The worst is they discover they've both grown apart. On the other hand, they reconnect and rekindle their love." Glen cut into his steak.

His words sank into Delia's heart, lessening her despair. "You are a hopeless romantic, Glen MacPhee."

He chuckled. "Now you know something about me no one else knows."

"I feel more people know than you think." Delia took a bite of her salmon, savoring its delicious flavor.

"You're probably right." Glen cut another piece of steak, lifting it to his lips.

"Tell me something else about yourself. What made you decide to move to Atlanta?" It was only fair, Delia asked. Glen already knew more about her than she did him.

He took another bite, chewing slowly. She could practically see the wheels turning behind Glen's eyes.

"Three years ago, I realized how disenchanted I was with my job and turned in my notice with the yard. I twiddled my thumbs for a while, trying to figure out what I wanted to do. My cousin approached me with the offer of running Daemon Securities." He motioned toward her. "Your turn."

"I'm terrified of Ouija boards."

His eyebrows arched. "Seriously? You're afraid of a toy?"

"It's not a toy," she continued. "One night, my college roommate pulled one from under her bed. Afterward, strange stuff started happening and continued until I moved out."

"What sort of strange things happened to you?"

"Items went missing, an earring and a photo of me with my parents from when I was a child. Nothing of monetary value, only sentimental value to me. Then one morning, Tara and I woke up with chunks of our hair cut. That was the last straw. I don't know if someone was pranking us or if she opened some doorway to another dimension, but I moved out."

"You didn't feel someone cutting your hair? Wild girl's night?"

"Studying late, but no, I didn't feel anything. Come to think of it, I was so tired the next morning that I was almost late for class. But I hadn't anything stronger than ginger ale to drink the night before. To be honest, I chalked it up to cramming."

"What happened to your roommate?"

"I tried to get her to move into the apartment with me, but she wouldn't. I'd see her around campus, and we would talk, but we weren't close friends. After graduation, I saw her a few more times when we took the same classes Scott taught. Blast it. I said his name."

A deep, rich laugh rose from Glen. "It's no' like speaking his name will conjure him up."

"I don't know. He seems to pop up more in my life now than when we were married. Anyway, Tara was also in the sculpting class. Once the class ended, I never saw her again until recently. She found me on Facebook." Delia slid her empty plate aside.

"Would you like dessert?"

"Not if we're going to The Joint." Besides, she couldn't eat another bite if she wanted.

Glen's grin widened. "*Dinna* laugh at my dance moves." He motioned for their server.

"I'll be right back." Delia slid gracefully from her seat. As she strode toward the restrooms, she could almost feel Glen watching her. Every second she was with him, her feelings toward him intensified.

Was it wrong to fall for a younger man? She knew of several famous couples who made it work. Edna was right. It was time to take a chance.

Delia checked herself in the ladies' room mirror. Surprisingly, her makeup hadn't caked in any of her wrinkles, and her lip stain still looked good. She reapplied it anyway, staring at her reflection. She looked darn good for her age. Delia drew in a deep breath and stepped from the restroom. She'd never felt this excited when she was around Scott. Damn it! Not saying or thinking about him.

"Cordy." Chills coursed through her at the sound of *his* voice.

"Scott, stop following me."

"I'm not following you. I'm here with Britney. I guess you're here with your boy toy?"

"Pot calling the Kettle?"

"You know, Cordy, the cougar look isn't attractive on you."

Chapter Seven

Glen paid the bill as he waited for Delia. Everything was going better than he'd expected. Her exhibit was in ten days. If fate was on his side, she'd be his completely by then. Most in the family had mated within a week after meeting their true mates except for Vaughn, Royce, Cat, Victoria, and Quaid. Hmm, looked like he'd be joining them in the "Delayed Mating Club." Glen finished his glass of wine.

Delia's shame swept through him. The tiny drops of blood he'd given her were enough to help heal her and let him sense her powerful emotions. Before searching for her, he scanned the table and chairs, ensuring Delia hadn't left anything.

Glen turned down the hall toward the restrooms, struggling to restrain his daemon.

He is harming our mate, the creature's growl echoed in Glen's mind.

The closer he drew, the more he smelled the sickeningly sweet scent of fear drifting from Cordelia.

"*Mo gràdh?*" Glen slipped his arm around Delia's waist as he eyed Scott, pressing into the man's weak mind. "If I didn't know better, I'd say you were following us. What did you do? Call all the restaurants to see if we had reservations?"

Scott flushed. "You're the security specialist. Maybe you're the ones following Britney and me." He stormed off toward the bar.

Gently cupping Delia's face, Glen caressed her soft cheek with his thumb. "Did he threaten you?" It had to be the reason for her fear. If Scott had, the daemon would get his wish.

"No. I'm okay. I know we'd planned to go dancing, but would it be okay if we call it a night?"

Keeping his eyes locked on hers, he slid his hand down her arm, lacing their fingers. "If that's what you want."

Delia adverted her eyes and nodded. "Please."

Look at her. Look at the fear in her eyes. He's frightened our mate. We should kill him.

Glen led Delia from the restaurant, wrestling with his daemon, trying to force the creature back into his mental cage. The bloody thing was formidable. *If we kill him here, we risk exposing our kind.*

We fade into his dwelling and kill him there, the creature argued.

What part of no, do you not understand? Glen handed the valet his ticket.

Our mate reeks of fear. He needs to die.

"Stop growling," Delia snapped. "You sound like a bear."

See what we've done? Glen reprimanded his beast before giving Delia his full attention. "I will not lie. Yes, I'm angry at Scott for putting that look of hurt on your face, not because of the change in plans."

She gave a tight-lipped nod before hurrying down the steps toward the car. Before he reached her, the valet had opened the door, and Delia slid into her seat.

Glen handed the valet a twenty. This was not how he'd planned for their evening to go, but there was nothing he could say to ease the situation. He slid behind the wheel, closing his door.

"I'm sorry," Delia whispered. "for snapping at you. I'd like to know how he keeps following us."

"No need to apologize. I understand." Glen pulled into the line exiting the carpark. If he made a left, it would take time with traffic. If he made a right, it would add more time to the drive, plus take them toward the nightclub. "As for how Scott knew where we were, I think he did what I accused him of, especially from how red he turned."

From the line of traffic, there was no way he could make the left turn. Never thought he'd be thankful for Atlanta traffic. "We're taking the long way home."

"Fine. You think I'm giving in to him again, don't you? I mean, for ending the night early."

"The truth?" Glen glanced at her.

"Yes."

"I think Scott will be incredibly pleased when the video doorbell on Britney's house alerts him to our returning home before him."

Delia crossed her arms and leaned back against her seat. "It's just—never mind."

"Delia, what do I have to say or do to convince you of your worth?" Even if he could have made it, he stopped for the yellow light and pissed off the ass behind them. The prick waved his middle finger out the window and laid on the horn.

"My worth? Really?" Delia laughed and rolled her eyes.

"Yes, really. Delia, you're beautiful, you're sexy, you're talented, intelligent, and screw it. I'm just going to put it out there. I'm extremely attracted to you, and I *dinna* want to hear a bloody thing about the difference in our ages."

The ass behind them laid on his horn the second the light turned green. Glen took his time driving through the intersection. The ass made the turn for the club. At least someone would enjoy their night.

He watched Delia in his periphery stare straight ahead and fidget with her purse strap. As much as he wanted to show her off, Glen wouldn't force the issue. Tonight was all about her, not him.

After we take our mate home, can we kill the male?

It's tempting. Bloody hell, if the daemon wasn't sharpening his claws.

"Glen, you're right. Scott has manipulated me again. I'm through with his crap. If you still want to go to the club, we can. I mean, I'd like to. If you still—"

"Say no more." He took the next right.

"Glen! This is a one-way."

"I'm going one way." He came to the end of the street, slowed, and made a right onto another one-way, but this time he was going with traffic.

"You know that's a good way to get a ticket."

"I do." He turned into the crowded parking lot. "It wouldn't be my first."

"This place is packed."

He didn't miss the disappointment in Delia's voice. "We'll get in, *mo gràdh*."

"*Mo gràdh*, that's twice you've called me that. What does it mean? Truth."

"Truth or dare tonight, *verra weel*," he slipped into his natural Scots. "Just a wee term of endearment. We Scots have some wonderful words, such as bonnie and jobby."

"I know bonnie means beautiful." Delia laughed.

"Dae ye?" He pulled into one of the last parking spaces. "I have pockets, so let me have your mobile, license, and lip color so you no' have to keep up with your purse."

Her curious, liquid brown eyes studied him before she pulled her mobile from her bag. "Lip color is a stain, and my temporary license is in my phone case." She handed over the device. "So, you just need my phone."

"Thank ye. Let me come around to ye."

"You realize I'm an independent woman." Delia arched her eyebrows at him.

"I'm an auld fashioned man." Glen leaned toward her, quickly bussing her lips. He hurried to her side. "Mo bonnie lass." He opened her door, offering her his hand.

Delia grinned, allowing him to help her from the car. She laced her fingers with his, looking up at him. "Okay, so…jobby? The meaning is what? Lover?"

Damn, he'd do anything to keep that look on her face. "Na. It means poo."

She furrowed her brows, twisting her lips like he remembered Edna doing years ago. "Like Pooh bear?"

"No. No. Not that." Glen chuckled and led Delia around the people waiting in a long line. "It means shit, but it sounds a lot nicer."

Delia snorted as she pointed to the line. "Shouldn't we..."

"Cade's on the door."

"Hey," someone shouted at them. "Line's back there, bub."

Glen glanced at the guy. *If I pissed the bleeding ass off at the light, he'll be raging in the next second.* "Cade," Glen greeted.

"Hey, boss, Ms. Parsons." He opened the door for them. "By the way, boss. I turned in my vacation to Fiona."

Glen patted Cade's shoulder as he passed. The cat always had his expense receipts in on time, but it took an act of God to get Cade to take a vacation. "Good. One less murder I have to worry about her committing."

"Oh, and Sue's here somewhere."

"Not keeping tabs on my employees." Glen didn't need to with their blood bond.

"Why do they get to cut? And you didn't frisk him." The ass shouted.

"Buddy," Cade's deep voice overrode the music filling the club. "we've reached our asshole limit. Go on back to your car."

"I take it Daemon provides the security here," Delia stated.

"We do."

"One of the perks, I guess." She tilted her head, looking up at him. "So, are you packing?"

"Hmm, want to frisk me and find out?" He jiggled his eyebrows.

Instead of laughing, she rolled her eyes. "Not particularly."

He gave her his best pout. "You wound me."

"You'll get over it." She patted his arm.

He chuckled, loving this playful bantering side of her.

"Wow." She paused in her tracks. "This place *is* packed."

Glen blinked a couple of times, adjusting his vision to the strobe lighting near the stage. Delia was right. There was a huge crowd tonight. Then again, anytime or place Alejandro played was a sellout. He wasn't on stage yet, which was good. They hadn't missed the first set.

"Oh, my stars." Delia gripped Glen's hand with more strength than he'd thought she had. "Is that Alejandro Botela? I love his music."

"Really?" He had no idea. "Then it's a good thing we came."

"Yeah, I'm a huge fan of Latin Jazz." Delia's pulse quickened the longer she stared at Alejandro. "Is he waving at us? Oh, heavens! I think he is."

"Looks like you're right." Glen nodded, letting Alejandro know they saw him.

Delia squeezed Glen's hand tighter. His little mate had a grip.

"He's coming toward us," she said beneath her breath. "Okay, Delia, breathe. No fangirling allowed."

"Amigo!" Alejandro held his hand out to Glen. He pulled him in, pounding his back. "I was worried you wouldn't show." He eyed Delia, smiling. "But I see you would've had a good reason. Please, join us." Alejandro motioned to the club's VIP area, where Summer, Alejandro's wife, sat with a few band members. "I insist."

Glen glanced at Delia, trying to gauge her reaction. He'd think she'd stopped breathing if he didn't know better. He slipped his arm around her waist, hugging her to his side. Possessive move? Maybe, but it also kept her from face-planting due to the lack of oxygen. "Breathe," he whispered. In a matter of half a heartbeat, Delia drew in a deep breath, giving a faint nod.

"We'll be happy to join you," Glen answered. "But first, Alejandro, I'd like you to meet my date, Cordelia Parsons. Delia, Alejandro Botela."

Delia leaned more into Glen as she extended her hand. "It's a pleasure to meet you, Senor Botela."

"Alejandro to my friends, please." Smiling, he took Delia's hand as he perused her. "Have we met before?"

"No."

"Are you sure? You look so familiar." He frowned. "Your name is remarkably familiar to me. Are you sure we haven't met?"

"Trust me, I'm a huge fan." Delia's cheeks pinked. "I would remember meeting you."

"Hmm." Alejandro tapped the side of his head. "Cordelia Parsons. Parsons..." Recognition showed in his eyes. "The artist! You created the Crying Woman piece on the billboard."

"Guilty as charged."

Glen smiled. Delia's cheeks glowed bright red in the dark lighting of the club. Apparently, she didn't handle compliments well, probably because of her ex.

Told you we should kill the ass, Glen's daemon muttered. Instead of commenting, Glen focused on the conversation between Alejandro and Delia.

"I have to say," Alejandro continued. "The billboard doesn't do it justice. I was at the gallery the other day. The statuette spoke to me. I could almost see the tears flowing from her eyes. You are quite an artist."

Delia's flush deepened to crimson. "Thank you."

Glen pressed a kiss to her temple. "I told you so."

"Yes, you did." She rested her hand over his heart.

"Ah, my friend." Alejandro slapped Glen's back. "You have yourself a special woman."

"I know it." He just had to convince Delia to take a chance on him.

"Come," Alejandro motioned to the tables again. "I'd like to introduce you to my wife before I take the stage. She is a huge admirer of your works."

Once Alejandro made the introductions, Glen lost Cordelia. Summer whisked her off to a circular booth, then peppered Delia with questions about the sculpture. Apparently, Summer grew up in Nantahala and was a massive fan of the falls' legend.

"Ya know," Summer drawled. "My mee-maw used to tell us stories about people who lived on the mountain who could turn into bears. Can you imagine having the ability to change into an animal?"

"Bears?" Glen repeated. He guessed it was possible. After all, Toby shifted into a gator. He'd have to ask Aunt Gwyn.

"What I said. Bears." Summer batted her lashes at him.

"How did you two meet?" Delia glanced from Summer to Alejandro.

"Oh, he and a few of his guys were driving through town when their car broke down. Lucky for me, it was my turn to operate the tow truck." Summer flashed her husband a grin. "In a way, you could say I picked him up."

"Yes, you did, my love." Alejandro leaned down, giving her a quick kiss. He strode toward the darkened stage, followed by his band members.

Glen stood there like an *eejit* for a second before sliding in beside Delia, his knee brushing against hers.

"I was wondering if you planned on standing all night," Delia whispered.

"Just wanted every mon to see you're with me." Cocky? Perhaps, but his reply brought an even bigger smile to her lips. "Would you like something to drink? Wine? Beer?"

"We playing twenty questions?" A mischievous gleam sparkled in Delia's eyes. "Hmm. Boxers or briefs? Truth."

"Boxer-briefs when I wear them." He dropped his gaze to her full chest. "Turnabout is fair play. Front closures or back?"

"Neither. Pullover sports bra." Delia batted the long lashes framing her liquid brown eyes.

He wasn't expecting an answer from his little minx. Damn, if her reply didn't shut his mouth.

"Left you speechless?" A faint laugh rang in Delia's voice. "Just an FYI," she whispered. "I don't do butt-floss."

Summer giggled. "Oh, my stars, from your teasing, I'd say you two have been dating for a while. Hope we get an invite to the wedding." She lifted a glass of green liquid to her lips.

Delia flushed and pointed to the glass in Summer's hand. "What are you drinking? It looks interesting."

"Absinthe. I order a glass and sip it all night long. Do you like black licorice?"

"Oh, I love it. To the point, I buy a few bags of the black jellybeans this time of year."

Glen cringed. Black licorice was his least favorite candy, followed by candy corn. *I like licorice, especially on our mate's lips.* His bloody beast chimed in.

Summer handed Delia the glass. "Taste it."

Delia took a sip, closing her eyes. "Mmm. This is so good."

"Be careful," Glen warned. "Or you'll be seeing the Green Fairy."

Delia's eyes snapped open. "The what?"

"The Green Fairy," Summer repeated. "They say Absinthe is a hallucinogen. It's made from Anise, which gives it the licorice flavor, wormwood, and fennel. As much as I drink it, I've never had a hallucination, but I do sip it."

Glen caught the attention of a server. "A glass of Absinthe."

"And a Perrier, please," Delia asked. "I've learned to drink water when I drink alcohol."

"Smart woman. Two bottles of Perrier."

Summer tapped her glass. "Tell Kyle to make it like mine," she told the guy, taking the order, then gave a dismissive wave. She shifted in her seat, eyeing Glen. "Every time I've seen you, Glen, I've never seen you drink. Does this make you uncomfortable?" She motioned to her drink.

"Not at all. I had a glass of wine earlier tonight." He could drink every drop of alcohol in the club, resulting in a slight buzz for a few minutes. The inability to get drunk was a blessing and a curse of his kind. Over the centuries, there were many times he wished he could get steamin' and forget. But no such luck.

"Ma'am." The server brought their drinks.

Delia took a long sip before licking her lower lip. "That's delicious. Think I just found my new favorite."

We should taste her lips. The daemon groaned.

At least Glen and the creature were on the same page. *Patience, my friend, patience.*

Alejandro started playing, and people flooded the dancefloor. Summer excused herself, hurrying to the front of the stage, dancing for her husband.

Delia shifted her attention from Glen to the dancers as she moved to the beat of the music. "I feel like dancing."

"As you wish."

"Ah, that phrase could get you into trouble."

"Promise?" It'd been decades since Glen danced with a woman other than one of his sisters or cousins. Hopefully, Delia wouldn't call him out for his fossilized moves. The moment he slipped his arm around her waist, losing himself in the desire burning in Delia's eyes. Bloody hell, he was instantly hard. Jeans were so much better at hiding a boner than dress pants.

"You know, you're a liar, Glen MacPhee?"

"Excuse me?"

"You said you didn't know how to dance."

"I said, not to laugh at my moves. I never said I couldn't dance." He spun Delia around, then caught her, dipping her. Glen pulled her back up into his arms. Her thigh brushed against his arousal, and her eyes grew huge. Her cheeks turned blood red.

Keeping with the rhythm of the music, he spun Delia so her back pressed against his front. She instantly stiffened. "I'll not apologize for how my body reacts to you," he whispered against her ear. "You're gorgeous and sexy as fuck, and I'm the luckiest *mon* here." He spun her away, then pulled her back into his arms.

The song ended, but Alejandro quickly went into another. Glen looped his arm around Delia, moving her in a rusty

Bachata. Not surprisingly, Delia was a thousand times better than he was.

"Where did you learn to dance like this?" Delia slid her hands slowly up his chest until she looped her arms around his neck. Her moves turned more sensual.

"Mum insisted I take lessons."

"Really?"

"It's the truth." It was. His mum insisted he'd be up on the latest country dances such as the La Boulanger, Teasing Made Easy, and, of course, The Scotch reel. After all, he was the son of the MacPhee. "Where did you learn?"

"Going to clubs in my college days." Delia shimmied her hips, leaning back in his arms.

His heart soared, seeing this more free-spirited side of her. "Are you having fun?"

"I am, but I could use a drink."

He danced them to the edge of the floor, then led her back to their table.

Summer motioned to two bottles of Perrier and another glass of Absinthe. "I took the liberty of reordering for y'all. No disrespect to your men, Glen, but I don't trust any glass left unattended."

"None taken." He picked up a water bottle, unscrewed the cap, and handed the bottle to Delia.

"Especially with men like that." She tipped her glass toward the dancefloor.

"Isn't he the same jerk from the line?" Delia asked.

"I thought Cade sent the jerk on his way."

"Ouch," Summer gasped. "That's going to leave a mark."

"Girlfriend just slapped some sense into him." Delia took a sip of her drink. "Oh, I think this is stronger than the first."

Summer threw her head back, laughing. "This is why I love to people-watch. Too bad we don't have popcorn."

The woman hurried from the bar, followed by the ass. "I know I will sound like a male chauvinistic pig," Glen glanced at

Delia. "But how do women move in dresses that tight, let alone breathe?"

"Spandex," Summer and Delia said in unison.

Delia took a larger sip of her drink.

Glen winced. Someone would have a headache in the morning, and it wouldn't be him. He opened the second bottle of water and handed it to Delia. He enjoyed listening to the two women joke and laugh. It also allowed him to gleam bits of information about Delia, like she loved playing music while working.

"This is my favorite song." Delia covered his hand with hers. "Let's dance."

They swayed to the soft ballad, her body fitting snuggly against his. She rested her head on his chest.

With each breath Glen took, he savored her exotic fragrance, citrus, and something uniquely Cordelia. "I love how you smell." He nuzzled her neck.

Sighing, she leaned into him. "It's nothing special. A little vanilla, a little citrus and—"

"The Big Lebowski," a woman screeched.

"Not them again," Delia groaned.

Glen turned, spotting the same jerk from earlier. "Bloody hell!" If Delia's ex wasn't causing trouble, it was assholes like this guy.

"Don't be a hero," Delia whispered, tightening her arm around his waist. "Let's head back to our table."

He understood the risk of getting in the middle of a domestic argument. Hopefully, he wouldn't have to. Glen searched the area for Cade. The cat was good. Cade pushed his way through the gathering crowd the second their eyes met.

Mitch was more subtle, weaving his way toward them on the outskirts of the crowd.

"I'd say it's more like Tiny Tim." The woman shoved the guy, causing him to stumble into Glen.

"Bitch! Don't dis me." The ass grabbed the woman's upper arm with one hand as he lifted his other.

Shit, he'd have to get involved. Glen pushed Delia behind him as he blocked the man's downward motion, preventing him from striking the woman.

"Buddy," Cade snarled. "I told you once to leave." He twisted the prick's arm behind him. "Now, I'm making you."

"Get your hands off my Wally." The guy's date attacked Cade, kicking and clawing at his arms.

Sue rushed up and caught the woman's wrist. "And you're leaving, too."

The woman spun around, trying to scratch Sue's face.

"Bitch." Sue caught the woman's other wrist. "I will so rip those acrylics off one at a time."

"Fine." The banshee snatched her hand free, darted around Sue, and kneed Cade.

To his credit, the cat didn't flinch...much. At least none of the humans noticed. Glen bit the inside of his cheek. It was wrong to laugh...seriously wrong. Poor Cade. From the looks of it, every person had their phones out, recording the altercation. Glen bet it was all over social media by now. Sucked to be Cade. At least Percy wasn't blowing up their mobiles...yet.

Brett, the club's manager, pushed through the crowd, apologizing as he moved forward. The kid didn't have a mean bone in him. Good thing Cade was working tonight.

"Get them out of here," Cade ordered.

Brett cleared his throat, drawing all eyes. "Both of you are permanently barred from ever entering this establishment."

"Yeah?" Dick for brains puffed out his chest. "We'll see about this. I'm friends with the owner."

"Bullshit." Glen glared at the asshole. "I am the owner. Sue, Mitch, get them out of here."

"With pleasure." Sue followed the two toward the exit. She glanced over her shoulder at Cade. "You should ice those babies."

"You owe me double for tonight," Cade murmured.

"Should have worn a cup." Glen chuckled. "Proper planning and practice prevents piss poor performance. Or, in your case, cracked nuts."

Cade flipped them off as he sulked off.

Brett snickered. "I'll make sure he gets hazard pay. Before I forget, Vic called but didn't leave a message, just said to tell you she rang." The kid had questions. Delia was the first woman Glen had brought to the club. "If you need me, I'll be in the office."

"Brett, before you go, I'd like you to meet my date, Cordelia Parsons. Delia, Brett Moss, the best manager we have."

The kid blushed. "Your only manager. Ma'am, it's a pleasure." He pushed his hand through his auburn hair. "I'd best get back to work." Brett hurried away quicker than when he arrived.

Delia shook her head. "Is he old enough to be here, much less work?"

"He's old enough." Brett's boyish looks had more than one woman dropping their panties for him every night. Delia best not fall for his charms.

We should kill him. Glen's baser side growled.

Naw, we'll send his ass to Texas.

Delia tugged on his hand. "You're growling again."

"Only because our dance was interrupted."

Alejandro belted out a fast-beat tune Glen hadn't heard before. He slipped his arm around Delia's waist, moving her across the floor to the song's rhythm.

She peered up at him, and the look in her eyes had his daemon cowering. "So, Brett runs this place, but you own it. And I take it you also own Special-Grams. Why am I not surprised?"

"Is it a problem?"

Chapter Eight

Delia stared deep into Glen's eyes as he moved her across the floor. Was it a problem he had money? Not a darn bit. It did, however, raise the question again. Why her? In the club alone were countless younger and, to be honest, more attractive women than she'd ever be. Heavens, the night they first met, he was at her house because he'd lost a bet. Was this also some twisted wager?

"Stop it." Glen pulled her tighter against him. His hard shaft pressed against her hip. "You're in my arms, lass, because I want and desire *you,* not because of any bloody wager. *You* are the only woman who makes me hard."

"I…" How the heck had he known what she was thinking?

"I could see the wheels turning behind yer eyes." Glen dipped her, then pulled her back into his arms. "I'll answer all of yer questions."

His suggestion intrigued her. "All of my questions?"

"Every single one, honestly," he whispered against her ear. "I'll never lie to ye, Delia." Glen nipped her where her shoulder met her neck, and she nearly came right there on the dancefloor.

The bar lights brightened, causing her to blink. "Why are they turning up the lights?"

"The club's closed, and they're chasing out the stragglers."

"Why so early?"

"Early?" Glen laughed. "Lass, it's past two. Alejandro and his band have already packed up and left."

"But the music?"

Glen pointed up at the speakers overhead. Someone had turned the chairs over on the table where they'd sat. A female server pushed a broom across the deserted floor. "Guess time flies when you're having fun."

A huge grin split Glen's lips, and his eyes shimmered under the harsh barroom lights. "You enjoy being with me, and I make you happy. Yes?"

"You're cute, you know that?" She couldn't remember the last time she'd genuinely enjoyed herself with a man. Maybe it was the Absinthe, or perhaps she felt so happy being with Glen, but whatever the reason, she rose and nipped his lower lip.

Desire flared in Glen's eyes, sending a delightful shiver of wanting through her. Was she flirting with danger? What would it be like to make love with him? Her pulse quickened at the speculation.

What was she thinking? She was fifty-five, saggy, and wrinkled. Glen would take one look at her and run screaming into the night. It'd probably take the poor man years of therapy to get over the sight of her.

"You're the only woman in the world I want."

"I'm calling blarney." She leaned against him as they strolled toward the exit.

"Scottish, not Irish, lass. I even have the kilt to prove it."

"Do you, now?" Delia's mind flashed with the image of a long-haired Glen, wearing a Black Watch kilt and nothing else while wielding a broadsword. Blast Edna for leaving her romance novels strewn throughout the house.

Glen pushed against the metal bar, opening the door for her. As they exited, he threw up his hand, giving a wave. "Picturing me on the cover of a romance book. Are ye, now?"

"Nope." At least not at this exact moment. "Boxer-briefs or commando under the kilt?" She looked up at him, purposely batting her lashes.

His deep, rich laugh filled the night air. Glen slipped his arm around her, and she leaned against him. She hadn't thought they'd parked this far from the door. Then again, her feet didn't ache when they'd arrived. Delia couldn't wait to kick off her shoes.

"Not going to answer my question?" she teased.

"Will ye think poorly o' me?"

"I promise I won't." One look at Glen's carefree smile had her forgetting her achy feet. But, heck, the man was undoubtedly handsome.

"*Verra weel.* If I'm participating in the games, I wear black exercise shorts. If I'm mucking around the keep, then..." He leaned down and nipped her ear. "Depends on if I need to do the wash."

"Games? As in highland games?"

"Aye, or a good game of rugby."

"Oh, I love rugby. Edna got me—"

A driver revved a car engine, drawing her attention. The jerk flipped on his high beams, blinding her. Once again, she stared at Glen's back. Dang, if he didn't appear to grow taller and broader. Maybe there was something to what Summer said about hallucinations.

"Your day's coming, rich man!" a male shouted from the car. Tires squealed as the driver peeled from the parking lot and nearly sideswiped a passing car.

What a jerk!

Glen swung around, facing her. He gently tipped her face up toward his. "Are you all right?"

Delia should be used to how Glen's eyes appeared to have a red glow whenever he was mad, but she wasn't. Maybe it was because of a health condition? High blood pressure?

"Delia, are you okay?" The amount of concern in his eyes and voice warmed her.

"I'm fine. I hope Wally and his Big Lebowski make it home without killing someone." And just because the situation couldn't get any worse, her stomach growled. Great. Simply great.

The corners of Glen's lips twitched as he helped her into the car. Great. He'd heard her stomach. Wonderful. Next, she'd be tooting with every step she took like Edna. Getting old sucked, but it was better than the alternative.

Glen closed her door. He stood beside it as he scanned the parking lot. Outwardly he appeared calm, but she could see the tension radiating through him. Glen turned, catching her watching him, and smiled. He casually strolled to his side of the vehicle and slid behind the wheel. "Here, before I forget." Glen held out her phone.

"Thank you. I'd forgotten you had it." She slipped it into her purse.

Glen started the engine. "I'm a little peckish. What do you say we grab a bite before I take you home? I know this quaint little place that makes a top-notch omelet."

"Knowing Edna, she's waiting up for me. I should really get home." Delia slid her seat back then toed off her shoes, easing her throbbing feet. She peered over at Glen, noting his expressionless face, making her feel like a killjoy. To make matters worse, her stomach growled. "As you can tell, I'm a little hungry myself. What's the name of this place?"

"Glen's condo."

Delia fought hard not to laugh at the stunning man beside her, attempting an innocent little boy look. Something told her that look would forever be her downfall. "Is this something like come up to my place and look at my etchings?"

"You wound me, lass. You have my word I will be on my best behavior. Unless you demand differently." He jiggled his eyebrows and gave her a lecherous grin.

"Fine. How far is Glen's condo?"

"A couple of blocks. Not far."

Delia watched as a stream of cars went by before Glen could pull out onto the street. For it being so late, she couldn't believe the amount of traffic. Sighing, she closed her eyes and stretched her legs out, wiggling her toes, trying to get the blood back in them. The feeling slowly returned to her feet, and she tilted her head back, enjoying the Atlanta skyline. "The city's beautiful at night. No sirens. I guess Wally made it home safe."

"Let's hope."

"I have a question. Why do men name their….?"

"Cars?" Glen glanced at her with arched eyebrows.

"No. Their…" Heat flamed her cheeks, and she knew she blushed to her roots. Delia flicked her hand toward his lap.

"Dicks?" Amusement rang in Glen's voice.

At her age, she shouldn't be embarrassed. "Yes."

"There's nothing to be ashamed of, my bonnie lass. Tis proof you're a classy lady." Glen glanced at her with a Cheshire cat grin. "The reason males name their…*members* is that no *mon* wants to be led into trouble by a stranger."

She couldn't control her burst of laughter if her life depended on it. Glen's rich baritone laugh joined hers, making her laugh even harder until her sides ached. "Oh, my. I needed this."

His smile glowed in the dim light. "What? Finding out why men name their junk?"

"No. Laughing, enjoying life."

"Living?" Glen reached over, covering her hand with his.

She turned her palm up, giving his hand a squeeze. "More than just living. Thriving."

The light changed, and traffic rolled to a stop. Several cars moved through the intersection as they waited their turn. "My place is to the left, down this road."

"Wait, you have a place in the chair factory?"

"I do. Are you afraid of the ghost stories concerning the place?" The light changed, and he made the turn.

"No, not at all. Maybe a bit envious. Everything is within walking distance, restaurants, theaters, and shopping. The gallery is a few blocks away. I can't wait to see your place."

"Hmm, I hope I remembered to pick up my dirty laundry." Glen chuckled.

Delia peered out the windshield at the large brick building coming into view. She bet his place was immaculate.

"Some would say it looked like a prison with the tall ornate fence surrounding it, but I like it. It reminded me of my flat in London when I saw the beauty in the old masonry work."

She'd heard the top floor condos had their own private sections on the Terrace roof, and somewhere on the grounds was a garden grotto with a to-die-for saltwater pool. Nice. "I don't get the prison vibe. I see beautiful craftsmanship in the stonework. What floor are you on?"

"The top." He turned on his indicator and slowed.

A car flew up on their rear before passing in a no-passing zone. A loud bang startled her as Glen's window shattered. Her seatbelt snapped, and she ended up on the car's floorboard. She peered up at Glen. Never mind seeing the green fairy, she stared at the devil himself—no more Absinthe for her.

"Stay down," the glowing red-eyed, horned demon ordered as he spun the car around a corner, tossing her against the door. "Were you hit?" Fangs peeked from below his upper lip.

Her blood chilled, and her breath caught. This was no hallucination.

"Delia, were you shot? Are you okay? Damn it, Cordelia, answer me." He sniffed the air and seemed to relax some.

Her fear ebbed the longer she stared at the monster, at the vampire, at Glen. Perhaps he was using his glamor on her, or whatever vampire mind control was called. No, somewhere in the deepest part of her soul, she knew she was safe with him. Or maybe she was just gullible. No. She was safe. Funny, she never felt safe with the *human* ass she'd married.

"Damn it, Delia!" Glen slammed on the brakes, causing her to slide even more into the floorboard. He turned in his seat and sniffed the air, his eyes glowing even more. "I can't smell blood, so I ken you were no' shot. Are you hurt anywhere else, love?"

In the dim light coming from the street, she noticed blood splattered on the side of his face and a dark stain blooming on his upper left arm, near his shoulder. Despite being hurt, Glen worried about her. There was no denying the concern in his voice. Nothing made sense. The longer she stared at the stain, the darker everything grew.

***

Glen turned in his seat, trying to assess any injuries Delia may have received. She lay slumped in her seat, mainly on the floorboard. Hell's bloody bells. He'd mucked up big time. No, he hadn't. He'd bet his last tenner *Wally* was to blame. Wally and the bloody daemon sharing Glen's soul.

The bullet might have hit our mate if I hadn't taken over. Your body is nothing more than a pillow.

Instead of arguing with the beast, Glen pulled out his mobile while keeping an eye on Delia. She was gorgeous when she slept. Only she was passed out, not sleeping. At least her breathing was even, and her heart rate had returned to normal. She no longer reeked of fear. But her beautiful brown eyes were closed. Damn, why couldn't anything ever be easy?

At least his bonnie mate didn't scream her bloody head off. Her thinking him a monster, a vampire, didn't faze him, but the fear in her eyes gutted him. Perhaps when she woke, it would be best if he wasn't in the car with her. He got out and went around to her side. He'd give her a second to wake, compose herself, and perhaps scream bloody murder in the meantime.

Glen stared at the blank screen on his mobile for a millisecond before sending Angus a quick text. *Pick up Dragon. Drive-by, windows shattered. ENHANCE CAMERA.* Maybe there wasn't a need for all caps, but what the hell? He hadn't had time to see if there was one shooter or two. Wally would pay along with whoever else was with him. But right now, Delia was more important. An average person would have revived by now.

He opened her door, then gently brushed the small granular pieces of glass from her. "Come on, love. Wake up. You're safe." He lifted her back into the car seat, hating she had to go through this tonight, of all nights.

Delia's eyes fluttered before snapping open as wide as saucers. She stared at him, measuring him, weighing him, and by the saints, he hoped she didn't find him wanting.

"You're not supposed to exist."

"But I do. And the term is Dhampir, not Vampire."

Her eyes grew wide, and there was no mistaking the anger brewing behind her brown orbs. "Have you been reading my mind? According to lore, vampires have that ability."

He held up his hand, forefinger barely touching his thumb. "Just a wee bit."

"A wee bit? That's like being a wee bit pregnant. You either are, or you're not. You know you're a dick." Delia swung her legs, sitting on the edge of the seat with her bare feet resting on the garage floor.

"Most men are dicks, and why are you barefooted?"

"At least you don't deny it." She bent over, retrieving her heels. "I took off my heels because my feet hurt." Delia upended her shoes, dumping out several pieces of broken glass.

He cringed as she tried to force her swollen foot into the unforgiving leather atrocity. "I'm afraid, Cinderella, the slipper won't fit." That earned him a formidable glare from his bonnie lass.

She huffed, shoving her foot into the shoe. "You weren't driving erratically, didn't flip anyone off, and didn't cut anyone off. Why were we shot at?"

"I surmise Wally took exception at being tossed out of the club, so we should get somewhere safer." Glen offered his hand to Delia, and a scintilla of hope rose in his heart when she took it. He helped her to her feet, catching her when she stumbled. The sooner he got her inside, the better he'd feel.

"You're hurt." Delia's hand hovered near his arm.

"It's nothing. We should—"

"That amount of blood *is something*."

"Dhampir." He pointed to his face, knowing his eyes glowed.

She gasped. "Dick!"

Delia was right. He was a dick, especially for being pleased she'd worried about him. The bullet nicked him, but he'd already healed. Out in the open wasn't the place to have *the talk*. "Which is why I think we should get someplace safer."

"Safer for whom? Me or you?"

"Delia." He dropped his chin to his chest. Any moment, the shooter could circle back. Glen didn't have time for this shit. He swung her into his arms. "Safer for you."

Chapter Nine

Delia shoved against Glen's shoulder as he stepped inside an elevator car. The moment the door closed, he unceremoniously set her down. Her feet instantly throbbed in protest, and she leaned against the wall. As dangerous as the situation appeared, she wasn't afraid of Glen. What did it say about her psyche? When it came to men, she was a crappy judge of character. If she survived this, she was swearing off men for good, no matter how hot they were.

The door slid open, and lights flickered on inside Glen's spacious open-plan condo. She'd been right. From what she could see, the place was spotless and looked professionally decorated with a mix of mid-century modern and antique furniture in earth tones. Directly in front of her was a wall of floor-to-ceiling windows with a spectacular view of the Atlanta skyline. What she wouldn't give to have a studio with such lighting.

To the left was a brick wall and a fireplace. Mounted above was the biggest television she'd ever seen. She almost laughed at the bagpipes resting on the hearth, likely more for decoration and not to play. There were two doors on either side of the enormous fireplace, probably leading to the bedrooms. A fantastic kitchen was to the right of the room. Delia remained firmly planted against the far wall, despite wanting to explore the condo. "Are you going to bite me?"

The smoldering flames in Glen's eyes as he licked his lower lip startled her, but not as much as his fangs. "Only if we make love."

It took everything in her to fight the overwhelming desire to scream yes. "Then, that's a no."

"After you, my heart." Still smiling, Glen made a sweeping motion. The action brought his bloody arm into focus again.

"Your wound needs tending. Can I convince you to go to a hospital?"

"I would do anything for you except waste a trip to a hospital." He shrugged and motioned to himself. "Like I said, this is nothing." He stepped from the elevator.

"How can you say that?" She followed him into the spacious unit. "Your shirtsleeve is soaked."

"You're right, and cooking for you like this wouldn't be sanitary." Glen strolled across the room to a door closest to the windows. "Give me a moment to clean up."

"But your arm?"

"Make yourself at home." He closed the door behind him.

"Glen—Damn him!" What was it with her? If this were some cheesy horror flick, she'd scream for the woman to get out of there. Instead, Delia was worried about him. Whatever Glen was, he wasn't a monster, but what was he? Kind. Trustworthy. A flipping boy scout. No wonder she felt safe with him. Safe and, dare she say, even cherished? Those emotions were impossible for her to logically explain.

His home looked nothing like his office, void of any personal touches. In the corner between the wall of windows and his kitchen was an ancient and large grandfather clock, standing a good eight feet. The wooden case featured an elaborately carved hunting scene with wolves chasing deer and rabbits. Engraved on the clock's bonnet was a hunting horn resting on oak leaves. The clock face featured the phases of the moon and the zodiac. "Is it that late?" She glanced at her phone. "Guess it is."

Delia ran her hand over a wool plaid draped across the dark brown, reclining leather sectional. If she had to guess, the red, green, and yellow plaid was his family's tartan. The Christmas photograph on the sofa table confirmed her suspicions. Everyone in the picture wore pajamas of the same plaid.

Glen had an enormous family. And all the kids. She counted thirteen. Delia set the picture down. Did they know he was a vampire? Another photo caught her eye. Glen was grinning as he cradled an infant. The loving look on his face made Delia's heart ache. She would never be a mother. She set the picture down, only to snatch it up. Her eyes had to be deceiving her. Delia stared at the photo. Nope. She wasn't seeing things. The baby had fangs and a tiny drop of blood on its lip. There were also two tiny drops of blood on Glen's throat. "Vampire babies? Maybe I am in some alternate universe."

"It's Dhampir—"

"Oh jeez!" Delia nearly dropped the photo. "Make some noise next time."

"Sorry."

"No, you're not." She eyed Glen. He'd changed into a pair of worn jeans and a black pocketed t-shirt. From his wet hair, she figured he'd grabbed a shower. "How's the arm?" She couldn't see where he'd bandaged it.

"See for yourself." He pulled off his shirt and flexed his muscles. "All better."

Delia's breath caught. Good heavens. Her imagination was seriously lacking. She had his tattoos correct, right down to the clan badge inked over his heart that she distinctly remembered biting in her dream. But heaven help her, Glen's muscles had muscles. His serratus anterior muscles were clearly defined, and she could easily count all eight of his abdominals. Faint scars crisscrossed his abdomen and peeked from the waist of his jeans. She wondered what had caused the wounds. She would have kissed them. Damn it! Now, she sounded like Edna.

"I take it I meet with your approval."

Cocky man. His words had the same effect as ice water. She ran her fingers lightly over the vee where his deltoid met his biceps. There should be a wound, but his skin wasn't marred.

"Just trying to wrap my head around what I'm seeing. I can't tell where you were wounded." Maybe he was trying to gaslight her. A blood capsule under his shirt would explain the blood, and he could have rigged the car windows to explode. But why? Maybe Snot hired Glen to mess with her. Again, in her heart, she knew she could trust Glen.

He jerked. "That tickles."

"Sorry."

"No, you're not." He winked. Glen pulled his shirt back on and headed to the kitchen. "Would you care for some tea while I cook?"

"Tea would be nice, but you don't have to cook." She wanted answers, not food.

"I understand. You want my full attention. And Scott didn't hire me."

"Stop reading my mind."

"Sorry. I…" Glen sighed. "It happens before I realize I'm doing it. Again, I apologize. I will never harm you. I would give my life to keep you safe. Before you say anything, yeah, I know…I sound like a stalker."

"Just a little. Look, Glen. I…" She sank onto the sectional, stretched her legs, and toed off her shoes. What could she say? She probably didn't have to say anything with him strolling through her mind all the time. Yet, she believed he'd keep his word, which was the crazy part. Common sense said she should get as far away from Glen as possible, but the tiny piece of her brain kept reassuring her she was safe. Her heart agreed.

Looking around his place, she noticed a door on the other side of his kitchen. "What's that? Pantry?"

"Laundry and lavatory." He filled an electric kettle, took a tray of something from the refrigerator, and slid it into the toaster oven. "Master," Glen pointed to the door he'd hastened through earlier. "And that door leads to the guest room." He pointed to the door on the other side of the fireplace." What type of tea would you like?"

"Whatever you're drinking will be fine."

Glen leaned against the counter, crossing his arms over his chest. "I'm having O positive," he said smoothly, with no expression. "Would you like yours cold or warmed? I prefer mine at body temperature."

Jerk. But Glen was right. Delia hated it when she asked Edna what she wanted and got whatever. "I deserved that. What kind of tea do you have?"

Grinning and not turning around, Glen reached up behind him and flipped open the cabinet next to his refrigerator.

"You have more tea than my grocery store."

He chuckled. "In my defense, I haven't purchased any of this. My sister visits regularly and brings a few boxes. Then my clients tend to gift me teas whenever they come into the office. I'm not as obsessive as this appears."

The mouth-watering scent of something baking teased her nose. "What's in the toaster? It smells wonderful."

"Raspberry scones that Fiona made."

"Then, Earl Grey, and it doesn't matter what brand. No sugar or cream, please."

"Brilliant." Glen turned around and took down a tea tin. Then, after a few moments, he set a tray with two cups of tea and two plates with the scones down on the coffee table. He handed her a cup and a scone before taking a seat as far from her as possible on the sectional.

"Thank you." Delia sipped her tea as the silence stretched between them. One of them had to say something. "I thought you were having blood." Okay, so that wasn't the best opener.

Glen set his cup down. His mouth spread, showing his awfully long and sharp-looking fangs. "I changed my mind. Blood and raspberry scones just *dinna* go together." Glen's fangs retracted back into his gums. "Ask away. I know you have a zillion questions, and no, I haven't peeked into your mind. However, when your emotions are heightened like they are, it's pretty damn hard for me not to hear your thoughts."

Every question Delia had. Heck, every thought she had fled her mind. "I...I. Oh, damn it! What the devil are you? A Dhampir is the child of a vampire and human, right?"

Glen popped the rest of his scone into his mouth and held up a finger while chewing. Slowly. Very slowly. The irritating man. He was also confusing. Everything she heard, read, and watched about vampires he contradicted. He wasn't supposed to eat or go out in the sun, yet he did. Maybe he could because of his human side.

"Not the child of a vampire," Glen finally said. "But yes, that is the accepted definition of Dhampir." He took a sip of tea. "I heal quickly, have an extremely high metabolism, and I have to drink blood. Human. Blood."

Those two words affirmed something inside of Cordelia was broken. No sane person would remain sitting in the same room with anyone who'd just uttered the fact they drank human blood. Yet here she sat like some poor twit in a horror movie. "Is that why you've been so persistent I go out with you? You want to drink my blood? In exchange, I get what? A fountain of youth? I take it from your impersonation of a fish. The answer is yes to all the above."

She couldn't run. He'd catch her. She could scream, but she bet the place was soundproof. She was frigging screwed.

"You're not, Delia. I am, and yes, I heard your thoughts. You're broadcasting them in stereo." He tilted his head back and mouthed something before meeting her eyes again. "You can run. I will not chase you. You can scream. The neighbors will call the police. Delia, I will not harm you."

She believed him. Deep in her heart, she knew Glen would not hurt her, and yet. "My mind keeps repeating the story of the Scorpion and Frog."

Glen leaned back, sizing her up. "Well, my little scorpion, I trust you with my life."

"Wait—what? No. You're the scorpion, and I'm the frog." The poor frog only agreed to ferry the scorpion across the pond if the scorpion agreed not to sting him.

"Am I?" He folded his arms behind his head and casually stretched his long legs before him. "Anytime my people reveal ourselves to humans, we risk persecution and extermination. History is full of accounts, such as the Spanish Inquisition, the witch trials. When my ancestors first landed on this planet—"

"Wait a minute. Landed?" Delia sat up straight, staring Glen in the eyes. She couldn't believe what she was hearing. "You're an extraterrestrial? An alien? Are you one of the Roswell guys?" What if he was? What if this wasn't what Glen really looked like? What if he was some lizard or... dragon in disguise? Glen had horns, after all, and he purchased her Guardians piece.

"Noo jist haud on! I'm na dragon." He crossed his arms and glared at her.

"You look like one right now." Delia pointed to his forehead.

"Woman." Glen dropped his chin to his chest, shaking his head. "Forget everything." He stood and held out his hand." Come on, I'm taking ye home. Angus has already dropped off another vehicle."

She stared at Glen's out-reached hand for a second before crossing her arms and leaning away. "Not until you answer a few questions."

"Fine. I drink human blood because if I don't I suffer. Before you run screaming, I *do not* kill for the blood. It's donated by trusted friends. I was born, not made. My mither is Dhampir, my faither is human. I have an adopted brither an' sister and two biological sisters. I'm the middle child. An' I was born in 1776, so you're the youngster in this relationship."

Delia stared up at Glen. There was no doubting the raw hurt glittering in his pale blue eyes. Had she had this discussion with Scott, he'd have thrown his latest affair at her, snatched up his keys, and slammed the door behind him as he stormed out. But

Glen spewed information at her that piqued her curiosity even more. Especially the fact he was born in the 1700s. And she'd unintentionally hurt him. She had many reasons to fear Glen, mainly the horns and the blood thing. But there were so many reasons for her not to fear him. "I'm sorry I was insensitive. I'm not trying to make an excuse, but you must admit the whole landing on this planet statement was… unexpected. On top of that, the I drink human blood thing." She patted the cushion beside her. "Please."

"Why *dinna* ya fear me?" Glen loomed over her, staring at her with blood-red eyes.

If Glen MacPhee thought he rattled her, well, he did. "You haven't done anything to make me fear you unless you're keeping me safe for some nefarious reason." Damn it. She didn't mean to say that. Open mouth, insert foot, way to go, Delia.

"Haud yer wheesht!" Glen huffed. "Cordelia, answer me a question. Would you prefer never to have met me?"

Her heart and brain both screamed no. Glen didn't fit the mold of a vampire, but something told her he had the power to make her forget him. Delia couldn't deny the truth any longer. Maybe it was the power and energy Glen projected that drew her to him, or perhaps the undeniable bond between them that had formed in the short time she'd known him. Whatever the reason, she could never forget him no matter what mojo he pulled. Most importantly, she didn't want to forget him. "Never in a million years. You know when you get mad, your brogue gets really thick."

He nodded and sat beside her. "Lassie, ya making me daft."

"Yeah, if you think I make you crazy, put yourself in my shoes. How would you feel if the guy you're attracted to just dropped the Dhampir, alien, blood-sucking bomb on you? Were you honestly born in the 1700s?"

"Aye. The thirty-first of December. On Hogmanay." The shimmer returned to Glen's eyes, and a grin spread across his lips. "You're attracted to me? No denying it. I heard you with my own ears."

Cocky man. "Hmm. Hogmanay. Fitting, seeing that you're a tall, dark-haired man. I bet you're the first one to cross the threshold after midnight."

"Woman."

"Yes. I'm attracted to you. But why are you attracted to me? The truth now, Glen. Why me?"

He sat sideways, facing her, and drew his knee up on the cushion. With the back of his hand, he stroked the side of her face. She leaned into his gentle caress. The man was more addicting than chocolate, and he was stalling.

"Like I said," he sighed. "My ancestors came to this planet when your ancestors still lived in caves. We are the foundation of the legends of vampires, shapeshifters, and gargoyles. Like the legends, we have certain abilities. All of us have telepathic and telekinetic powers. Some more than others."

She didn't want to sound skeptical, but. "You can make things move."

Glen's eyes twinkled with mischief as he stared at the tray with their plates and cups. The dishes rattled as the tray lifted from the coffee table, flew over to the counter, separating the kitchen from the living room. The tray dropped to the counter, and Delia was sure a dish or two broke.

"Still having problems sticking the landing." Glen shrugged.

"Wow. That trick comes in handy. What else can you do?"

"A few of us can fly. Some can take the forms of animals that have existed and are of the same mass as the person, so no dragons. Others of my kind can fade, moving through solid objects."

"Since no dragons, I take it you're the gargoyle?" Dang, she bet Glen would have made a sexy dragon.

"I am. I can't fly. I fade." Glen slowly became transparent with each word until he was nothing more than a wisp of mist that vanished.

Delia sat frozen in anticipation of what he'd do next. The cushion behind her dipped, and warm breath teased the back of her neck. His ghostly hand grew more solid as it slid down her arm. Finally, a warm, solid hand covered hers. She leaned back into the warmth of his hard body. "If you ever tire of running a security company, you could always do a residency in Vegas as a magician."

He tightened his arms around her waist and rested his chin on her crown. "Did that during the Depression—not in Vegas, but with a traveling show."

This amazing man who held her had lived more lifetimes than Delia could imagine. The undeniable and dreadful fact pierced her brain. She was fifty-five. Glen was so much older than her, but. "You may be immortal, but I'm not."

"Delia—"

"No." She pulled from his embrace and shifted in her seat to face him. "Glen, I have had so much fun, and you have breathed life back into me, but I'm going to grow old, and I don't want you remembering me as an old hag who's lost her faculties."

"Longed lived, not immortal, and I will never see you as an old hag."

She regarded Glen with the somber reality with each passing day, she would age, and he would not. "It doesn't change the fact I will age much faster than you."

Glen drew in a deep breath, exhaling on a sigh. "Delia, my *da*, is human and was born around 1685. He and my mum were handfasted in 1713." He reached behind him, took a photo from the sofa table, and handed it to her. "That's a snap of him and Mum skiing last winter on holiday. Not bad for a human over three hundred."

Delia held the candid photo, staring at a couple who she would guess were in their mid to late forties if she hadn't known their ages. "You have your father's smile and your mother's eyes and hair color." She handed the picture back to him. "But what does this have to do with the fact I won't live to see a hundred, much less three hundred?"

"Do you believe in love at first sight?" He returned the photo to its place.

"No, and I'm not sure if I believe in love anymore." Her admission even shocked her, but it was the truth. Or was it? "I don't know if it was love or if I idolized Scott. He was charming and was always pushing me to improve my art. The sad part, I wanted our marriage to work more than he did. Even before we were married, I suspected Scott of having other lovers. I was stupid and believed his lies. He wasn't having affairs, those women were his students, and because of my insecurities, I imagined things."

Glen rested his hand lightly over hers. "Scott is a predator. He recognized your talent and wanted to either possess it or eliminate it. Trust me. I know a thing or two about predators." A smile bloomed beneath Glen's pale blue eyes.

"Do you believe in love at first sight?" Delia asked with a sick feeling she already knew his answer.

"I do. I've told you we are long-lived, drink blood, and have other special abilities."

"Such as reading people's minds?" She teased.

"Yes." Glen chuckled. "But we also sense our true mates. Our soul mates. The one individual who the Creator made especially for us."

If this wasn't a ration of bull, she didn't know what was. "Let me guess, I'm your mate?"

He nodded. "You can accept what I am, but not this." Glen propped his elbow against the back of the sectional, resting his head in his palm. "The first night I went to your house, I groused the entire way there. Ten minutes, that's all I had to do. Ring the doorbell. Once inside, I hit play and shook my arse while stripping to The Beatles - Birthday. At least the song had a fast-paced beat. If I was lucky, I'd be in and out in less time."

Delia couldn't help but laugh at the memory. Glen was so cute and looked ridiculous in the stupid costume he'd worn. "Instead, you ended staying much later."

Glen swallowed hard, his Adam's apple undulating. "I stared at your blue painted door, breathing in your scent and feeling like I'd just been sucker-punched in the nads. I was about to meet my mate while stripping in front of her. I knew the Creator had a sense of humor, but bloody hell."

"Then you saw me and knew you were being punished." She wiped at her eyes. Tears from laughing and from what could never be.

"No. I saw you and thanked God for blessing me with an incredible woman who was brave, intelligent, and beautiful. I wanted to kill the bastards who put their hand on you. That's when I went to your refrigerator for an ice pack."

They'd reached a point in the conversation where their relationship had to be resolved. Delia's stomach churned, knowing she'd hurt him. But what Glen deserved, she could never give him. "A mate. To raise a family with someone you love and cherish for all your life?"

He nodded. "When my kind claims our mates. When we make love for the first time, I will take your blood, giving you my blood in return. This act will bind us as well as change you physically. You will age as I do. I will never, ever forsake your love. I will be at your side until we both leave this world."

Tears spilled from her eyes and rolled down her cheeks. "I'm sorry. I can't give you that."

"Delia." He leaned closer, reaching for her.

"No, Glen. I'm sure your blood can do amazing things, but I doubt it can regrow a uterus."

Chapter Ten

Glen struggled as he reined in his daemon. The tears shimmering in Delia's eyes had the bloody beast roaring. Glen didn't like her crying any more than his daemon. "You're right, Delia. Our blood can cure just about everything except death or regrow severed limbs and organs. If it could," he pointed to a photo he'd taken last fall. "Quaid wouldn't be sporting that steampunk prosthetic. Drive a stake through my heart. If I'm lucky, I can pull it out, and my heart will repair itself. The skin over the wound will heal and, over time, fade, leaving no trace of the injury. But, cut off my head, I'll turn to a pile of ash. Cutting off an arm or leg isn't as fatal, but the limb turns to ash and doesn't grow back. The same goes for kidneys, gallbladder, appendix, tonsils."

Anger and hurt flashed in Delia's eyes. "If you're telling me this because you think I'll try to kill you, I won't. Let me tell you something, mister. I'm not your mate. Anyone with eyes can see from those pictures you love children. It isn't fair to you if you want a family that some pheromone you sniffed told you I was the woman of your dreams. I'm not! As much as I would love a house full of kids, I can't give you children."

"Are you finished?" he asked.

Delia pressed her lips together and motioned for him to speak. "By all means, continue."

If he accomplished one thing tonight, it would be to get it through her stubborn head. He didn't give a bloody hell about her uterus or age. He loved the woman. "Good. Yes, I love kids. I love my nieces and nephews *very* much."

"Point made—"

"Bloody hell, woman! Would you let me say something?"

"Say what you want." She pulled her phone from her purse."

"What are you doing?"

"Calling a ride share to take me home."

"Not until you hear what I have to say." He snatched the phone from her and tossed it across the room. Not his best choice of action, but if he didn't tell her now, he'd never have the courage later.

Delia crossed her arms. Angry brown orbs bored into him. "Speak."

"We can sense others of our kind, and if we have shared blood with them...June 6, 1944. Sword Beach. There were 142 of us—Dhampirs. Royce and I were part of the beach clearing team. The tanks had successfully made it ashore, providing us with cover. But the bloody Germans—war is war, right? They'd heavily mined the beach and peppered it with anything they could. It's not like we thought securing the stretch of land would be a stroll in the park, but...." He rubbed his side as memories rushed forward. "Even if you could bear children, I couldn't sire them."

His daemon roared. *Shut-up. If she knows we're weak, she'll leave.*

She needs to know.

Delia scooted closer and laid her hand on his thigh. Compassion replaced the anger in her eyes. Thank God it wasn't pity. He wouldn't be able to handle it if she pitied him. "The scars on your stomach are barely noticeable. How badly were you wounded?"

"The most severe injuries and vital organs heal first. Scars and less vital parts heal last. Sometimes they never heal." He should have died. "Eighteen of my people died that day, including my nephew. I staggered when I felt his death. The next thing I knew, I was face down in the sand. The raging battle around me sounded muffled. I couldn't move. I couldn't feel anything below my waist, and I was a bloody coward. I *didna* lift my head to check the damage, fearing what I'd see. I waited for my body to turn to ash, then welcomed the darkness as it took me."

"But you survived."

"I did. I woke up to Royce and Vaughn taking turns feeding me. There were several dead German soldiers piled in the house with us. Royce and Vaughn had found me and somehow got one of our medics to me. They'd removed so much shrapnel from my body that they didn't know if I would live, much less walk. I lost my spleen, a kidney, half my liver, but that grows back even in humans. I have a laundry list of injuries I will not go through. So, here I am," he motioned to himself. "Alive and *whingeing* when so many died." Damn, he was a bloody wanker, yet a sense of peace flowed through him for the first time since that day.

"Are you sure—"

Before Delia could utter another word, he placed his finger over her lips. He would love to have silenced her with a kiss, but from the look in Delia's eyes, she'd bite his tongue off. "A little over three years ago, I was injured in a blast again. This time I lost my vision temporarily. Once I regained my sight, our healer rechecked me. Not much had changed."

Delia batted his hand away. "Next time, I'll bite the finger."

"Ah, foreplay." Glen flashed his fangs, trying to lighten the mood, but from her expression—he failed miserably.

"You're an ass. You know that?" Her face flushed, but amusement flickered in her eyes, and her lips twitched before spreading into a full smile.

"But, I'm your ass."

"Glen—"

This time, he did lean forward, silencing her with a quick kiss. "Hear me out, please." He rested his forehead against Delia's.

She shifted, snuggling against him and resting her head on his shoulder. "I like you, Glen. I seriously do. But I'm not in love. I mean, we've been on one date."

"Technically, two." He slipped his arm around her, causing her to rest her head on his chest.

"Whatever. The point is, you can't expect me to say yes, let's get married, mated, or whatever you call it. *You're* drawn to me because of some chemical reaction in your brain. I'm human. I need time to get to know you, and even after that, there's no guarantee we'll end up getting along, much less loving each other. You may take one look at my naked body and bolt. Like I told you before, I'm not a twenty-something. Gravity has taken a toll, Glen. My body is ugly."

That's it. He'd told her he would be honest. Glen slipped his arm from around Delia and stood. She eyed him curiously as he pulled off his shirt, then toed off his shoes. At least he hadn't gone commando tonight.

"What are you doing?"

"Showing you ugly." He undid his jeans, dropping them to the floor, and shifted.

***

Show her ugly? Delia was too startled by Glen's words to object. She'd already told him his scars were barely noticeable…Unless. Dear heaven, had the landmine blown off his—no, she'd clearly felt his erection when they danced. Her mouth dropped open, and she was too stunned to scream as Glen changed. Hell, she couldn't even breathe. She was sadly mistaken if she thought she'd seen his true self in the car.

Horns grew from his forehead, curving back like a ram's horns. Glen's fangs were massive and protruded from his mouth. His fingernails were deadly curved talons, as were his toenails. Glen was a tall, muscular man who was over six feet tall. But this form…he had to be closer to seven feet tall with width and bulk to match. The longer she stared at him, the closer to hysteria she inched. He didn't move, remaining still as a statue. She met his eyes, and the tenderness in his red eyes removed all fear. No matter the form, this was her Glen. Her Glen? *Damn it, Delia. He isn't a puppy. But...* "The windows. People will see you."

Glen glanced toward the windows and shrugged. If he wasn't concerned, she wouldn't be either.

Delia panned down his body again, taking in his incredibly muscular torso. She wanted to sketch it! Heck, she wanted to immortalize him in bronze. Never had she seen a more exemplary male specimen in her life. Her gaze dipped lower, and she bit her lip at this…gargoyle wearing boxer briefs and his jeans pooling around his ankles. And yet…those boxer-briefs stretched to the point of tearing—if he was that gigantic relaxed, there was no way his package would *ever* fit in her mail slot. Delia swallowed. "Gargoyle?"

Glen shrugged again, keeping his eyes locked on her. He had a look in them that said he'd bolt if she uttered boo. What did he have to fear? She was perplexed about Glen not uttering a word since his transformation. Perhaps he couldn't speak, especially with a mouth full of sharp fangs. She wondered if all his teeth were pointy, but maybe some things were best not answered.

Gargoyle. No, Glen didn't look gargoyle-esque. "No, you're not a gargoyle. I just can't see it." Her comment got a raised eyebrow.

She stood and took a step back to see him better. Then she eased around the coffee table to study him from a slightly different angle. She wanted, no, needed, to see more of his incredible muscles. The horns and claws, not so much. The Barberini Faun sculpture came to mind. Glen could have posed for it had he been around in 537AD. Hmm, maybe the Billy Goat Statue at the Zwinger Palace in Dresden? Nope, he wasn't born then. "You're a Satyr or a Faun."

He scoffed. "I'm no bleeding, gormless prancing faun, and I'm not a bloody goat."

"You can talk?"

"Aye." Glen grinned, revealing more of his exceedingly long fangs and regular-looking teeth. "Someone has watched too many horror movies." He held his arms out like Frankenstein's monster. "Thinking I should only growl." Glen took a step toward her, stumbled over his pants, and smacked his chin on the cushion. Laughing, he peered up at her through his dark lashes. "So much for my monster persona." The amusement intensified in Glen's eyes as he regarded her.

"You did that on purpose," she accused.

"Guilty." He chuckled and, with a fluid motion, pushed up and flipped around, sitting on the couch. "But, *not* a goat."

She didn't need mind-reading abilities to know Glen was leaving where their relationship would go to her, which was the million-dollar question. Where did she want it to go, and what did she want from this incredible man? She liked him and enjoyed his company. Since she'd met him, Glen had occupied nearly every thought, both waking and wet-dreaming. But lust wasn't love.

"How about Zeus-Ammon?" Delia eased down beside him, crossing her legs at the ankles. The moment she covered his hand with hers, Glen exhaled. Even though he'd visibly relaxed, he kept his horned appearance. From his boyish glances at her, she guessed he wanted her more comfortable with this form. Silly boy.

"Zeus? I like the sound of that." He flashed her another boyish grin.

Still a satyr, though. She smoothed a finger down his clawed index nail as she examined it. "I know a great nail technician who could take care of these for you. As for the toenails, I bet they're hard on sheets."

He pulled his foot from his pants, held it up, and wiggled his toes. "You have no idea."

Dang, her goofy satyr was big. Correction. Enormous. "I thought you said you had to shift into an animal of the same mass as you?"

"The shifters do, but for some reason, those of us with DuMond or Lucard blood tend to be exceptions to rules." Once more, his expression grew serious. "Does my size frighten you?"

Frightened wouldn't be the word she'd use. "A little. Is this how you look when you have sex?"

"No. This is my battle form." A lazy smile spread across his lips. "This is how I'll look when we make love."

Glen's horns slowly sank back into his forehead as he returned to his more normal-looking self. Normal, if she ignored the red eyes and fangs. At least he didn't need a mani-pedi anymore. Still, Delia's heart pounded more erratically than when he looked like Lucifer's kid brother. Her gaze dipped to his lap, and she quickly averted her eyes. Some parts of him hadn't shrunken in the least bit. Delia cleared her throat, pretending not to be affected by him, and vacated her seat.

"Delia?"

She strolled to the windows, looking out at the Atlanta skyline. "You can pull your pants up anytime now. It's awful bright out there. Is it like that all the time?"

Strong arms wrapped around her waist, tugging her back against a hard bare chest, and she gulped. "Only from dawn to dusk, my bonnie lass."

She turned in his arms, and yep—heart attack in the making. It was one thing dancing in a clothed Glen's arms and totally another standing in the arms of a half-naked Glen. "Wouldn't it be better security if you had the light on at night?"

"Humm." He rested his forehead against hers. "Then, my lass, the night would be day, and the day would be night, for that light through yonder window is the sun."

"Kinda butchering William there, aren't you?"

Glen shrugged. "A little, but Willie was no Rabbie Burns."

"Bless your heart." She glanced at the grandfather clock. "Please tell me the time isn't correct?"

"It's not." She breathed a sigh of relief. "That old clock is slow."

"What?" Oh, for heaven's sakes, she'd been up all night.

"It's about a quarter past seven, and one of us is calling into work today."

"Sorry. I'll see you a Fiona and raise you an Edna." Delia dropped her head to Glen's chest. "She'd gonna have kittens when I get home."

"You can always spend the day here."

Delia wouldn't deny the offer was very tempting. Blast her treacherous body. Her heart and lady parts were all on board, too. "I'm not going to lie to you. I like you. I like you a lot, but I'm not... I dated Snot for six months before we ever." She closed her eyes and drew a deep breath, breathing in Glen's cologne and natural scent. She wanted to clear her mind, but the action had her hormones in full gear. "If what you say is true. If I'm your—"

"You're my mate, Delia."

"If what you say is true," Delia placed her finger over his lips, and he promptly sucked it into his mouth. "Then," she cleared her throat. "We can take it slow and date for a while. I'll even let you escort me to this little thing I have on Saturday."

Glen leaned down to kiss her, and she wet her lips in anticipation. Her heart dropped when he pressed his lips to her forehead. "If I kiss you like I want, I'll have you naked in my bed before we come up for air." The desire in his eyes said he wasn't joking. It also pissed her off.

"Sure of yourself?" Delia stiffened at Glen's challenge. She tilted her head back and glared at him. "A little kissing and a flash of fang, and you think I'm dropping my panties for you? Think again, boy scout." Dang, the red in his cheeks practically matched his red eyes. At least he was remorseful for his comment.

"I'm sorry. I..." Glen's fangs retracted, eyes returned to their brilliant blue, and he flashed her the innocent look that would probably have her cutting him slack for the rest of their lives together—not. "At least I'm honest with you." His innocent grin turned carnal. "I can't wait to be yours for all time. I want to love you, worship you, watch your eyes as you scream your release over and over again."

Her panties instantly became damp, and she squeezed her inner muscles. "Yes, well, unless your fetish is sex with an unconscious partner, which raises more red flags than your fangs, eyes, or even your horns. Then yeah, it ain't happen today because I've been up for over twenty-four hours. I'm guessing so have you, which means if we had sex—"

"Make love."

"It would be over in 0.25 seconds with you passing out, leaving me to finish things on my own." Why in heavens had she vomited that?

Glen chuckled. "Lass, my stamina is a lot stronger." His eyes twinkled as he hugged her to him. "I'm giving you fair warning. Double up on your vitamins. You'll need your strength because I want to bind myself to you as your mate for as long as we live and make love to you every night. All. Night. Long."

Delia slid her hand up his bare chest and around his neck. "Since you put it that way." She nipped Glen's lower lip. His blue eyes turned crimson. "I suggest you take me home so we both can get some sleep."

"Together? In your bed?" He grinned.

"In a word…Edna. Oh, my. Edna." Panic raced through Delia. "There is no way we can ever let Edna find out about you."

"Don't fret," Glen said matter-of-factly. He leaned forward, brushing his lips against hers. "Edna already knows."

Chapter Eleven

Traffic heading into Atlanta was at a standstill, making Delia glad she didn't have to commute to work. The traffic heading toward her place wasn't moving much better. But it gave her time to mull over what Glen spewed. He was Edna's Glen, something Delia had already figured out. "You all gave Edna some of your blood, but she's aged. Granted, she looks younger than her years, but I always thought it was due to good genes."

"We healed her, not transformed her. That only happens when we claim our true mates." Glen glanced at Delia. Even behind his dark aviators, the longing in his eyes was unmistakable.

"I have to know. Why? Why risk exposing yourselves to save her?"

"We first met her in London. Edna was part of the Anti-Aircraft Battery, protecting the city against the blitzkrieg. We were all drawn to her can-do spirit. We met up with her again in Brussels. That's when we discovered she and Whitaker were fond of each other."

"You saved her for him."

"To be honest. We saved her for us. We'd grown fond of the lass."

"Because of your blood, Edna has perfect hearing, sight, and all of her wits about her."

"Right." Glen laughed and took her exit. "Yesterday when she called me on the carpet," he shook his head. "Edna said she doesn't have dementia. She only pretended to be eccentric because people spoke freely around a crazy old woman. Her words, not mine. I would never call her crazy. Manipulating, but not crazy."

Delia loved her aunt dearly. Every time Edna did something odd, it worried Delia even more. Bothered her to the point she'd gone behind Edna's back and spoken with her physician. Delia knew the man couldn't and wouldn't violate Edna's HIPAA privacy, but the man had to know about her eccentric behavior. "I'm going to kill her."

Glen rolled to a stop behind a school bus. "No, you're not."

"You're right. Besides, you'd probably just revive her again." Delia tried to suppress a yawn and failed miserably. Even in her college days, she hadn't stayed up this late.

"Can't heal death," Glen replied as he turned down her street.

She stared out her window at the houses. Her neighborhood hadn't existed fifteen years ago. Would it still be here in a hundred? Glen had explained several times to her, to the point of almost sounding like a broken record, once she claimed him...Bless his heart. Her boy scout was putting everything in her court. Glen had explained she would live as long as he did. But what about Edna? He'd given her his blood, as had Royce and Vaughn. "But your blood can extend life."

"To a degree." Glen pulled into her drive, killing the engine. "Before you ask. I gave you a few drops of my blood to heal you." He caressed Delia's cheek, pushing a stray wisp of hair behind her ear. Instinctively, she leaned into his hand. "You were hurt, and I couldn't bear to see you suffer." His knuckles brushed her cheek as he withdrew.

The thought of drinking Glen's blood should have her heaving her guts out, but it didn't. Instead, knowing he cared about her enough to heal her injuries endeared him to her that much more. "How long?" Delia reached over and slipped Glen's dark glasses from his face so she could see his eyes. "How long will Edna live?"

"Only the Lord knows." He took his glasses from her, catching her hand in his. "To be honest, the longer time passed, the more I gave up on finding her alive."

"I still have to tell her about Whitaker. I haven't found the right time, and well, to be honest, I've had other things on my mind."

"Your exhibit this weekend?"

Delia could be coy, but that wasn't her. "More like a particular sexy blue-eyed boy scout."

Hints of crimson colored Glen's eyes. "I've been thinking about an artist I'd *verra* much liked to kiss goodnight."

"Hmm. Since it's morning…maybe a good morning kiss?"

Glen leaned in, brushing his lips against hers in a light, feather-soft kiss. His eyes were dark red when he drew back, and a faint smile curved his mouth. Reclaiming her mouth, his kiss demanded a response from her, and she parted her lips. His hand gently cupped her cheek as he captured her lips in a heart-stopping, toe-curling, soul-scorching kiss.

Glen's tongue explored the recesses of her mouth, sending shivers of desire racing through her as she ran her fingers through his silky locks. Delia tried to get closer, but her seatbelt and the SUV's blasted console prevented her. Her seatbelt gave way. The console flipped up, and in one fluid motion, Glen snugly cradled her in his arms. All the while, he kept kissing her thoroughly until one of his fangs scraped her lower lip.

"Sorry," Glen murmured before reclaiming her mouth again. This time, his kiss was surprisingly gentle. When he drew back, his uneven breathing fanned her cheek. "I hurt you."

"You didn't." Delia snuggled, resting her head against his muscular chest and enjoying the feel of his arms around her. She had no desire to leave Glen's embrace, though she couldn't stay in the car forever.

"I should have more control. It's just with you, I *dinna*." Glen smoothed his hand down her arm.

She peered up at Glen. His fangs peeked below his lips. His eyes were closed, but she knew they glowed. How could she be so content with a man she hardly knew? Was she seriously considering binding herself to Glen for the rest of her life? Maybe. "Good thing you have dark tinted windows."

He drew in a deep breath, exhaling slowly. His fangs retracted, and his eyes returned to their beautiful sky blue. "It's just—"

"I get it. When you get horny, you really get horny."

"Let's get you inside before I throw this car in reverse and take you back to my place." Glen opened his door.

She caught his arm, halting his exit. "You don't have to get out. I can see myself in."

Glen leaned over, kissing her. "I'll not have your ex or neighbors thinking badly of you." He got out and strode around to her side.

Bless his heart. Scott or her neighbors already had ideas if they'd watched her and Glen make out like two hormone-fueled teens in her driveway. However, she didn't give a darn what anyone thought. For the first time in her life, Delia knew how it felt to have a man desire her. Even with her fine lines and less-than-perky boobs.

Glen opened her door, smiling at her. He arched his brow. "Second thoughts?"

"Coming." She slung her purse over her shoulder, then grabbed her shoes. She'd toed them off in the car and wasn't about to make her feet suffer again.

"Here, I thought you'd changed your mind about going back to my place," Glen teased and slid his hands around her waist, helping her out of the jacked-up SUV. Even with her height, hopping down from the thing was a stretch. He set her feet softly on the ground, keeping an arm around her waist. "Call me when you wake. I'd like to see you again."

"I'd like that." She slipped her arm around Glen's waist as they strolled across the lawn toward the door. The morning dew felt terrific on her bare feet. Shoes were so overrated. "Maybe Edna isn't up yet."

"She's been peeking out the window since we pulled up." Glen nodded toward the picture window. Sure enough, Edna's silhouette was clearly visible behind the sheer. "She wasn't our only voyeur." He threw his hand up in a greeting at Scott. "Beautiful morn, isn't it?"

Delia smiled, leaning closer to Glen. Scott just glared. If looks could kill, she and Glen would be dead. "Being civil or trying to goad him?"

"Neither. I was being a typical male and letting your ex know we're a couple. Like you did when you smiled at him and leaned your head against my arm."

"Here, I thought I was just neighborly. Besides, Scott isn't the brightest bulb in the lamp. You may have to spell it out for him several times."

"I can do that." Glen kissed her, a slow, smooth, gentle, just lips pressed to lips kiss. He smacked his lips when he lifted them from hers. "You make me drunk."

"I'm sure lack of sleep has something to do with it."

"You're back from breakfast already?" Edna shouted loud enough to be heard miles away. "I thought you'd be gone longer."

A school bus rolled down the street. Several of Delia's neighbors stood in their yards to see their little ones off to school. Laura and Kelly wore knowing grins and gave Delia a subtle thumbs-up as they openly eye-groped Glen.

"Same ole, Eddie," Glen murmured and slipped his arm around Delia's waist, leading her toward the open door.

Edna stepped back and eyed Glen. "At least he didn't let you do the walk of shame alone." She shut the door behind them.

Delia kissed Edna's cheek. "Hmm, I wouldn't call it the walk of shame. From the looks on Kelly's and Laura's faces, I'd say it was more like a you-go-girl strut."

"Cordelia Anwen Parsons, I can't believe you said that."

"Anwen, huh? It's fitting. You are gorgeous."

Delia hated her middle name passionately, but couldn't be mad at Glen for his compliment.

"You should have called me or something," Edna continued. "I could have had a heart attack and died before you returned home."

Oh, no. After years of listening to Edna's ailments, it was ending now. "Are heart attacks possible?" Delia peered up at Glen. "I mean, you gave her so much Dhampir blood."

He shrugged. "It has been several years, but I'm no healer."

Edna's eyes nearly fell out of her head, and she gasped. "You told her? It took you bloody damn long enough. Right. Well, tea's ready." She looped her arm with Delia's. "Did you have a good time? This one," Edna jerked her head toward Glen. "Was my favorite of all my boys, you know."

"Edna," Glen chuckled as he followed them into the kitchen. "You were my favorite ATS girl."

"Don't think flattery will get you out of trouble. I would have appreciated a phone call or text." She patted Glen's cheek as she poured the tea. "Now tell me about your evening. I was so worried Snotface had ruined it. Not a minute after you left, he was pounding on the door, demanding to know where you'd gone. I told him I didn't know, which was the truth. Then I told him to get his arse off my property before I dragged out my old Sten. I'd called the police to come get his carcass. Ole' Snot skedaddled straight away. Ten minutes later, he dragged that poor stupid girl behind him, shouting at her to hurry. Next thing, I heard tires squealing. Man nearly hit the *Amazon* truck."

"Eddie," Glen pinched the bridge of his nose. "First, threaten no one with a gun. You could be arrested. Second, do you even have that old relic?"

"I do," Edna snapped. "I keep it in good firing order. Took it to the range just last week. You know women get to shoot for free on Wednesdays. Now," She patted Delia's hand. "Tell me you didn't encounter that tosser."

Delia nodded. Maybe it was time for her to persuade her lawyers about the restraining order. "We ran into him at the restaurant. I'll call Patsy and Luke after I get some sleep."

"Please tell me he didn't cause a ruckus."

Edna would no doubt have a conniption. As for Glen, Delia peered over at him. He stared at her. His pale blue eyes were red as he lifted his cup to his lips. What she wouldn't give to know what he was thinking. Of course, that could make her an accessory to a crime.

"Scott just called me a cougar. If I'm a cougar, what's he? A pedophile or a sugar daddy?"

"Desperate, if you ask me," Edna crooned. "But calling you a cougar, it's bloody damn time he gave you a compliment."

"What?" Delia nearly dropped her cup. "How in the hell is calling me a cougar a compliment?"

"Cougar is a far better name than that other feline reference *men* use."

Delia couldn't deal with her aunt with so little sleep and was almost afraid to ask Edna what she'd meant. "What other feline reference?"

Edna shot daggers at Glen. "Pussy!" she shouted.

Glen sputtered, spraying tea. He snatched up a handful of napkins. "Sorry." He held up his hand as he laughed. "For the record, I've never used that word regarding a woman, Eddie."

"I bet," Edna huffed. "Pussy, pussy, pussy," she continued her rant. "Oh, look, there goes a hot pussy. I'd sure like to tap that pussy. I'm so sick of the word. The next time I hear it, I will take my cane and use it as a pool cue, racking a couple of balls."

Delia knew it was wrong to laugh at her aunt, but Glen's laughter was so contagious she couldn't hold back. "Edna, you don't have a walking cane." Tears rolled down Delia's cheeks as she tried to get her amusement under control.

"Then I'll borrow Mary's."

"Mary uses a walker."

"Good, four tips instead of one."

"Edna, will you please stop? My sides hurt from laughing, and you're frightening Glen."

"He ought to be afraid." Edna shook a bony finger at him. "Mind you, use that word in my presence, and you'll be hitting high notes."

"See what I have to put up with?" Delia covered her mouth, fighting an overpowering urge to yawn. "Sorry, it's not the company, I assure you."

"I should leave and let you get some sleep." Glen took his cup to the sink.

"I'll walk you to the door." Delia slid her chair back.

He held out his hand to her, and when their hands touched, she laced her fingers with his. The warmth of Glen's hand inched up her arm. Damn, she craved his touch worse than she did chocolate, and all they'd done so far was kiss.

Bright morning sunlight bathed the family room in its warm glow. Another school bus rolled down the street. Delia rested her hand on the doorknob, pausing short of opening it. "Are you going to be okay driving? You can always crash in the guest room."

"I'll be fine. I've gone longer with no sleep." He slid his arm around her waist, hugging her to him. Glen's lips slowly descended to meet hers.

"I bloody well hope you two aren't snogging again," Edna shouted. "One would think you got enough of that, sitting in the car."

Delia rested her head against Glen's chest, listening to his heart pound. "I'm going to kill her."

"Let me," he chuckled. "I have experience."

Edna stomped her foot. "I heard that."

"I meant for you to hear." Glen flashed his fangs.

"Oh, stop it, both of you." Delia rose on her tiptoes and kissed his cheek. "Get some sleep." She opened the door.

"I can take a hint." Glen pressed a kiss to her forehead. "Get some sleep, as well. Call me." He slipped on his sunglasses as he strode toward his car.

Delia watched until he drove away. She stepped inside, closing the door. Sighing, she faced her aunt. "Edna, seriously?"

A huge grin curved her aunt's mouth. "You're his one. Right?"

Delia exhaled a long sigh of contentment. Blissful happiness filled her despite her exhaustion. "He says I am."

"Oh, bloody marvelous. This is the best news ever. You know, he was my favorite. Glen will treat you like you deserve to be treated. Now, off to bed with you."

"Good night, Edna." Delia paused on the steps. "What do you know about the Dhampir?"

"Nothing set in fact, only the stories and legends I heard as a wee girl. The Dhampirs were our version of the superhero, children of vampires and werewolves who protected the innocent. I never thought they existed until that night."

Cordelia didn't know all the details of the night Edna's battalion was overrun by the Nazis but had learned over the years that asking questions only led to Edna shutting down and doing a thorough housecleaning. "How do you know they are the good guys and not...monsters?"

"I listened to my heart." She patted Delia's hand. "Just like you have. Dilly, don't question your heart. You deserve someone who adores you and will kiss you and treat you with love and respect. You also deserve a bloody dragon who will roast everyone who has wronged you." Edna grinned. "Though, I never saw Glen breathe fire. Does he?"

She didn't know how but knew the answer. "No, and dragons don't exist." Then again, until tonight, Delia didn't think vampires did either.

"No, they don't. Though Glen has the horns." Edna wrinkled her nose. "Gives a new meaning to horny?"

"Edna!"

Georgiana Fields

"Well, it's true." Her aunt giggled. "Get some sleep."

Getting some sleep was easier said than done, even after a lavender-infused bath, which relaxed her and had her yawning. Despite her exhaustion, each time she closed her eyes, her mind relived the warmth and intimacy of Glen's kisses, making her body ache for his touch. Hugging her pillow, Delia tuned out the faint ringing of Edna's phone and exhaled.

Glen's thick brawny arm pulled her against his warm, naked body as he spooned with her. His hand cupped her breast. "Dream of me, lass."

"Cordelia!" Her door banged against the wall, startling her, and she bolted up in bed. Edna stood in the doorway.

"What's wrong?"

"You." Edna glared at Cordelia with burning, reproachful eyes. When crossed, Edna's temper could be uncontrollable. "How could you?" Tears streamed down her withered cheeks.

"How could I do what? What's this about?"

"Whitty! He's alive, and you knew it. You *knew* it!" She left, slamming the door.

Chapter Twelve

If you hadn't been such a gentleman, we'd be mated. Glen clenched his teeth as he maneuvered through the last of Atlanta's morning rush hour, trying to ignore the creature who shared his soul. *We should have never left our lair. We should have claimed what was ours. Our mate enjoyed our touch. She —*

"Enough!" Glen gripped the steering wheel so tight it cracked. "Cordelia has had one male ride roughshod in her life. She doesn't deserve an overbearing daemon, forcing himself on her. If she doesn't want to mate us for a hundred years, we wait a hundred years."

The damn beast paled, his mouth hung slack, and his red eyes grew huge. *A hundred years*, he sputtered. *But it will rot and fall off.*

Hell's bloody bells! Glen's mum was right. His daemon was a snot-nose fledgling. "Do you want Delia to love us or fear us? If we show her how special she is, treat her with the love and respect we have for her, she will welcome us into her heart."

And her bed?

"You have a one-track mind." Glen drove through the opened security gate and glanced in his back mirror. Good, no one was following him. He'd grab a couple hours of sleep. If Delia hadn't rung him back by the time his alarm sounded, he'd call her.

We could bring takeout to her and flowers.

"We could do that." Glen pulled out his mobile as he strode toward his elevator. He punched the up arrow as he made the call. An icy chill ran down Glen's spine. Why did Vic have to visit now, of all times?

Fiona picked up on the first ring. "Are you all right?"

"I'm good." The door slid closed, and he leaned against the wall. "Give me the deets."

"Cade said he's working on the footage Angus gave him. It's grainy, but Cade thinks he can enhance it enough to ID the perp. The Millers sent over their payment along with a bottle of whiskey, and Victoria's in town, other than that, same old same old."

The elevator door slid open, and Glen stared at the chaos scattered through his home. Victoria had kicked off her black heels centimeters from the door. Her black skirt littered the floor, and she'd tossed her gray blouse across his sectional. His sister didn't need a mate. She needed a bloody maid. "Hold down the fort, Fiona."

"I always do."

Glen disconnected and kicked Vic's shoes out of the way as he headed toward his bedroom. He'd deal with his sister after he had a few hours of shuteye. Vic best not say or do anything to hurt Delia. Otherwise, he'd wring his sister's bloody neck. He flung open his door. "What the bloody hell are you doing in my bed?"

Victoria bolted upright, yanking the sheets to her chin. "Sleeping," she hissed past her fangs.

"You're naked."

"How I always sleep," she snapped.

"In my bloody bed!"

"Well, if your guest bed had clean sheets, I wouldn't be in *your* bed."

"They are clean. My cleaning service changed them after you left the last time, which was last month."

"Exactly! They aren't fresh."

"For the love of—" He backed from the room, slamming the door behind him. Had Victoria been born when William wrote *The Taming of the Shrew*, Glen would swear the story was about her.

"Glen! Glen!"

"What?" He whirled around before he thought. Thank heavens Vic had the decency to wrap the sheets around her.

"Who's the woman? I could smell her the moment I entered."

"What are you doing here?"

"Business." Vic's signature condescending smirk spread across her lips. "What's her name?"

"Delia. She's an artist."

"Well, just because she can paint by numbers doesn't make her an artist."

He opened the door to his guest room. "She's also my mate."

Vic's fingernails bit deep into his shoulder, stopping his retreat. "Does she know?"

Glen reached up, removing her hand. "Delia can't have children, if that's what you're asking."

"And about us?" For once, his sister's voice held a hint of compassion. Or perhaps it was dreaming on his part.

"She knows." Glen stepped into the room, closing the door and locking it. Being a flyer, Vic couldn't fade through the door. Even if she could, as siblings, they had rules. No picking on one who was down. There was no snitching to the parents and no fading into bedrooms when the doors were closed and locked, unless the individual inside was in mortal peril.

He stripped, then crawled between the sheets. Vic was right. They didn't smell fresh, but they were clean and crisp. Glen folded his hands behind his head and exhaled, staring at the ceiling. If there was one good thing about the last ten minutes, the painful erection he'd been sporting since kissing Delia had lessened. At least Vic was here on business and wouldn't be in his way, even if part of him wanted to show Delia off. Perhaps before Victoria left, he'd arrange for her and Delia to meet. Before he did anything, he needed a few hours of sleep.

Glen rolled over and closed his eyes, imagining he spooned against Delia's naked body. He could almost feel her warmth as he draped his arm across her waist, his hand cupping her breast. His thumb teased her nipple, and she giggled.

Delia slammed her derriere into him, and he was instantly hard again. "Stop it," she murmured. His mate was ticklish. At least she was in his dreams. Humm wondered if she was ticklish for real.

"Dream of me, lass," he whispered.

The shrill sound pierced his brain, jarring him awake. Whoever was ringing him had better have a good reason. Glen fumbled for his phone, knocking his wallet to the floor. "Speak."

"Glen. I—"

"Delia?" He sat up, dragging his fingers through his hair.

"I didn't mean to wake you."

"No, you're fine." From her voice, something had clearly upset her. Or someone. Scott's life expectancy just shortened. "What's wrong?"

"It's Edna."

"Edna? Is she all right? Do you need to take her to emergency?"

"No. No. It's not her health. She received a call from Whitaker," Delia's voice hitched. "I've never seen her this upset in my life. I should have told her the second I found out...but."

He shouldered his phone and pulled on his jeans. "I'm on my way. I'll ring Percy and see if I can figure out things from that end. Will you be all right?"

"I'm fine. I'm just worried about her. Edna's locked her door, and I could hear her crying. I'm sorry. I shouldn't have bothered you with this."

"Delia. Delia?" Damn it, she disconnected. He tossed the phone to the bed and grabbed a shirt, yanking it over his head. Glen snatched up his wallet as he stepped into his shoes and headed toward the door. He reached into his pocket for his phone. "Shite!"

"What's wrong?" Victoria lifted a cup to her lips.

Glen returned to the room, retrieving his phone from where he tossed it. *On my way.* He sent a text to Cordelia, then threw his hand up in goodbye to Vic as he stepped into the elevator. Glen didn't have time to play questions and answers with her. He needed to get to Delia.

His daemon growled a warning at Vic's attempt to ease into his mind.

If you need me, I'm here. His sister's concern-laced words echoed in his head, silencing his snarly beast.

Thank you. Glen pulled from his space. "Call Percy." Ten rings. Percy wasn't answering. The man always answered. "Disconnect. Call Fiona."

"It's a bloody cluster," she answered mid-ring. "Dad apparently overheard Percy and me. How Dad found Edna's mobile number is beyond me, but he did and rang her. All I know is, at first, Edna thought it was a cruel prank from someone she called Snot. The ugly tears started, followed by angry words at Dad for not finding her sooner. The woman disconnected before Dad could tell her Mum passed away years ago."

"Did Whitaker ring her back?"

"He tried. Edna shut off her mobile. Glen, you should know she threatened to drive a stake through your heart and shove garlic up your bum."

"That's Edna. Have you spoken with Delia?" Glen took her exit, thankful for once the traffic was in his favor.

"Haven't had the chance. I just got off the phone with Viktor."

"I'm on my way to her place. Set up the conference room for a video chat, then ring Viktor back. Luckily, we can get these two lovebirds together and smooth out some feathers."

"On it."

Glen ended the call. If everything worked out, Edna and Whitaker would reunite, perhaps have the happy ending they should have had years ago, making Fiona and Percy Glen's in-laws. He slowed, turning into Delia's neighborhood. If Royce could deal with Mattie, Glen guessed he could manage Edna. The positive thoughts had him in a much better frame of mind for two seconds.

Delia stood in the doorway, with one hand on her hip and the other gripping her door so tightly her knuckles were white. "What business is it of yours, Scott?"

"Everything you do reflects on me." He thrust a finger in her face. "You're my wife—"

She knocked his hand away. "Ex-wife!"

"Who's acting more like a—ow—ow!"

Glen gripped the offensive digit between his thumb and forefinger, hyper-extending it backward. A little more pressure and he could snap the bone. Even more pressure and the prick would lose a finger. "I warned you."

"Stop!" Tears streamed down Scott's face as he kneeled on Delia's porch.

"Now that I have your attention, listen carefully to what I have to say. You fucked-up. Thank you. Because now I'm Delia's."

Delia crossed her arms. "Let him go, Glen."

"Delia and I are together," Glen continued. "Get over it. Disrespect her again…" He turned loose of Scott's finger only because Delia cleared her throat and arched her brow. Glen knew the look well.

Clutching his hand in the other, Scott scooted back and scrambled to his feet. "I'm suing."

Glen withdrew his wallet, then pulled out a business card, flicking it at Scott. "Have your lawyers call mine." He stepped up on the porch and lowered his lips to Delia's. "You all right?"

"I'm good."

Glen slipped his arm around her waist, escorting her inside, then kicked the door closed behind them. He kissed her more thoroughly.

She shoved against him. "What's that alarm?"

"Bloody hell." He pulled out his key fob. "Forgot to kill the engine."

"You forgot to shut off your car?" She wrapped her arms around his waist, resting her head against his chest.

"You were being threatened and—"

"It's a good thing you wear dark sunglasses." She peered up at him.

He shrugged, retracting his fangs. "Simple minds are easy to manipulate."

Delia ran her finger down his shirt as a smile teased her lips. "Why is your shirt inside-out?"

He shrugged again, looking down at his polo. Heat warmed his cheeks. "You needed me?"

She laughed. "What am I going to do with you?"

He had some ideas involving them naked in his bed, which had his body responding. "I have a *verra* long list."

"I bet."

"You," Edna yelled, hurrying toward him with her fist clenched.

Glen set Delia from him, focusing on Edna. Her red, swollen eyes and splotchy red cheeks gutted him.

"You knew." Edna pounded Glen's chest, and he noticed she no longer wore Whitaker's ring. "They said he died." Her body shook with each sob.

Edna's knees buckled, and Glen scooped her into his arms and sat on the couch, cradling her. She clung to him, mumbling. It was difficult to understand everything she said through tears, even with his keen hearing, but he understood enough that Edna lamented the heartache she'd endured all these years. Her love for Whitaker had never waned.

Delia sat beside them, smoothing her hand up and down Edna's back. "I should have told you. I'm so sorry Aunt Edna. But I didn't know how to tell you. I'm sorry."

Edna pushed from Glen, turning toward Delia and taking her hand. "It's not your fault. I'm just an old fool."

"You're not an old fool," Glen corrected, handing Edna a tissue.

"Then what do you call grieving someone who replaced you as quick as a wink?"

It wasn't Glen's story to tell, but Whitaker's. However, Glen could give Edna the facts as he knew them. "Eddie." He took her hand in his. "As you know, when the war ended, it wasn't truly over. A few diehard Germans refused to believe they'd lost. Others marched hundreds of miles to surrender to the Americans or us rather than the Russians. Compounded with the fact, information was only as good as the clerk filing it. Delia explained about your name being screwed up, which is why we couldn't find you. We searched. We all did."

"You looked for me?" Edna's bright green eyes searched his face.

"We all searched, Eddie. After the war, Whitaker and I spent two years over here going through immigration records, coming up empty. We never gave up, Eddie. Whitaker never gave up." Glen let that bit of information sink into her. "Whitaker insisted we search marriage licenses and... and death certificates. The problem, we were looking for Edna Cooper, not Parsons."

Edna crossed her arms over her chest. "So he could marry this new woman with a clean conscience." She huffed, reminding him so much of Hope, Percy's daughter. Edna's bottom lip quivered. "He said he'd love me for...ever." She leaned forward, snatching a tissue from the box, then blew her nose.

"Eddie—"

"Don't Eddie, me." She punched his arm. "Men. You're all alike. Mangy mutts the lot of you."

"That would be my cousins." The second the words tumbled from his mouth, he cringed. Now wasn't the time for humor.

Eddie stared at him. Her mouth gaped, and a sound any banshee would have been proud of escaped her. She fell against Delia, bawling even harder.

Glen glanced at Delia, and she glared back, mouthing, *fix this*. Fix this? How the bloody hell was he supposed to fix this? He dealt with problems in two simple ways, threatening the person causing the problem, or killing them. What the hell was he to do? He didn't have a bloody magical wand, and he couldn't very well threaten or kill Whitaker.

Edna glanced over her shoulder at him. "Hang Whitty and the trollop he wed."

"Whitaker married Martha Sullivan," the words ripped from Glen. "Ye'll na speak ill o' the dead, Edna Cooper."

"Martha, but she was engaged to Andrew, Whitty's cousin. They were closer than brothers, they were." She snatched another tissue.

"Aye, they were. Andrew received serious injuries when he crashed. Even with us helping, he never fully recovered. Andrew promised Martha they'd wed as soon as he was healthy. He died three years later. Before he died, Martha found herself pregnant with his child. They never married."

The anger faded from Edna's green eyes, and her crying stopped. "Because of Whitty's honor, he married Martha."

"Aye, he did." Glen nodded. "Not wanting Andrew's son to carry the stigma of a bastard. You know how tongues wag." In for a penny, in for a pound. "Ten years later, Martha gave Whitaker a daughter. Sadly, Martha died shortly after Fiona's birth."

"Oh, I'm such a fool. I have to ring him back."

"I have a better idea." Glen handed Edna another tissue. "I've asked Fiona to prepare the conference room. Come with me, and you can see and speak with Whitaker."

Edna's eyes lit. "Give me a moment. I have to fix my face first." She stared at her left hand, and her bottom lip trembled. "My ring."

"Edna," Delia grasped Edna's hand. "What did you do with your ring?"

"It may have fallen down the garbage disposal." Fat tears rolled down her cheeks again.

It took Glen a shorter amount of time to dismantle the garbage disposal, retrieve Edna's ring and then reassemble the bloody contraption than it did for Edna to fix her face and change outfits a million times. It was a bloody good thing she hadn't turned on the disposal or flushed the ring down the lavvy.

Finally on their way, Glen glanced in his back mirror at Edna. Outwardly she appeared calm, but he smelled the sickeningly sweet odor of fear coming from her. "You all right, Eddie?"

She stared out the side window. "Perhaps this wasn't such a good idea. It's been a few years since Whitty last saw me." Eddie sighed. "I'm not young anymore."

Glen pulled into his parking space. "Neither is Whitaker." Before killing the motor, he looked in his mirror. "If you wish, Eddie, I'll take you home."

She twisted the ring on her finger. "I didn't run when the Nazis attacked. I'll not run now." Edna unfastened her shoulder harness, then flung open the door. "Are you coming?"

Chapter Thirteen

Delia couldn't imagine what Edna was thinking or feeling or the emotions of the last five hours. She'd believed all this time the love of her life had died in battle. Then suddenly, she discovered him alive and, because of a series of errors, not finding out the truth for decades. There was no telling how Edna would react when she met with Whitty after all these years, even through a videoconference. Or what Edna would say when she met Fiona, Whitaker's daughter.

The first set of mirrored doors slid open, and Edna stopped. She stood there, staring straight ahead. The doors closed again, but she still didn't move.

"Aunt Edna," Delia placed her hand on her shoulder. "We don't have to do this if you don't want to."

After a long moment, Edna drew in a deep breath and held her head high as she squared her shoulders. "Right. Shall we get on with it?" She took a step, and the doors opened again.

The second pair of doors opened, revealing a crowd in the reception area, making an already stressful situation more uncomfortable. Paul and Cade stood near the elevators. Paul held a file while Cade stared expectantly at Glen. Mitch leaned over Sue's shoulder, pointing at something on the computer screen. Fiona stood in front of the reception desk, smiling yet appearing as nervous as Edna. The only person Delia didn't see was Angus.

She glanced up at Glen. His eyes glowed, and his fangs peeked from below his lip. She reached out and clutched his hand. "I think they're here for Fiona's moral support," she whispered as they strode into Daemon Securities.

Glen glared at his employees. "No need to whisper, *mo gràdh*. They can hear."

The elevator doors slid open, and Angus exited, carrying a small black object. He grinned and hurried across the lobby toward them. "That drive-by was no random attack, boss." He pushed the device in Glen's face, making him back up. "They targeted you."

Delia's heart stopped. "Are you talking about last night's incident?" she whispered, not wanting to add more stress to the situation for Edna.

"Yes, ma'am. See." Angus tapped the device where black tape covered it.

Glen let go of her hand, snatched the device, and turned it over, examining it before handing it back to Angus. "I'll be down after I take care of other business."

Angus gaped but gave a quick nod before striding toward the elevator.

"We have a situation." Cade stepped forward.

"You really need to look at this." Paul waved the file as he followed Cade. "It's all related." He nodded toward Angus, standing near the elevator.

Glen held up his hand. "If I *dinna* deal with it at this moment, will someone die?"

Cade chuckled. "Naw, they'd just get to live a little longer."

"Then they get a reprieve until I call you." Glen turned his attention from Cade and Paul and focused on Mitch. "What are you two doing?"

"We're coordinating schedules with Ryder, boss." Mitch straightened. "Do you need us?"

"Since you all are here," Glen offered his arm to Edna. "I'd like you to meet Edna Cooper, the best bloody damn ATS soldier during the war."

"Oh, you," Edna gushed, patting Glen's arm. "You men were the actual heroes." She beamed up at Glen. "Did they serve like you and my other boys?"

"No. They were too young, but Sue was a Women's Airforce Service Pilot."

Edna nodded at Sue. "My best mate was a Women's Auxiliary Air Force member." She sighed, turning her attention toward Fiona. "You, my dear, look so much like her. It's like seeing her ghost."

"They know," Paul exclaimed, drawing Delia's attention.

Wasn't Glen supposed to tell her? No one appeared upset, so what was the issue? She eased closer to Glen.

"They know." Glen slipped his arm around her waist. "I told Delia last night." He leaned down and bussed her cheek. "As for Edna, she recognized me right off."

Cade's eyes shimmered, and a grin spread across his lips. "Delia—"

"Ms. Parsons," Glen snapped.

"Stop it. Cade can call me Delia if he wants."

Glen arched his eyebrows at Cade.

"Ms. Parsons," Cade began again. "That wolf you painted was amazing, but have you ever painted or sculpted a mountain lion?"

Glen had said some Dhampir could shift into animals. Staring at Cade, she could envision him as a feline. "No. Sorry. I take it you can…" She couldn't get the words past her lips.

"Shift into the most amazing cat you've ever seen."

As much as she wanted to see him shift and cement this new reality into her brain, she had more important issues to deal with. "We'll talk later. Okay?"

Giving a quick nod, Cade left with Paul fast on his heels.

"I'm sorry about…," his words trailed off, and his brows furrowed. Glen nodded at something behind Delia.

She turned and gasped. Edna cupped Fiona's cheek. "Aunt Edna?"

"I can't get over how much you look like Martha. You even have her green eyes. Oh, Martha. She was the plucky one." A sad smile curved Edna's lips, and her eyes shimmered. "You must be her and Whitty's granddaughter."

Smiling, Fiona took Edna's hand. "They're my parents."

Edna glanced at Glen and tapped Fiona's wedding ring. "Then your husband is…"

"Human. My brother, Percy, and I, well," she shrugged. "Let's just say we have good genes."

Amusement flickered in Edna's eyes, and she laughed. "Yes, I would say you come from excellent stock. Whitty and Andrew introduced me to your grandfather and great-grandfather. The men were still strapping, given their age." Edna's smile slipped. "Glen said your mum passed. I'm so sorry, love."

"Mum loved flying." Fiona's eyes shimmered. "From what I was told, she was flying Great-grands and Grands to Scotland. All of us were to have gone on the trip. But Percy had the stomach gripes, and father thought it best if Percy and I stayed behind with him." Fiona wiped her eyes. "I was barely a year when she died, so I don't have any genuine memories of her or my grands, only the stories I've been told."

Edna patted Fiona's hand. "Your mum was a blooming, marvelous pilot. Better than some men who flew. I can tell you all I know about her and our exploits. I even have some old photos. If you'd like."

"I'd like that." Fiona glanced at the clock. "Shall we? Don't want Father thinking you'd changed your mind. You haven't, have you?"

"Oh, Heaven's. No."

"Then let's not keep Dad waiting." Fiona motioned toward the elevator. "We can take the lift."

"Why, when there's a perfectly good staircase?" Edna winked. "I'm old, love. Not decrepit. I run the stairs at home," she cupped her mouth and whispered. "Don't tell Dilly. She'll get miffed."

"Oh, for the love of…Edna, you could get hurt." There was no getting miffed. Delia was already there.

"See what I mean?" Edna tipped her head in Delia's direction.

Fiona chuckled and motioned toward the stairs. "After you, Edna."

Delia had so many questions spinning around in her mind. She reached for Glen's hand as they ascended the stairs. The second her hand brushed against his, he laced his fingers with hers. She couldn't explain it, but she craved his touch. When they reached the first landing, she squeezed Glen's hand. "Edna, Fiona, we'll be up in a second."

Glen arched his black eyebrow and tipped his head. "Problem?"

"No—Yes. Last night's incident was not an accident. Are you sure you don't need to see what your men have discovered?"

"It can wait."

"But they shot you," she whispered, waving her hand at him. "I know you said it wasn't serious, but darn it! I don't want anything to happen to you." How had she come to care so much about him in such a short time?

"Oh, Hell's bloody bells." Glen hugged her to him, giving her a quick kiss. "You're not going to lose me, and I won't allow anything to happen to you or Edna." He pressed his lips to hers once more.

"Are you two snogging again?" Edna bellowed from the top landing.

Snorting, Mitch quickly darted out the front sliding door while Sue snatched up the phone. Great. Simply great. "Nothing like being embarrassed in front of your boyfriend's employees." Delia peered up at Glen. "Why are you grinning?"

He looped his arm around her waist. "Come on. Let's not keep *Whitty* waiting any longer."

They followed Fiona and Edna down the hall, past several offices. Fiona opened a door and ushered Edna inside. Delia didn't know what she had expected, but not this. The elegantly carved mahogany table would have been better suited to a castle than a conference room. The high-end leather executive chairs just added to the opulence. Decorating the walls were flags she didn't recognize. "What countries are these?"

"Not countries, love," Edna replied. "Football banners."

"Aye," Glen confirmed. "Part of Fiona's agreement to work with me was that I allowed her to hang that atrocity." He pointed to the white and blue banner with a red rose.

"Oi, the Blue and White are older than your pitiful Berwick Rangers and far better." Fiona pointed to a black and gold banner.

"Aye, the Blackburn Rovers do play like a bunch of old men."

Fiona glared at Glen and snatched the remote from the table.

Delia shook her head. "I guess I'll hang the Five Stripes up in here. Gotta support the local team."

"You like football? I knew you were perfect."

The enormous television screen flicked on before she could tell Glen baseball was her sport, not soccer. A thin-faced elderly man with gray hair and steel-gray eyes nervously stared at them. The man was wearing a tux. Seriously? A tux, more specifically a morning suit. Delia had thought Edna had gone all out.

"Oh, Eddie, you're as beautiful as ever," he said.

"Whitty." Edna rushed toward the television with her arms wide. Her steps faulted, and she glanced over her shoulder with tears shimmering in them. "Cordelia, this is Whitaker." Edna blinked and wiped at her cheek before turning back to the screen.

"A pleasure." Whitaker inclined his head.

"It's nice to meet you as well," Delia greeted, staring at the image of a man in the mirror behind Whitaker. She'd swear she saw Glen's blond twin if she didn't know better. But he said his brother was adopted.

"Oh, Whitty, I'm such a fool. I died that day they told me you were gone. I believed them." Edna wiped at her eyes again.

Whitty reached his hand out as if to wipe her tears. "When they told you, why didn't you go to Wyvern House?"

Fiona handed Edna a tissue.

"Me? A nobody turning up at the lord's stoop?" Edna tsked. "When they told me, I lost my senses. Ida, God love her, spoke with the Americans. One moment I was standing at their base. The next, I was on a ship crossing the Atlantic."

"But Royce would—"

"Whitty, the bombs took everything. All I had were my uniforms and my mum's favorite cup and saucer. That was all. My mum and dad died during the blitz. Ida was leaving for America, and I found out you were dead. There was nothing left for me in England. I didn't start living again until I held Charlie junior in my arms."

"I looked for you, Eddie."

"I know." She sniffed. "Glen told us how you and he searched. It never occurred to me that anyone would look for me. I didn't change my name back to Cooper until I became an American citizen." Edna twisted the ring on her finger.

"I never married, Whitty. I never dated." She pulled the ring from her finger. "I never stopped loving you." She placed it on the table.

"Edna," Whitty cooed. He glanced away, "Would you give us some privacy

The man in the mirror moved away, as did someone else in the room. A door clicked, and Whitty shifted his attention to Fiona. "Do you mind?"

Delia placed her hand on Edna's shoulder. "Do you want me to stay?"

"No, dear. Whitty and I have much to discuss."

"Edna." Fiona opened the door. "I'll be right next door if you need anything. In the meantime, would you care for some tea?"

"Thank you." Edna eased down into one of the leather chairs, never taking her eyes off Whitaker.

"Come along, *mo gràdh*." Glen slipped his arm around Delia's shoulder, leading her from the room, but not before she caught Whitaker's surprised look.

They strolled down the hall toward his office, and she paused. "Precisely what does *mo gràdh* mean?" Delia knew it wasn't some simple term of endearment, not from the expression on Whitaker's face or the faces of Glen's team. *Mo gràdh* meant something significant.

Glen cupped her cheek. "It means—"

"There you are." A tall, slender woman in her mid-twenties or early thirties emerged from Glen's office. The woman wore designer clothes. Delia recognized the skirt as one she'd admired. Whoever this woman was, she had money. She also had the same piercing blue eyes and ink-black hair as Glen, but her complexion was fairer, reminding Delia of fine porcelain. The woman perused them as she approached. Her blood-red lips pulled back in a smile. "I was wondering where you were hiding."

Glen slipped his arm around Delia's waist, drawing her close to his side. "Love, I'd like you to meet my sister, Victoria."

Love? Delia extended her hand. "Cordelia Parsons. It's a pleasure to meet you."

Glen's sister took Delia's hand. The woman's nails were two-inch long stilettos. "Parsons. Parsons." Her smile widened, becoming warmer. "You're just the person I'm here to see."

Chapter Fourteen

"I thought you were here on business, Victoria." Glen tightened his arm around Delia. If his sister said or did anything to upset her, he'd rip Vic's heart out and take her head. He didn't give a rat's arse if it pissed off his mum.

"Stop it." Delia pinched his side. "You're growling again."

"Oh, please," Vic rolled her eyes. "You said your mate was an artist. You didn't say she was a renowned sculptor."

Delia blushed. "I wouldn't consider myself renowned."

"I like your modesty, but it's misplaced." Victoria pulled Delia from his arm. "I've seen your work. When Margo rang me, I looked you up. I also paid a visit to Nantahala City Hall yesterday. I first went to the art gallery, but two lovely sisters pointed me to City Hall." Victoria flicked her wrist as if the world understood everything spewing from her. She led Delia into his office and to his desk, where she pulled out the chair for Delia. "Have a seat. I want to show you something." Vic started typing on *his* keyboard.

"What are you doing?" Glen didn't keep the daemon from his voice.

"Using your computer. What does it look like I'm doing? Don't you have a company or something to run?"

"I do, but someone is using *my* computer."

Delia glanced between him and Victoria. "Would you like us to go someplace else?"

"You're fine." He glared at his sister. Damn her for manipulating the situation.

She rolled her eyes. "Glen still hasn't forgiven me for putting his hair in ringlets, even if it was the style then."

"Oh, my," Delia laughed. "I would have loved to have seen that."

"Too bad there weren't cameras back then." His sister winked.

"Vic," he warned.

"Yes." She finally straightened and batted her lashes at him before turning her full attention to Delia. A genuine smile graced his sister's face, not her typical smirk. "See. Renowned sculptor Cordelia Parsons. How long did it take you to create this fountain?"

"Not quite a year. This was my healing piece." Delia shrugged. "I donated it to the town, and they raised the money to cast it. It was their sheriff who suggested turning it into a fountain. I have the model in my studio, along with everything else."

"You keep everything in your art studio?" Victoria asked. Her tone had him wondering why.

Delia nodded. "Models and all my sketch pads."

"Hmm, we should talk," Vic replied. "I know. Let's do lunch."

Glen could see the wheels turning in his sister's mind. He eased around Victoria and peered at the screen. He couldn't believe his eyes. The only sculptures of Delia's he'd seen were the ceramic ones at Ivy and Rose Art Gallery. He knew she cast some of her commissioned pieces in bronze, but this...Wow. "This is your Crying Woman Falls piece. It's gorgeous. Where is this again?"

"The town of Nantahala," Delia replied. "North of Dahlonega, and slightly east of US Highway 19. It's a wonderful little town with a rich history and lore."

Glen leaned over, enlarging the picture. "This one's different from the others you've created."

"You're right. The four tabletops each represent a season." Delia covered his hand, moving the mouse, turning the photo 360 degrees. "Because of the size, I could incorporate all four seasons."

Vic pointed at the screen. "See, right here," she glanced at Cordelia. "I can call you Delia?"

"You can," She replied. "Just not Cordy. You do, and I might stake you."

His usually composed sister tossed her head back, laughing. "Oh, blessed be! I like you. A lot, and that's saying something." Vic tapped the screen with her long nail. "Here you did a nod to spring, with the daffodils and this cute little bear cub. Over here is summer with the butterflies. The leaves and nuts scattered on the ground represent fall." Victoria clicked the mouse. "Here, you carved a few snowflakes for winter. All-in-all, most people looking at the fountain straight on only see the woman's face, not the different seasons or the many tiny details you included."

"True. Most people only see the falls." Delia sat back in the chair, staring mindlessly at the screen. "I sometimes worked around the clock on this. I can't tell you how often Edna found me sound asleep in my studio. I made this in eight sections." She looked up at him. "I took photos up to the gallery in town one weekend. The women there raved about it, but the Wolverton sisters who run the hotel, they were the ones who spoke with the mayor. And everyone in town." Delia laughed. "I was shocked by how much the town wanted my work. Before the weekend was over, I'd donated it to them. They would have to come up with the money if they wanted it cast. The town raised the money in no time, then it was off to the foundry. After the pieces were cast, I spent a week welding it together. At one point, I thought about buying a house up there, but I couldn't leave Edna."

"Edna is?" Victoria asked, staring at Glen.

"Delia's aunt. Edna Cooper." He watched Vic's eyes widen.

"Whitaker's Eddie?" Vic pointed to the left, towards the conference room. "That's who's in there?"

"Yes," he replied.

"Marvelous," she exclaimed. If Glen didn't know better, he'd swear their cousin Miranda was finally rubbing off on Victoria. "Delia, how about I take you *and* your aunt to lunch once she finishes speaking with Whitaker? We'll even kidnap Fiona, making it a girls' thing. After we eat, we can swing by Margo's. What do you say?"

Glen shook his head. "Vic. Delia's not going anywhere without me. But you're more than welcome to join us."

"I think that's a wonderful idea, Victoria." Delia tilted her head back, peering up at him. Her eyes were as black as the Earl of Hell's waistcoat. "Why don't you see what Cade and Paul wanted to show you? If you finish before *we* leave, *you* may join us."

Hell slapped it to him. He should have known better than to overstep what Delia did or didn't do. He'd stepped over the line and was now in the doghouse. "Are you sure?" He didn't enjoy leaving her with his sister, not that he thought Vic would harm Delia. But Victoria could be bitchy.

Seriously? What? Are you afraid I'm going to tell her all your bad habits? Vic's words slammed into his mind.

"I'm positive." Delia's smile didn't hide her annoyance with him.

Glen leaned down to kiss her lips, but she turned her head, making him kiss her cheek. "Sorry for being—"

"Controlling?" She arched her brows.

Hell's bloody bells. He'd have to make this up to her. Glen nodded, then kissed her again. "I'll text you when I'm finished. If and only if you want me to meet up with you, I will." He tossed his keys to Victoria.

Glen strode from his office, pausing and glancing back at his sister. *Their safety is in your hands.*

I meant what I said. I like Delia a lot, so I can assure you I'll keep her and Edna safe. Vic's reply even soothed his beast.

Glen strode from his office. He paused outside their view, watching them laugh as if they were old friends. The scene was odd to him. Delia, he understood. She seemed to get along with everyone she met. Whereas Victoria, his sister, didn't let people get close to her. Even her fated mate. Glen could easily eavesdrop on Delia's and Vic's conversation, but he'd let them have their secrets.

He rode the elevator down to the basement level, where his team would be waiting. He'd expect Cade and Paul to be sparring in the ring and Angus tearing apart some motor. The doors slid apart, and three sets of eyes stared expectantly at him. Oh, well, he couldn't be right all the time. "Show me what you got."

"*Now,* you want to hear what we have to say." Angus marched toward him. "If you're not too busy, look." He shoved the rear camera from what was left of the Bentley in Glen's face.

Glen counted to ten. He wouldn't bust Angus for his attitude. Yet. "You took Dragon apart?" He handed the camera back to Angus.

"Not the first time. Doubt it'll be the last." Angus turned, strolling back to the Bentley.

"Cade, Paul, what do you have?"

"Oh, you have time for them, too?" Angus shouted from under a chassis. "Must be our lucky day, lads."

The daemon tore from Glen. He grabbed Angus by the ankles, yanking him from under the vehicle. Glen bent down, snatching Angus by the throat, then slammed him against the cement support beam. "Here or the cage?" Blood pooled where Glen's claws dug into Angus's neck.

Angus tipped his head in submission. "Mercy," he rasped out.

Glen opened his hand, dropping the kid to the floor. "I was tending to the needs of my mate's family, not that I owe you an explanation. But know this, all of you. As long as there is no immediate danger, my mate will *always* come first."

The kid rose to his knees, tipping his head back as far as possible. "They targeted you or her. Your safety and hers are my concern." Angus met Glen's gaze. "You can't die until I repay my blood debt."

"Haud yer wheesht!" Glen's bloody daemon was hell in a fight, but a wuss when it came to sentiment. Fangs and claws retracted. Glen dropped his chin to his chest and exhaled. "Getting your bloody arse out of that hellhole does no' constitute a feckin' blood debt." Glen held his hand out to Angus, helping him to his feet. "You're family, now." Glen patted the man's back.

"So, what do you two have for me?" Glen strode toward Cade and Paul.

Cade tipped his head back. "Don't know if it's because I hang with Karma, but I don't talk to dudes with their wangers out."

"Yeah, man." Paul turned his back. "Put some clothes on."

Glen's daemon was hell in a fight, even worse on clothes. "Seriously?" He headed toward his locker.

"You're pussies, the both of you," Angus shouted.

"Purring and proud." Cade shifted his ears and popped his whiskers.

"Hey, I'm not feline," Paul shot back. "You know I'm a wolf. Like you."

Glen pulled on a pair of jeans and grabbed another polo, making sure it was right-side-out before tugging it over his head.

"Just because you shift into a wolf doesn't mean you're not a pussy." Angus laughed, then made a hissing noise.

Glen chuckled at their ribbing. Two years ago, Cade, Paul, and Angus were literally at each other's throats. Today, they had each other's backs. Glen slipped on another pair of boots. Had he and Angus settled their dispute in the cage, Glen was sure Cade would have been in there with them, keeping the fight clean.

"Satisfied?" Glen joined his team standing near a computer screen. "Show me what you have."

"We're not ready yet." Paul gave him a sideways glance. "Waiting on the popcorn."

Angus thumped Paul, causing his head to bob forward.

"Hey! Why'd you hit me?" Paul rubbed the back of his head.

"'Cause yer acting like a loco pup." Cade pointed the remote at the screen. "Not much to see, boss, until here. Watch that area to the left."

After a moment, the car's security picked up a dark figure placing something over the rear camera. The other cameras instantly started recording. The feed was too dark to see the perp's face, but Glen bet he wore a mask. A bloody skeleton mask. From the shape of the perp's dark outline, he had the same body size and shape as Luka. The stupid kid was going to get killed one day. "Is this all you have?"

"Nope." Cade's expression was one of amusement as he clicked the remote again. "You'll hear audio from the interior."

"The top." Glen listened, hating the sound of his voice. Next was the distinctive sound of glass shattering. "Stay down! Were you hit? Delia, were you shot? Are you okay? Damn it, Cordelia, answer me."

The exterior cameras captured the view of a dark-colored Lexus. The passenger side window was down. With the glow of the streetlights, he clearly saw the driver wearing a dark hoodie and a skeleton mask, just like Luka wore the night he tried to carjack Glen. Stupid. Stupid kid.

"Right. Make me a copy, with date and time stamps. Also, include a copy of the footage from the carpark at my condo."

Paul held out a thumb drive. "This fast enough?"

"No." Glen pocketed the device. "You should have handed it to me before I asked."

"You'll need this." Cade held out a slip of paper.

"What's this?" It wasn't Petrov's home address.

"One of Edik Petrov's businesses. It's an import-export near here. He's been inside for the last ten minutes. We'll ring you if he moves."

"Here boss." Angus held out a set of keys. "Take Odin."

"Thanks, but it's just a good stretch of the legs." Glen faded, pushing through the brick wall of the building. With luck, he'd be back in time to take Delia and the ladies out to eat.

Staying in the wraith zone, the space where everything in the solid world appeared foggy and voices muted, he strode toward the business dodging people in his path. The air surrounding him was thick, and he couldn't wait to escape the zone. Glen shivered as a man ran through him to catch a bus. Bloody hell, he hated it when that happened! One of the biggest drawbacks of the wraith zone, humans in the solid world have no idea about the zone and don't realize they can pass through those inside the zone.

Glen stopped in front of the address. It was a high-end looking shipping store. Worldwide Shipping. Hmm, no real imagination with the name, but that could be on purpose.

His phone vibrated, and he glanced at it, reading the text. *Edik Petrov should be inside. Fiona said to deliver the drive, then come straight away. She's got this.* Okay, whatever the bloody hell that meant.

According to the hours of operation, the place should be open. However, from the darkened interior, it appeared closed. He tried the door. Locked. Not a problem. Glen faded into the business. No dead bodies. That's always a good sign.

It was bloody hard to hear anything in the zone, but muffled voices came from the back of the building. Glen headed toward the sound, fading through the closed metal door.

"Your job," shouted the man behind the desk. He looked like an older version of Luka. Had to be Edik Petrov. "Is to keep my son out of trouble." The target of Petrov's anger was none other than the messenger boy.

"Kids will be kids." The wanker shrugged.

This should be fun. Glen strode back to the front door, unlocked it, then faded from the building. The camera on the door had to show him entering for this to work. Good thing the business backed up to an alleyway with no surveillance cameras. Petrov probably didn't want any evidence of what went on back there, unlike in front where Glen counted four cameras. He strode out front, ensuring he smiled and nodded at the people he passed. He propped his foot on a hydrant and retied his bootlace before entering again. Maybe the cameras got his good side.

"We're closed." Messenger boy stepped from the shadows.

"I have something for Edik Petrov concerning his son, Luka."

"You. How did you get in here?"

"Through the door. It was unlocked," Glen replied.

"Show him back, Arman."

The man stepped aside. As Glen entered, Arman grabbed Glen's arm. "You got some balls coming here."

"Perhaps I wouldn't be here if you did a better job babysitting." Glen jerked free and strode into the office.

He stared Edik Petrov in the eye and placed the thumb drive on the desk. "I suggest you hire a new babysitter or *mon* up and be a father."

Glen's face slammed against the top of the desk, and his arm forced up behind his back. "You do not speak to Mr. Petrov in that manner."

In a smooth motion and using a tad more strength than he should, Glen reversed position with Arman. "Come by my office, and we'll go a few rounds in the ring. Who knows, you may even learn something." Glen arched his eyebrow at Petrov. "I hope you *dinna* pay this tosser a lot."

"My sister's son." Petrov shrugged.

Glen shoved Arman aside, knocking him to the ground, then looked Petrov in the eyes again. "Watch the videos. Make your own conclusions." Glen straightened and tapped the thumb drive. "Because the next time the kid in the video is involved in a drive-by, it may be his last."

Petrov pushed from his chair, sending it crashing into the wall behind him. "Are you threatening my son?"

"I never hurt kids. Never have. Never will, including the little wankers who take potshots at me." He glanced at Arman, who'd finally made it to his feet. "Adults are another story."

Glen half expected to see Atlanta's finest waiting for him when he exited the building. Surprisingly, they weren't. However, his least favorite FBI agent was standing in the lobby of Daemon Securities and being glared at by Fiona.

"Agent Trammell." Glen extended his hand, sizing up Deneen Trammell again. The woman was determined, feisty, matter-of-fact, and by-the-book. She had a little more gray in her hair, but the stress of the job didn't seem to age her. She had lost weight since the last time Glen had seen her.

Trammell frowned. "I'm not here for tea, MacPhee."

"Hey, iron pants rhymed," Paul joked, causing Fiona to crack a smile.

Deneen cut her eyes at Paul and flipped him off.

Glen dropped his hand. "What can I help you with, Trammell?"

"Why did you pay Edik Petrov a visit?"

Fiona huffed. "Oh, for the love of—I've already explained this to you."

"Fiona." Glen shook his head. "I dropped off a flash drive."

"Containing what?" Trammell pressed.

"Video of Luka attempting to carjack me the other night and of someone driving a dark Lexus wearing a hoodie and skull mask similar to what Luka wore, taking a potshot at me and my date."

"Did you report this to the police, or are you taking the law into your own hands? *Again*?"

"The carjacking—yes. The drive-by—no. Before you ask…" Glen exhaled. "It's not Luka's fault he has shitty parents. Do you want a copy of the thumb drive?

Trammell nodded and held out her hand. "The flash drive, the casings, and the vehicle involved."

"You can have the drive and casings. As for the vehicle, you'll have to pry it from Angus's hands."

"Not a problem." She grinned. "Don't mind if I drive around to your garage."

"Suit yourself." Paul dropped a thumb drive into Trammell's hand.

She folded her slender fingers around the thumb drive. "Thank you. As for the car, I'll ensure my boys take good care of it."

As soon as Trammell left, Glen glared at Fiona. "Care to explain?"

"Sure. I was speaking to Edgar and mentioned what had happened. He told me to tell you to stay clear of Petrov because Trammell and her partner had Petrov under surveillance. It seems someone in his organization has turned, feeding the feds all sorts of juicy tidbits. I told Edgar it was too late. You'd already left. I'm not going to repeat what he said."

Glen could imagine. "You and Edgar devised this plan to inform Trammell?"

"I wouldn't call it a plan, per se. More like Edgar ringing off." Fiona grinned. "I'll forgive him as long as he's in town when Percy and Dad arrive."

"What?" Glen knew he hadn't heard her correctly.

"That's why I didn't go to lunch with the ladies. I was making travel arrangements with Percy. He and Father will be here in a few days."

Chapter Fifteen

Delia wiped her eyes, then stared at the cobweb near the ceiling, trying to clear her mind of her nightmare. The cobweb fluttered in the breeze from the spinning ceiling fan. She guessed Edna missed it during her kamikaze cleaning spree. Delia swore she'd throw a conniption if Edna came in once more to clean. Good grief, why did Whitaker have to arrive today of all days? Why couldn't he come tomorrow or the next day?

Cordelia rolled over and peered at the clock on her nightstand. It was another sleepless night, and she really needed to sleep. The last thing she wanted was dark circles under her eyes. Well, that's why concealer was invented. She fluffed her pillow, then flopped down. She had too much on her mind. Glen, her exhibit, Edna, but mostly Glen.

Whenever Delia closed her eyes, she pictured blood dripping from Glen's arm or a stake through his heart. Why wouldn't he tell her what his team discovered? Every time she'd asked him what he found out, he'd sidestepped the subject. Which meant it was serious. Terrible, considering the incident at Francine's. The man with the switchblade screamed mafia, and they were sending Glen a message to back off. That's why someone shot him. Maybe they were after him because they knew what he was? "Oh, lord, love a duck! Perhaps I should be a writer instead of an artist with all the crazy crap in my head." *I'm talking to myself. That's it. I'm crazy. And it's all Glen's fault.*

She'd known him less than a month, in reality only three weeks, and worried about him. It didn't matter how often he assured her he was practically indestructible. She'd still worry. Of course, she worried about him, she liked him, and they were friends. Who was she kidding? Delia's feelings toward Glen were deeper than friendship, and it was time she admitted it. Her problem was perception. It didn't matter if he was several hundred years older. She still looked like an old woman. Granted, she wasn't that old. But every morning when she looked in the mirror, she found a new line etched on her face. She needed to talk to him face to face, not over the phone, and not where Edna or Victoria would interrupt.

She and Glen hadn't had any alone time since their date. Once Edna spoke with Whitaker, Delia's life turned into a whirlwind. She'd been busy attempting to stay out of Edna's cleaning-frenzy way and finalizing things with Margo. Delia really needed to do something special for Victoria. She'd been a great help with everything for the exhibit, which would take place in a little over thirteen hours.

According to Margo, the meet and greet was from six to eight. The gallery would open at five today instead of its usual time, giving them ample time for a final once-over. Even with the careful planning, Delia still worried something would go wrong, or worse yet, no one would show.

Her sculptures and a few oils were displayed, with prices to fit any budget. She had her whimsical cats, woodland brownies, and mischievous ravens. Then there were her high-end pieces, including *Untitled* and Glen's *Guardians of the Isle,* which were not for sale. *Untitled,* her nod to Agatha Christy had sold, but Margo wouldn't say who purchased it because of confidentiality, but the buyer agreed to keep it on display and pick it up at the show.

To add to Delia's already chaotic week, she'd spent hours on the phone with Percy, reviewing the personal information he'd removed from the internet. From speaking with him, she liked the man and his wicked sense of humor and couldn't wait to meet him in person. Though the thought crossed her mind about his motivation for helping her. Was it because of her relationship with Glen, or because she was Edna's niece? Either way, she guessed it didn't matter since Percy did what her lawyers could not.

No wonder her mind was spinning. Delia glanced at the clock and groaned. In a few hours, Percy and his father would arrive. Fiona and her husband would pick them up from the airport and take them to Glen's complex, where Daemon Securities owned another unit. She wished she could meet them before tonight's event, but time wouldn't allow it.

Another reason for her inability to sleep. She was a nervous wreck, worrying that Whitaker and Percy liked her. They were, after all, Glen's family. Yes, they were coming because of Edna, but they were part of Glen's family, not blood relation but family nonetheless, and Delia wanted them to like her. She didn't need Glen's mind-reading abilities to see how much he loved and missed his family.

No wonder she couldn't sleep with everything going on in her head. Cordelia tossed back the covers. She might as well get up.

She unlocked her studio, then closed the door before turning on the lights. There was no need to advertise to the neighbors she couldn't sleep. Lord knows, the last thing she wanted was to have Scott screaming at her.

Time slipped by, and she reached for her cup, lifting it. Dang-it! "Empty." She set her cup aside only to have it disappear. Heart pounding, she spun in her chair. "What are you doing here?"

Glen set her cup down. "The silent alarm went off, and I was worried. Plus," He bent down, giving her a quick kiss. "I missed you."

"Silent alarm? What silent alarm?" Delia tipped her head back, taking in Glen's disheveled wet hair, unshaven face, and the dab of toothpaste at the corner of his mouth.

"The one we installed at the same time as the cameras." Glen hooked his thumbs in his belt loops, eyeing her. "When the alert went off, I rushed over here."

Yet, he had time to shower, get dressed, and brush his teeth. "Rushed over here, huh? You have toothpaste right there." She slid from her chair and pointed to his lower lip.

His tongue darted out, licking away the white smidgin. "Been up since three, couldn't sleep." His appreciative gaze traveled slowly down her pajama-clad body to her bare feet before returning to her face. A hint of red-tinged his blue eyes. "I do like what you're wearing. Cute little, short-shorts, tank-top," He licked his lips. "No bra." His deep bedroom voice had her body tingling.

Focus, girl. "How I sleep." She motioned to herself. "Back on track. I don't remember telling you to install an alarm." The man was a sexy devil who knew how to distract her.

"I was going to suggest it, considering your ex." Glen shrugged and grinned, his gaze traveling over her body once more. "Mmm, I do like what you're wearing."

She snapped her fingers at him. "Focus. Alarm system?"

"Edna requested them. Good thing she did."

"Of course she did. Why's it a good thing? So you'll know where I am."

"Because you were so engrossed in your work, you *didna* hear me call your name?" He arched his dark eyebrow as he slipped his arm around her waist, pulling her to him until their hips met. Her arms instantly went around his waist. "Nor did you realize I've been here for nearly an hour."

"You've been here an hour?"

Glen nodded. "Almost. Watching you work. You buzzed around your shelves, organizing them, before turning your frustrations loose on that poor lump of clay." His lips twitched. "Mind telling me what it did to piss you off so much?"

She rose on her toes and kissed his chin. "Nothing. I'm wedging it to remove the air and get it smooth and pliable."

"Looks more like torturing it." He chuckled. "What's it going to be?"

Delia straightened her shoulders and smiled. "You."

"Me?" Glen peered at her. "Don't see it."

"Silly. I haven't started sculpting. Let me finish wedging, then we can talk." She cupped the clay, pressing it down and away from her.

"How many times do you do this?" Glen wrapped his arms around her from behind. His warm breath fanned her nape. She shivered with desire as she continued working the clay into a ball. Each time she pulled the clay back, her rump rubbed against his erection.

"A hundred times." She set the clay aside. "Now it's ready to use."

"Would you like me to strip and model for you?" Glen's eyes glowed red, and his fangs peeked from below his upper lip.

Yes, please. She wet her suddenly dry lips and slid her hands up his chest and around his neck.

"Or would you prefer to tell me why you couldn't sleep?"

"You really know how to kill a mood."

"Not my intention." Glen lifted her, setting her on top of the workbench.

She spread her legs slightly and reached out toward him. "Hold me for a moment."

Glen stepped closer, wrapping her in his embrace. "Delia, if you're worried about the jobby next door, don't. Margo has assured me Snotface did *not* get a ticket. Should he get in tonight, I'll sic Victoria on him."

"Stop it. Victoria has been a great help, finalizing everything with Margo."

"Then why are you out here and not in your bed, sleeping?" Glen arched his dark eyebrows, staring at her. "I could stroll through your mind if you'd like."

"Fine." Delia huffed, knowing Glen would, too. "It's nothing, and it's everything."

His eyebrow inched closer to his hairline, and he tilted his head. "I don't follow."

"I'm worried about you. You never explained what your team found out about the other night. I know you keep saying being shot was nothing, but it was something for me. I care about you. Add in my nervousness about meeting your family and about my showing. Every time I close my eyes, my mind spins like crazy. Then there's Edna. I deal with stress by coming out here." Delia waved her hand, motioning to her surroundings. "Edna deals with it by cleaning. She's scrubbed the house so much it smells like a lemon factory. Do you realize she came out here and cleaned? That's why I was re-organizing my shelves." Delia tilted her head, peering at the magnificent man in her arms.

"You're fretting over nothing, lass." Glen flashed her a panty-wetting smile as his hand skimmed down her bare arms.

"The other day, we waited for you. Fiona finally came in and told us you were *dealing* with the situation and for us to go to lunch without you. Since then, you've evaded the question whenever I've asked about it. So, when I closed my eyes, visions of you being staked danced through my head, along with Scott smashing all my works and Edna killing everyone with lemon cleaner. To top it off, I envisioned standing alone in a gallery with all my art destroyed." There, she'd voiced her fears aloud, but it didn't make her feel any better.

Glen's mouth twitched, and he shook his head. "Lass, what am I going to do with you? I gave Luka's father a copy of what the cameras captured. He called later, saying Luka denied he shot at us or was the one who carjacked you. No surprise there. Luka couldn't deny trying to carjack me." Glen shrugged as his thumb toyed with the strap of her shirt. "As for you being alone. Never. I will always be with you. And no one is going to destroy your art."

"This explains why I'm here and not asleep. Wedging clay prepares it for sculpting and is a great way to release tension."

"I know a better way." He lowered his lips to hers, silencing her.

Delia cupped his face, nipping and sucking on his lower lip. His breath was hot and minty. She ran her hands down the hard plain of Glen's muscular back until she cupped his firm rear. Marble was softer than his butt. She groaned, and he slipped his tongue between her lips. When he caressed her tongue with his, she mimicked the action. She felt his kiss through every cell in her body, but mostly in her pink bits. Perhaps it was time to take their relationship one step further.

Glen lifted his lips. His eyes were so red, they appeared molten. His breathing was erratic as hers. "If you say stop. I will."

Desire racked her body, and she rocked against him. Glen answered her slight tilt of hips with a rumbling growl. He captured her mouth once more and thrust his hips against her, driving home how much he wanted her. His kiss turned demanding. He cupped her cheek with one hand, moving her head as he wished. His other hand caressed her arm. His thumb brushed against her breast. She ached so much with desire, her nipples hardened. His jean-clad shaft rubbed against her center, building the sensation. He moved his hand, cupping one breast in his palm as he pinched her hardened nipple.

The sensation had her bucking against him. "Touch me," she moaned.

Glen lifted his lips from hers. He stared into her eyes expectantly.

"Please," she whispered.

Glen pushed her pajama top up and pinned her down onto the bench in a smooth motion. He trailed kisses down her neck, then gently bit where her shoulder met her throat. Delia wasn't into pain, but Glen's bite made her moan with pleasure. He sucked and lapped at the area as he kneaded her breast.

Delia gasped as Glen took one breast into his hot mouth. His tongue lapped at her nipple as he sucked hard, making her shiver and moan. She hooked her legs around his, rocking against him.

Her hands tugged and pulled at his shirt, wanting to feel his skin against hers. "Want more."

"How much more?" he asked as he moved to her neglected breast. One hand slid down her, palming her mound. His fingers slipped up the leg of her shorts, twining with her short curls. "Delia?"

She spread her legs further and bucked with each touch. She dug her heels into Glen's rear as he fingered her. She pulsed and rocked against him, begging. "Yes. Yes. More."

"I've got you. Let go, love." Glen kissed and nipped her neck.

The second he bit her, she arched her back, dug her nails into his shoulder, and experienced an orgasm like no other. Then, she couldn't help herself. She bit down on Glen's shoulder. He roared and thrust his hips against her. He held her while she rode out the last tremors of her release.

"Sorry for biting you," she gasped out. Spent, Delia relaxed against the unforgiving surface of her workbench, enjoying Glen's weight as he blanketed her. She ran her fingers through his thick hair with one hand, smoothing the other up and down his back under his shirt.

"Never apologize for biting me. But I should for losing control and biting you."

"Don't. It was...I liked it." She shivered as need filled her again. "I want you."

"You have me, lass. All of me. Mind, body, and soul." He rose on one arm. His eyes still glowed as he stared at her. Others would see Glen's red eyes as demonic and run screaming into the night. She saw them as proof he desired her so much he'd lost a bit of control. The greater evidence of his desire for her was his throbbing cock pressing against her center.

"You know what I mean." She stared into his crimson eyes. "Make love to me."

The door banged, and she jumped. "What the hell?"

"Delia! Delia, are you in there?" Edna shouted.

Delia groaned. "Could her timing be worse?"

Glen dropped his head, resting his forehead against hers. His shoulders shook with his laugh. "No." Glen smoothed her shirt down, then gripped her around the waist, lifting her from the table. He hugged her, their bodies snug as she slid down him. His hard erection pressed against her through his jeans until her feet touched the cool concrete floor.

"I feel bad." She cupped him, and he hissed as he inhaled. His hand covered hers.

"You shouldn't. I enjoyed watching you. Your eyes were shut, lips parted, and a wanton flush colored your gorgeous face." A purely masculine, prideful grin curved his lips. "I put that look on your face and intend to do it again. *Often*."

Wow. Okay, then. "But don't you—" She fingered the button of his jeans. "At least let me return the favor."

He shook his head, lifting her hand to his lips, kissing her fingertips. "When we make love, I want to worship you in the comforts of a bed." He glanced toward the door. "Without Edna standing at the door."

"But—"

"There is no but." Glen's thumb brushed Delia's neck where he'd bitten her, instantly arousing her. "You're mine, and I'm yours."

She rolled her eyes and squeezed her thighs. Damn Glen. How could someone arouse her and piss her off at the same time? "Even after we mate, you won't *own* me, and I won't own you."

Glen grinned, and his eyes shimmered. "You've just made me the happiest man alive. You've agreed to be my mate."

"I just said you won't own me, and I won't own you."

"You said, even after we've mated. So, you've agreed." His thumb brushed her shoulder again, hitting that very arousing spot, causing her to shiver.

Stubborn, one-track-minded man. Had she agreed? Possibly. Maybe. Darn it, yes. Glen had captured her heart before she knew he was Dhampir. Then he tied his heart in a bow and held it out to her for the taking. But… she still had doubts and needed to ask one last time. "You don't mind being saddled with me?"

"Delia?" Edna pounded on the door again. "Are you in there?"

"Good grief, I'm going to kill her," Delia whispered. "Edna, I'll be out in a minute."

"What are you doing in there?"

Glen stepped back, taking his warmth with him. As he tucked his shirt back into his pants, he replied, "Edna, she's teaching me how to wedge clay."

"Glen? You in there, too?"

He chuckled and shook his head. "She's gone back into the house." Glen's expression turned serious, and he took Delia's hand, pulling her back into his embrace. "When I look at you, I see the most gorgeous woman in the world. A woman who isn't afraid of what I am."

"I have wrinkles," she informed him.

"I have horns," he countered.

He did, but gravity hadn't been her friend. "My boobs—"

He placed his finger over her lips, silencing her. "Are beautiful." Glen flashed his fangs. "And tasty."

Heat rushed to her face. "Be serious."

"I am." His expression filled with longing and need. Glen wanted and desired her, but he needed *her* to want and desire him. He pressed his lips to hers in a brief, gentle kiss. "When I look at you, I thank God for blessing me with such a wonderful, beautiful mate."

Staring into his blue eyes, seeing the emotions there, Delia wanted Glen. Her age didn't define her, nor did her looks. Was it okay to bind their lives together? "I'm not worthy of the pedestal you've put me on."

"Lass, it's not a pedestal but a throne I've placed you, for you are my lady, and I'm your servant."

"Oh, for the love of…"

"Come on, my bonnie mate, before Edna wears a hole in your floor."

"It's her floor, and you know she's pacing how?"

He opened the door, then tapped his ear. "If she stomps any heavier, she'd be treading on Old Scratch's head."

Sure enough, Edna paced in front of the kitchen window, glaring at the studio each time she passed.

"On second thought," Delia looped her arm with Glen's. "let's go back."

He pulled her back around, slipping his arm around her waist. "Nope. Best to rip the plaster off fast and get it over with." He turned the doorknob.

"The plaster?"

"Bandage." Glen pushed open the door.

Edna spun on them, clutching a lint brush in hand. "From the noise, I thought the neighbor's cat was locked in there again."

"Oh, for heaven's sakes, Edna." Delia lifted the lid on the teapot. There was enough tea for a few more cups. "I couldn't sleep and decided to do some work. I didn't know Glen installed a silent alarm system in my studio." She glanced over her shoulder at her aunt. "But you did."

"I did?" Edna grinned, waving the brush around like a wand. "Must have slipped my mind."

"It went off," Delia continued and poured a cup of tea. "Glen rushed over to ensure it wasn't Scott destroying stuff and found me wedging clay." She handed the cup to Glen.

"Is that what it's called now?" Edna aimed the brush at Glen's crotch. "Don't think you want me to dust him off. Though I wouldn't mind."

"Give me that." Heat rose in Delia's cheeks, seeing her prominent gray handprint covering his crotch. Good grief, he was still erect. She looked up, meeting Glen's eyes shimmering with humor. "Do you always have to wear black?" She snapped.

"Everything matches." Glen chuckled. He wrapped his fingers around hers, taking the brush from her.

"Don't forget his rump." Edna winked and strolled from the kitchen.

"I've got this." Glen leaned forward, brushing his lips against hers. "Go get dressed. I'm taking you and Edna for breakfast."

"Don't like my pajamas?" Delia teased.

"On the contrary, lass. If you wear your jammies to breakfast, I'll remain hard enough to drive nails, as every time I look at you, they'll remind me of how you responded to my touch." A wicked grin curved his lips, and his eyes glowed red.

She went up on her tiptoes and pressed a kiss to his cheek. "Your way was far better to release tension."

"Forgot the furniture cleaner," Edna said, strolling into the kitchen. "By the way, Snotface was smoking on his deck when you were…." She flashed them a devilish grin. "Wedging clay."

The thought of what Glen did had Delia aching for his touch again, and she shivered. "Good, maybe Scott realizes I'm with Glen. By the way, he's taking us to breakfast."

Edna frowned. "But Whitty will be here soon. How do I look?"

"You look fine."

"Eddie." Glen turned his back to them as he dusted his front. "Their plane doesn't land until eight. Then he'll have to go through customs, followed by Atlanta traffic. I wouldn't expect them before ten."

Delia had debated which would be better, to meet them this morning or tonight at the exhibit. Her logical brain said this morning, her sleep-deprived brain screamed tonight would be best.

"Whitty called while you two were *busy*. They've landed and are on their way here. Delia, unless you want to meet them in your nightclothes, I'd suggest you get dressed."

"Oh, dang it." Delia dashed from the room and up the steps. She quickly dressed, deciding on jeans and a tunic rather than a dressier look.

"Delia." Edna rapped on the door before opening it. "Do you want me to ring them back? We can meet them later." There was no denying the disappointment and regret in Edna's voice.

"No. Everything is fine, Aunt Edna," Delia replied as she pulled her hair back into a messy bun. "Give me a second, and I'll be down." She wasn't meeting the Queen of England, just Glen's family. Delia stared in the mirror at her reflection. Yay! No dark circles under her eyes, so she could forgo makeup this morning. But maybe she'd apply little lip color and a touch of blush.

Edna's shriek of delight followed by muffled masculine voices had Delia hurrying from her room and down the steps, wishing she could shake the feeling that something would go wrong tonight. With her luck, a meteor would crash into the gallery right at six.

Delia paused on the landing, staring at Glen's doppelgänger. She'd seen Edna's old photos many times but seeing Royce and Glen in person, standing side-by-side. Wow! Twins.

"The ex?" Royce asked.

Glen nodded.

"Problem?"

"Nothing that can't be eradicated." Glen closed the door.

Royce chuckled, slapping Glen on the back. "Then I won't do the honor and take away your fun."

Delia groaned and continued down the steps. It was easy to see Glen and Royce were close.

"Whitty!" Edna threw herself at Whitaker.

He caught her, raining kisses over her face. "You're just as beautiful as I remembered."

"Oh, you," Edna gushed, staring up at him. She then hugged Percy. "You're the spitting image of Andrew. You even have the Westmorland dimple."

"That he does." Whitaker beamed, revealing his dimple. He slipped his arm around Edna's waist, tucking her against him.

Edna glanced around the room. "Fiona didn't bring you?"

"No. Her husband was called back to Washington, so I drove," Royce replied. He shifted his gaze, meeting Delia's, and smiled.

She drew in a deep breath and stepped down. Time to join the party.

"And we survived," Percy stated.

"My boy!" Edna hugged Royce for so long Delia didn't think her aunt would turn loose.

"Eddie," Royce gasped. "Hugs have to end."

She stepped back, wiping her eyes. "I'm so sorry I didn't see you right off."

"That's all right, Eddie." He chuckled. "I realize you only have eyes for Whitaker."

"Oh, you."

Glen was at Delia's side the moment she stepped from the stairs. He slipped his arm around her waist, tucking her against him. A rumbling growl vibrated from him.

"Hush," Delia whispered, lightly pinching his side, then resting her hand around his waist. She raised up and kissed his cheek. "I can't get over how much you two look alike. Other than your hair coloring and darker eyes, you're twins."

"Yes, but I'm the better-looking one. Right?"

"No need to fish for compliments. I prefer tall, dark, and," she whispered. "Horny."

Royce roared with laughter. "I'm delighted you have accepted Glen for what he is."

Heat warmed her face. "I don't think I'll ever get over your supersonic hearing."

Glen pressed a kiss to her temple. He motioned to Royce. "*Mo gràdh*, my cousin, Royce Lucard. Royce, my mate, Cordelia Parsons."

His mate? Victoria had explained some things to Delia. Being a mate was more than being a fiancé, and being mated was more than being married. Mating bound a couple's heart and soul. Victoria also explained *mo gràdh* meant my love.

Royce smiled, his gaze dipping to Delia's neck where Glen had nipped her.

She'd checked the area in the mirror, making sure he hadn't given her a hickey. There were only two very faint and tiny pin-size white scars. But there was something in Royce's eyes that told her he saw more. Delia held out her hand to him. "It's a pleasure to meet you."

Royce took her hand, lifting it to his lips, then handing her hand to Glen. "I hope our early arrival hasn't disrupted your day."

"Oh, no. Not at all." She chuckled. "Your arrival is a wonderful distraction." Otherwise, she'd be chewing her fingernails and pacing.

"Breathe." Glen smoothed his hand down her back.

"Brilliant," Royce said. "Then shall we have brunch, giving you the rest of the day to relax?"

"Delia," Edna called. She patted Whitaker's arm. "This is Whitty and his son, Percival."

"Gentlemen, it's wonderful to meet you face to face. Percy, thank you so much for everything you've done. I wish I could repay you somehow."

A wicked grin curved his lips. "Do you have an issue with puce?"

"Purple-brown. Not my favorite color, possibly because it's French for flea, tick, or some other blood-sucking insect?"

"Flea. It's French for flea." Percy scrunched up his face. "That never occurred to me."

"Besides, it's spring." She winked at him. "Go with something vibrant. Something to make your blue eyes pop."

"Percival?" Whitaker frowned. "You promised."

"I love puce," Edna said. "Is that the color you plan on dying your hair? Victoria said to expect you with vibrant hair color, so seeing you," she motioned to him. "So dull was off-putting."

Delia tried not to laugh. She honestly did, but when poor Percy mouthed *dull,* she laughed so hard that tears rolled down her cheeks. Maybe the world wouldn't end tonight.

Chapter Sixteen

The prolonged anticipation was unbearable. What was taking her so long? Glen rocked back on his heels, staring up the staircase, waiting for Delia. He couldn't believe how well she got on with everyone. Hell, even Victoria liked Delia. And Percy...Thank God the man was gay and mated. Otherwise, Glen would have to kill him to eliminate the competition. Glen glanced at the wall clock. Delia would be late for her exhibit if she didn't hurry.

Relax, his daemon growled.

Glen looked up. His breath caught as Delia stepped onto the upper landing. "You're beautiful."

"Thank you," Delia said, slowly descending the steps. "Sorry I took so long. I just couldn't wear what Victoria and Percy suggested. I opted for this." She motioned to the simple sleeveless black turtleneck dress she wore. "When I couldn't decide on pearls or a simple gold chain, I decided on this colorful statement necklace I made."

"You made that? It's beautiful."

"Thank you. So are you." Slowly and seductively, Delia's gaze slid over him. "Damn, you make that suit look good." She straightened his tie, then kissed him. "We could lock the doors and stay here all night."

The thought had his zipper cutting into his dick. That would teach him to go commando. "We could." He grinned, knowing Delia saw his fangs. "But I'm afraid we'd have to face my sister's fury if we did that."

"You're right. I think she's more excited about tonight than I am." Delia strode to the door, not waiting for him.

Glen followed, trying to analyze her odd statement. They didn't have time to discuss it here, not if he wanted to get her there on time. Glen followed Delia out to his Bentley. Once inside and buckled, he closed the door for her. She sat as stiff as one of her sculptures. Discussing it in the driveway was not an option. She'd be out of the car, and they'd never make it on time.

"I see Angus repaired Dragon."

"He did." Glen merged onto the interstate and glanced over at her. He didn't need a blood connection to feel Delia's tension. It increased vehemently with each passing second. "I'm going to ask a stupid male question. Why are you so anxious?"

"Excuse me."

He glanced at her, kept his mouth shut, and waited.

"Fine," she huffed. "I can't shake the feeling something bad is going to happen. Damnit, Glen. I'm not a pessimist, but I can't shake the feeling. I mean damnit! Someone carjacked me, Scott moved in next door, and someone shot at us. What else can go wrong?"

"Nothing is going to go wrong." Glen reached over, taking her hand. "Cade and Paul are already there covering the inside while Sue and Mitch secure the outside perimeters. I'm not going to leave your side, but if something comes up and I must leave, Victoria or Margo will be with you. You will not be alone."

"Wait a minute. Why do you have so many people there if you're not expecting trouble?"

"It's normal for a private events like this. I'm here because you're my mate—"

"Not officially." Delia laughed, and he sensed most of her anxiety draining away.

"You're right. I need to put a ring on it, so everyone will know you're mine."

Delia turned in her seat, smiling at him. "Hmm, you mean your fang marks aren't enough? Victoria explained why Royce would glance at my neck and grin during brunch."

Glen had marked Delia without her permission. It took all of Glen's strength to rein the bloody daemon to keep from going further. Delia deserved to be well-loved in a bed when they mated, not laid out on a table like a feast for his taking. "Is that why you wore a turtleneck, to hide my bite?"

"Hell, no." She leaned across the seat, kissing his cheek. "I chose this dress because it's forgiving and hides my imperfections. That and it's comfortable and classy. Besides, according to your sister, only your kind can see your bite from when we got frisky. So, mister. If you are serious—"

"Delia." Glen pulled into the full carpark, thankful Margo had reserved a space for them. He killed the engine as his sister hurried from the building. His heart pounded so loudly that Delia surely heard it. "I've never been more serious in my life."

Victoria rapped on Delia's window. "Save it for later. People are asking about you," Vic shouted. She crossed her arms, glaring at them.

Delia reached for the door handle. "I guess it's showtime."

"Let me get the door for you, please."

Before he could get out, Victoria had Delia's door open, escorting her inside. He really loved his sister about as much as he loved pestilence.

"Not the dress Percy and I picked out, but it will do," Victoria said, giving Delia the once-over.

She exhaled. "I wanted to be comfortable."

Vic nodded. "Understandable. I love the necklace." She opened the gallery door.

Margo ushered Delia inside. "Ladies and gentlemen, thank you for coming tonight. May I present the artist who created these wonderful sculptures, Cordelia Parsons."

The second Delia stepped over the threshold, a round of applause greeted her. Glen's heart swelled, and pride filled him hearing the sound.

Vic grabbed his arm, halting his entrance. "Give her a second. This is *her* moment."

It was long overdue. "Thank you for not giving Delia grief over the dress she chose."

"Aunt Gwyn has taught me the bless-your-heart look. I wasn't about to push the issue. I knew Delia was nervous about tonight. That's why we've kept Edna entertained today. Everything will be perfect, Glen. You can breathe." Vic flashed him a smile, then nudged him forward.

Summer Botela hugged Delia, giving her a kiss on the cheek. "I just wanted to tell you, I got my falls. I chose Spring. I love the cute little bear cub."

"Thank you, Summer." Delia visibly relaxed.

Margo approached, handing Delia a flute of champagne. "A word, please."

"Something wrong?" The color drained from Delia's face.

Margo's gaze shifted to the entrance as Scott strolled in with Britney on his arm. "They're here with the Bouviers."

Boss, we have a problem. Cade's voice echoed in Glen's mind.

Give me a sec. Glen slipped his arm around Delia and whispered, "Do you want me to ask them to leave?"

We don't have a second. Paul sniffed C4.

Bloody freakin' hell.

Delia shook her head. "Scott would love that. Just don't leave me."

Victoria. Now. "I'll be back in a second."

"But—"

Glen pressed a quick kiss to Delia's lips. "Vic will be at your side." He hurried off, catching Royce's questioning expression.

Glen shoved through the swinging storeroom door. "What do we have?"

Cade and Paul looked up from the inconspicuous small white package barely big enough to ship a cricket ball.

Cade pointed to the box. "We haven't attempted to open it. We didn't want to risk detonating it, but we have taken photos of the mailing label. I wish we had x-ray vision, like comic book heroes, to see inside the damn thing."

"That's for damn sure," Paul replied. "Whoever shipped it made it difficult to open. Look at all the tape they used."

Glen met Paul's eyes. "You're certain it's C4?" The man was a wolf with a hell of a nose.

"Positive."

"How much?"

Paul's tight-lipped expression was answer enough. Enough to cause one hell of a bang. Possibly maim a few, if not kill. Bloody frigging hell. Glen had promised Delia nothing would go wrong. "Give it to me."

"You have a mate," Paul argued.

He did, and Delia's life mattered more than anything. "Give it to me."

Paul gently lifted the box, handing it over. "What are you going—"

"Taking it into the wraith zone." Glen faded. He didn't know if his plan would work, but in all practicality, it should. People and objects become mere ghostly apparitions in the zone containing no solid form. However, those in the wraith zone could still die. He hoped to hell he didn't blow himself up.

In this world, Glen barely made out Cade's shadow, opening the heavy metal door leading into the alley, then running toward the dumpster. Cade slid the door open.

Glen held his breath, tossed the box inside, and quickly pushed from the zone. He closed the door and exhaled. "Let's hope this works."

Cade glanced back at the dumpster as they headed toward the gallery. "The dumpster is far enough away, and the bomb's in another dimension, so we should be safe. What if we're mistaken, and this was some poor idiot's art?"

"Then they should've chosen a different medium," Glen snapped, entering the warehouse and meeting Royce's red glare.

He shoved against Glen's chest. "You took a bloody risk pushing your luck like that. You're two for two. Let's not risk it again, shall we?" His horns retreated, and his eyes slowly faded to normal.

"What would you have suggested?" Glen asked. It wasn't like Royce to lose his control.

His lips thinned, and he shook his head. "The same bloody thing you did."

Glen patted Paul's shoulder. "You and Cade were brilliant. I want all surveillance footage downloaded and gone through. I doubt a carrier delivered this package. I'm going to speak with Margo."

Royce caught Glen's arm. "If you go out there now, you'll cause more harm than that device, which was a dud."

"You know this how?"

"The device?" Royce shrugged. "It didn't go off when you tossed it. As for you walking through that door? Delia's ex has her cornered."

Glen jerked free, only to have Royce grab his arm again.

"Don't. Your mate has things under control. Besides, Victoria and Percy are with her. Now, fill me in about this." Royce motioned toward the exterior door and the dumpster on the other side. "Personal, or does this concern us?"

Us, meaning the Dhampir. After all, Royce was in attendance. However, other than family, no one knew he'd be here. Bloody hell, Glen didn't even know until he opened the door this morning. "This doesn't concern us. I have two suspects, Delia's ex and a certain father with poor parenting skills."

Royce propped his hip on a table and crossed his arms. "The ex doesn't have the brains the Lord gave a piss-ant. Tell me about the father."

If Glen wanted to get to Delia's side, he'd have to appease his cousin. Bloody hell. He loved Royce and hated him at the same time. "Name's Edik Petrov. Businessman. Runs an import-export, amongst other things. I suspect his son Luka was the one who carjacked and pistol-whipped Delia. I also believe he's the prick who took the potshot at us the other night. Daddy may have taken exception to my dropping off a copy of junior's activities."

"What proof do you have of this kid's involvement?"

Glen flexed his hands and exhaled. "The kid tried to carjack me. I have the footage if you want to see it." He snapped his finger. Cade hurried to his side.

"No need." Royce waved Cade off and slid from the table. "You mucked up the fingerprints. You touched the box, as did Paul. Neither of you wore gloves, so obtaining proof that Cordelia's ex was involved will be difficult, but not impossible. The ruffian would have known to wear gloves."

Glen wasn't about to crawl into the dumpster and retrieve the bloody box. He wanted to get back to Delia. "Dud or not, I'm not crawling into that dumpster and smell like garbage. No. It stays where it is, where it can do no harm."

Royce laughed and patted Glen's back. "Just checking. But you should ask who wants to kill your mate. Who's saying her attempted carjacking was not staged to cover up something more sinister?"

"I think you've been involved in one too many conspiracies. Either that or you've read a few too many penny dreadfuls."

"Hear me out." Royce flung his arm around Glen's shoulder as they strolled to the door. "Look out there. Delia's ex and his date are standing at the farthest point in the room. Perfect alibi, wouldn't you say? Being in the building during the blast would eliminate him as a suspect. I don't suppose you see this Edik Petrov chap lurking about?"

"No, and he wasn't on the list either." Glen searched the faces to make sure. That could mean they were the ones responsible.

"As for the shooter the other night," Royce continued. "Didn't you tell me the kid's bodyguard saw you and Delia together? I find it interesting that her ex was at the same restaurant at the same time as this lad. Makes me wonder if Delia's ex didn't hire them to eliminate her."

"You make a valid argument." Glen studied everyone's position. Margo and Delia stood near the center of the room. Alejandro and Summer examined a display of naughty ravens while others wandered about the gallery. "What would her ex have to gain? *If* something happened to Delia, Edna would inherit." He and Delia had already had this conversation. Scott would gain nothing from Delia's death.

"Unless this isn't about money." Royce pushed the swinging door open and paused. "We know what Margaret Keane went through. From what you've told me, Delia's ex is just as ruthless."

Glen followed Royce from the storeroom. What if Royce was right, and this was about Delia's art?

A muffled bang echoed in the building.

Royce glanced over his shoulder. "Hmm, bloody good thing you didn't go back."

Chapter Seventeen

Delia knew disaster would strike tonight. It had. Why did Scott have to show up? Stupid question. Because he enjoyed watching her suffer. She expected something like this from Scott, but Glen? Delia couldn't believe *he* was abandoning her right as Scott appeared.

Glen pressed a quick kiss to her lips. "Vic will be at your side." He hurried off before she could utter a word. Royce glanced at her as he pursued Glen.

"Ladies and gentlemen," Scott raised his voice, drawing everyone's attention. "I'd like to introduce my newest protégé." He lifted his glass. "Britney Goldman."

Summer tapped Delia's shoulder. "Who is that?"

"The man is my ex, and the poor girl with him is his newest girlfriend."

"From her red face, she's embarrassed, as she should be, so bless her heart. I'll pray for her. As for your ex, I have a few cousins who would be more than happy to take him hunting for a six-pack and a pick 'em up truck. Five would go in, four would come out."

"Don't tempt me." Delia laughed and took a sip of champagne.

Summer winked. "I'm serious." She exhaled, shaking her head. "Sweetie, Alejandro is flapping his arms like a chicken trying to fly. Let me see what he wants. You going to be okay for a second?"

"Oh, I'm good. Go see what he wants." Delia glanced at the door leading to the storeroom. Where the devil had Glen run off to?

"He's taking care of an issue." Smiling, Victoria looped her arm with Delia's. "You should stand over here, next to that gorgeous piece. Pity my brother purchased it as I would have loved it for myself."

"The only problem is I'll be closer to Scott."

"I didn't take you for one to back away from a challenge."

Victoria's words snapped the invisible thread of doubt keeping Delia a prisoner of Scott's, even after all these years. Courage and determination infused her very being, straightening her shoulders and allowing her self-confidence to radiate.

"You're right. I'm not." Delia headed toward the *Guardians of the Isle*. It was one of her favorite works. She glanced around the room. There were more people in attendance than she expected to appear. The Bouviers were old southern money and huge contributors to the arts. Apparently, Snooks Bouvier invited several friends and acquaintances, including Scott.

"Delia," Percy singsong as he sauntered toward her. "I can't decide." His bright teal hair literally lit up the room.

"I thought you were going with puce."

"I was, but since Father kept badgering me." A wicked grin lit his face. "I went with something bright and cheery."

"Well, I like it. What can I help you with?"

"I want to get my daughter Hope something, but I can't decide between the raven wearing the jewels and that cute brownie."

"Well, the raven, I did as a nod to Merlina, Queen of the Tower Ravens. Thus the little diadem she's wearing and tiny scepter under her wing. Edna was so upset when the poor thing died."

"Hope loves the Tower Ravens." He peered around. "Where are Tweedledee and Tweedledum?"

"I'm assuming you mean Glen and Royce. According to Victoria, they're dealing with an issue and should return soon." Delia hoped. Her mind had conjured up all sorts of issues, including a wormhole. "As for this Brownie," she continued, trying to get her mind on something positive. "The large eraser he's holding and his scrunched-up face are supposed to conjure up the image of him checking homework."

Percy mimicked the brownie's expression. "Humm, I think he's cute. Hope needs a brownie checking her lessons after Viktor, and I do. Modern math." He grinned. "Decision made. I'm getting both." Percy leaned over, pecking her cheek, and whispered, "You're being watched."

"I know," she whispered back. "I don't care."

"Bloody good for you." He raised his hand, catching the attention of one of Margo's assistants.

Delia looked up, meeting Scott's glare and signature cynical smirk. Seeing the hate in his eyes gave her strength. Tonight was about her. Not him.

He strode toward her, dragging Britney by the hand. Scott flicked the dragon's wingtip on *The Guardians of the Isle*. "Still doing fantasy art. What's this? Your ode to Tolkien?"

Delia kept her smile firmly plastered in place and eyed her work of art, trying to hide her annoyance. The base was in the shape of England, with the English lion, Scottish unicorn, and Welsh dragon placed at their locations. Flowers representing its country surrounded each creature. The Tudor rose for England, thistles for Scotland, and daffodils for Wales. How the devil had Scott seen Tolkien in this? "No. It's not."

Victoria casually eased closer. She lightly caressed the dragon's wingtip. "Good thing this is cast in bronze. Otherwise, you'd be reimbursing the owner."

"You are?" Scott sneered.

"The proprietor of Sterling Gale Art Galleries."

Montreal, Scott mouthed, thrusting out his hand. "Scott Haynes. The Scott Haynes. The artist who created *Phoenix Rising* and *Unhinged*."

Victoria's lips pulled into a red slash across her face as she stared at Scott's outstretched hand. "Yes, I know." She turned on her stiletto heels and sauntered away.

"What a bitch." Scott lifted his hand, pretending to examine his nails. "Snooks said it would be a who's who here tonight, and she was right. But some men don't care how their women look."

Delia glanced sideways, smiled, and nodded at Danielle DuMond. Her husband glared at Scott. Darn it, Magnus must have heard Scott. "Just an FYI Scott. The DuMonds are extremely wealthy and powerful, so I'd lower my voice if I were you." Delia softened her smile for Britney. It wasn't her fault Scott was a snot. "How are you doing?"

"She's doing fine," Scott replied, finding something amusing behind Delia. "Your crone is assaulting one of your patrons. Poor man."

Delia glanced over her shoulder. She'd never met the man Edna spoke with but had seen his photo countless times. Delia smiled as she wove her way around displays, making eye contact and nodding at attendees as she made her way to her aunt. Damn, she'd smiled more tonight than she had in her life. Her cheeks ached, and it felt fantastic!

"Cordy," a feminine voice called.

Heaven's! Delia hated the nickname but smiled and nodded in the voice's direction as she continued toward Edna.

Someone grabbed her shoulder. "Cordy?"

Delia swiveled quickly, throwing off the person's hand, and met a set of familiar brown eyes. For the life of her, Delia couldn't remember who this woman was or come up with a name.

The woman wore a smile but blatantly scrutinized Delia from head to toe. "You don't recognize me. Do. You. *Cordy*?"

The woman's high-pitched whine catapulted Delia back to her old Stanford dorm room. "Tara! Oh my stars, we haven't seen each other in ages. You look good. Do you live here in Atlanta?"

"I'm here on business. Your art must do quite well to afford a billboard. I saw it as I was coming in from the airport. The reason I'm here."

"I'm glad you made it." A muffled bang made Delia jump. "What was that?"

"Sounded like someone needs a new exhaust silencer." Glen slipped his arm around her waist, and she leaned into him, welcoming his warmth.

"Whatever it was, it made me jump." Delia laughed. "Glen, I'd like you to meet a friend from college. Tara…"

"Browning," Tara supplied. "Never married. Is this your son? He looks nothing like you or Scott."

Delia gasped, too startled to say anything. Lack of sleep made her look older, but dang it.

"No," Glen replied. "I'm the lucky man whose heart Delia holds." He leaned over, kissing her firmly on the lips in front of everyone. *You look gorgeous. Even better naked.* His voice and lecherous laugh echoed in her head, instantly making her grin.

"I'm so sorry," Tara stuttered, blushing to her roots. "I thought I saw Scott and you speaking earlier. I just assumed."

"It's okay, Tara." Delia leaned closer to Glen, slipping her arm around his waist. "Scott and I divorced fifteen years ago. But you saw him. He's here with his girlfriend."

"Divorced and still getting along. Wow! Few couples can do that."

"Well, Scott and I have gone our separate ways. Tara, it's great speaking with you, but I really need to see my aunt."

Tara's face lit. "I'm going to be in town for a few days. How about I call you? We can do lunch or something."

As much as Delia didn't want to go down memory lane, what did she have to lose? "That will be fine. Let me give you my number."

"Oh, I have it. I Googled you. Here, let me show you." She pulled out her phone, then showed Delia the number.

"That's it." Perhaps it was time to do as Glen had wanted when he gave her the new phone and change her number.

Tara slipped her phone back into her purse. "You really should be careful about protecting your privacy."

"Yes, I have someone taking care of that now." She glanced up at Glen, hoping he'd do his mind-reading magic and get her away.

He flashed Tara one of his kilowatt smiles. "It's a pleasure to meet you, but if you'll excuse us."

As they made their way to Edna, Delia noticed several women giving Glen the once over. Even Snooks Bouvier stripped him with her eyes, then stepped in front of them. Snooks was old enough to be Delia's mother.

"Cordelia. I didn't realize you and Glen knew each other, much less were dating." Snooks' wandering gaze slipped over Glen once more. "This is marvelous. Simply marvelous. I wanted to say hello and congratulate you on a very successful event before Henry and I take our leave."

"Thank you, Snooks, and thank you for coming."

Snooks's eyes roamed over Glen once more before she strolled away.

Glen leaned closed to Delia's ear and whispered, "Why do I feel like I was just accosted?"

"Because, my love," she whispered back. "you were. Well, eye-groped at least."

His mouth quirked before he erupted in laughter, drawing more attention to them.

"Oh, Dilly." Edna beamed, and for a brief second, Delia saw Edna as the young woman serving king and country. She reached out, taking Delia's hand. "My three boys. Dilly, this is Vaughn Madoc and his lovely wife—"

"Cordelia Parsons." Vaughn's wife thrust out her hand. "Sorry, Rose Madoc."

"Forgive my wife." Vaughn chuckled. "She's a huge admirer of yours."

"Only because I turned Rose on to Cordelia." Danielle winked. "This is fantastic, Delia. You deserved it."

Dang it, Delia hated brain fog. Rose Madoc? Where did she know that name? Then it clicked. "Victorian Dreams Restoration and Remodel. It's a pleasure to finally meet you in person."

"Thank you," Rose gushed. "We've talked so much on the phone, I feel as if I already know you."

Glen wagged a finger between Rose and Delia. "Wait a minute. You two know each other?"

"This is the first time Rose and I have met in person," Delia replied. "But, yes. Remember the sculptures of the four children I told you about? They were Danielle's and Magnus's sets of twins, Megan, Maggie, and Danny and David."

"But you two—three," Glen pointed to Danielle. "know each other."

"Okay, once more for the slow ones in the class." Rose huffed and shook her head. "Dani showed me Cordelia's sculptures of the children, and I started following her on social media," she clarified. "I have to confess, Cordelia. I'm in love with your *Untitled* piece. But it's already sold." Rose bit her lower lip and glanced over at Danielle. "You didn't purchase it, did you?"

"I wish." Danielle glanced at Vaughn. Her eyes widened, and she pointed to one of Margo's assistants carrying the sculpture to the back counter. "It looks like it's being packed up."

"Well, poo." Rose rolled out her bottom lip. "If you were the one, Dani. I would have arm-wrestled you for it. Delia. Can I call you Delia?"

"You can."

"By chance, did you create a second one?"

Delia shook her head. "I'm afraid not."

"Magnus, Vaughn. Did you know they knew each other?" Glen demanded.

Vaughn's expressionless stone face didn't hide the humor glistening in his green eyes. "Yes, Glen. Magnus and I knew our mates knew one another." The corner of his lips twitched. "And deliberately kept you out of the loop."

"Bleeding bawbag."

Edna cackled. "You boys are still giving each other what-for."

"All the time," Percy said, joining them. "Edna, are you and Father ready?"

"Fiona and Percy are taking Whitty and me to dinner. Don't wait up, Dilly." Edna looped her arm with Whitakers and left, laughing at something he'd said.

"You two are mates?" Dani elbowed her husband. "Why didn't you tell me?"

Delia looked up at Glen. Did he want them to know? Did she? She and Glen had only known each other a month, if that long. She searched his eyes, his beautiful, compassionate, and, dare she say, loved-filled blue eyes. Then she met each woman's anticipation-filled expressions and nodded. "We haven't made it official yet."

"Let's go out for dinner and celebrate," Danielle suggested. "I can make reservations at the Coach and Six or the Abby for tomorrow night. What do you say?"

"Excuse me." Margo smiled at Vaughn. "Mr. Madoc, I'll have someone carry out your purchase when you are ready."

Rose squealed, throwing her arms around his neck and kissing his cheek. "*You* brought it!"

Margo cringed and mouthed, sorry.

Vaughn laughed, staring down at Rose. "I have no idea what you're talking about."

Delia stifled a yawn, forcing a smile to her face. "If you all will excuse me, I must make my rounds before everyone leaves."

"We're leaving, as well." Dani hugged her. "Got to rescue the babysitter."

"Us too," Rose replied. "But we'll see you tomorrow night. Right?"

"I'm looking forward to it." Even before tonight, Delia had an easy rapport with Dani and had longed to meet Rose in person, knowing they'd click. And they had. The fact Delia would have others she could confine in made her relationship with Glen seem like divine intervention.

"Thank you so much for coming." Delia exhaled as the last patron left.

Margo closed the door, locked it, and flipped the sign. She stared out the glass door before turning around and squealing. "Oh, my stars! Delia, this was the best exhibit we've ever had!" She rushed forward, hugging Delia so tight she felt a vertebra or two pop. "We have to make plans for your next event. But right now, I want a word with Glen." Margo's entire mood shifted from let's celebrate to going to kill someone, and from her glare at Glen, he'd best run. "What did you find out?"

A door slammed, causing Delia to jump and turn, startled by Paul, Cade, Sue, and Mitch. She hadn't seen any of Glen's people all night, and from the sour looks on their faces, perhaps it was a good thing. "What's going on?"

Margo planted her hands on her hips. "I want whoever was responsible found." She snapped her fingers. "Now!"

"Baby." Margo's husband came from behind the register and slipped his arm around her waist. "Bring it down a notch."

"Don't tell me to bring it down. You don't do shit like this. What the hell is wrong with people? Trying to blow up our business. I'd like to shove that bomb up their asses and blow them up."

"Bomb!" Delia's knees buckled, and Glen caught her.

"The threat was minimal," he said, holding his hand up, his thumb and forefinger barely touching. "Think firecracker."

"I'm fine." Delia pulled away. Minimal her derriere. "That boom we all heard wasn't a car backfiring, and it sure as the devil sounded bigger than a firecracker. Good grief! Monterrey all over again. I knew something would happen tonight. I just knew it."

"Monterrey? What happened?"

She huffed. "That had nothing to do with tonight." It couldn't.

"Delia." Glen leveled his eyes at her, his brows drawn, and his lips thinned. "Humor me."

She glared right back at him. After a few minutes, she blinked. "When I was a student, all the art schools held a show. The individual colleges submitted the works of their top students. At the height of the event, someone set off fireworks, causing the crowd to panic. In the wake of the chaos, countless works were destroyed. The police never caught the ones responsible and chalked it up as a practical joke."

Cade pulled out his phone. "Do either of you recognize this person?"

Margo shook her head and peered up at her husband. "Do you?"

"I can't tell if it's a man or woman. Do you have a better image?" he asked.

"This is the best one," Cade replied. "What about the clerk? Is she here tonight?"

Margo shook her head. "She's gone back to college. From the date stamp, that was her last day."

Delia studied the image of a person wearing a black overcoat and hat. "There was no need for them to wear a coat that day, and it appears too big. I'd say this was either a teen or a petite woman from the width of their shoulders."

Glen's stern-faced expression grew darker. "Delia, was Scott there in Monterrey?"

"I don't know. Scott could have been a judge. It was before we started dating."

"Was your art destroyed?"

"No. My work wasn't submitted. I was there as a student volunteer. You think Scott had something to do with tonight?"

Glen exhaled and nodded. "I can't rule him out."

Delia could. "Well, not unless he hired someone or picked up some skills in the past years. When we were married, he didn't have the ability to change a light bulb."

"Hired someone, like maybe…Britney?" Glen's eyes were glowing orbs.

"Wrong body type to be Britney."

"Doesn't mean she's not helping him," Glen snarled.

Delia bit her tongue and pulled out a stool. She wasn't going to call Glen on his snarly self. She glanced at her watch, wondering how long Glen and his team would stare at the computer screen. Getting no rest the night before was one thing, but going from an ultimate high of a successful show to realizing somebody tried to sabotage the event left her exhausted with a throbbing headache. Though she couldn't see Scott building a bomb, he had tried to kill her once and almost succeeded.

Victoria glanced up from her phone. "How are you holding up?"

"Tired. Could you take me home?"

"Sure. Glen."

"In a tick." He didn't even bother to look up.

A satanic smirk curved Victoria's lips. "Cover your ears," she whispered. Victoria placed her thumb and forefinger in her mouth and whistled. Delia knew the shrill sound had rendered every glass and crystal object in a mile radius to sand.

"Hell's bloody bells, Vic!" Glen yanked on his ear.

"Delia's knackered. I'm taking her home. Ciao."

"Delia." Glen rushed over to her. He tipped her chin up and kissed her. "I know you're tired, but I don't want you going back to your house alone."

"I won't be. Your sister is taking me." She kissed him back. "I'll see you tomorrow."

"Delia, someone tried to kill you."

She stopped and drew in a deep breath. "No. They tried to sabotage me." She met Glen's glowing eyes, thankful neither

Margo nor her husband noticed. "I'm not going to live in fear. Been there. Done that. Not doing it again."

"Delia—"

"No. Glen, for all we know, this isn't about me but the Gallery. Until you can prove otherwise, I'm going home. I'll see you tomorrow."

Delia sat quietly and closed her eyes as Victoria wove through Saturday night traffic. The easy jazz and rocking of the car helped ease some tension, but Delia's mind kept spinning. Who would want to sabotage her show? Scott. But planting an explosive and hanging around didn't seem his style. However, it would destroy her art. He would do that to get back at her.

"We're here." Vic pulled into the driveway. "I don't sense anyone inside, so I guess Edna is still out with Whitaker."

The moonless night left the house cloaked in darkness. Delia hadn't even turned on the porch light, and the streetlights didn't help.

"Do you want me to come in and wait with you?"

"No, but thank you for bringing me home and everything you've done. I'll see you tomorrow."

"No, you won't. I'm flying out first thing in the morning. I think it's time I stop running."

"From?"

Victoria shook her head. "Get some sleep, love. I'll see you in a few weeks."

"Have a safe flight. Call me." Delia leaned across the seat, giving Victoria a hug before sliding from the car.

At least with the new locks Glen installed, Delia wouldn't have to dig around in her purse. She locked the door behind her and flicked the porch light for Edna. She should be home soon— or not. She and Whitaker had a lifetime of catching up to do. In the meantime, a hot shower and soft bed were calling Delia's name.

She glanced at her phone. It was nearly midnight, and she still couldn't get her mind to stop racing. Maybe warm milk would help. She headed toward the kitchen, passing Edna's room. She still wasn't home. Edna and Whitaker must still be with Percy and Fiona. If anything was wrong, Glen would call. Delia went back and snatched her phone, just in case. The way her luck was going, if she didn't, she'd break her neck running back up to answer it.

With the phone in hand, she strode into the kitchen. The glass of milk and maybe one or two of Edna's oatmeal cookies sounded good. Delia's hand hovered over the light switch as she stared out the window. A soft glow came from around her studio door. Damnit, she'd left the light on all day. Again. Well, it could stay on for a few more hours. But what would it take for her to go out there, turn off the dang thing and make sure she locked the door? If the light was on, it was a sure thing she'd left the door unlocked.

Her phone dinged. Maybe it was Edna saying she's on her way home. Delia swiped her thumb over the screen and read the text as she headed toward her studio. "Oh, hell no!" She tapped out his number.

"Delia, I didn't think you'd still be up," Glen's too sexy voice answered.

"I don't need a babysitter." She pulled on the studio door, and just as she thought, she'd left it unlocked.

"I just need a place to sleep. Not a problem. I'll crash at the office."

She guessed with everyone in town, Glen was out of a bed. "Come on over." She stepped into her studio and pulled the chain, flipping off the light.

The doors slammed. "Glen."

"Delia, where are—"

"Glen! This isn't funny." If this was his idea of a practical joke, he had a pretty sick sense of humor. She turned the handle, pushing on the door, only to have it slam shut again. "Glen, open this door now!" She tried the handle again, but something was jamming it. "Glen!"

An orange glow and smoke filled the small space. "Help!" She banged on the door. Panicking, she called 911. Nothing. No reception.

The crackling of the fire was deafening. "Help!" Delia took several steps back to get enough momentum. She ran, slamming into the door, trying to force it open. "Help!" she screamed, pounding on the door as black smoke filled the building. "Help," Delia coughed. Her lungs burned as she continued pounding on the door.

Chapter Eighteen

"Percy, take my bed. Don't worry about it." Glen pressed the button of his elevator, and as the doors slid together, he couldn't keep from grinning. If fate was with him, he'd be cuddling with Delia. Never had he been so thankful for Percy's dramatics as tonight.

Glen pulled from his complex. In fifteen, he'd be at Delia's and in twenty in her arms. With luck, naked.

We should be guarding our mate, not the mutt. His daemon pouted. *She painted his picture.*

No, she didn't. But Paul is going home. Glen pressed the call button on the steering wheel. "Call Paul."

"Glen, dang it. Ain't nothing changed since you called ten minutes ago."

Right. Maybe Glen had been a tad overprotective, calling so much. "I'll be there in less than ten. You can take off."

"Why?" There was so much disappointment in that one word.

"Percy's crashing in my bed. With luck, I'll be on Delia's couch. The last thing I want is for her to peer out her bedroom window, spotting you pulling away as I pull up."

"Make sense. If I were you, I'd send Delia a text. You can play dumb in the morning, saying you took it as a yes since she didn't respond."

That wouldn't fly with Delia, but it would be worth a shot. "Not a bad idea." He ended the call.

It's an awful idea. Our mate will be furious.

"Then we can make it up to her. Text Delia. Crashing on your couch. Send."

A second later, his phone rang. "Delia, I didn't think you'd still be up."

"I don't need a babysitter," she snapped.

Yup, she was pissed. Time for the pity-poor-me routine. "I just needed a place to sleep." He exhaled as dramatically as possible. "Not a problem. I'll crash at the office." Who said you couldn't learn from kids?

Delia huffed so loud he could feel her breath through the speaker. "Come on over."

The sound of a door slamming was overridden by Delia's shout, "Glen."

"Delia, where are—" Static. Shit! He sped down the interstate. Flashing blue lights lit the interior of his car. For once, this wasn't a bad thing.

"Call Paul."

"Toss your ass out?" Paul chuckled.

"Get back there now. Something's going down." Glen ended the call. He gave the intersection a quick scan before running the traffic signal. He turned down Delia's street, and his heart stopped at the orange glow lighting up the sky. *Delia. Delia.* He tried to reach her mind. Nothing. "Please, God. Please, *Yeva,* keep her safe."

Glen's daemon fought to break free. Red haze blurred his vision. Sirens blared as red and blue flashing lights joined the orange glow in the sky. He was out of the car, vaulting over the six-foot fence into Delia's backyard. White plastic zip ties secured the two handles, locking her inside her flame engulfed studio. He gripped the handles, scorching his hands, and yanked. Delia lay on the ground, coughing and gasping. Glen scooped her in his arms, carrying her to safety as the fire brigade rushed through the open gate.

"Anyone else in there?" a female firefighter asked.

"No." Delia coughed, shaking her head.

Glen set her on the ground, propping her against the house. Thick smoke hung heavy in the air, along with the distinctive odor of kerosene. The crackling and popping of the fire drowned out the shouts from the firefighters.

"Sir," a paramedic tapped his shoulder. "Are you injured?"

Glen's hands stung, but his body would heal them. "No. Just Delia."

The paramedics nudged Glen out of the way to tend to her. One spoke quietly as another pressed an oxygen mask to her face. Glen stood, but he'd be damned if he'd leave her side. This was no accident. This was a blatant attempt on her life.

"MacPhee," Marks bellowed as he stormed through the open gate. "Under the circumstances," Marks said, arching his dark brows. "I'm going to ignore the numerous traffic violations."

Several more officers filed through the gate along with a familiar fedora. Detective Gannon's dry humor and no-nonsense attitude reminded Glen of his old boss.

"Why's CID here? Did someone call you?" Usually, the Criminal Investigations Division didn't just show up. They were called to investigate and follow up on a crime. Considering the circumstances, Glen was glad Gannon was here.

"Marks called me, said you were breaking the sound barrier. That doesn't happen unless there's a body." Gannon's displeasure turned from Glen to the medics tending Delia to the fire. The man's lips thinned the longer he stared at the burning structure sprayed down by the fire brigade. Finally, he shifted his attention back to Glen. "Care to enlighten us?"

"I was on the mobile with Cordelia. I heard a door slam, her scream, then static. Gannon, this is arson and attempted murder."

"It always amazes me how you make my job so easy. Got a suspect for me to arrest?"

"Holy shit." Paul strode through the gate.

Glen slammed Paul against the side of the house. "What the bleeding hell happened?"

"Hey," Marks shouted, straining to pull Glen from Paul.

MacPhee, let him go," Gannon barked. "Damn, here I thought you'd be worthwhile to work for when I got sick of this job."

Glen released Paul and backed away. His daemon would have ripped the wolf's throat if he hadn't. "Explain."

"After you called." Paul rubbed the back of his head. "I got out and checked the surrounding area. Everything was fine. Cordelia's house was dark, and the neighbor over there," he pointed to the house on the left. "Turned off the light in the kitchen as I returned to my car."

Delia yanked the oxygen mask from her face. "What did you say?"

"Your neighbor—"

Delia paled, and fear glistened in her wide eyes. "Glen." She reached for him. "That house is a rental. It's empty. "Where's Edna?"

Gannon jerked his head toward the house. Marks, along with three other officers, took off.

Glen knelt beside Delia, wrapping his arm around her shoulders. "She's safe. She's with Whitaker. Percy and Victoria won't allow anything to happen to them."

The paramedic frowned. "Ma'am, please reconsider."

"Thank you for everything." Delia coughed. "But I am not going to the hospital. Thank you."

"Sir," the man pleaded to Glen. "Her lungs could be—"

"Could be," Delia retorted. "Doesn't mean they are."

Glen sympathized with the man. Delia was stubborn. "I'll make sure she receives the proper medical care." *With a couple of drops of me.*

"I'm not going—"

"Cordelia," he warned.

"Fine. I'll be a good little girl." She held out her hand to the medic.

Glen bit his tongue. He'd prefer naughty, but now wasn't the time for sarcasm.

"Ma'am." The man handed her the oxygen mask. "If you won't go to the hospital, at least use this while we're here."

"Go on." Gannon eyed Paul.

"Miss Parsons," Paul stammered. "I let you down."

Delia removed the mask. Again. "You didn't do any of the sorts." She coughed, pointing at Glen. "And *he* apologizes for being a jobby."

The corner of her lips twitched before she hid them behind the mask. Delia was right. Glen should have been protecting her, not Paul. "I'm sorry for crackin' *her siding* with your head."

Paul slightly tilted his head, baring his throat. "Once I assumed everything was okay, and yes, I know what assume means. I left. It couldn't have been over four minutes since I spoke with you. Meaning, whoever did this—fuck it—was watching me." *I didn't scent them.* Paul mentally added.

This wasn't good coming from a wolf with a damn good sniffer. "Check the cameras to see if we got something." *Enhance the footage and send it to Viktor if needed. Don't bother Percy unless necessary. He's keeping an eye on Edna.*

"On it." Paul strode through the gate, only to rush back. "When I made my final rounds, I didn't check the area between the building and the privacy fence. When we installed the cameras, I didn't check for a dark zone back here. I screwed up."

"It's done. Download the cameras."

Delia removed the oxygen mask again. "If what you're saying is true, they knew I was in there."

Paul nodded. "Making what happened tonight directed at you and not the gallery."

The fear rolling from Delia stabbed Glen's heart. "Paul. Now." Glen took the mask from Delia's limp fingers and placed it back on her face. "Keep this on. Please." He kissed her forehead.

"Miss Parsons, may I use your kitchen table?" Paul asked.

She nodded, keeping the mask firmly on.

"Good girl." Glen kissed her forehead again.

"What about tonight?" Gannon looked up from his notebook. Yeah, the man would catch that tidbit. "Was there another attempt?"

"Detective," a firefighter shouted. "You need to see this."

"Coming." Gannon pocketed his notepad as he strode to the back of the yard. He squatted, examining something on the ground. "MacPhee."

Glen squatted, carefully examining the jammer trampled deep into the mud. How the bloody hell had he missed it? *We were rescuing our mate*, his daemon rumbled.

Gannon pulled on gloves, then took a plastic evidence bag from his pocket. "What's your take?" He carefully pried the device from the mud. Then examined it for a second before dropping it into the bag.

"Short-range Wi-Fi jammer. It's a low-end model, probably purchased off the internet. The range is approximately fifty yards, which explains why Delia lost mobile reception."

"What happened tonight that you weren't going to tell me?"

Glen wouldn't bust Paul for his slip, but damn. There was no way Glen would retrieve the bloody thing from the wraith zone. "We found a noisemaker at Ivy and Rose Art Gallery. Delia was having an art exhibit. My team dealt with it, and no one was the wiser. Those attending thought it was a car backfiring."

"What else aren't you telling me?"

"I didn't want to say anything where Delia could hear, but the door handles had been zip-tied to keep her from escaping, and there was a strong kerosene smell." Glen stared at the pile of smoldering wet ash that had once been Delia's studio. He'd replace everything.

"Yeah, the captain already mentioned that." Gannon stood, pulling off his gloves. "Any ideas who would want her dead?"

He had a pretty good idea. "I have two in mind. The first, Edik Petrov."

"You can cross him off your list unless he ordered the hit from the grave."

"What? When?" This meant Scott was to blame.

We should've killed him. His daemon rumbled.

They still might. Glen swallowed the lump in his throat. He could have lost her if he had not been on the phone with Delia and slept on his couch. Scott was a dead man.

"Three nights ago," Gannon replied. His eyes turned vacant, emotionless, and his tone robotic. He must have seen the bodies. "We collected over a hundred casings from outside the car. Petrov, his son, Luca, and their bodyguard. The kid's the only survivor, but he's in a coma. I'm not giving much hope to his pulling through. Damn, he's the same age as my grandson." Gannon glanced back at Delia, then at the smoldering building. "From what Marks said, I thought you had someone on Petrov."

"I did until the Feds called me off."

"That stopped you?" Gannon chuckled.

"Not when Trammell ordered me." But when Edgar cautioned, Glen listened. But he'd keep that to himself. "Higher-ups threatened to send my arse back to Scotland. Permanently. I kinda like it here."

"I can see why. She's a real looker."

"We're a couple." *We should blind him for coveting what is ours.* Glen's bloody beast roared.

"You're what, thirty-five?" Gannon eyed him. "She's what? Twenty years your senior?"

Ah, Gannon was smooth, really smooth. "Delia's a classy, graceful lady, full of life, and has her head on straight. What can I say? Fate. So, let's hope you find the bastard who did this before I do."

"I'm going to forget you said that because I feel if you find them first, that body won't be found." Gannon peered up at him from under his fedora. The man seriously needed to buy a new hat. "So, who's your next likely candidate for this?"

"What the fuck, Cordy?" Scott stormed through the gate. Good, Glen wouldn't have to hunt the bastard down. But with so many witnesses, he'd have to kill him later. "Are you trying to burn down the neighborhood?"

Delia pushed to her feet and yanked off the oxygen mask. "I have enough going on without dealing with your crap." She coughed, trying to draw breath.

Glen rushed to her side, snatching the mask from the medic. "There's a property line, Scott. I suggest you get on your side of it." He held the mask to Delia's face.

"Or what?" Scott sneered. "You'll assault me? Again?"

She knocked Glen's hand and the mask aside. "No, Scott, I'll sue you for trespassing."

Gannon stepped between them and Scott. "And you are, sir?"

"Who wants to know?" Scott curled his lip.

Bloody hell, Scott was not only stupid but also blind if he couldn't see Gannon's badge dangling around his neck.

"I don't have to answer a pretend cop." Scott's voice rose in volume and pitch to the point the surrounding commotion stilled. Even the fire brigade paused in rolling up the hoses.

Maybe they'd all get lucky, and Gannon would do the world a great service and shoot the arse. One could hope.

"Detective Joe Gannon. Atlanta PD. I'll ask again. Who are you?"

Delia yanked the mask off once more and handed it to the paramedic. "At this rate, you can keep it. Detective Gannon, he's Scott Haynes, my ex."

Gannon weighed Delia with a calculating expression. "*You* called him?"

"No," Scott bellowed. "I saw the damn fire from my house. What happened, Cordy? Did you leave your kiln on while passed out drunk from all the champagne you guzzled tonight?"

Glen lunged, but Delia darted between him and Scott, shoving Scott with both hands.

He stumbled back, falling against the fence. "Did you see that, Officer?" Scott sneered. "She assaulted me."

Delia lunged at him again, but Glen caught her around the waist, pulling her back. She struggled with him trying to get free as she shouted at the jobby, "You tried to kill me, you sawed-off cockwomble knob! Just like you did fifteen years ago."

"You were drunk and fell down the damn steps. I was nowhere near you. I was with Megan, so stop blaming it on me."

"You lying bastard. I stared up at you as I cradled my stomach, pleading for help." Delia's voice hitched, and tears streamed down her face. "You thought I wouldn't know it was you because you hid your face. How dumb can you be?"

"Because it wasn't me."

"I smelled your nauseating cologne—"

"DaVinci is a hundred dollars an ounce, you stupid bitch."

Rage and the daemon took over, punching Scott. The man half spun as he stumbled back, smacking his face against the open gate.

Scott screamed as blood painted the gate post. "I'm suing! My nose is bleeding."

Gannon scuffed. "We all witnessed you tripping over your own feet."

"No! He punched *me*," Scott shrieked.

Gannon glared at Scott. "The man never moved. Perhaps you're the one who's had too much to drink."

Delia gripped Glen's arm. The muscles in her jaw twitched. She squared her shoulders until her back was ramrod straight and her head held high.

Glen had enough. He wasn't about to subject her to more of Scott's insults. "Delia, go inside."

"I'm fine." She glanced at him with a cold, vacant look in her eyes. The same look Glen had seen countless times on the dead. "Scott, you stood over me, pouring that cheap wine you always drank on me while I lost our—No. He was never your child. He was my child. You never wanted him. But don't ever tell me again you weren't there. I. Saw. *You*!"

"You're as delusional now as you were then. And I'm bleeding!" Scott shouted, glaring at the paramedics. "Don't any of you give a damn?"

A paramedic removed an icepack from the kit, activated it, then handed it to Scott. "Hold this on your nose."

"My taxes pay for this shit." Scott snatched the ice pack.

"Mr. Haynes," Gannon cleared his throat. "I'd like you to come to the station with me."

"Are you arresting me?"

"No, sir. I'd just like to ask you more questions."

"Then I think I'll pass until after speaking with my lawyer." Scott turned on his heels, striding toward the gate. He paused and glanced over his shoulder. "Cordy, too bad you lost everything. Now you know how it feels." Scott marched through the gate as a uniform entered, bumping into him. "Watch where you're going."

"Ma'am, how many years?" Gannon asked, still staring at where Scott had stood.

"Married for ten, divorced for fifteen. Scott moved here ten years ago. Detective," a hoarse sob escaped with her words. "May I go inside? I'd like to…I'd like to clean up."

"That will be fine, ma'am."

"Thank you."

"MacPhee, if you don't mind hanging with us a little more."

"I'll be fine, Glen." Delia pulled from his embrace, glancing up at him. Dark soot mottled her face, and her eyes were dull and broken. She slowly made her way toward the house.

"Delia?" He pointed after her.

"I'm sure she can manage on her own for a few more minutes. Marks, what did you find?"

Marks? Glen turned. Where the hell had he come from?

"The back door to the house was unlocked. We didn't see any evidence of forced entry. We entered, and everything appeared okay. There was contact information from the real estate agency, so I notified them and left a voice mail. From the breakfast nook, you have a perfect view of this backyard. But you need to see this." Marks motioned to the fence. "Come with me."

Glen followed, keeping his mouth shut. He was a civilian, and Gannon didn't have to share any information.

"Watch." Marks strode a couple of feet past Delia's studio. He gripped a fence board and tugged, exposing an area big enough for a person to squeeze through. "From here, the building would block the security camera's view. My guess is the perp used the vacant house as a lookout. As soon as your man left, they came out, removed these boards, and waited. When Miss Parsons entered, they locked her inside and set the building on fire before going back through the hole. If we're lucky, the camera caught whoever did this."

Gannon tapped his pen against the notepad. "Why did she come out of the house, and how did they know she would?"

That was something nagging Glen, as well. He pulled out his phone, scrolling through it for alerts. "The silent alarm didn't go off this time. Which means it was unlocked." He went into the app, not liking what he saw. He was the last person to unlock the door when he came over last night. Meaning Delia's studio had been unlocked this entire time.

"We can assume something alerted her. MacPhee, do you know what Haynes meant when he said, "Now you know how it feels to lose everything?"

Glen shook his head.

"You know, MacPhee, my grandfather was a Scott. He had a saying, "a nod's as guid as a wink tae a blind horse.""

Glen chuckled. "You kinda botched the brogue there. To answer your question, I don't. I know that since their divorce, Haynes has been harassing Delia. In fact, his current girlfriend purchased the house over there on the first of the month. She says she didn't know Delia lived here."

"Fifteen years?" Gannon removed his hat, wiped his brow, then replaced his fedora. "Any idea why he's still stalking her after all this time? Not that any sane reason would matter. I've seen this type of shit a million times over. People like him have to have someone to blame for their shortcomings."

"My sister has a theory. She says this reminds her of the Margaret Keane case."

"Interesting." Gannon nodded. "Very interesting. Margaret Keane was the actual artist, but her husband claimed her work. We'll see what Mr. Haynes says when he's brought in."

"Gannon, as soon as Paul downloads the camera feed, he'll bring you a copy. If you need me, I'll be inside." Glen turned away, not waiting for an answer. He needed to check on Delia. Lack of sleep made her physically exhausted. Now, thanks to her ex, she was emotionally drained as well.

Paul didn't bother looking up as Glen strode into the kitchen. "You need to see this."

"Where's Delia?"

"Said she was going to take a bath. She's been in there a while." Paul clicked the mouse, enlarging the video, clearly showing Delia talking on her mobile. She yanked on the door handle and was instantly bathed in light. The light had to be what drew her out. Delia stepped into the building, and a dark figure rushed into view, slamming the door closed. After a tick, the individual turned, shooting a bird at the camera, then ran between the fence and building.

Paul paused the video. "Skeleton mask. It has to be Luca."

"Except, he's in hospital, and daddy is dead, so is the bodyguard." Glen jumped when the rear of Delia's studio burst into flames. "Make a copy of this and give it to Gannon. Then send a copy to Viktor and Percy. Yeah, I know I said to leave Percy alone, but I want them to calculate everything they can about this person."

Damn, Glen couldn't shake the chill of almost losing Delia. The thought of what would have happened if he'd crashed on his couch or simply headed into the office kept spinning in his mind. Delia would have died. From now on, he wasn't letting her out of his sight until they found and dealt with the guilty, preferably putting them six feet under. Delia could argue with him all she wanted, but he'd rather have her pissed than dead. As long as she was alive, he could beg for forgiveness.

"Delia." He knocked on her door, listening. "Hell's bloody bells." Glen stepped into her room, kicked the door behind him, and followed the gut-wrenching sound. He pushed open the bathroom door. The steam billowing from the room was so thick he could barely see. "Delia." Glen pushed aside the shower curtain.

She leaned against the shower wall, head bowed, body shaking with each sob.

"*Mo gràdh.*"

Delia peered up at him. The anguish in her eyes sliced through him more profoundly than the shrapnel on Normandy. "Go away."

Chapter Nineteen

Delia clutched her sides, coughing. She'd coughed so much she thought a lung would fly out of her mouth. It made her throat hurt even more. If she could just eliminate the smell, perhaps she'd stop hacking up a lung. No matter how much she scrubbed herself, she couldn't wash away the odor and reminder she might have died tonight. She would have if Glen didn't pull her from the building.

How much longer was she going to fight Scott? What if he found out about Glen's nature? Scott would stop at nothing to expose the Dhampir. He'd finally won. To save Glen, Scott could have her art.

The realization stabbed her, and she sagged against the shower wall.

"Delia." Glen pushed aside the shower curtain. "*Mo gràdh.*"

She peered up at him. Grief and humiliation tore through her, finding her naked and defeated like this. She tried to cover as much of her body as possible, swallowing hard and biting back tears. "Go away."

"Nope." Glen snatched a towel from the rack, wrapped it around her, and lifted her into his arms.

"Glen, please." She pushed against his shoulder. "I don't want you to see me like this." The last shreds of her control shattered, and she buried her face against his shoulder, yielding to the convulsive sobs wracking her body.

She clutched the towel around her as Glen cradled her on his lap. His large hand gently smoothed up and down her back. If her earlier hysterics hadn't frightened him away, surely bawling like a spoiled child would.

Delia drew in deep breaths, trying to stop her tears. The effort only had her hacking like an old woman. "I hate my body," she sputtered between coughs.

"Personally, I adore it." Glen pressed his lips to her temple. "Paul's brought up a pot of tea for you."

"I'm naked." It was one thing for Glen to see her like this, but no one else. She clutched the towel tighter.

"Be assured, I would never allow another man to see you nude." Glen cracked open the door, then bent and retrieved a pot and cup from the floor.

"What about my doctor? Hmm." That was a bit contrary of her, but blast him for his alpha-male attitude.

He closed the door, setting the small teapot and cup on her nightstand. "There are excellent female doctors."

"Dominating much?"

"Just a tad." Glen shrugged. "My question to you, do you want my blood in the tea, or would you prefer straight from the source?" He said that last bit with a sigh.

"Try neither," she retorted.

Glen exhaled, his eyes turned red, and he crossed his arms over his chest. Whoopi-skip, he was pissed. So was she.

"I can hear the rattle in your lungs with every breath you take. I will not stand here and continue watching you gasping for air."

"Fine, if you don't want to hear me cough, there's the door." She pointed. "Leave."

"I almost lost you tonight," he bellowed. The muscles in his jaw twitched. His fangs protruded from his upper lip and his horns pushed from his forehead. Glen opened and closed his fist, visibly struggling with his Dhampir side. His shoulders expanded, the threads of his clothes popped, and an unnatural growl emitted from him.

Okay, perhaps she'd tweaked his buttons a little much. "Look, Glen." Delia slid from the bed, securing the towel around her. "I'm tired. I haven't slept in over twenty-four hours. I just want to go to sleep." Right on cue, a cough wracked her body, causing her to nearly lose the towel.

A clawed finger gently caressed her cheek, then urged her to look up into glowing red eyes. Eyes filled with tenderness and concern. "The daemon is livid that someone tried to kill you."

"Yeah, I'm pretty pissed about it, too."

"I can't keep him—" A growl tore from Glen as his other self took over, leaving him in shredded clothes. Glen could deny it all he wanted, but he was her Zeus-Ammon. "You're my heart and soul. I can't lose you."

The raw emotion in those words had her leaning more into his embrace. She stroked his back, savoring the warmth that enveloped her. "I'll take the tea."

Glen leaned down and softly kissed her. "Probably cold," he grumbled.

She brushed his hair out of his eyes, then ran her hand over a horn and giggled when he leaned into her caress. Giggled? Well, laughing was better than crying. "Yes, it probably is. And as you prepare your concoction, I'm pulling on some clothes."

"It's just chamomile tea."

She shimmied into a pair of jogging shorts under the towel, then dug around looking for a dark t-shirt. Smiling, she pulled out one of her favorites. Giving Glen her back, she dropped the towel. When she turned around, the desire in his eyes did more for her self-esteem than her gallery showing. His white dress shirt and slacks were in tatters.

Glen handed her the cup, his warm fingers brushed against hers. Even though he'd shifted back to his more human self, his eyes still glowed. "Drink it all, please."

She took a sip, and the minty flavor exploded across her tastebuds. This was probably the best tea she'd ever tasted. "This is wonderful." She took another sip, savoring the flavor and enjoying the warmth inching through her body. "Did you put alcohol in this?"

"Nope. Just tea and a little bit of me."

A logical person would heave their guts out, knowing they'd just drank tea laced with blood. "Rhyming, are we? Huh."

He exhaled and briefly closed his eyes, frowning. "I've got to go speak with Gannon again. Are you going to be all right?"

"You're going to speak with the detective?" She finished her tea, trying not to laugh.

"Yeah. Paul said Gannon needed to ask me a few more questions." Glen's black eyebrow inched higher as he tilted his head, perusing her. "Why?"

Delia flicked his tattered shirt. "Hmm, how are you planning to explain this?" She stared up at him, grinning.

Even in the darkness of her room, humor was shimmering in his eyes despite his stone expression. He shrugged, and a smirk played at his lips. "Going to tell him you couldn't control yourself." He chuckled. "Actually, Paul brought up my go-bag. I'll change in the bathroom." Glen opened her door and retrieved a black backpack.

"That's fine. In the meantime, I'm going to bed. Wake me up next year." She pulled back the blanket, then slid beneath the sheets and comforter.

Glen padded into the bathroom and closed the door. Not completely. Nope, he'd left enough of a crack that she could clearly see him strip. She shouldn't look. She should close her eyes and not ogle. But damn, he had a nice ass. Very nice…He flexed his butt cheeks. She tore her gaze from his sculpted back to the mirror in front of him, meeting his eyes.

"Like what you see?" He grinned.

She could deny it, but. "I do, actually." She swore his head swelled three sizes.

"Good." He pulled on a pair of jogging pants, followed by a white t-shirt. "Because it's all yours."

"Is it now?" She wiggled into a more comfortable position under the covers and yawned.

Glen leaned over her, brushing a kiss on her lips. "Get some rest." He left, pulling the door shut behind him, leaving her in a dark room with her thoughts.

The mattress cradled her as the duvet's weight lured her into that place between sleep and wakefulness.

Something creaked, and a shadow moved across the wall. Delia bolted upright with her heart pounding and the sheet clutched to her chin. For heaven's sake, she was fifty-five, not two. She shouldn't be afraid. But she was. Scott's little prank had rattled her, leaving her jumpy and…frightened. He'd stolen her art and now the feeling of security in her own bed. She could what? Get out of bed and go downstairs and fall asleep on the couch? That would go over like a lead balloon.

The floor creaked, and her heart jumped into her throat once more, pounding wildly as the door handle slowly turned.

"Delia, what's wrong?" Glen poked his head inside her room.

"Nothing?"

He shook his head and stepped inside, closing the door behind him. "Let's try this one more time." Glen brushed aside her locks, tucking them behind her ear. He gently stroked her cheek. "What's wrong?"

"I'm fine, except I'm scared out of my ever-loving mind." She was a crappy liar and glad for the room's darkness. Perhaps Glen hadn't noticed her flush. Then again, he had supernatural senses, so he probably could see her as if she were in the noonday sun.

"You're emotionally drained, for good reasons."

"Oh yeah, let's see if I can count the ways, first solo show ever, that someone tried to blow up but failed, so they attempted to turn me into a crispy critter." She pointed toward the door. "Then I acted like an idiot in front of you and everyone out there arguing with Scott, giving a clear definition of a hysterical old woman." She blinked, not giving a damn about the tears trailing down her cheeks.

"Scoot over." Glen gripped the edge of the blankets.

"Why?"

"I can hold you until you fall asleep." He tugged on the blanket. "Scoot."

"Why can't you come around to the other side?" Not that she didn't want him in bed with her, but the other side was cold, and she had a chill.

"Because the door is on this side. Your scooting is a lot easier than me turning the bed around. Scoot." Glen toed off his shoes, then pulled off his t-shirt. He slipped under the covers, and she wiggled against him.

"What did Gannon want?" Delia nuzzled Glen's chest as she closed her eyes. Her mind still spun with everything that had happened. Thank goodness tomorrow was Sunday, and she could sleep in. Maybe if she didn't have to speak with the police, fire, and insurance. Damn Scott.

"Sleep. We'll discuss everything when you wake."

"I don't know if I can sleep. Every time I close my eyes, I go back inside the fire. You sure Edna is okay with Whitaker?" Glen's chest shook with his laugh, and she raised up on her elbow, looking down at him. "What's so funny?"

"Lay back down. I'll tell ya'." Glen gently pulled her toward him until she practically lay on top of him. He exhaled, draping his arm across her back. "When I returned to my flat, I walked in to find Percy screaming for bleach to wash his eyes out and Victoria laughing like a hyena. I soon found out Percy walked in on Whitaker and Edna on the floor in front of the fireplace in the guest flat."

Good for Edna. "What? Percy couldn't stand seeing his dad snogging Edna?"

"Love, they were past snogging and well into the getting off stage. Edna was straddling Whitaker and shouted tally-ho as Percy walked in on them."

"Oh, my gosh! I bet it mortified Edna. And thank you for that image, though I think I'd prefer the burning building in my mind."

Glen laughed and smoothed his hand down her back. "You're welcome. Don't worry about Edna. From what Percy said, she and Whitaker were so into the moment they didn't notice him. Even if Victoria said he squealed like a little girl."

Delia giggled. She didn't think she'd get the image out of her mind. "Poor Percy."

Glen kissed her head as he stroked his hand up and down her back. The gentle tattoo of his heartbeat had her relaxing in his embrace. She wouldn't sleep, but maybe she'd catnap for a few moments.

Delia exhaled. Her head rested on her pillow instead of Glen's chest. She ran her hand over where he'd been. The sheets were cool. She should get up, too, but a few more minutes of basking in the morning silence wouldn't cause the world to end. Unfortunately, the doorbell ringing shattered the peace and quiet. Whoever was leaning on it was an impatient jerk. Dang, she didn't want to get up. Glen could deal with them if he was here. If not, perhaps whoever it was would go away. She closed her eyes, only to be jarred by squealing brakes. This was Sunday morning. Usually, her neighborhood was quiet except for the occasional leaf blower or mower.

Delia crawled out of bed, then peeped through the slats of her blinds. Good grief! More SUVs were parked in her drive and on the street than at a car dealership. Why in the devil was a school bus rolling down her street on a Sunday? The bus stopped in front of Kelly's house. Her daughter, Lacey, jumped from the bus and ran to her mom's open arms. Today was Sunday, though. Maybe the school had a special field trip. Either that or Delia had stepped into another dimension. With her luck lately, that was probably the situation. The only way she'd find out what was going on was to go downstairs, which meant putting on something other than boxers and a t-shirt. Oh, joy.

Muffled voices and the clanging of pots and pans rose to greet her as she descended the steps.

"I told ye haud yer wheesht," Glen snarled. "You've awakened her."

Delia padded through the living room, nodding at Percy sitting on the couch and flipping through the slew of documents strewn across the coffee table. He also had two of Edna's TV trays in front of him, each with a laptop. He glanced up, giving her a rather sad expression before blowing her a kiss. Great. Simply fantastic, just what she needed. More bad news. Maybe she should have stayed in bed.

Delia barely stepped into the kitchen when Glen turned and faced her with a huge grin. She'd expected his smile when he saw her. What she hadn't expected was the desire to feel his warmth. She went to him, resting her cheek on his chest, and exhaled. Through the kitchen window, Delia clearly saw the charred remains of her studio. So much for hoping it had all been a bad dream. No matter what, she would get through it. Safe in Glen's arms, she peered around the room.

Edna's small kitchen was even smaller, packed with too many people. Whitaker wore Edna's Union Jack apron and pulled a tray of freshly baked scones from the oven while she poured a mug of tea. Dani and Rose sat at the table, eyeing something on a tablet. Detective Gannon leaned against the counter, jotting in his notebook. Though no one uttered a word, they all greeted her with tight smiles and nods.

Well, not everyone. Gannon's expression was as stern as ever. "Good afternoon, Miss Parsons. Glad you're finally up and about. I have a few questions for you. Is there someplace we could go that's more private?"

Delia pulled from Glen's embrace, though he didn't let go of her entirely. Instead, he slipped an arm around her waist and pulled out an empty chair.

"Fresh from the oven." Edna sat a plate of delicious-smelling scones on the table.

"Where are Vaughn and Royce?" Delia had assumed they'd be here too.

"Golfing," Dani replied, moving her tablet, making more room on the table. "With Magnus and my dad, since Glen didn't want to leave you. Victoria rang. She said to tell you she's landed and not to worry."

Delia glanced over her shoulder, meeting Glen's warm eyes. "You could have gone with them. You don't get to visit with Royce often."

He sat a cup of tea in front of her, brushing a kiss on her cheek.

"Miss Parsons," Gannon raised his voice as if she'd not heard him the first time.

"Tea and scone first." Mouth-watering to taste it, she slathered clotted cream on the delicious-looking pastry. "Questions after. As for going somewhere else, I have no problem with them hearing what I have to say." She took a bite and knew she'd died, for this was the best tasting cranberry and orange scone she'd ever had.

"Fine," Gannon grumbled as she took another bite. "Can you explain what Mr. Haynes meant when he said?" Gannon flipped through his notes. "Too bad you lost everything. Now you know how it feels."

Delia wiped at her lips. She didn't want to go down this road again, but she guessed she must. "I hope you get paid extra for working on Sunday."

"It's Monday." Gannon eyed her. "Monday afternoon."

"Monday? Well, that would explain the school bus." She'd slept *all* of Sunday and most of today. "Okay, then." Delia took another sip of tea and closed her eyes, gathering her thoughts. "I was young and stupid when I married Scott. My credit rating was excellent. Scott's...not so much. He'd ruined my credit and blown through our money within a year. I was the only one working because he had to devote all his time to his art. I stayed with him until I caught him having affairs with several of his students."

Gannon paused in his writing. "How many affairs?"

"You don't understand," Edna cackled. "Snotface was boinking three girls at the same time. Delia found out when they all showed up on the same night, demanding she grant Scott the divorce he'd begged her for. That's the lie he was telling those stupid girls. Didn't they know if he cheated on his wife, he would cheat on them too someday? Oh, what I would give to have been a fly on the wall that night."

"Together?" Gannon stared in utter disbelief. "They showed up together?"

It was hard not to laugh at the poor man. "No. Katherine Higgins showed up first. Before she left, Amy Boil arrived. That was interesting because I thought I'd have to separate them. I was never one for hair-pulling and scratching. Anyway, about twenty minutes later, Buffy Smith rang my doorbell. Things got really interesting ten minutes later when Scott showed up. I went to bed when the wailing started, leaving him to deal with them. From the shade of pink on Scott's neck, I'd say he was with conquest number four."

"Why did you stay married to him?"

"Like I said, I was stupid. That, and I found out the next day I was pregnant."

"The child was his?" Gannon asked.

"Yes. Scott wasn't happy. He said a baby would distract him from his art. Anyway, Edna planned to help me when the baby arrived. That's what we told Scott, anyway. Our actual plan was for Edna to fly out to California. She and I would return to Atlanta, where I would file for divorce. But things didn't go the way we'd planned. I would have died if Edna hadn't arrived a day early and found me. She phoned Scott, as did the police, telling him what had happened. He informed them he couldn't leave his art show for Edna to take care of *it*." Delia glanced up at Edna, wrapped in Whitaker's embrace and wiping her eyes.

"When I opened that door, I thought you were dead. With that bloody alarm blaring, I couldn't think. Thank God the police arrived when they did." Edna sniffed. "While Delia was in the hospital, I packed everything she owned. Everything except her models. Those I smashed like she'd asked. Every. Last. One. I made damn sure he could never use them, but I touched nothing belonging to that murdering bastard. He cared more about Delia's bloody models than about the loss of his child or Delia's injuries."

Gannon's lips thinned even more as he read through his notes. He finally looked at her. "Here's the thing. I spoke with the detective who handled your case. He's retired now and living in Marietta."

She knew what Gannon was going to say. "That would be Detective Kerr. He told you countless witnesses stated Scott never left the art exhibit, and there was no evidence he hired anyone to break into the house. In fact, there was no evidence of a break-in at all. His conclusion was that I slipped and fell down the stairs. Because I smelled of wine and the empty bottle beside my body, I was most likely drunk. There was no alcohol in my system because of the time lapsed before they collected my blood. Yes, I know what he told you. He also informed you he thought it very suspicious that my parents left all their wealth to Edna when they passed, not me. Well, to answer your questions. They did that to keep Scott from blowing through my inheritance."

"Delia." Glen squeezed her shoulder, and she welcomed his touch, kissing his hand.

"Glen, it doesn't matter." She exhaled. "Scott's won. For what it was worth, my studio is gone, and I'm tired of going to court every time I create a piece of art."

"We'll discuss you quitting in a tick. Go back, Edna. What did you say about the alarm? Was it sounding when you arrived?"

"No, I set it off when I used the key and opened the door."

"I see." Glen's eyes darkened, and he stared at Gannon. "Did Kerr say anything about the alarm?"

"I never asked. Why?"

Glen's red-rimmed eyes met hers, and his teeth were pointy. So, so, not good. "Delia, what type of security system did your home have?"

"Alarm on doors and lower windows, and motion detection on the lower floor."

"That doesn't mean anything," Gannon snorted. "When she fell, if the motion detectors were high enough, they may not have been triggered. Already thought of this, MacPhee."

"Oh, no." Delia wasn't going to have this blamed on her again. "I wasn't allowed to have pets because of that blasted alarm system. Scott wouldn't even let me have a damn goldfish because swimming around in its bowl would set off the motion detectors. No. I don't care what Kerr told you, nor do I care about your theory. I set the alarm, then went to bed. Something woke me up, and I thought Scott had come home early. When I reached the steps, Scott pushed me from behind. He ran after me, but not to help me. He stood over me, pouring the cheap wine he liked to drink on me. Scott left me on the floor and headed toward the kitchen. I screamed for him to help me, but he left. I either fell asleep or passed out at some point, but I woke with the alarm going off and Edna standing over me. Don't you dare," Delia lunged to her feet, shaking the table and sloshing tea. "tell me that the system was on when it was not! And if it was, then what? I fell down the steps, got up, turned on the alarm, then laid back in my own blood?"

Gannon opened his mouth like the damn goldfish she'd never had. He snapped his mouth closed and slid his ratty notebook into his pocket. She didn't need Glen's mind-reading abilities to know what was going through Gannon's head.

"You don't have to answer. I know what you're thinking. I shut off the alarm, came downstairs, grabbed the bottle of wine, drank it, turned on the system, and staggered up the steps. I was so drunk that I slipped, fell, and landed on the marble floor. The only thing wrong with this theory is, my fall didn't set off the motion detectors." She stared into Gannon's dark brown eyes until someone rang the doorbell. "If that's Scott, I'm wringing his damn neck!" She started for the door, glad for the chance to get away from Gannon.

Glen snagged her hand, pulling her back. "Percy has the door." His eyes bled red for a microsecond before he turned on Gannon. "Do yer job, Gannon. Or I will. Find ou' abou' the alarm system an' also if Scott had a life insurance policy on Delia. Never mind, I'll get *my* team on it."

Gannon flinched as if Glen had punched him. He picked up his hat from the table, placing it on his bald head. "MacPhee, your brogue gets thick when you're pissed. Miss Parsons, I'll be in touch."

"Cordy," Tara sang as she dashed into the kitchen. She skidded to a halt. "Oh, my stars. Are you okay?"

"Ma'am," Percy snapped, following Tara. Maybe it was his candy-apple red hair, but the man looked pissed and ready to kill. Which was okay with Delia. She had a list started.

Delia plastered a smile on her lips for Tara. "Did we have a lunch date or something?"

"Oh, no." She craned her neck, peering out the kitchen window. "I was in the area…did you have a fire?"

"Whatever made you ask that?" Percy sassed. "The fresh scent of charred faggot in the air or the blackened building wrapped in yellow crime tape beyond yonder window?"

"I'm sorry." Tara panned back to Percy, giving him the evil eye. "Am I interrupting something?"

"Kinda," Delia replied. "We were speaking with Detective Gannon, and I'm not sure if we have to talk to the arson investigators or not."

"Arson investigators? Do you mean the fire was intentional?"

"No, we roasted marshmallows," Percy murmured, smiling beguilingly.

Tara rolled her eyes. "It's possible your solvents ignited. You know that happened before."

"I remember when the community center caught fire that way."

"Community center? What happened, Miss Parsons?" Gannon stared at her while pulling out his notebook again.

Why did Tara have to show up now, of all times? Delia finished her tea, wishing it would instantly refill with something more robust, like—espresso. "When I was in college, the local community center caught fire. The investigators said it was because the center stored solvents too close to a heat source."

"*Mo gràdh*," Glen squeezed her shoulder. "Did this happen before or after Monterrey?"

"Oh, a year after. But the fire occurred during an art exhibit the center held." A vivid recollection pushed to the forefront of her mind, and she shivered. "Glen, Scott was a judge. I remember because that's when he first introduced himself to me. You don't think…"

"That it was a coincidence. Maybe." From Glen's dark expression, he didn't believe it was a coincidence any more than she did.

Gannon stared at Tara as if he were committing every line of her face to memory. "This is all quite interesting."

"Detective Gannon," Edna chimed in as she refilled Delia's tea. "Would you care for another scone, and when can we remove the debris?"

Gannon waved off Edna, never taking his eyes off Tara. "And you are?"

"Ah, Tara Browning. But I'm not from here. I live in California and have known Cordy since we attended college. I'm just here on business."

"California? I have a few questions, if you don't mind."

"But—I."

"Tara." Delia almost felt sorry for her. Not. "Why don't we plan on having lunch sometime next week since you're still in town? That should give me plenty of time to deal with this mess."

Her lips pulled into a sour frown, and she gave a curt nod. "I guess that'll be fine."

"Good." Gannon motioned toward the door. "I'll see you out, Ms. Browning, and you can answer a few questions. For starters, did you also know Scott Haynes?"

"Yes," Tara replied as Gannon ushered her from the room with Percy fast on their heels.

The front door slammed a second before Percy strode back into the kitchen. "That friend of yours elbowed me and nearly struck my lower regions when I told her you were busy."

"She's an acquaintance from college, Cuz."

"Cuz?" Percy batted his lashes. "I like the sound of that."

"We kinda are because of those two." Delia pointed to Edna and Whitaker.

"Well, Cuz." Percy clapped his hands together. "Before we have any more interruptions, shall we get down to business?"

Delia dropped her head to the table. She didn't want to get down to business. She wanted peace and quiet. She wanted... "If you must. What business?"

"Whitty has asked me to marry him. Again. And go back to England with him. I said yes." Edna beamed, smiling up at Whitaker.

"Oh, Edna!" Delia leaped from her chair. She couldn't be happier for her. "That's wonderful. Congratulations."

"Thank you, dear. We plan to leave in a week. Percy says they can have the house packed in less than a day and shipped. Everything is happening so fast. This really doesn't give us much time. Does it?"

"No, it doesn't, Aunt Edna." Delia knew her aunt would probably go back with Whitaker when he rushed here to see her. But...wow. She didn't think it would be so soon. Could the world just stop for a second for her to breathe?

"Splendid. Rose and Danielle are here with photos of some homes we all think you'll like. Rose said you could move in as early as the end of the week. Personally, I love the English Tudor."

"Excuse me. What?" Moving was the last damn thing Delia wanted to do with everything going on.

"English Tudor, dear. It's a style of house."

"I know what it is, but why should I move? I'll just buy this one from you."

Chapter Twenty

"You're not staying in this house." Glen would be damned if Delia stayed here alone while Scott still breathed. Of course, tearing Delia's ex into tiny pieces and mounting his head on a pike would solve the problem.

But then, she wouldn't be in our bed. His daemon groused.

"Stop growling." Delia's wide-eyed gaze collided with his, and her doe-brown eyes reflected the unmistakable stress and pain she endured answering Gannon's questions.

By the saints, she didn't need his ire. Drawing in a deep breath, he tempered his tone. "I'm not growling." Yeah, he still was.

"You kinda are," Rose muttered. "And don't flash your fangs at me."

Delia rubbed her temples and sat. "Rose, Dani, I appreciate what you've done. Honestly, but I don't understand why I can't stay here."

He didn't have to read her mind to know Gannon's questions had been a biting icy wind to an old wound. "Because—" Glen started only to have Edna hip-check him out of the way.

"Delia." Edna's expression stilled and grew serious. Her eyes darkened, and her lips thinned into a faint slash across her face. "As much as I love Whitty, I cannot go with him, leaving you here if I don't feel you are safe. You staying in this house while Snotface lives next door is not an option."

"Fine. I'll move, but it doesn't matter if I live here, with Glen, or under a rock. Scott will always be able to find out where I am. Heck, anyone can. You pay a fee to some online company and download the information. Think about it. I never gave Tara my info, and yet she showed up here. She even had my phone number. She told me at the gallery she'd Googled me. And..." Delia glanced up at Percy. "what you did for me, removing all my sensitive info, was wonderful, but we both know once something is out there on the internet, it's out there for good."

Glen blamed Scott for doxing Delia. Who else would have had access to her sensitive information? It certainly wasn't Eddie. Hell, Glen blamed the asshole for every ounce of pain Delia had endured. The man's days were numbered. Perhaps it was time to pay him a visit.

"This is where Rose and I come in," Dani announced. "As you stated, if you or Glen purchase a home, the information becomes a public record anyone can access. However, if a corporation purchases the property, the only available information would be the company's ownership, not who lives in the residence. This is one method the Dhampir uses to protect themselves."

"That's all fine and good." Delia shrugged. "Scott knows Glen owns Daemon Securities, so Scott will figure it out if his company purchases a residence."

"Ah, yes." Dani grinned. The woman really got off on crap like this. "But, Daemon Securities is a subsidiary of Wolfmoon Enterprises and the DuMond Corporation. We own several hundred properties around the world."

"Victorian Dreams is even under their umbrella," Rose added. "Glen's looking at the five properties we think you'd like to see."

"Four. The condo's out." He handed Delia the tablet. "I think you'd like one of these. If not, we can find something you do like. And," he really didn't want to say what he was about to, but, "if you'd prefer me not living under the same roof as you, these two have guest homes." He tapped the screen, bringing up the image of the first house. One he doubted she'd like. It just didn't look like her.

"I kinda enjoy having you under the roof, so not a problem." She scrunched up her face. "This one has nine bedrooms." Delia swiped her finger across the screen. "It's nice, but I can't see myself living here. Glen," she glanced up at him. "I'm a simple person. Do we honestly need an eight-car garage and a guest house?"

"You can use the guest house when Glen plays the pipes," Rose teased.

Delia laughed. "Those bagpipes weren't for decoration? You really do play them?"

"Aye. Perhaps I'll serenade you one night."

"I'd like that," she said, though her tone said otherwise. Delia swiped her finger over the tablet again, flipping through images of the second house. Her lips twisted with each photo. "This one's more ostentatious than the first."

"May I?" Rose held out her hand. "Tell me what you're looking for in a house, Delia."

"Not a mansion to rival the governor's."

"An outbuilding for her art." Glen cupped Delia's chin, tilting her face up to meet his. "I willna have you quitting because of that jobby."

"Glen—"

"No. If Scott wants to drag you to court—fine. I have the resources to bury him." He bent down and stole a kiss. "You're good, and it brings you joy. I willna have him stealing that away from you."

"Very well." She nodded. "Rose, if you have a place that has an outbuilding with plenty of natural daylighting, office space for Glen, at least three bedrooms for when family visits, and a decent kitchen, I'll be happy. Oh, and the commute can't be more than an hour for Glen."

"How about this one?" Rose turned the tablet around, revealing a photo of a familiar-looking Georgia granite American Foursquare home. "Denny and the guys are finishing up on this one. If you want, we can look at it today. The lower level has your entry, kitchen with breakfast nook, dining room, living room, and a library you could use as office space. There's also a den with a fireplace. Both the den and kitchen have half baths off them. All bedrooms are upstairs, and the master and in-law suite have private ensuite baths. There are four other bedrooms and two more full baths, giving you six bedrooms and four bathrooms upstairs. Your laundry room is also on the second level." Rose grinned. "Here's the best part. It has an in-ground pool, and we converted the old garden house into a four-seasons room, complete with gorgeous—I'm envious of—skylights."

Delia's eyes sparkled. "It sounds perfect. Where's it located?"

"It's in an older neighborhood close to here. Most of the homes are on several acres of property. This one is in the middle of," Rose tapped the screen. "Here it is. It's on—"

"Eleven acres." Glen knew the home well. Vaughn and Rose were considering moving closer to Dani and Magnus and him. "Rose, I—"

The bloody doorbell chimed, and Delia was out of her seat and heading toward the door. "I've got it this time." She darted around Percy, hurrying toward the door. "Don't want to risk your lower regions getting elbowed," she called over her shoulder.

The second Delia was out of the kitchen, Glen turned to Rose. "Thank you. But we'll not take a home you've fixed up for yourself. We'll find something else."

"Glen, don't be ridiculous."

***

Hang politeness! If this was Tara again, Delia was slamming the door in the woman's face. "Britney," Delia blurted, too shocked to say anything else.

"Don't slam the door, please," Brittany rushed out. "I just wanted to tell you I'm so sorry for everything Scott has put you through. It's stopping now. I told him to let you go or pack up and get out. Cordelia, don't get upset about what I am about to say."

"I'll try not to," Delia replied dryly. If she could deal with Gannon, she could deal with Britney. "Go on."

"I don't think Scott ever loved you as a person. It's your talent he loved. And still does." Britney sniffled.

Delia gripped the edge of the door, debating whether to slam it. She didn't need Scott's girlfriend telling her what she already knew. "Oh."

"You give life to each piece you create," Britney continued, her hand resting on the flat of her stomach. "The other night, when I saw your works, Cordelia, I could see the ravens ruffle their feathers. I saw smoke curling from the dragon's nose. Each piece was alive. Scott's talented. But his pieces don't have life. So, I just want you to know. It's over. He either leaves you alone, or he leaves *my* home." A sad laugh escaped her. "He helped me move in and never left. Anyway, it's over."

Wow. Delia didn't see that coming. "I don't know what to say. Thank you." Delia stepped back to close the door but stopped. "I have to ask, has he ever raised his hand to you?"

Britney lunged forward, hugging her. "Daddy's a retired Marine," she whispered in Delia's ear. "He told Scott if he ever laid a hand on me, he'd vanish from the face of this Earth, and no one would give a rat's fart." Britney stepped back, releasing Delia, and wiped her eyes. "I'm a fool, but I love him."

Maybe it was Glen's blood or because she was his fated mate, but whatever the reason, Delia didn't need to see him to know he was right behind her. She leaned back slightly, and his muscular arms wrapped around her waist.

Britney glanced up at Glen. "You won't have any more trouble from Scott. I promise." She stepped off the stoop and slowly made her way across the lawn.

Delia closed the door, then turned in his arms.

"You all right?"

"I'm good. I'm worried about Britney, though."

"Why? Not that I hold a grudge against her."

"She's pregnant, Glen."

"Pregnant? When did she say anything about a bairn?"

"I don't know for certain, but I suspect. The whole time Britney was here, she kept a hand over her stomach." That's a pretty good tell. Delia remembered doing the same, even before the doctors confirmed her suspicions.

Glen tucked a strand of hair behind her ear. "Could mean she has the gripes."

"And you call yourself a detective." Delia laughed, staring up into his baby blues.

"Are you all right?" His eyes searched hers.

"Are you reading my mind?" Her silly, wonderful boy scout was worried about her.

He shrugged. "I can." Translation, he was.

"Stop worrying. Does it bother me she's pregnant? No." It didn't. She was happy for Britney. "Did I get emotional with Gannon? Yes. But, Glen, I'm good. So, let's go look at this house."

His eyes left hers. "About the house—"

"What about the house?" Damn it. She knew it sounded too good to be true. "Someone's already put a bid on it?"

"Glen," Rose snapped, hands planted on her hips. Dani stood behind her, shooting daggers at Glen. Whatever it was, they were both pissed at him.

"Rosie, we're not taking your house from you."

"Your house?" Delia asked. Well, crap. She knew it was too good to be true.

"Augh!" Rose tossed her hands in the air. "Men, sometimes you can be so damn dense."

"I blame it on the chromosome." Dani grinned, batting her lashes. "Just saying."

"Look, Glen. Never mind." Rose turned her attention to Delia. "Vaughn and I have already talked about it. Neither Kimber nor George wants to move. To be honest, I don't either. We only considered it so Vaughn wouldn't have to drive an hour to harass Glen." She giggled. "He's so happy to be back in the States. Anyway, we're good. Besides, you having a pool gives us a good reason to visit. Often. Like every other day." Rose looped her arm with Delia's. "What do you say? Shall we take a look?"

"Dani, are you coming with us?" Delia asked, noticing Dani had her purse on her shoulder.

"Sorry, no. My day to pick up the kids from practice. Glen, ring me and let me know if you decide on the house. I can send Fiona the paperwork and have it finalized so you can start moving in as soon as possible. Maybe even by tomorrow or the next day."

"Tomorrow?" Delia couldn't believe how fast things were moving. "That's wow. Tomorrow."

"Only if you like the house." Glen kissed Delia's crown. "Dani, I'll let you know."

***

Delia lazily dragged her fingers down the smooth polished banister as she descended the stairs. The rich dark wood had her thinking back to her childhood when she'd raced down her grandmother's steps at Christmas. This house offered everything she wanted. The open, bright gourmet kitchen might entice her to cook more often. She planned to stock the shelves in the library with all her favorite authors. Glen said he'd take the den as his office. The master bedroom was something else! Delia couldn't keep the smile from her lips. Of course, the master bath with an enormous shower and the clawed tub, big enough for two, gave her some wicked ideas.

She stepped down and stared up at the stained-glass chandelier suspended overhead. She loved everything about the house. True, it was much larger than the one she shared with Edna, but not too big. In fact, the size would be perfect for when Glen's family visited.

"What do you think?" Delia leaned back against Glen, knowing he was behind her. She angled her head, looking up at him. He hadn't shaved this morning, and she liked his unkempt look. Then again, there wasn't much about him she didn't like.

His rich laugh bubbled up from him, vibrating his chest as it escaped. "I could say the same about you."

"Hmm, reading my mind?"

"I plead the fifth. Now that we've seen the entire house, let's go back and look at your new art studio."

As much as Delia loved everything about the house, she didn't want to get her hopes up, which she'd already had, but...she needed to know how Glen felt. He'd been too quiet since they arrived. "Not until you tell me what you think. Do *you* like this house? You haven't indicated how you felt about it. And I don't have your mind-reading abilities."

"I think." Glen buried his face in her neck, drawing in a deep breath, then slowly releasing it. His breath tickled her neck. "It's in a good part of the city. Not too far from the office or what the city offers. I can tell you like it. I'm already thinking about how we'll christen each room." When she faced him, his eyes were darker red than she'd ever seen.

"Christened as in...?"

"You. Me. Naked—"

"Oh, there you are." Rose strolled from the den.

Glen dropped his head, resting his forehead against Delia's. "Alone."

"What do you think so far, and is there anything you'd like to change or add? What about the garden shed? Will it work for your art studio? 'Cause," Rose grinned. "Denny said he and the guys can make any changes you want. Build shelves, platforms, worktables...anything you want. Change out the garage door if need be. Just say the word."

Delia laughed and pushed against Glen's chest. "There's nothing here in the main house I would change." If she had to describe her dream home, this would be it. "I love everything about it." She peered up at Glen. "Let's do it."

"Good, because I've already called Dani and told her we'd take it. Come on, let's look at your new studio." Glen snagged her hand, leading her toward the door. "Denny's waiting for us."

"What a second." Rose stepped in front of them. "I'll give you six months, Delia, then I'll ask again what you want to change. Glen, anything you'd change?"

"From a security perspective, nothing. Well, that's a lie. I'd like to install a fence around the perimeter. What are the covenants concerning fences?"

"No chain-link, and nothing over six feet tall. And…" Rose blushed. "Snooks Bouvier spotted me. I didn't realize she lived in this neighborhood. She may try to rope you into being an officer in the HOA. Sorry."

"Not an issue." He squeezed Delia's hand. "The only other thing I'd like is a sink in the mudroom off the kitchen."

"Why?" Delia didn't understand since the kitchen sink would be a few steps away.

"Because, my love, there's a permanent stain on your kitchen doorframe from you dashing in with clay on your hands."

"Guilty. But in my defense, you don't know how often Edna has put the kettle on, only to fall asleep." She and Whitaker strolled into the foyer as if saying her aunt's name conjured her. Her lips were slightly swollen, and a faint ruby smear was on Whitaker's cheek.

"So, what have you two been up to?"

"Snogging in the larder like teens," Percy replied dryly as he emerged from the kitchen.

"That's because we have decades of catching up to do." Edna patted his cheek. "Isn't that right, Whitty?"

"Okay, then." Delia headed straight toward the door. The less she heard about Edna's sex life, the better. "Let's go speak with Denny." Heaven help her. She was really going to do this.

"Wait for us," Edna called. "You know, our old bodies aren't what they used to be." She giggled as she and Whitaker drew abreast of them.

"You're as lush as the day we first met," Whitaker whispered.

Rose motioned toward the door. "Before deciding about the mudroom, you should look at the garden shed."

Her foreman, Denny Smith, waited patiently for them at the garden... no, at what would be Delia's new studio. "From your grins, I take this old gal will be your new home. Congratulations."

"Thank you," Delia's voice came out as an excited squeak.

In a wink, Denny pulled out a notepad and pen. "Rose called this a garden shed, but I think it was once a boathouse that subbed as a pool house, especially with the double garage door and gravel path. As you can see, the door is frosted windows, providing ample lighting inside and the skylights. We can keep it or replace it with French doors."

"Glen would probably want the French doors for security, but if I do an immense piece, having the garage door would be handy for getting the sculpture to the foundry."

"Then it stays. Let me show you this area over here." Denny pointed to a small section of cabinets. "We've refinished the solid oak cabinets already, but if you'd like a different stain, we can do it. It has a nice space for a coffee maker, toaster oven, and you could plug in a small refrigerator over here. The sink is small, but we can install a deeper one if you'd like."

"No, this is fine. I was hoping there'd be running water, so I don't have to lug a bucket anymore."

"Good. Good. As for the countertop, it's quartz, the same as the ones in the house." Denny turned a knob, opening a door. "In here's a full bath, sink, toilet, and shower."

Delia stepped into a smaller bathroom than the one she had at Edna's but a lot nicer. "I like the floor-to-ceiling subway tile in the shower. Nice. Hey, Glen, come look."

Glen's firm hands gripped her shoulder as he peered over her head. "I like it. Guess there's no need for a sink in the mudroom then." Glen's deep laugh had her tilting her head back and dislodging his chin from her crown.

"Smartass."

"Just stating the obvious." Glen angled his head and kissed her lips.

Denny grinned. "Now, what would you like us to do with the rest of this area?" He made a sweeping motion toward the massive space of the building.

Delia shook her head. She knew Glen didn't think about money, but she did. She could easily say what she wanted if she had unlimited finances. The question was, what did she need?

"Denny, give us a minute," Glen asked. The second Denny stepped from the room, Glen shut the door. "*Mo gràdh,* don't think about the cost. Just tell Denny what you want. Not what you need, but what you want. You get me?"

She nodded, not knowing what to say.

"Good." Glen opened the door. "Now, tell Denny what you *want.*"

Okay then. "Denny, I'm going to need a platform here...Do you have some graph paper? It'll be easier if I draw it out for you."

"Now, ya' talking." He set his leather briefcase down and pulled out a pad of graph paper, handing it to her.

While she and Denny went over her ideas for the studio, Glen and Rose wandered off, whispering. Probably discussing what he'd like for his office.

"Now, about these ovens you use," Denny said. "Do you need 120-watt or 240-watt outlets?"

That was the question. She'd love to have a large kiln for her more significant projects, but those were too expensive.

"Run a power supply for both," Glen answered, strolling toward them. He slid the graph pad around, studying it. "Hmm, shelves over there. Kilns in the back. What are you going to do with this large space here?"

"I haven't decided yet, but I'm thinking—"

Her phone rang, and she glanced at the caller ID. "It's Gannon." She answered, putting the call on speaker. "You're on speaker, Detective."

"Just a quick question for you, Ms. Parsons. After that night, did you have contact with Katherine Higgins, Buffy Smith, or Amy Boil?"

"No. I never saw or heard from them again. But again, I left California less than a year later. Why do you ask?"

"Following a lead." He disconnected.

"What do you make of that, Glen?" She glanced up at him, following his line of sight to Percy. His fingers rapidly tapped on his phone. After a second, Percy shook his head. "What?" she demanded.

Glen nodded. "Tell her."

"Buffy Smith died in a road rage incident east of L.A., Katherine Higgins was a victim of an apparent home invasion. She suffered a severe brain injury that left her paralyzed and unable to communicate."

"And Amy?" Delia was almost afraid to know what had happened to her.

"Amy Boil's parents reported her missing fifteen years ago. The case is ongoing, but with no new leads."

She clenched her fists until her nails bit into her palms. After all these years, this confirmed her worst suspicions. "Glen. He did it. Scott's a killer. Oh my God, Britney."

Chapter Twenty-One

Why in the bloody hell did God make women so blasted stubborn! No, not women. Woman. One particularly determined, beautiful, intelligent woman. The same woman had him itching to go down to the police station and murder her ex.

The edge of the counter cracked under his grasp. Something else he'd have Rose's team repair. Too freakin' bloody bad they couldn't fix his current situation. He'd asked Delia to spend the night at his condo, where she'd be safe. She refused.

Soft footfalls reached him, but he didn't dare turn around. If he did, he'd cave under her pleading eyes. Just like he had in his condo. In front of Royce and Vaughn. He'd deal with them later for their comments. Right now, Glen had to deal with Delia and this so-called plan of hers.

Bloody hell. He loved her and hated the idea of her being in jeopardy. He'd almost lost her. The proof was the blackened building he glared at. "Explain to me once more why we're here?" Glen caught Delia's reflection in the window, still wearing that stubborn expression.

"To protect Britney." She wrapped her arms around his waist from behind and rested her head against his back. "I've closed all the curtains and turned on the porch light and the lamp by the stairs, just like I always do when Edna's out, and I'm here alone."

Stubborn! At least she did as he'd asked. Whoever Scott hired had to think Delia was here alone for her plan to work.

"You remember Gannon forcibly taking Scott in for questioning? Right?"

"I also remember Gannon saying he couldn't do anything for Britney because nothing had happened to her. However, with me being here, alone and unprotected, he'd be sending a cruiser by tonight. By the way, you scared the bejesus out of me when you ghosted through the wall."

He shrugged. He had the life frightened out of him when she'd nearly died the other night. "Gannon knows I won't leave you *unprotected*."

"Yes, he does. Scott's an idiot and a chauvinistic jobby. I really like that word, jobby. Anyway, Scott had a solid alibi for my attack. I'm sure he has alibis for the others as well. This would be the perfect time for him to arrange for something to happen to Britney or me. Being interrogated by the police makes the perfect alibi."

"True, but why do you think he'd go after Britney? He just introduced her as his newest protégé?"

Delia huffed, and her breath ruffled the hair on his neck. "Because Britney threatened to kick him out. When any of his conquests break up with him, he takes revenge. He has to be stopped, and before you say anything. I know you'll keep me safe, so there's no danger to me with you here. Plus, I know you have one of your guys stationed somewhere outside."

There were two.

Glen turned in her arms. Delia's lips were pressed together, and her head tilted in that determined angle he was becoming all too familiar with. Well, he was just as stubborn. "You could have stayed at the condo while I staked out the place."

"That would have looked suspicious to whoever is working with Scott. My plan is better. As soon as Scott was in the police car, you kissed me and left. They think I'm here alone." Delia raised up. Her warm lips pressed against his. "This is a win-win."

"Do you plan on seducing me?"

She leaned back in his arms with a smile curving her lips and laughter in her eyes. "Hmm, can't do that. Not until after we talk. Then…who knows."

When a woman said she needed to talk, it always meant trouble. "About?"

She pulled from him and sashayed away with a little more wiggle in her stride. Delia filled the electric kettle. He watched her rummage through Edna's tea stash before taking down the box of Earl Grey. She was stalling, which didn't bode well for him.

"Delia?"

She exhaled, and her shoulders slumped forward for a second before she faced him. "The house. Me moving in with you. Us. Your sister, Rose, Dani, and even Percy have told me that once we...once we're intimate, it's a done deal. You're perfect, Glen. If I had to create the man of my dreams, it would be you."

Okay, so maybe it wasn't as bad as he thought.

"But..."

Bloody freakin' hell, there's a but.

"They also told me how wonderful you are with kids. I saw their disappointment when I told them I can't have any."

Bloody hell, he'd not thought of the women. "Delia—"

She was in his arms in two steps and gasped as he lifted her and plopped her bum on the counter, bringing her eye-level with him.

"I'm fifty-five years old, Glen. I can't have children. I will always—"

He placed his finger over her lips. "I don't give a bloody damn about your age or uterus. You will always, *always* be beautiful to me, Delia."

"But—"

"But, nothing. I'm a lot older than you, and I've already told you I can't father any kids. However," He tipped her chin up so she could see the truth in his eyes. "If there comes a time when we're blessed with a child—"

"Glen—"

He silenced her with a kiss, just a light touching of lips. "You met Michael and Hope this afternoon when Percy face-timed Hope, right?"

Delia nodded.

"You know they're adopted."

"I can't imagine the horrors they lived through before you rescued them. Hope and Michael seem to miss their dads and Whitaker."

"Only because Hope and Michael have Whitaker and their fathers wrapped around their little fingers. Viktor and Jenny, not so much."

"They are so lucky you found them."

"Royce and I have gone over the files we acquired. There's a lot of missing information. We think there could be other children out there. Other Dhampir children hiding in the shadows or being used for heaven knows what. If we find such children, they will need loving homes. It's something to think about."

"I'd like that." Delia slid her arms around his neck.

"I would, too." He lowered his head and brushed his lips across hers in a light caress. "You're it for me, Delia. You're my world. My life. My love."

Delia licked her lips, and the tiny action had his dick standing at full attention and pressing against his zipper. She brushed his hair from his eyes and smiled. "In the month I've known you, you've become as important to me as air."

She hadn't said she loved him, but it was bloody damn close enough for him. He reclaimed her lips, crushing her to him, demanding and taking, marking her as his with his kiss.

Delia parted her lips, giving herself to him as he controlled the kiss. He savored each taste of her sweetness, each trace of her natural essence, showing her how he planned to make love to her.

He couldn't wait to claim Delia as his. To slide in and out of her wet heat, pleasuring her with each stroke. Delia wrapped her legs around him as their passion built, digging her heels into his bum and pulling him closer to her. His dick throbbed, demanding to sink into her as his fangs ached and lengthened. Her blood called to him, and his daemon demanded they claim her. Glen was in control, not his beast. *Him.*

That thought went out the window when Delia slid her hand down his chest. She flicked the button on his jeans, then freed him from his denim confines.

"Delia?"

"Hmm?" Her hand encircled him, stroking him. Moving up and down to the rhythm of their kiss.

Glen moaned as his balls drew up against him, and he fought to hold off his release. He broke off their kiss and covered her hand, stilling her motions and pissing off both his dick and daemon.

Delia peered up at him. "Why?"

"When I come with you for the first time, I want to be buried balls deep in you with my fangs in your throat, claiming you as mine."

A smile slowly curved her swollen lips before she struck. Delia bit down hard where his neck met his shoulder.

He roared and bit. Delia's blood filled his mouth as he bathed her with his release. His bloody daemon roared with delight.

When his tremors ceased, he lapped at the wound he'd made in her throat. She did the same to him, sending shivers down his back.

"Delia," he rasped out.

Smiling, she peered up at him. His blood colored her lips. "I wanted to pleasure my man."

Her man? Well, bloody hell. His dick was ready to go again until he noticed the mess coating her stomach. "I'm…"

"Stop it, boy scout. All of this," she motioned to herself. "Will wash off in the shower." Delia slowly drew her tongue across her lower lip. "However, if you're feeling guilty, you could wash my…."

"I can do that," he rushed out. "Who told you to bite me?"

"Dani." Delia nipped his lower lip. "I wanted to—"

The kitchen door flew open.

"Boss—Ah, shit. Sorry." Paul quickly slammed the door.

"What do you need, Paul?"

"We have a situation," he replied from outside.

Glen dropped his forehead, resting it against Delia's. "Of course, we do."

"Go. See what they want then…maybe…if I'm still in the shower…"

"Say no more." He quickly kissed her. "Stay away from the windows, and do not. I repeat. Do not open the door to anyone and do not leave the house."

"Aye. Aye, captain." She saluted.

He turned, reaching for the doorknob.

"Hey," Delia yelled. "Zip it up, boy scout. I don't want you flashing what's mine to the neighbors." Her lyrical laugh filled the air as she hopped off the counter.

Heat inched up his face as he yanked up his zipper. Glen flung open the kitchen door, and his gaze collided with the wolf's smirk. "I will gut you."

Paul swallowed his laugh. "Understood."

"Tell me about the situation?" The sooner he knew what was going on, the sooner he could wash Delia's back and every other part of her.

"Cade and I were checking the perimeter and heard Britney's car startup with the garage door closed. The car was still running, and the garage door closed when we circled back. Cade's ringing the doorbell. Do you want us to kick in the side door?"

Bloody hell, he hoped Delia liked long showers. "No. I'll ghost in and see what's going on. For all we know, the *numpty* could be stupidly checking her emails while sitting in a closed garage."

Glen faded, rushing toward the back of Britney's home. Her and Delia's homes were mirror images, with the master bedroom over the garage. They also had doors leading into the garage from the rear side of the house, making it easy for someone with ill intent to break in.

He faded through the rear of the garage. Even in the wraith zone, he smelled the exhaust fumes. He peered into the car. Both front and back seats were empty. Next, Glen eased from the zone, opened the car door, killed the engine, then pressed the garage opener. He always hated this next part. Drawing a deep breath, he pushed the trunk release, exhaling in relief when Cade gave a thumbs up. Britney wasn't dead in the trunk. Where the bloody hell was she?

Glen pounded on the kitchen door before trying the knob. "It's unlocked," he replied as he opened the door, entering her kitchen. "Britney?" Where the freakin' hell are you? He closed his eyes and concentrated, hearing a faint heartbeat above.

He ran up the stairs, and a mass of blond hair had him sprinting forward. "Britney!" He knelt beside her and rolled her onto her back. A large welt was on the back of her head, and she barely breathed. He lifted her, carrying her downstairs. She needed fresh air and medical attention. *Cade, we need an ambulance.*

Already on the way.

Glen was barely at the door when the wail of the sirens reached him. The medics were rushing toward him by the time he exited the house. "Possible carbon monoxide poisoning," he informed the paramedics as he laid her on the ground.

"Suicide attempt?" Jones asked as she approached.

"I'm thinking more like stupidity. She left the car running in the garage with the door closed. I shut off the ignition and opened the garage door. I found her upstairs in the hallway, passed out. She has a pretty good knot on her head."

Jones eyed him. He could see why her fellow officers gave her a wide berth. "What's *your* take on how she received the welt?

"It could have happened when she passed out. Or someone could have knocked her unconscious," he said that part under his breath. From her expression, Jones caught it.

"Hey," she shouted at a fireman, "is it safe to go in?"

"We haven't cleared the house yet. You can check the garage."

"Thanks. Walk me through it again." Jones strode toward the garage, not waiting for Glen to follow.

"Like I said, I heard the car running and noticed the closed garage door. About five minutes later, if that long. The car was still running, and the garage door still closed, so I came over to investigate."

"You had a driving need to investigate, hmm?" Sarcasm dripped from each word, but Jones had a teasing twitch on her mouth. "How'd you gain entry?"

Damn, the woman didn't miss anything. Wonder if she wants to go into private security? "Through that door." Glen pointed. "Which was unlocked, so was the kitchen door I used to enter the house. As for my driving need to investigate, Britney Goldman gave Haynes an ultimatum."

"Did she? Interesting." Jones peered into the car. "You know, you can start this model remotely with an app on your phone or by pressing the key fob."

"True, but runs for a few minutes before shutting off."

"True." Jones strolled to the door, examining it. "All right, what else did you do?"

"I called out Britney's name as I entered. I didn't see her in the kitchen, so I went upstairs and found her lying in the doorway. She was on her right side, more on her stomach."

"Show me."

"You want me to lie on the garage floor?"

"Not like I can examine the crime scene. Plus, you found the body, and you're a hell of a lot younger than me. On the floor, boy."

He laughed and did as she'd asked. He even placed his arms and legs in the exact position of Britney's. Anything to speed this along because Delia would be out of the shower and sound asleep at this rate. "About like this."

"Don't move." Jones walked around him, stepping over his legs as she circled, making a rough sketch in her notes. She squatted and stared at him for several minutes. "How much of her was in the hall? All of her?"

"Mostly. Her knees were in the doorway."

"How far was the door opened?"

"All the way."

"Okay, you can get up." Jones stood, but her attention stayed on the floor where he'd lain. "Hmm. It's possible she hit her head and pitched forward."

"Possible." *Doubtful.*

Glen stepped from the garage and surveyed the chaos. If it wasn't for the fire trucks, police cars, an ambulance, he'd say the neighborhood was having a block party. Everyone was out and milling around, including his mate.

His mate was *not* safely locked inside her home. She was hovering over Britney while Officer Davis asked questions. Ordering Delia to go back now wouldn't be wise. Anyone could have slipped into her house and laid a trap. Paranoid much? He had every bloody right to be.

Glen didn't need to shout for his men. The second he made eye contact, Paul and Cade strode toward him. Glen wanted answers. He wanted to know how Britney was struck on the back of the head. Even more importantly, how had a human been able to sneak by Paul and Cade?

"What the bloody hell happened? How did a human sneak past the both of you? Again! This is the second time this has happened."

"If you give them a second to answer," Delia slipped her arm around his waist. "You might get the answers to your questions."

Glen's daemon was ready to tear into anyone and everyone. It was pissed. Delia didn't follow his orders and had put herself in danger. "I told you to stay away from the windows and not leave the house."

"Stop being a dick and stop growling," Delia whispered.

His mate was feisty, and he loved it. "I can't let anything happen to you." Glen slipped his arm around her, tucking her as close to him as possible.

"You won't, Glen," she sighed, relaxing against him.

The soft whisper of his name calmed his pissy daemon and had his fangs retracting. "Your hair is still wet."

"Yes, it is, Captain Obvious. Now, do you want to know what we found out?"

"We?" Glen watched the medics load Britney into the back of the ambulance.

"Yes, we." Delia pinched his side hard, digging her nails into the fleshy part of his hip. "Britney wasn't forthcoming with info until I asked if there was anyone she wanted me to call. I don't think the officer appreciated it. Whatever. I handed Britney my phone, and she called her father. FYI, the number is still in my call log. She didn't delete it. She *spilled* to him what had happened."

"According to Britney," Paul started. "Dinner Delivery rang the doorbell after Scott left with the police. Apparently, Haynes is always ordering takeout from some restaurant and never tips. Her father said, once a cheapskate, always a cheapskate."

"Scott never tips," Delia scoffed. "It's a wonder he's never been poisoned by waitstaff."

Cade picked up. "Britney told her father she remembers going up to get her purse, and the next thing she was waking up outside. Daddy dearest wants to meet you, by the way."

"I'll put it on my to-do list." Glen thought back. "There was a delivery bag on the counter, but I don't remember smelling food when I went inside."

"Could have been a salad," Cade surmised.

"Possible," Delia replied. "If Scott's on one of his health kicks. However, I'm wondering if he indeed ordered dinner. Or did he order a hit?" She teasingly squeezed his side before strolling away. "I'll let you figure that out."

"Where are you off?" He grabbed for her hand, but she dodged him. "I'm going back to the house."

"Delia."

"You worry too much. I'll be fine."

"MacPhee," Davis shouted, running toward him. "A word."

"Cade, go with Delia."

"And your men, too."

"Shite." Glen searched, finding Delia talking with two neighborhood women. Good. She was where he could see her. "What do you need, Davis?"

"Did any of you see this delivery person?"

Paul nodded. "Older model silver Civic. It wasn't in the drive long." He glanced at Paul.

"I'd say about three minutes tops before the driver returned to the car and drove away." Paul shook his head. "Jeans, black hoodie, red kicks. Red baseball cap. Oh, and sunglasses."

"Male or female?"

Both Cade and Paul shrugged. Cade pulled out his phone, tapping the screen several times. His lips thinned, and he shook his head again.

"I was hoping Delia's cameras may have caught an image as the driver returned to his car. Nothing. They didn't even capture the vehicle."

"Thanks. If we have any more questions—"

"You know how to get hold of us." Glen searched for Delia. She wasn't with the women anymore.

Delia's moan jerked his attention toward the house.

"Excuse me." He sprinted toward Delia.

Hunched over, she shuffled up her driveway with her arms wrapped around her waist.

The powerful scent of her blood drifted on the wind. "Delia!"

Chapter Twenty-Two

Pain in the ass! Glen saw everyone and everything as a risk. Delia got it. In his line of work, everyone could be a danger. Considering everyone on her street, and she meant everyone, was standing in their little clicks, gawking. Glen's daemon was probably about ready to have—whatever daemons had. Geeze. Maybe she should return to ensure he didn't transform into the devil himself.

No.

This was not how the rest of her life would be, no matter how many centuries she'd live. Glen would just have to get over it. Maybe she'd convince him to take yoga. Delia laughed at the thought. For some reason, she saw him finding inner peace by blowing something up, not doing peaceful warrior.

"Cordelia," Kelly and Laura shouted, waving her over.

Smiling, Delia crossed the street. She liked the two women. Even though she was twenty years older, they were always friendly. "Hey, ladies."

"Is she going to be all right?" Kelly lifted a glass of red wine to her lips.

"I hope so." Delia cringed as the ambulance pulled away with lights and sirens blaring.

"No matter how screwed up a man is, that's no reason to kill yourself," Laura said. "Just hire a damn good lawyer. Atlanta's full of them."

"Suicide? Oh, no." Britney might not be one of Delia's favorite people, but she didn't want this going around the neighborhood rumor mill. "From what I found out, this was an accident."

Laura rolled her eyes and huffed. "I don't know which is worse, trying to kill yourself or being so damn stupid you almost kill yourself. I mean, who is dumb enough to start their car in the garage with the door closed? Seriously?"

Kelly raised her hand, wiggling her fingers. "I do it all the time. You never know who could be lurking around, ready to carjack you. Nope. I start my car, make sure the doors are locked, then open the garage door. Besides, my garage door opener won't work unless my car is running. I never shut off the motor when I pull inside until the garage door is closed. Someone could slip inside. You see it on the news all the time."

"You're a mess, Kelly," Laura teased. "There goes that new kid, jogging again."

"Have you met the family yet?" Kelly finished her wine.

"Nope," Laura replied. "I think they purchased a house a couple of streets over. Dang, I'm going to have to go back inside and refill my glass. Cordelia, would you like a glass?"

"No, not tonight. Thank you." She glanced across the street. Glen was still speaking with the officers.

"I don't blame you," Kelly replied. "If I had a hottie like that waiting on me, I wouldn't want to hang with us either."

Laura stared dreamily over at Glen and sighed.

"Laura!" Kelly gasped. "You're married."

"Yes, I am, but I wish Todd would look at me once the way your man looks at you, Cordelia. Every time I see him watching you, I swear he looks like he wants to eat you with a spoon."

"True," Kelly agreed. "It shows in his eyes how much he adores you. Not that we've been staring out our windows or anything." She giggled. "How did you two meet?"

Wow. Delia had thought Kelly and Laura didn't see past Glen's expensive car and clothes. Guess she missed judged them. "Edna introduced us. She's known him a while."

"Where is Edna?" Laura lifted her empty glass to her lips. "I haven't seen her around for a few days."

"Enjoying time with old friends. Ladies, it's been a pleasure." Delia wiggled her fingers in farewell. The ambulance and fire engine were gone, as were most of the neighbors. Glen was still speaking with the police. He could be a spell, seeing Cade had his phone out.

Delia paused on the sidewalk. The streetlights illuminated most of Edna's yard, but not the driveway. Maybe she'd ask Glen—nope. No need to install a light over the garage if she and Edna weren't going to live here much longer.

The jogger grew closer. Kids nowadays all dressed alike, in sweatpants and hoodies. There was no individuality. Delia continued across the street, staring at the house she'd lived in for the past fifteen years. Leaving here didn't conjure up any feelings of melancholy. In fact, the more she thought about it, moving to the new home and starting her life with Glen had her excited. She couldn't wait!

Someone bumped her, and searing pain sucked her breath. Delia twisted and gasped as the agonizing pain nearly brought her to her knees. She staggered, pitching forward and catching herself against Glen's car. Never pausing, the jogger rounded the corner with a huge dog fast on his heels.

Fighting through the pain, Delia reached behind, brushing something protruding from her lower back. She tried to get her fingers on the handle, but the pain was so severe that she gasped for breath.

Groaning, she withdrew her hand. Blood coated her fingers. Oh, God! Her vision blurred, and she broke out in a cold sweat. He'd stabbed her. Warmth trickled down her leg, pooling at her feet.

Blood.

Delia had to get inside. A few feet. That's all she had to travel to make it inside. Just a few more feet. She pushed from the car, wincing against the pain, and staggered forward.

"Delia!" Glen swung her up into his arms.

The action sent pain coursing through her with fear, freezing her heart. "Glen." She slipped her arm around his neck and struggled to breathe through the agony.

"Shh, I've got you. Cade," Glen whispered, barely loud enough for Delia to hear. He shifted her slightly, jarring her as he turned the knob. "Sorry," he murmured, opening the door.

"The jogger," Delia rasped. If she was going to die, she wanted Glen to catch the bastard. "He stabbed me. You were right."

"Remind me to mark it on the calendar." Glen kicked the door shut behind him and carried her to the couch. He eased down, still cradling her in his arms. Fear reflected in his eyes, confirming her trepidations. She was dying.

"You've given me the best month of my life." She forced a smile despite the pain.

"And I swear every day from here on out will only be better. I swear." Glen gently brushed the hair from her face.

She closed her eyes, wanting to escape the anguish.

"*Mo gràdh,* open your eyes."

"Sleepy."

"Delia, look at me."

Prying her eyelids apart was like bench pressing two hundred pounds. But she did it, wanting her last image to be Glen's handsome face and his beautiful blue eyes.

They were red. And he had horns. Still hers.

She stared up into his eyes and smiled. *I love you.*

Cade squatted by Glen's knees, drawing her attention. A frighteningly serious expression replaced Cade's customary casual one. "Move your arm off the rest."

Glen dropped his elbow, tilting Delia's head back slightly.

"Let's place this here." Cade shoved Edna's needlepoint Union Jack pillow under Glen's bloody arm.

"I'm seeing the German Shepherd that chased the jogger." Damn it, she was hallucinating.

"You're not hallucinating. It's Paul." Glen shifted his nail into a claw.

"Thirsty," Delia rasped out, focusing on Glen's face. Her vision blurred. She licked her dried lips. The lure of sleep called to her.

"We're losing her," Cade hissed.

"Delia," panic rang in Glen's voice. "Open your eyes. Focus on me."

She tried to pry her eyelids apart, but exhaustion won.

"Do it now," Cade ordered.

Warm liquid filled her mouth and ran down Delia's throat, quenching her thirst. A hand pressed against her back, followed by excruciating tugging.

She screamed against the agony.

"Shh, I've got you, *mo gràdh*," Glen murmured. "I've got you." His voice faded.

More of the warm, sweet liquid filled her mouth and trickled down her throat, sweeping her into a phantasmagoric realm. Strange and vivid images filled her mind of Glen biting into his wrist, pressing it to her lips. He repeated the action over and over each time his wounds healed.

Cade glanced up. His eyes were red, and blood coated his lips. "Her heartbeat is strong, and she's no longer bleeding. It's time to stop."

"I can't lose her," Glen shouted.

"Stop." Cade's hand gripped her wrist. No. He grabbed Glen's. "Stop before she loses you."

Her strange dreams changed, carrying her on a journey through time. Delia whirled across a dance floor. Next, she was skiing down a Swiss slope. Pain tore through her heart at the loss of her nephew. Aileen and David would be heartbroken. Delia stumbled in the sand. An explosion shook the ground. The force catapulted her through the air as shrapnel shredded her lower body.

Delia was dead, and she knew it. Cold sweat beaded her forehead, and she forced her eyes open, dreading what would envelop her. "I'm not dead? I saw my death."

Her head sure as hell felt like she had died. Damn. What happened? Oh, Scott tried to kill her. Again. The bastard.

She blinked, trying to focus and clear the cobwebs from her brain. Her room was dark. Darker than usual because someone had closed her curtains and that someone was in bed beside her, growling worse than a bear.

The longer Delia watched Glen sleep, the clearer her mind grew. She hadn't been dreaming. She'd been in his mind, experiencing his life through the years. Not just his life, but his hopes and dreams. She knew the depth of his love for her. Glen would have willingly died to save her if it had not been for Cade. That sweet, sweet boy.

"Glen," she whispered, shaking him a bit.

"You're awake. How do you feel?" He stretched and rolled toward her. "Let me hold you."

Delia snuggled against him. The muscles in her lower back protested, but the pain wasn't unbearable. She rested her head on Glen's chest. The steady rhythm of his heart made her realize she'd come too close to losing him. "Tired, but other than that, a heck of a lot better. How many days have I been out this time?" Lying in Glen's arms made her realize she was naked, and so was he, which had her girly parts thinking about other things.

"A few hours." Sleep edged his deep baritone, making her regret waking him. Until he shifted, rubbing his bare skin against her.

"Why are we naked?"

Glen shrugged, and his eyes briefly flashed red. "Once I knew you were out of the woods, I carried you up and bathed you. I figured you wouldn't appreciate it if I put you to bed soaked in blood."

"I have pajamas."

"I didna want to snoop through your things." His hand trailed down her back in a gentle caress. "As for why I'm naked too, I didna think you wanted me to soil your sheets."

He was right. "Did you catch the guy?" Delia trailed her finger down the thin black line from Glen's navel.

"No." He captured her hand, placing it over his heart. "Which is why you're moving today. Wanted to move you last night, but Cade convinced me it wouldn't be a good idea."

"I don't get a choice?" Yes, she was looking forward to moving. She hated feeling she had no option. Delia peered up at him, waiting for his answer.

"I failed to keep you safe. Again." Glen exhaled and hugged her to him.

She hadn't missed the hitch in his voice. Glen hadn't failed to keep her safe. If there was fault to be had, it was hers for not taking his warnings seriously and not staying vigilant. "No. You've done everything to protect me. I'm the one who didn't listen."

"Your ex lives next door."

"You don't have to remind me. By the way, do you know how Britney is doing?"

"No, I don't. She didn't return home, and Scott is still with Gannon. Delia, you're the most precious person in my life. I can't lose you."

"You won't." She traced the clan badge tattooed over his heart. Glen's skin twitched. For all his strength, her man was ticklish. Her man? Possessive much. Yes, yes, she was.

"I almost did." The trace of certainty in his tone had her pausing.

Delia pushed up, ignoring her protesting back and not giving a damn if Glen got a good look at her saggy boobs. She wanted to see his eyes. "I almost lost you. If it hadn't been for Cade stopping you, Glen. You would have died."

"I would willingly give my life for you." She felt the truth of Glen's words in her very soul. "But I wasn't in danger," he sighed.

"I was in your mind, seeing things through your eyes," she challenged. Damn it, Glen could pull his macho crap with his men, but not with her. "I know better."

"What you saw was when I gave Royce blood to save his life."

"Because he's the leader of your people, but mostly because you look at Vaughn and Royce as brothers." Delia rested her head on his shoulder. "I guess I know this because of all the blood you've given me."

"You're right on all counts. I do consider them my brothers. As for how you know this, it's the blood bond. When we mate, the bond will be stronger."

"The visions were so real. I was there. I felt the loss of William. When you stepped on the landmine, I felt your pain. I saw Cade with blood coating his lips."

"You lost a lot of blood." Glen kissed her crown. "They stabbed you in the kidney. They drove the shank in up to the hilt. When Cade pulled the thing from you, it caused more damage."

"That would explain my aching back—"

"You're in pain?" Glen glared at her.

Really? Bless Glen's boy scout heart. He'd just told her Cade ripped out part of her kidney. "A little. But why did I see Cade with blood on his mouth?" Now that she asked, she wasn't sure she wanted to know.

"You were bleeding out. Cade gave you blood by biting his hand, pressing it to your wound."

"Am I now also bound to Cade?" God, she hoped not. She liked the boy, but—no.

Glen growled, and his eyes glowed. He captured her hand, bringing it to his lips and kissing her fingertips. "Mine."

"Then don't do anything stupid, like nearly killing yourself."

"*Mo gràdh*, I wasn't in danger. Unlike Royce and Vaughn, my body can replenish a blood loss."

"A small blood loss and even then, to an extent." Something else she'd gleaned from Glen's mind. "Promise me you'll never risk your life for mine."

"I'll not watch you die."

"I don't want to live without you. So there!"

"Delia—"

"No. End of discussion. Now, were you able to get fingerprints off the shank? Maybe with Percy's help, you could find out who'd stabbed me and capture the bastard."

"Because you're in pain, I'll end this discussion. For now." Glen glared at her, and she didn't care. "As for prints. The only ones were yours."

"Mine? I remember brushing my hand against it. I guess I got a better grip on the thing than I thought."

"Cade said the handle matched the carving tools you had in your studio. It resembles a long, thin, bent-tipped trowel. It's still downstairs if you'd like to see it."

"I do, but not at the moment." Delia snuggled closer, enjoying the warmth of Glen's bare skin against hers. She'd almost lost him because of her stubbornness, which was unacceptable. It was time she grabbed life by the horns and went for it. "You know, I'm naked. You're naked. We could…" She trailed her hand down his abdomen again, finding him fully erect.

"*Mo gràdh*," Glen groaned. His horns pushed from his forehead as she ran a finger over his tip. "You enjoy torturing me." He shivered, rocking his hips.

"Mmm, not at all." She drew his nipple into her mouth, gently nipping, then sucking before letting it slip free. "Make me yours, Glen."

"Delia, I want to claim you so much, but you're not fully healed."

Yes, her back ached, but nothing worse than when she had menstrual cramps. Her heart, body, and soul were in complete agreement. It was time to make Glen hers. She pushed up, ignoring her back, and nipped his lower lips. "I'm healed enough to make love."

"I love you, but I have to ask. Are you sure, Delia? I'll take your blood, giving you mine. We will be one forever, even past the grave."

She slipped her arms around his neck and stared into his red eyes. "A month ago, I told you I didn't believe in love anymore. Right now, I can't imagine my life without you in it. I'm sure."

Glen seized her mouth, making her shiver as his hot lips locked on hers in a sensual kiss, drawing her into a foray against his tongue. He rolled her to her back, and she stiffened, breaking off their kiss.

"You're in pain," he ground the words between his fangs.

"So, you can do all the work." She grinned. "And make me forget my pain."

"Bloody freakin' hell." He cringed and dropped his head, resting his forehead against hers.

"What?" She shoved against his shoulder.

"We have company," he groaned, flopping to his back.

"Who," she demanded.

"Delia, Whitty said you'd been stabbed," Edna shouted and rattled the doorknob. "Why's your door locked?"

"I'm fine Edna. We'll be down in a minute." Good grief, cock-blocked by Edna again.

Glen laughed and tossed back the covers. "I'm giving the order to shoot to kill when we move to the new place."

"Not going to argue with you on that one." Delia laughed.

"Open this door," Edna shouted again.

"I'm naked." Delia bellowed back. "Let me get some clothes on."

"It won't be the first time I've seen you starkers."

"Edna, please. Glen and I will be down shortly."

His shoulders shook as he pulled a pair of jeans from a duffle bag. Glen glanced over at her, grinning. "To be continued."

"Count on it," she whispered.

"He can see you, but I can't? Open this door, or I'll—I'll get my key."

"No. Glen's getting dressed, too."

"Now you're really tempting me."

"Edna!" Delia tossed back the covers, sitting up. She cringed as her lower back protested the sudden movement. Perhaps Glen was right about the extent of her healing—but she'd keep that to herself. "Would you please go?"

"Fine. But you best be down in two shakes."

"All right?" Glen eyed her.

"I'm good. Let me get some clothes on and deal with Edna. What time is it, anyway?"

"Too bloody early for them to be here, if you ask me," Glen replied, pulling on his jeans.

Delia stepped into the bathroom, closing the door behind her. She would not kill her aunt. At least not where there were witnesses.

Chapter Twenty-Three

Glen tucked his throbbing dick into his jeans as he watched Delia rush into the bathroom. Edna interrupting them was probably a good thing. Delia wasn't fully healed. He knew. He'd felt her pain when she stood. He was an ass, thinking with his dick instead of his heart. He should have never tried to seduce her.

Our mate craves our touch. She seduced us, the beast murmured.

Our mate isn't healed, Glen informed his ignoble side. *We should have been stronger.*

Her needs come first. Therefore, if she craves our touch, we take care of her desire.

Do we? Glen questioned. *Even if it causes her more pain?*

Pain? Our blood eases our mate's pain. You've already given her enough blood to form a mating bond. Therefore, you know her desire for us, her feelings for us. You also know each time we don't claim her, she feels we don't desire her.

Debating with his primitive daemon was daunting on a good day. *I desire her more than anything. But Delia hasn't healed, and her health and welfare are primary above anything else.*

Are they? Then why did you give her so much blood the first night unless your intentions were not to heal her but to purposely create the bond? If that's the case, you've finally started listening to me. The damned beast grinned.

Delia was in pain. I wanted to ensure she'd heal by the morning. If we hadn't given her so much blood, then we'd be no better than her ex.

You protest too much. The bloody damned creature laughed.

Sometimes Glen hated the beast sharing his soul, but at least his dick had shivered back to normal.

His daemon continued, *We're far better of a mate than that arse. We tended to our mate, healing her. We did not leave her to suffer. Once we claim Delia as ours, we will make love to her anytime and anywhere she desires.*

Glen's zipper bit into his dick once more. He really hated his beast.

The creature laughed.

There wasn't time for this foolishness. They had a busy day ahead, and if they didn't muck it up, perhaps they could finish what they started with Delia, providing she was fully healed.

I'm not the one mucking about.

Why couldn't I be born a flyer?

Because they're boring and we are not.

"For the love of—"

"You know, you growl a lot when talking to Zeus." Delia leaned against the bathroom door frame with her arms crossed over her chest, a huge smile curving her lips.

"Zeus? Who the bloody hell is Zeus?"

"Zeus-Ammon. What I named your other half. Of course, Zeus was bearded, but you're not, which is a good thing cause I'm not into beards. Just saying." Delia grinned, pushing away from the wall. "Hmm, I'm thinking of doing a sculpture of him."

I'm Zeus! King of the gods.

"Brilliant. Simply brilliant. You don't need to encourage him, and he doesn't have a name."

"He does now. I'm calling your other half Zeus-Ammon, and that's that since you won't let me compare you to the Barberini Faun sculpture." Delia drew her finger down his chest. "You *are* a lot sexier."

It was one thing to call his beast after the king of gods, but also saying he was sexy had his daemon preening like a bloody peacock and his head swelling ten sizes. There'd be no living with him now.

Glen brushed his lips to hers, then reached behind him and opened the door. "Come on, let's get this debriefing over with."

From the landing, Glen surveyed the group. Royce sat on the couch in the middle. Edna and Whitaker occupied the loveseat, and Percy worked away on his laptop in the armchair. Paul and Cade leaned against the doorframe to the kitchen, leaving no place for Glen or Delia to sit or stand. Yep, he was being called to the carpet. Bloody brilliant and in front of Delia.

"Royce," Glen greeted as he and Delia descended the stairs. "Percy, I see you're busy at it. Edna, Whitaker, good morning."

"I guess it is," Edna snapped. "seeing Delia is up and about."

"We've been informed," Royce started without pleasantries. "the perpetrators used a scent block. Do they know about us?"

Us, meaning the Dhampir, but no concern for our mate. The arse.

For once, Glen concurred with his daemon. "My mate is still healing. Move."

"Cordelia." Royce stood, motioning toward the vacant couch. "Please, sit and forgive my rudeness."

"Why do you think the attacks on me are related to the Dhampir?" Delia flinched as she eased down.

"What can I do?" Glen sat beside her, feeling helpless to ease her pain.

"I'm fine. Honestly, it's getting better. Royce, if I understand you, what you're saying is whoever is behind the attacks had to know I was Glen's mate even before I married Scott."

"No, that's not what I meant." His cousin smiled beguilingly at Delia, giving her the same look Royce often used with his son Michael. "Because of the use of scent block, I was making a presumption."

"Already explained to him, Glen," Paul grossed. "That there's been a growing trend among criminals using scent maskers. They think it will throw off police dogs. This guy smelled of clove."

"It worked on you," Royce countered.

"Naw, there, you're wrong. They got away 'cause I don't shift into a Greyhound. Even if I did, I doubt I could catch a speeding car. Delia's attacker jumped into a waiting silver 2006 Toyota Camry with an aftermarket window tint and no tags. My guess is it was stolen. Oh, one more thing. The driver was the same female who set fire to Delia's studio."

"Why are you just now telling me this? I swear I will rip your heart out, Paul, and mail your ashes back to your mum with an apology." Royce shifted his attention from Paul to Glen. "Did you know about this?"

"I did, which is why we are moving into the new place today." He glanced at Delia. "What do you want to take?"

She shrugged. "Just what's in my bedroom."

"Moving? Today? Do you think that's a good idea, Delia?" Edna sputtered. "From the amount of blood I saw, it's a miracle you're alive."

"And yet, Aunt Edna, I see no blood."

"That's because when we arrived, *their* people had finished cleaning the carpet and brought in a new couch." Edna's lips thinned. "They even replaced the needlepoint pillow I made sixty years ago. That one," she jabbed her finger at the offending pillow. "Holds no sentiment."

"What about the firestarter? Did she use a scent block?" Royce asked, ignoring Eddie.

"Nope." Paul shook his head. "She's evaded my wolf twice. There won't be a third time."

"Why," Edna asked. "Are you quitting? Doesn't surprise me. The lot of you are no better than the officers who investigated Delia's case when Snot tried to kill her the first time. Just as now, he has an alibi. I don't understand why you won't kill him and put an end to this nonsense."

As much as Glen would like to do that, he couldn't. Not without solid proof. "Because, Eddie, murder is illegal."

She snorted. "Only if you get caught."

"Here, this should take the edge off." Cade handed Delia a glass of water and some pills.

Royce eyed Glen with a calculating expression. *You gave her enough blood to form a mating bond, yet she's still not healed. How severe was her injury?*

"Thank you." Delia took the drugs Cade offered her.

"Why is she not fully healed?" Royce asked again.

"Because you can't do anything right," Edna blurted. "For being supernatural beings, you've allowed mere mortals to get around your defenses and attack my girl. And you think I'm leaving her in your care?" Edna glared at Glen, "Think again."

"Edna!" Delia snapped.

"Don't Edna me. They're in a tizzy to head back to England, leaving you completely unprotected."

"I'm not unprotected. Glen is—"

"Glen is doing nothing. With all his high-tech machinery and supernatural abilities, he's still allowed Snotface to get to you. I swear he and his employees are as gormless as the detectives who handled your case from the start."

"As much as it pains me," Royce pinched the bridge of his nose. "I must agree with Eddie, as I don't understand how these attacks keep occurring."

Edna's words cut deep. Royce's rubbed salt, lemon juice, and vinegar into the wound.

"Because they are hiding in plain sight," Delia replied. "Last night, there was so much commotion going on, all my neighbors were outside. I saw the jogger. I didn't look at his face. I just assumed it was the new kid. After all, most of the kids wear sweats and hoodies."

"That makes sense," Royce agreed. "Do you have anything linking Cordelia's ex to her attackers?"

"If I may." Percy glanced up from his computer. "Fiona, Karma, and I have scoured Mr. Haynes's finances. We cannot locate any large transfers of cash, offshore accounts—"

Delia snorted. "Sorry, Percy. I know you're doing everything you can, but if Scott had that kind of money, he wouldn't have been making my life a living hell for as long as he has."

"True," Percy conceded. "Unless he's been after you all this time because you left him."

"What about his new romance?" Royce asked.

"Britney?" Delia gasped. "Scott tried to kill her last night. I bet her food delivery person and my stabber are the same."

"No," Cade replied. "The food delivery person matches the same height and body type as our suspect from the gallery and the arsonist." He nodded at Delia. "Thanks for the tips you gave Paul and me. Your art lesson really helped." He panned back to Royce. "The jogger slash stabber was taller and heavier set. In fact, his body type resembles Scotts, but as we know, he was in police custody."

Glen leaned forward, resting his arms on his legs, staring at his feet. "The arsonist and bomber are possibly the same person. Do we have any footage of Delia's carjacking? If I were a chancer, I'd say Delia's carjackers and Britney's food deliverer were the same."

"We do, and I'm thinking the same." Percy nodded.

Delia leaned against Glen. "Why not kill me then?" Her voice trembled.

Glen wrapped his arm around Delia, hugging her to him. Pieces were falling into place, and he didn't like the picture he saw. "Because they wanted your death to appear to be an accident."

Edna rolled her eyes. "How was stabbing Delia supposed to have been an accident? She what, accidentally tripped and fell against the knife?"

"No, Edna." Glen met the old woman's irate expression. "Last night's attack was out of frustration. I'm wondering if Scott isn't the actual killer—"

Edna snorted. "As if."

"Perhaps a Judas Goat," Glen finished.

Cade whistled. "Damn, that's dark. But considering what Percy uncovered about the other women, I think you're on to something."

"What's a Judas Goat?" Delia asked, shifting her attention from Cade to Glen.

"Oh, I can explain," Paul chimed in. "It's a goat that leads an animal to slaughter, so the creature isn't stressed. Pop uses one when he's slaughtering steer. When you're talking about criminals, usually it's two people. One person, in this case, Scott, dates the women, earning their trust, probably stealing their money like he did you." Paul nodded toward Cordelia. "When finished, he sits back and watches as his partner torment then kills—"

"Oh, God. It's one thing to think Scott wanted me dead. It's another to think...." Delia buried her face in her hands.

Glen smoothed his hand up and down her back as he stared over her head at Paul. *Remind me why I haven't killed you yet.*

Sorry, boss.

"Stop threatening Paul." Delia wiped her eyes.

"Do you think Miss Goldman, Britney, is the newest target or the accomplice?" Royce asked.

Delia shook her head. "If I had to guess, I'd say target. Britney's too young to have been involved with what happened fifteen years ago, and her body type doesn't match the woman on the security feed. Plus, she almost died last night."

"True," Percy agreed. "Last night, her father and another man, possibly a brother, returned to the house around midnight. They changed the locks, pushed Haynes' car from the garage, and deposited several bags of items in the drive. I'm assuming Miss Goldman's family was evicting Mr. Haynes from the premises. Miss Goldman did not return to the house. According to hospital records, they discharged Britney, and she left in the care of her mother."

Edna huffed. "I'm not hearing anything that will convict that poor excuse of a human."

"Eddie," Whitaker cooed. "Percival isn't leaving any stone unturned."

Glen agreed with Edna. They were coming up with more victims and nothing linking Scott to the attacks. "You have valid reasons to rule her out, but it doesn't mean she isn't involved. What about her finances?"

"You have a point," Royce agreed. "Haynes could be grooming her."

Percy hammered away on his keyboard. His lips pulled thinner with each stroke. "From what I see, she put everything she had into buying the house. Before you ask, her parents don't have the funds, either."

"That could be your motive." Royce patted Percy's shoulder. "Brilliant work."

Glen wasn't hearing anything, putting Scott behind bars or, better, six feet under. "Yes, well, before we congratulate ourselves, Percy, is there anything connecting Scott to Delia's attacker or to any of the other women?"

Percy gave a curt shake of the head. "There's no apparent hit on Cordelia that I can find on the web. Also, no evidence Haynes is contacting anyone. It appears he's using a burner, limiting our abilities. I see nothing suspicious on Haynes or Goldman's phone."

"In other words, all you know is where he gets his hair cut. The world of good that will do ya. Like I said, worthless." Edna crossed her arms over her chest and huffed. "If you think I'm leaving my girl unprotected, think again. I'm not going anywhere until Snot's dead and Cordelia's safe."

"Edna," Delia snapped. "You're not helping. Percy, I have a crazy question. What if this isn't what you said, Judas Goat or whatever, but a plain old hit? What if this is the same hitman Scott hired all those years ago? From the movies I've seen and books I've read, hitmen get paid half in advance and the rest once the jobs are done. I'm still alive. Maybe I screwed up his record or something."

It wasn't good to laugh at one's mate. "Not likely, love." Glen slipped his arm around her shoulder. "If it were me and Scott didn't pay the rest because you survived, I'd break his hands and call us even. As for screwing up a personal record, they wouldn't have waited fifteen years."

"True," Percy agreed, clicking away on his keyboard. "Hmm, it appears Gannon's put in a request to examine the case files on Buffy Smith, Amy Boil, and Katherine Higgins."

"Wasting his time on old cases, he should concentrate on Delia." Edna snorted. "Like I said, worthless."

"Edna, you're not being fair," Delia tossed back.

"Not fair?" Edna stood, planting her hands on her hips. "Since you've met him, you've been carjacked, shot at, nearly blown-up, burned alive, and now shish kabobbed!"

"You can't blame Glen for the carjacking." Delia stood, pointing at him. "I didn't know him, and besides, you were the one all about having him change the locks when I wanted to go to bed."

"Only because you were too self-conscious about turning fifty-five, you didn't see the man's tongue dragging the floor every time he looked at you."

"Edna!" Scarlet stains colored Delia's cheeks.

"It's the truth, and damn it, I thought it a bloody brilliant thing. Glen being so attracted to you and all, I figured he would protect you from that tosser. Snotface is a bloody bad penny, always showing up."

"I will, Eddie." Glen stood, drawing Delia to his side. "Cordelia is my heart. I won't allow anything to happen to her."

"And yet, you have. None of you care anything about my girl." Edna turned her ire on Royce. "All you care about are dance recitals."

"Enough." Glen fought to contain his beast and failed. His horns pushed from his brow, and he knew his eyes glowed.

Edna paled, and tears welled in her eyes as she continued to stare at him.

"Eddie." Whitaker wrapped his arm around her, turning her in his embrace. "I love you, but Percival and I promised Hope. It's her first recital."

Edna nodded and drew her hand across her eyes. "I know. You should be there for her, but I can't lose my girl, and I'll not leave until I know she's safe."

"Aunt Edna." Delia placed her hand on the old woman's shoulder. "Glen will keep me safe. Return with Whitaker to England. The two of you have been apart for far too long. That will give you a chance to reconnect with friends."

Edna shook her head. "I doubt any are still alive. Delia, I'll not budge on this. I'll not leave if that tosser is free and breathing."

"Perhaps Detective Gannon will have enough evidence to hold Haynes for some time," Percy offered.

"We can wish," Whitaker replied.

Edna turned in Whitaker's arms and nodded, smiling at Delia. A single tear rolled down Edna's withered cheek. "Every time Scott shows up, you end up hurt. I can't lose you."

Glen hugged Delia tighter to him. "Percy, place a call into the cleaners."

Someone pounded on the door, and Glen had a good idea of who it was. He drew a deep breath, slammed his daemon back into his cage, and strode to the door.

"I cannot sanction a hit on a human," Royce drawled. "Even if it appears warranted."

Glen bet if Royce had to be in Scott's company more than a second, Royce would rip the jobby's heart out without a thought. Glen turned the knob and opened the door. Yep, his favorite asshole glared at him.

"I don't know what the hell that old bitch—"

Glen slammed the door. "Apparently, Gannon didn't have enough evidence to hold him."

Royce cleared his throat. "It's sanctioned."

Chapter Twenty-Four

Delia dropped her chin to her chest and shook her head. While living with Edna, she kept her room clean, but Delia admitted sometimes it was a little cluttered, especially when working on a project. A little cluttered? That was putting it mildly. Her room was hoarder hell.

When Glen asked her what she wanted moved into the new place, she hadn't meant literally everything in her room. Well, the so-called *cleaners* had left the blinds and curtains as Glen requested. He wanted the neighbors to think she still lived there. As for Edna, Glen and Royce gave her twenty-four hours to list what she wanted shipped to England and what she didn't want anymore. Delia laughed because their demands might have short-circuited Edna's brain. At least until Fred, the person in charge of the cleaners, took pity on Edna, handing her a stack of sticky notes to place on everything. He instructed her to go through the house and mark items as to her wishes. He also assured Edna her mother's teacup would be packed with care. Delia would return tomorrow to help Edna sort through everything.

Cleaners. Highly efficient paranormal crime scene eradication team and movers. It amazed Delia how quickly they had packed, loaded, and moved all her belongings. First, they loaded their vehicles onto a flatbed, then drove away. When asked why, Glen explained he didn't want to risk the possibility of someone placing trackers on either car. After all, they had gotten to her twice. For once, Edna didn't complain.

After the flatbed drove off, Freddie backed a small moving van that barely fit into the garage. In under thirty minutes, his team had it loaded and driving away. Royce, Percy, Whitaker, and Edna left in the same car they'd arrived in. Delia believed they'd return to the agency where Angus would inspect the vehicle, ensuring its safety.

As soon as that group left, Cade pulled into the garage, driving a massive black SUV. Glen helped her into the back seat and climbed in beside her. She took in the spacious, luxurious leather interior and privacy glass between the front and rear seats. And wow, a bar with a coffeemaker.

Glen poured himself a brandy sniffer of a burgundy liquid. She had no doubt it contained blood. He tossed back his drink, turned the glass upside down on a small black ring, and instantly water rinsed the residual red film from the glass.

She glanced at Glen, and her breath stalled, catching his glowing eyes. At least with the privacy glass up, Paul and Cade wouldn't hear her conversation with Glen. "Hey." She laced her fingers with his, giving them a squeeze.

"Sorry. Would you care for something?"

"Yeah, to know what's got your kilt in a knot?"

His lips twitched. "Edna's right. I have failed to keep you safe."

"Oh, for the love of—Glen, I didn't precisely follow your instructions. I figured I'd be safe in my neighborhood, even if someone almost turned me into a crispy critter. I wasn't behaving exactly like the brightest Crayon in the box."

"Delia—"

"Stop. Scott is not smarter than you. I know you will keep me alive and safe. I also know you will get the evidence the police need to put him under the jail. Now, what's the game plan for when we get to the new place? I put away the things from my room, and you take care of your stuff?"

"If that's what you want." Muscles twitched in Glen's jaw. Yeah, her Zeus didn't like it when she called him on his bullcrap, and blaming himself for what had happened was a bunch of crap.

"What I'd like is to have a couple of un-cockblocked days with you. That's what I'd like."

A loud thump had her jerking her attention to the front. Cade's shoulders shook while Paul pounded on the dash, clearly laughing his head off.

"I thought privacy glass also meant soundproof."

Glen shrugged, and a genuine smile curved his mouth. "Dhampir hearing."

"Well, at least they know the boss *might* get lucky."

Glen's eyes turned the darkest red she'd ever seen them. "Might?"

She patted his cheek as they pulled through the gate of their new home. "Might."

Might? The Cleaner meticulously packed, moved, unpacked, and arranged *her* possessions just as they'd been in her bedroom and bathroom. Precisely as they had been. What had she expected? For Freddie and his team to strip and remake the bed, clean and dust everything as they unpacked? Nope, that would make her a diva.

Groaning, Delia removed a bra dangling from the bedpost and tossed it in the hamper. From what she could tell, they had hung her clothing in the master bedroom. At least she'd assumed they had since her things weren't in this closet. Freddie's crew had left her folded items in her dresser. She'd deal with moving that later, seeing this would be the perfect opportunity for her to go through everything and sort out what she wanted to keep, donate, and trash. She had more important things to do now, like hunting down Glen.

Delia strode across the hall. He grinned as she entered and motioned to the massive four-poster tester bed with curtains. She'd not seen Glen's bedroom when she visited his condo and had assumed the furniture to be mid-century modern, like his living room. Boy, was she wrong. "Wow. This was not what I had expected." She ran her hand over the massive dark oak poster as she studied the intricate carving.

"You don't like it." Glen's smile faded. "I'll have Fred bring something out of storage."

"No, silly. I love it. This bed isn't going anywhere."

"You like it?" His question sounded too hesitant. There was more to this bed than it being a magnificently well-preserved antique.

"I do. I can see us lying there with the curtains drawn, keeping out the butt-crack of dawn. Better yet, the curtains at the end of the bed opened, with us watching the crackling fire in the fireplace." She looked up at the underside of the oak tester. "Hmm, mirrored panels are the only things missing."

"Do you really want to watch my hairy arse as I make love to ya?" A too devilish grin curved his lips. "Though I could watch you too."

She laughed at the image forming in her mind. "No mirrors. Besides, they'd cover up all the woodwork. I especially love the carved thistles."

Glen looped his arms around her from behind. "No mirrors." He nipped her earlobe, sending shivers down her back and had her wanting to take the bed for a spin.

"Mmm." She turned, slipping her arms around his neck. "So, how many young maidens have you deflowered in this bed?" Was she jealous? No, what happened in Glen's past was his past. But that didn't keep curiosity from raising its head.

"None." Glen met her eyes and shrugged. "It's been my sanctuary since I acquired it from the craftsman."

"Which was *when*?" she prodded.

"1852 or somewhere around then. Don't worry, the mattress is new with one of those adjustable frames." He grinned, jiggling his eyebrows. "Multi-positional."

"Hmm, I like the sound of that." She toyed with his shirt until she'd slipped it free from his jeans.

"Do you, lass?" Glen whispered, claiming her mouth. His tongue traced the seam of her lips, and she opened to him.

The sensual taste of Glen's tongue overwhelmed her. Delia slid her hands up his broad, muscular chest until she cupped the back of his head. She kissed Glen with as much fervor as he'd kissed her.

Glen's arms tightened around her. One hand caressed her back as the other slid further down, cupping her rear. Still kissing her, Glen lifted her and took a step. The back of Delia's legs bumped against the edge of the bed.

Stop me now if you don't want to be my mate. Glen's voice resonated through her mind.

Make love to me. Claim me. She hoped he heard her.

"Ah, Glen?" A familiar deep voice broke through her foggy thoughts, and she pushed against Glen's chest, breaking off their kiss. Paul stood in the doorway, staring down the hall.

It was one thing to be interrupted by Edna, but now Paul. What the hell? Did the universe suddenly deem them celibate?

Unfortunately for Paul, Glen didn't like being cockblocked again any more than she did. Horns sprouted, nails blackened, and he bellowed, sounding more like a bull moose, looking more like the devil.

"What?"

Paul instantly dropped to his knees in the hall and bared his throat. "Ah," his voice trembled. "Denny said to tell you he's finished and for you to take a look. If he doesn't hear from you, he'll assume everything's as you want it," Paul rushed out.

"Stop growling." Delia squeezed Glen's granite hard forearm.

He glanced at her before turning his fury on Paul. "Never barge into our chambers for any reason."

"The door was open," Paul stammered.

Bless his stupid heart.

"I will kill you and send your ashes back to your mother!"

This time, she reached up and tugged on Glen's hair. "No, you're not."

Glen focused on her, arching a single brow. "No?"

"No." She patted Glen's cheek. "We should thank him. The door was open. He didn't barge in." She arched her brow. "And to forbid him from ever entering a room we're in is nonsense. What if you're hurt and need him?"

Glen snorted. "If I'm injured, he'll know. We've shared blood."

"Okay, I didn't know that. But what if it's me? I haven't shared blood with Paul." At least, she didn't think she had.

Glen's burgundy eyes slowly returned to their gorgeous sky-blue, though his frown remained. He huffed as he continued to stare at her. "Fine. Paul, next time, quietly close the door and leave. Never interrupt Delia and me unless someone's life depends on it. And even then, it had best be someone we care about. Understood?"

Paul scrambled to his feet. "Understood." He reached for the doorknob.

"You can leave the door open," Delia told him. "We'll go look at the studio now. Thank you, Paul."

Glen snapped his mouth shut. "One more thing." He faced Paul. "Report."

The man snapped to attention. "Cade and I have secured the parameter. Security cameras are in place. We've installed the com and," He winked at Delia. "Audio systems in your studio. Currently, we're setting up the command center in the guest house."

"We'll discuss a permanent place later, thank you. That's all." Glen's attention slowly drifted back to her. The questioning look in his eyes had her sighing.

Yep, cockblocked again, for now. Delia lifted on her tiptoes and kissed Glen's chin. "You going from horny, and let's get it on, to horny, and you're going to kill someone in less than a heartbeat is kind of a mood kill. Though I will say, your homicidal possessiveness is a little sexy." She held up her hand, thumb, and forefinger, slightly touching. "Barely."

A slow, lazy smile curved his lips. "You thought I was sexy?"

"I said barely." She patted his cheek. "Stop fishing for compliments." She groaned, staring into his blue eyes. "Pouting is so unbecoming."

"No' pouting. Tis scowling, lass."

"Now, you look constipated."

That earned her a grunt as Glen slipped his arm around her waist. "Let's look at your studio, so we can send a text to Denny and perhaps have the rest of the day without interruptions."

Delia liked the sound of that, and so did her lady parts. "To do...?" She practically purred.

Glen shrugged as they descended the staircase. "Considering the only furniture in the house is what's in our bedroom and what came from your room, I figure we'd go through the catalog Fred left and see if there is anything we want from storage. If not, we'd venture out to a few furniture stores."

"That sounds...nice." Not. Delia hoped Glen would suggest they spend the rest of the day in bed becoming true mates, *finally*. But he hadn't, which meant she'd have to take matters into her own hands. Not. A. Problem.

"Now, if anything's wrong, you can blame Vic."

"Victoria?" Delia peered up at him. "Why?"

Glen shoved his hand through his hair, making it more unruly than usual. "Aye, she's the one who told me what you'd need. I called her last night while you were healing." He shrugged, opening the door. "What do you think?"

Delia hurried into the room. Denny and his men had built everything she'd asked for, just as she'd wanted. They'd done all of it in less than twenty-four hours. Talk about miracle workers. They positioned a platform under the skylights, allowing her to work on large pieces. Piled to one side were new furniture blankets so she could wrap her sculptures for transport. Shelves stood along the right wall. A drafting table, filing cabinet, and a kick-ass audio system were on the opposite wall. The small kitchen area had an electric kettle and a coffeemaker that allowed her to brew a pot or use a pod for a single cup. As if. She was a two-pot-a-day girl. Coffee, tea didn't matter as long as it was hot and intense. *Just like her man.*

"I can't believe this. It's amazing." Delia spotted not one but two kilns in the back and rushed toward them. One would be perfect for her smaller works and the other for her more substantial pieces. Both were top of the line and so out of her price range. Next, she inspected the shelves stocked with glazes, tools, more clay than she ever had at one time, and enough heavy-duty plastic to cover any size piece she might create. She'd described a simple workbench to Denny, but ran her hand across a beautiful piece of craftsmanship. Heck, even the wedging table was better than she'd requested. It was the perfect height, and Denny had stretched heavy canvas over the cement board. Delia took in every inch of the room, staring at everything she'd ever wanted or could need.

"Do you like it?" Glen asked, drawing her attention. Outwardly, Glen appeared relaxed and confident, but she knew he perused her, looking for any sign she wasn't happy.

"I love it. Never in my imagination did I think I'd ever have a studio like this. Thank you."

"You don't have to thank me." Glen picked up a drawing pad from Denny or Rose's desk. "Go on, check out everything." He flipped through the drawing pad.

Delia should call Glen on being nosey, but...later. Much later, after she seduced him a few times. She headed over to the garage door and slid the lock in place. Part one of her plan was securing every entry. Not getting cockblocked this time. Glen was so engrossed in his snooping he didn't bother looking up as she locked the door behind him. She leaned against the door, watching him slowly turn the pages. "What are you looking at?"

Glen looked up and held out the pad to her. *Her* sketch pad. "Is this how you see my daemon?"

Delia studied the drawing she'd made of Glen in his other form. "I find you very attractive in both forms."

"There will be no living with him."

Delia laughed and took the sketch pad from him. "I thought I lost this in the fire.

"One of the firefighters found it under some debris. The pages were singed, and it had water damage, but Fred thought he could salvage it for you."

"He did an excellent job. I need to do something for Victoria. If she hadn't convinced me to move my other sketchbooks and the few models I had to your facility, I would have lost them. I can't get over the fact Scott wants me dead. He has nothing to gain from my death."

"He will never get to you again. I swear it." Glen slipped the pad from her fingers and placed it on the drafting table. "Are there any changes you'd like to make?"

"Yes. Yes, there is."

"Oh?" Glen tilted his head as he frowned. "What?"

"You have on too many clothes."

"Do I?" His eyes instantly turned red.

"You do." She grinned, stepping closer to him.

Glen slipped his arms around her waist. "Is that why you locked all the doors? Because I know where a perfectly wonderful bed is waiting to be broken in." He hugged her closer to him. His arousal pressed against her.

"I know, but Paul and Cade—"

"Won't interrupt us." Glen lowered his head, brushing his lips against hers. "What do you say?"

"Here. Now." His eyes turned so dark they were nearly black, and his fangs peeked from below his lip. "Glen, I want to be mated to you before someone tries to kill me again."

"Never," he roared. "Mine."

She reached up and cupped his face in her hands. "We have a nice platform and some blankets for you to make me yours."

His lips contorted, fighting a grin. "Are you sadistic?"

"I don't know if I should cry right now or punch you. You're really killing my sexy mood."

Glen's deep baritone laugh echoed in the room as he swept her into his arms. "That's the last thing I want to do. While it looks like one of us will have splinters in their arse, it won't be you."

Glen was right. Denny had made her an incredible platform, but it wasn't sanded to perfection. "We have the furniture blankets."

"Splinters or rug burn?"

He had a point. Furniture blankets were stiff, but... "I'm afraid the second we step out of here—"

"Everyone and their brother will pull us in different directions." He slid her down every hard inch of him. "What we're going to do is this." Glen grabbed one of the folded blankets, arranging it on the platform. He toed off his shoes with a wicked grin, then faced her with his hands on his hips. "Your wish is my command."

"Make love to me, Glen."

The heat burning in Glen's eyes had Delia quivering with anticipation. He made quick work of his clothes, then pulled her shirt over her head.

"You make my knees weak, lass. I have a powerful need to wear your mark and put my mark on you, claiming you for life."

"Wear my mark?" She raised on her toes, teasing his nipple with her tongue, drawing a groan from him.

Glen's response was to flip the front closure of her bra, then shred her panties.

She was naked, and the heated look in Glen's eyes went up a notch. He cupped her breasts in his hands, then lowered his mouth, drawing on her nipple, licking and sucking and sending shivers of desire through her.

Delia ran her fingers through the hair at his nape, holding Glen closer to her, wanting him to do more, touch her more. "Glen, please."

He lapped at her breast once more, then shifted his attention to her other breast. Glen slid one hand down her torso until he cupped her mound. She spread her legs, encouraging him to touch her. His fingers ghosted over her slit, then he began teasing her nub. Her knees nearly buckled when his finger pushed into her.

Delia rode the pleasure of Glen's mouth, sucking and lapping on her breast and his finger stroking and plunging. Her muscles quivered, and she clung to him, unable to distinguish one pleasure from the other but knowing she wanted him. All of him.

Delia slipped a hand between them, circling her fingers around his stiff shaft. She wanted to please him as he did her.

He lifted his mouth from her breast and slipped his fingers from her. She whimpered at the loss.

"I want to come in you." He sat on the platform, drawing her down on top of him.

"Glen, I…" She'd never made love in this position and wasn't sure what to do.

"You're wet, but I'm big." He grinned. "So I'm going to tease your sweet pearl while filling your sweet honey pot."

She glanced at Glen's thick, long cock and knew no matter how ready she was, it would be tight.

Glen caressed her more intently until she squirmed, and her body only wanted him. Tugging on her hips, Glen slowly lowered her down onto his cock. The burning stretch was almost too much. He held her halfway down his thick shaft, his thumb teasing her nub until she couldn't stand it anymore, and she sheathed him entirely.

Glen sat up, the motion pushing him deeper, and she gasped, but not as much as when he latched onto her breast again. He rocked his hip so rhythmically she dug her nails into his shoulders. She buried her face against his neck, nipping and sucking where Glen's throat met his shoulder. Each time she nibbled, he thrust deeper, hitting her sweet spot. Delia wrapped her arms around him and bit, puncturing Glen's skin. He roared and sank his fangs deep. Her orgasm whipped through her. Each time he drew on her neck, the sensations intensified, sweeping her away on pulsating waves of sensation and emotion into blissful oblivion.

Strange visions of historical events again streamed through her mind, followed by carefree holidays and family celebrations. Instead of watching Glen's life this time, she lived it. She felt his pain, wonder, humility, and joy. As her tremors subsided, Delia dimly realized Glen had also experienced her life.

She leaned back in his arms and gazed at his horned visage. "Stop it."

Glen opened his eyes and his dark red orbs collided with her. "He murdered your child. I felt—"

She kissed him. "We can't change the past. We can only live and enjoy our future. I'm yours, you're mine, and we'll be together for a very long time."

"How did I get so lucky?"

"Losing a stupid bet." She laughed.

"Cheeky." Glen licked his bite mark on her neck. She gasped as inner muscles clenched around his shaft.

A wicked laugh erupted from him as he slowly moved inside her again.

Delia arched her back, peering up at the skylight. Her attention focused on the black object hovering overhead. "A freakn' drone! Are you kidding me?"

Chapter Twenty-Five

Glen peered up. He wasn't a voyeur, and he sure as hell didn't want anyone watching him, especially with his mate naked and straddling him. It didn't matter that the room was dark, and there was a film over the skylight, blocking anyone from seeing through the glass. Delia was naked, for his eyes only. Whoever was flying the bloody contraption would die.

He reached beside him, snagging another furniture blanket. The action had him slipping from Delia's warmth, drawing a displeased huff from her.

Yes, the jobby would die. Painfully. Glen tugged the stiff, rough covering around Delia's shoulders. This was not how he wanted their mating to end.

Cade, Paul, what the bloody hell is going on?

A million tiny bits of black plastic and metal rained down, sounding like an out-of-tune wind chime.

Neighborhood teens being nosey. We have the situation under control and will deal with the pissed-off parents if they show up. Paul's voice resonated in Glen's mind. *By the way, congratulations!*

Thank you. Notify me if the parents show.

Um, seriously? Delia's voice joined the conversation in his head. She cupped his face with both hands. When their eyes met, he didn't need the mating bond to know his gorgeous pissed-off mate had been in his mind the entire time he and Paul spoke.

Wow! You're a fast learner. Don't worry, we won't bother you. Chuckling, Paul faded from Glen's mind.

If Glen learned one thing from his father, it was how to grovel. "You're right, *mo gràdh*."

Delia arched her brows. "Paul said he and Cade had the situation under control. Are they not your best agents? Then let them do their job."

"I don't trust anyone a hundred percent with your safety. You are more precious to me than air."

"I love you, too. But if it happens again, I'll be dusting off my toys."

"Do I hear a challenge?"

His feisty mate pushed upward and latched onto his mate mark, instantly waking up his flaccid cock. Delia tilted her head, peering up at him. A devilish grin curved her lush lips before her slender hand slipped between them and circled his shaft.

He cupped her breast, toying with her nipple, enjoying how it pebbled. He leaned forward, nipping at her mate mark. Satisfaction surged through him as she moaned against his chest. "Challenge accepted," he whispered.

***

Glen had loved his lady well, but apparently not well enough because he no longer held a warm woman in his arms. He was cold and cracked open an eye, followed by the other. Faint light glowed from around the bathroom door, but Delia wasn't in the bathroom. She wore one of his t-shirts and sat against the headboard with her knees drawn up, resting her sketch pad on them. He drew a deep breath, pushing up and resting his back against the headboard. He wasn't bothered Delia had retrieved her pad. It bothered him he hadn't sensed her leaving their bed. Then again, he'd gotten up to speak with Paul and Cade, leaving her fast asleep. "I thought we left that in the studio."

"We did. But I woke up and needed to draw the image in my mind before I lost it." She smiled at him and scooted closer. "I guess Cade sensed my frustration because I heard him in my mind telling me to give him a second. Then he tapped on our door, leaving my pad leaning against it. Sorry if I woke you."

"You were frustrated?" He was furious at himself for not sensing Delia's distress.

"Frustrated might be too strong of a word, and don't blame yourself for not waking up." Closing the pad, Delia placed it on the nightstand, then snuggled against him. "I don't know if you gleaned this bit of info from my brain, but I usually wake up at night and doodle. Some of my doodlings have become sculptures. Tonight's the first time since my exhibit that I've been relaxed enough for my mind to dream. Anyway, I usually keep a pad next to the bed."

"Fred didn't pack it?" Odd. If the Irish ginger stole Delia's drawings, he'd soon be nothing but ash.

"Freddie and his team packed everything exactly how it was in my room. Dust and all. So you don't have to kill him. Besides, I like Freddie."

"You like Fred? Maybe I will kill him."

She chuckled. "You can't kill all of your employees that I like."

He could, but he'd keep that to himself.

Delia rolled her eyes and patted his cheek. "That's sweet in a creepy way. But if you killed everyone, you'd have to do all the work, leaving you with no time to make love with me."

"I'd make time for that."

"Besides, keeping Freddie around would be handy, as I'm so not Susie Homemaker, and he'd mentioned something about a cleaning service, which doesn't require the removal of a body."

"I use his crew twice a week for the same reason. Love a clean place. Just don't like cleaning. But that doesn't answer why your drawing pad wasn't next to your bed." Had Scott been in Delia's house without her knowledge?

"Relax. Scott didn't creep into the house. It was next to my bed until…Oh, gosh. Um, the night I branded you." Delia trailed a finger down his chest.

Instinctively, Glen touched his mate mark and shivered. "That was tonight."

"No, silly. The night I couldn't sleep, and you found me wedging clay. Remember, you had my handprints all over your black jeans. You're not wearing jeans now." Her delicate fingers circled his shaft. Delia licked her lips, then eased down his body.

"Oh, bloody hell!" he gasped as her luscious lips pressed against the head of his dick. Delia sucked him harder than a bloody vac. He arched his back, threading his fingers into her hair, pressing her closer.

Her mouth slid up and down while her magical fingers tapped the sensitive area behind his balls. His bloody daemon roared with pleasure.

Delia's brilliant tongue tantalized and stroked the length of him. Then she…she pressed her teeth against his head while squeezing his base with her hand. She caressed and teased him, her fingers getting awful close to his— "By the Saints, Delia!"

The pleasure had him shivering with need. His release was so damn close it burned.

The minx peered up at him with his dick in her mouth to his root. She flashed a smile, her teeth holding him tight in her mouth. The sight nearly had him coming.

Delia sucked, becoming more demanding as she cupped his balls. She gently squeezed and rolled them while continuing a rhythm, nearly killing him. He never wanted her to stop.

Then she tapped his forbidden hole. The ecstasy of his release tore through him. He gripped the bedding to keep from digging his claws into her head. He rode out each wave until he was utterly sated and blissfully spent.

Delia allowed his dick to slip from her lips, then she softly kissed the flaccid flesh before grinning at him. "Enjoyed that, did you?"

Her chaste kiss was all it took to have him hard again. She looked so sexy in his t-shirt with her hair rumpled from his fingers. She'd look even better, naked. Glen ripped the thin fabric from her, then rolled her onto her back. He kissed her, tasting himself on her lips. It was an aphrodisiac, making him so hard his shaft burned. He broke off their kiss, drawing a whimper from her. The sound urged him on. He sucked and toyed with her nipples, making her squirm beneath him. Slowly, he moved his lips down her soft body, branding her skin with feather-light kisses. Glen paid homage to every scar, blemish, mole, and freckle, memorizing her gorgeous body. Damn, he was a lucky bastard.

Glen moved even lower, and Delia spread her legs in invitation. He loved her, bringing her to completion. Before the tremors of her release ended, he pushed up and buried his shaft deep within her warmth. Delia cried out his name as she dug her short nails into his back and clamped her teeth down on his shoulder, which had him returning the bite.

Glen didn't know how often they'd made love, but he was a little drunk from her blood. He made his way back to her, crawling over the foot of the bed until he lay beside her. Delia instantly snuggled against him, resting her head on his chest. She threw her leg over his and sighed contentedly. He'd loved his lady thoroughly and well.

"Yes, you did, lover. I've been well wedged," she murmured, falling back asleep.

His sweet mate had mastered the art of strolling through his mind with no problem. He laughed, enjoying the knowledge she easily heard his thoughts. He kissed her crown before tucking her against him, where she belonged for as long as the Creator granted them. Glen prayed it would be for an extremely long time.

A shrill, irritating sound jolted Glen awake. After the third ring, the insidious noise ceased. Delia groaned. She squirmed, nuzzling against him. Her warm breath fanned his chest, pebbling his nipples. Delia's bloody ring tone could wake the dead, but not her.

The shrill noise started again.

"For the love of—Why won't people leave us alone?" Delia rolled on top of him, snatched his phone, and launched it at the door. "Good grief, it's not even eight yet."

He laughed. A soul-warming laugh. Glen couldn't love Delia more. "My bonny lass, it's your phone that's ringing. Not mine." He arched his brow, pointing toward his phone on the floor.

"Sorry. But it didn't sound like my phone." Delia dropped her head to his chest. The hideous noise sounded again, and she grabbed her phone. "Good grief. I guess it was. I have a ton of missed text messages from Tara, plus three missed calls from her. Doesn't the woman ever sleep? As for Edna, she sent a text saying she and Whitaker were heading to the house to go through the stuff she wants to keep, donate, or toss." Delia flopped back down, clutching her phone to her ear. "Tara's umpteenth text messages and voicemails are about her wanting to meet up today for lunch."

"If you don't want to meet her, tell her you don't have time." Delia wouldn't if he had anything to do with it. Waking up with a warm naked woman in his arms had him thinking perhaps they should spend the day in bed.

Delia rolled to her side, pillowing her head on his chest. "I like how you think, but I've been putting Tara off long enough, and I want to spend time with Edna and help her go through the house. She said there were things she wanted us to have. I can't imagine what, though." She sighed, fanning her warm breath across Glen's chest. He could quickly get used to waking up with Delia on top of him. She lifted her head, meeting his eyes. "After Edna and Whitaker leave, we can spend the day in bed. Besides, this bed is a mess from where someone shredded the sheets."

"Good thing I can afford to buy new sheets." He grinned and folded his arms behind his head.

"Smartass." Delia rolled from him, tossed the covers back, and slid from the bed. "I need another shower."

Glen could join her, but that would only lead them back to bed again.

And why is that a bad idea? His pain in the arse daemon demanded to know. As did his dick.

Because she didn't invite us, our lady needs some alone time. But we could dress and ensure our mate has coffee and a hot scone.

Another even more irritating noise blasted through the room.

Delia flung open the bathroom door. "That's not my phone. What is that horrendous sound? A fire alarm?"

"I thought it was your ring tone, but I think it's our doorbell."

"Oh, hell no. We're getting rid of that today." Delia slung the door closed.

Glen retrieved his phone and sent Vaughn a quick text. *Payback's a bitch.* Send.

LMFAO was his reply.

Laughing, Glen dressed, then headed downstairs.

Loud voices rose from the entry, and he paused on the landing, listening. Great. The pissed-off mother grousing about her kid's destroyed toy. She should have taught him about invading people's privacy.

Glen slipped into the kitchen.

Boss. Cade's angry voice echoed in Glen's head. *The cat wants to claw her face.*

You and Paul deal with it and fix that bloody doorbell. Glen turned on the electric kettle. As the water heated, he opened the cabinet near the sink, taking down his favorite tin of Earl Grey. When Fred handled Glen's move, he always knew where to find things. "Now, let's hope there're scones in the refrigerator."

"Don't tell me that's a dog. I know better. It's a wolf, and I'm calling animal control!" A woman shrieked.

Glen shut the refrigerator. He'd best intervene before he had to bail Paul out from animal services.

"I see you've never seen a Tamaskan before," Delia said softly.

Too soft for Glen's liking. When the women in his family used that tone, someone always died. Literally.

He rushed to the entry, finding Paul in his wolf, leaning against Delia. She wore a white t-shirt and faded distressed jeans that hugged her bum nicely. Her shoulder-length brown hair was still wet from her shower, and she was barefoot. Delia scratched Paul behind his ears with one hand as she extended the other, holding a clear bag containing the bits and pieces of the destroyed drone.

"I understand why Vaughn didn't move here." Glen took the bag from Delia and looped his arm around her waist, ignoring Cade's chuckle.

Glen sized up the woman and kid, darkening their doorway. He'd dealt with people like them before. The parents had more money than aptitude and assumed the world needed to bow down to them. The kid knew mommy and daddy would bail him out of any trouble. Same as Luka. He hoped this kid didn't come to the same end. "Good morning. I'm Glen MacPhee, and my wife, Delia. You are?"

"Pissed," the woman shouted.

We're not married yet, lover. Delia's voice purred in his mind.

Minor detail.

Glen drew in a deep, calming breath. He refused to allow anything or anyone to ruin his post-mating high. "Fine. What are you upset about?"

"As I was telling him." The woman jabbed her well-manicured nail at Cade, drawing a snarl from Paul. She glared at him, taking a step back. "Your dog destroyed a costly item. You will pay for it."

You told them our dog destroyed it? Glen sent his thoughts to Cade.

What? You wanted us to tell the crazy bitch we shot it down?

Glen shook his head, regretting moving Delia into the neighborhood. "A drone on our property, hovering around our windows. We'll get to that in a minute. As for this gentleman, he is one of my top employees. I neglected to mention I own and operate Daemon Security." Glen barely met Cade's eyes. "Report."

Cade pulled a pair of latex gloves from his pocket and a screwdriver. "According to the HOA and police department, there have been several complaints about drones buzzing residences in this neighborhood." He stepped out onto the porch and removed the doorbell. "After filing complaints, their homes and properties were vandalized."

The woman's face grew redder as each word fell from Cade's mouth.

"Are you accusing *my* son of being the vandal?" If the woman screeched any higher, Glen might have to kill her to protect his hearing. "Are. You?" she demanded.

The kid smirked, puffing out his chest. "Yeah, are you?"

Delia tsked, shaking her head. "You don't see a problem with your son flying a drone around someone's windows? You don't see this as a tad intrusive?"

The woman huffed and rolled her eyes. "When can we expect payment?"

"I believe there's a cup of tea with my name on it." Delia patted Glen's chest, then strolled toward the kitchen.

"As for payment." He met the woman's ire-filled eyes. "Never." And shut the door.

"How about Westminster chimes?" Cade asked.

Glen nodded and sought Delia. He found her at the kitchen bar with her elbows on the counter and her head in her palms.

She sighed and looked up. "I really love this house. But I'm warning you, I am over being bullied and harassed. If that woman is an example of the neighbors we'll have, I may start using them as armatures."

"Duly noted. I'll keep Fred and his crew on standby."

Chapter Twenty-Six

Delia was hotter than Hell, furious with herself for never fighting back. Hell, she didn't know if she had a fight response. Flight, yes. Fight…Hell. Maybe if she'd learned to fight back as a child, Scott would have left her alone all these years.

Glen squeezed her hand but didn't say a word. She turned away, staring out the window. He'd asked Cade to drive through the neighborhood, wanting to get a feel for the area.

"This is a nice place," she said, breaking the silence.

"It is, but if you want to move, we will."

If she said yes, she'd be running away again. "Both my parents abhorred confrontation. They always stressed my life would be easy if I put all my energy into art and not conflict. If I had a penny for each time one told me persuasion wins over force, I'd be a zillionaire instead of a doormat."

"Delia," Glen said her name on an exhale. "You're not a doormat. Choosing to walk away from a fight is often the bravest thing a person can do. This morning, you didn't argue with that woman. You didn't lower yourself to her level. You walked away. That alone told her she cannot intimidate you."

"I used to love people. In high school, I was a social butterfly. After I married Scott, I didn't realize how much he'd isolated me from my friends and family." Delia blinked, tears threatening to spill. "Scott even threw a fit when my parents died. He didn't want me to fly back to Georgia for their funeral, saying we were trying to start a family and the time away could mess that up. Even if deep down he never wanted children. The sad part, I stayed married to him, thinking it was just my imagination." She faced Glen, fearing the contempt she'd see in his eyes but saw only love and compassion burning in them. She scooted closer and leaned her head against his shoulder. "I don't ever want to be the person Scott made me. I want to enjoy life and live every day to its fullest. I want to connect with people." She sighed, knowing having close friendships with humans might not be possible. She was, however, grateful for the friendships she'd already forged with Dani and Rose and was looking forward to one with Karma, Morgan's mate.

A faint smile graced Glen's mouth, and he wrapped his arm around her shoulders. "Well, my beautiful Monarch, today you have busted free of your chrysalis. Just remember, I will always be your thistle."

"My mate, the smooth-talking poet."

"I'm no Rabbie Burns." Glen brushed a strand of hair behind her ear. "Is that the reason you agreed to meet with Tara today? To reconnect with her?"

Delia shrugged. That was part of the reason, but... "I feel a little sorry for her. Tara was one of those girls who wanted to please everyone in the world." Delia cupped Glen's chin, turning his face towards hers. She pressed a kiss to his lips. "Thank you for offering to treat us to Francine's. I was racking my brain trying to find a place for us to meet, and I think it made her happy you were joining us."

"Trust me, I had ulterior motives for suggesting it. Mainly because I'm craving crawfish etouffee and some bread pudding."

"Hopefully, this won't take long with Edna. I don't want to keep Tara waiting. I told her we'd meet at 2:30, but I feel she'll be there way before us."

"I wouldn't imagine it will take Edna long to mark the items she wants to be shipped overseas and anything she wants to give to a few of her friends."

"You don't know Edna." Delia laughed and patted Glen's thigh. "I feel we'll be coming back to finish up after eating."

"You realize we'll be flying to England several times a year. A perk of having a private jet at your disposal."

"I do." Delia stared out the window as they drove into the neighborhood. Britney's house had a small moving truck parked in the drive. Scott stood by the driver's door, facing off with Britney's father. Neither man looked happy.

"Odd." Glen frowned, leaning forward in the seat. "Percy isn't here?"

"He rang, saying Fiona asked if he'd run by the office." Cade stopped in front of Edna's home. The garage door was open, but there wasn't a car in the driveway. "I told him we'd left and would be here soon. However, that was before you decided to cruise through the new neighborhood. And shit. Don't look now, but our favorite police detective has pulled behind us. Want me to stay?"

"Nope." Glen unfastened his seat belt. "Drop this off with Angus, then be back by 1:30. I don't want to risk someone following us."

"You insult me." Cade huffed. "As if I wouldn't make a tail."

"Not doubting your abilities, just telling you what I want done." Glen held out his hand to Delia.

"Detective. Have you discovered anything new?" She slid from the vehicle, finding herself trapped between Glen, the opened door, and Detective Gannon.

"No, ma'am." Gannon took a step back, allowing her to ease away from the vehicle and Glen to close the door. "I just have a few questions for MacPhee."

Glen slipped his arm around her waist as he stared past Gannon. "You don't need Delia?"

"No," Gannon replied, following Glen's line of sight. Now both men stared at Scott. "I just have a few questions for you, and if you don't mind, I would like to run a theory by you." Gannon turned back to her. "In private, if you don't mind."

Scott slammed the door to the truck and headed toward them. "I have something to say!"

"That's my cue to go help Edna." Delia rose and kissed Glen firmly on the lips. "Don't kill him. I'll need you to rescue Whitaker and me from Edna." She strolled toward the house.

"No promises." Glen's deep laugh rang in her wake.

Delia paused with her hand resting on the doorknob. Melancholy darkened her heart for the first time since realizing Edna was leaving. It wasn't like Delia would never see her aunt again. In fact, Glen assured her they'd be flying to England and Scotland several times a year. Still, this was a significant change.

Chin up, Delia, she told herself as she took a deep breath and squared her shoulders. She opened the door, stepping over the threshold.

"Edna." Delia's foot stumped against a box by the door. Lying on top was a scrapbook she'd not seen for years. Picking it up, she read the sticky note attached to the cover.

> *Whitaker explained how Glen would live your life through the blood connection, but I thought he'd enjoy seeing you as I have all these years.*
> *Love you, Edna.*

Delia flipped through the pages of her life. Everything was there. Pictures of her holding her first art award in grade school, getting her driver's license, and summer vacations. Her dad wearing his favorite horrendous glow-in-the-dark orange socks with his sandals. Her mom, grandmother, and Edna standing in the kitchen laughing about something. Delia turned another page. The picture was her selfie in front of Auguste Rodin's bronze statues of Calais' Burghers. She turned another page, then another, and gasped. She didn't know an art critic was at her exhibit the other night. But Edna had found his review and printed it. It was the accompanying photo Delia couldn't stop staring at. She had no idea when it was taken, and perhaps it had been photoshopped, but she looked younger and so happy and full of life. The picture was of her standing with Glen beside *The Guardians of the Isle,* and in the background was Edna smiling, standing beside Whitaker.

Delia, what's wrong? Glen's voice echoed in her mind.

I'm fine. Just...I'm fine.

She closed the book and set it back on the box. She'd go through the rest of the stuff later. Delia laughed as she looked around the living room. "Lord have mercy." Every object had a sticky note with either the word ship or a person's name. The sticky note on the needlepoint pillow Edna had a fit over, read, '*Get your money back.*' Poor Fred, he and his crew didn't know what they'd be dealing with when it came to Edna.

"Edna, I'm here," Delia shouted, heading toward the steps. She paused and peeked into the kitchen, laughing at the sight before her. Just like in the living room, sticky notes covered everything. Perhaps Glen should buy stock.

Already own shares, his deep warm laugh sounded in her mind. *Bubble wrap, too.*

She laughed, examining Edna's ruby Wedgwood teacup and saucer. Someone had wrapped it in enough bubble wrap, Delia doubted it would break if it was dropped from the top of Big Ben.

"Edna, I'm coming up the steps." Better to warn Edna and Whitaker, just in case. Delia's hand touched the wall. The family photos were gone. Odd. It'd been years since Delia paid them any attention, but now that they were no longer there, she missed them.

She paused on the steps as memories of the holidays ran through her mind. The many times she and Edna hung garland on the step banisters and along the loft railing for Christmas. Edna loved decorating and had a treasure trove of holiday decorations, from Christmas ornaments to Easter eggs to Halloween ghosts squirreled away in the attic.

"Edna," Delia hollered once more as she ambled up the steps. It wasn't like Edna not to answer. Maybe she and Whitaker *were* taking the bed for a spin. Bad image. Bad, bad image. They were probably in the attic, going through all the holiday decorations. Poor Royce, there's no way Edna would be ready to leave on time.

Edna's bedroom door creaked open.

"Edna, Whit—Tara?"

"Surprised to see me?" Tara grinned, closing Edna's door. "Your aunt wanted me to tell you she and her friend were tied up."

Nothing like being blindsided. "I see. Did I miss a text?" Delia cringed at the tone of her voice. Hadn't she told Glen she felt sorry for Tara?

"I don't know. Did you?" Tara volleyed back.

"I'm sorry, Tara. I don't mean to sound snippy. It's just today didn't start out on a great note."

"Problem with the boyfriend? I saw him drive off." Tara's smile slowly turned creepy, sending chills down Delia's back and raising the hair on her neck.

Delia plastered a smile, hoping it appeared sincere. *Glen, we may have a problem.* God, she hoped he was listening. "No, nothing like that, Tara. Just one of those mornings where Murphy was playing havoc. But, yeah, I am a little surprised at seeing you here. I thought I'd mentioned I was helping Edna pack this morning."

"You did," she singsong. Her expression grew creepier by the second.

Glen, Tara's here, and I'm getting the creepies. Big time.
Let me get rid of Gannon.
Hurry, please.

Tara eased away from Edna's doorway, turning and blocking the rest of the hall. "I came by early so we'd have more time to catch up. You've been so occupied lately. I was afraid you'd *ditch* me." Tara's grin turned into a sneer. "Again."

Hell, she'd be upset if she were in Tara's place. Heat rushed to Delia's face, and she didn't need a mirror to know she was beet red.

"You don't seem happy to see me." Tara's laser-point gaze focused on Delia, studying every inch of her face for what? A sign of fear? Subterfuge? "Or is your lack of expression due to all your plastic surgeries?"

Delia smiled at the comment meant as an insult. "No plastic surgeries, just good genes."

"Of course, it's good genes. You always came out on top."

Delia had enough of acidic people for one day. Hell, she'd had enough for a lifetime. "Look, Tara, I'm sorry we lost touch after school. I'm sorry I haven't been able to spend much time with you, but a lot of unforeseen circumstances have occurred in the past weeks that were out of my control. If you want to stay and help Edna and me, I'd appreciate it. But if you don't want, I understand. Glen and I will meet you for lunch."

"Do you hear yourself, Cordy? Everything is about you. It's always been about *you*."

"Tara, I don't know what's going on, but I think it's time for you to leave." Delia took a step back, pressing against the wall, giving Tara room to leave.

Glen, where the hell are you?

Trying to get rid of Gannon.

"You want me to leave?" Tara's voice rose. "You don't get what you want this time, Cordy."

"You know the way out." Delia balled her fist as tension filled her, tightening her muscles. She didn't know what was going on with Tara, but enough was enough. Delia squared her shoulders and stepped toward Edna's room. A bloody fingerprint on the doorframe forestalled her momentum.

"Edna!"

A vicious laugh filled the hall. "I told you she's tied up." Tara glanced at the doorframe. "Oops. I guess I missed that." Her mouth twisted in anger as hate descended over her face. She reached behind her, withdrawing a gun, aiming it at Delia.

Glen, Tara has a gun.

Chapter Twenty-Seven

Glen enjoyed watching Gannon volley inquiry after inquiry at Scott, who squirmed worse than a child having to pee. The jobby sang the same old song. He had nothing to do with any of the attacks on Delia. But as much as Glen enjoyed the show, his mate needed him.

"Anything else, Gannon?"

"Hold on a sec, MacPhee. Look, Mr. Haynes, who did if you didn't have anything to do with the attacks?" Gannon held up a clenched fist. "Buffy Smith—killed in a road-rage incident." Gannon stuck up his thumb. "Katherine Higgins—paralyzed and left unable to communicate from a home invasion." Another finger went up. "Amy Boil—missing and presumed dead, Britney Goldman nearly died from carbon monoxide poisoning, and we have Cordelia Parsons. Five women." Gannon waved his open hand. "Five. Count them. Five women. *All* involved with you. So, tell me, who would want to harm these women?"

"How the hell should I know? As for my crazy ex, maybe she staged her attacks. She blames me for everything, anyway."

Zeus, Glen's daemon, struggled to break free. How dare the pathetic human slander their mate?

Glen stifled the growl rising in his throat. They couldn't kill Scott in front of witnesses, but later the man would die. Slowly, methodically, and painfully.

Zeus couldn't wait. Neither could Glen.

Gannon removed his fedora and wiped his brow. "Haynes, you're a magnet for unlucky, accident-prone females."

Glen, where the hell are you?

Trying to get rid of Gannon. Turning, Glen tossed his hand up. "When you're ready, I'll be inside."

"I said wait," Gannon barked.

"I've heard enough," Glen shot back.

Gannon's lips thinned as he studied Glen. "Before you go, I have one more question for you and Haynes." He pulled a photo from his coat, showing the picture first to Delia's ex. "Recognize this guy?"

Scott barely glanced at the picture. "Never seen him before."

"Take a closer look." Gannon shoved the picture at Haynes, nearly smacking him in the nose. "Maybe he's been at one of your art exhibits."

He shoved Gannon's hand away. "Like I said. I've never seen him before."

"What about you, MacPhee? Ever seen this guy?" Gannon turned the photo, giving Glen a better view.

Glen recognized the arse. "His date called him Wally." The longer Glen studied the photo, the more familiar the face grew. He glanced at Scott, then back to the photograph. The eyes were the same shape and color, and they had the same chin. Coincidence? Maybe. Wally was slightly taller and more muscular than Scott but still had a similar build. Perhaps Scott had the same shape when he was younger. Damn, he wished they'd had a better picture of the person who'd stabbed Delia. Even when he pressed into Delia's mind, her memory was blurry. "I don't have proof, but I bet he's the same asshole who shot at Delia and me."

"Did you report it?" Gannon slipped Wally's picture back inside his coat.

"If you're finished, I have things to pack." Scott headed across the yard.

Glen waited, but Gannon didn't call Haynes back. Nope, Gannon just glared at Glen. Damn, Gannon's expression made him feel like he'd cheated on him.

"Trammell, the day she cautioned me about Edik Petrov."

Gannon's lips thinned. "Damn feds. They're not supposed to interfere with a case unless we ask them! Guess they confiscated the cartridges."

"They wanted the vehicle too, but Trammell's men couldn't pry Angus's fingers from the bumper."

"Damn, MacPhee. You've got some crazy ass people working for you."

He wouldn't call them crazy, maybe a little eccentric, okay, a lot eccentric, but not crazy. "I trust each of them with Delia's life and mine."

Delia's panic slammed into him as her words froze his blood. *Glen, Tara has a gun.*

Glen sprinted toward the house, hitting the door with such force it flew open. He continued his momentum, vaulting up the steps until Delia's alarmed gaze collided with his. He stopped short, coming face to face with a crazy woman pointing a gun at Delia's head.

A woman who was responsible for burning down Delia's studio with her inside. A woman who stabbed Delia, nearly ending her life. The woman who'd slipped under his radar. A woman about to die.

Tara was thin with red hair and deeply sunken brown eyes, making her complexion pale and pasty. Sickly? Nothing about her screamed a threat. Nothing but the gun in her hand. Once Delia was out of danger, Glen would let his daemon kick his arse for not considering Tara a threat.

A step creaked, and he glanced at Gannon, motioning for him to stay back. Gannon's presence had Glen re-evaluating his next move. He couldn't take Tara down like he wanted. He had to do it like a human.

"Oh, goodie. The boy-toy," Tara sneered, waving her gun at Glen.

She was desperate, and desperate people were dangerous. He had to play this carefully. "Why are you doing this?" Glen kept his voice calm.

Tara sneered, waving the gun back at Delia. "Because she's a thief. Tell him, Cordy. Tell him how you steal everything!"

"I haven't stolen anything," Delia stated. Glen heard her struggle to sound calm.

"Liar!" Tara fired. The bullet barely missed Delia, lodging in the wall above her head.

Glen's daemon roared. He was so focused on Delia that he'd nearly seen her murdered.

"You stay back." Tara aimed her gun at Delia. "Or I'll blow her head off."

Delia straightened and calmly brushed the drywall from her hair and shirt. "What have I stolen from you?"

What the bloody hell was she doing? Antagonizing the bitch was no brilliant idea. When this was over, he and Delia were having a serious talk about how to act around nutters with guns.

The gun trained on Delia shook in Tara's hand, and her eyes grew wilder and wilder with each second. "What you stole?" she screeched. "You've stolen everything from me. The Dyer scholarship they awarded you. Mine! Do you hear me? Mine!"

"What?" Delia whispered.

"Delia," he warned, keeping his attention on the gun.

"If that wasn't enough, you stole Professor Lassitar's TA position. I applied to be her TA, but you weaseled your way in and stole *it*. You stole my job at the Cantor Center. They laid me off, and you were working in my place three days later!"

"Tara, I'm sorry. I didn't know. My counselor suggested I apply. I'm—"

"Liar!" Tara gripped the pistol so hard her hands were red and her knuckles white. "You're such a fucking liar. But you couldn't stop ruining my life there, could you? No, you had to steal Scott from me. He was mine!"

A snort rose from the first floor.

If Haynes caused Delia to get hurt, the man would die.

"Scott told me he wasn't dating anyone."

Delia, stop engaging with her.

"Dating?" Tara shouted. "We were living together. You took him away from *us*. But I got my revenge. I took that brat you carried from you. I wanted you to die that night, but knowing the pain and heartache you endured was even better than your death."

"You," Delia's voice hitched. "You pushed me down the stairs?"

Glen wanted to wrap his arms around her and take away her anguish. But there'd be time later. After he made Tara suffer. He studied the woman, looking for his opening. He could rush her, but he couldn't risk Delia.

Tara cackled. "Of course, it was me. I made sure you suffered. I made sure all the whores who threw themselves at Scott suffered. *He's* mine! But you're not suffering anymore, are you?" She swung the gun in Glen's direction. "What if I take your little boy-toy from you?"

"Don't, Tara. Please." Delia inched in front of him.

The steps creaked again.

What the fuck was Gannon attempting?

"Stop! Stay back! You're not taking this from me!" Tara waved the gun around, pointing it behind Glen. She must be aiming it at Gannon. "Put the gun down, or I swear I'll kill her. Put it down."

"I'm setting it down," Gannon rushed out. "Sliding it away. See. There's no need to hurt anyone, Tara."

A squeak, followed by a crash.

"Who else is in here?" Tara demanded.

"No one," Gannon lied. Glen clearly heard the pounding of a seventh heartbeat. He also heard a faint rustling from Edna's room. "It's just us," Gannon repeated the lie.

"I don't believe you."

"Trust me, Tara. It's just us. Look, I get it. Cordelia is a thief, and she needs to be punished."

What the bloody hell? Glen's daemon focused on Gannon's words, its fury pushing toward the surface.

"Let me arrest her."

"No!" Tara clutched the gun, her finger slowly tightened on the trigger.

Glen lunged, shoving Delia to the floor, covering her with his body as gunfire erupted.

"You barking slapper!" Edna shouted. Volleying another round of bullets.

Tara kicked Glen's arm, and he glanced up. Her eyes were wide, and blood soaked her chest. The gun slipped from her lax fingers, no longer able to grip the weapon. She stumbled backward, striking the banister. The railing cracked, sending Tara crashing to the floor below.

Glen pushed to his feet, reaching for Delia, but she scrambled to her feet and rushed toward Edna.

"*Mo gràdh*, are you okay?" He roared.

"You know I am." Delia tried to take the old rifle from Edna, but she jerked away. "Edna?"

"Not until I'm sure that skank is dead." Edna pushed the words past her swollen lips. Still gripping her old Sten, she peered down through the broken railing. "Been meaning to have that baluster fixed." She shrugged.

"Get her off—get her off," Scott screamed.

Glen gazed down. Scott was prone on his back as he struggled to shove Tara off himself. Her lifeless eyes stared at them.

The sickening odor of fear, urine, and feces had Glen stepping back. He gently took the rifle from Edna's withered hands. "It's over."

"Help Whitty. That ruffian with her worked Whitty over." Tears streamed from Edna's black and swollen eyes. They'd beaten the hell out of her.

The door behind her creaked open, then Whitaker slowly emerged. Edna was at his side, whispering he should have stayed put. His right eye was swollen shut. A hint of a smile graced his bloodied and bruised face. Whitaker wrapped his arms tightly around himself as he leaned against the wall. He coughed, and blood peppered his lips. Sweat beaded his brow as he slid down the wall, resting on the floor.

"Let me *help* you." Glen knelt beside his old friend. A few drops of blood would speed Whitaker's healing.

Whitaker shook his head. "I'm all right. Basher kicked like a babe." He nodded to something or someone behind Glen. "I think he needs you more than me."

"You get a good look at the assailant?" Gannon groaned, gripping his bleeding left shoulder. "MacPhee, show him this photo."

"Gannon, it's covered in blood." Glen applied pressure to Gannon's wound with one hand and pulled out his phone with the other. No sooner had he ended the call than sirens echoed in the house.

"I got a good look at him," Whitaker rasped. "He burst in through the kitchen. Got the drop on me before I could react."

"Dad!" Percy bellowed.

"Help me," Scott wailed.

"He's up here, Percy." Glen met Percy's panicked gaze as he bolted up the steps. "Beaten, but alive." Best to prepare the man.

Fiona and Edgar followed closely behind Percy, running up the steps.

Glen struggled with Gannon as he tried to get to his feet, despite losing an unhealthy amount of blood. "Sit your arse down," Glen ordered

"This is my crime scene, O'Brien," Gannon shouted.

"And my in-laws," Edgar snapped, rushing toward Edna and Whitaker.

"Fine, show him this." Gannon held out the bloody photograph. It slipped from his fingers.

"Don't worry, I'll have one of my men download the security feed." Glen called Cade.

"Pulling—Whoa! What the hell?" Cade exclaimed.

"Download all the security feed. Then I want everyone hunting the bastard."

"On it."

"Dead or alive," Gannon wheezed.

Glen shrugged. "Does it matter?"

Edgar arched his eyebrow and nodded as he stared at Fiona, gently smoothing Whitaker's disheveled hair.

Half of the Atlanta police force filled the house, making it feel tiny. A half a second later, the medics arrived.

Trammell appeared, which had Gannon declaring the crime scene his and his alone with Marks backing him up. Gannon refused to be loaded into the ambulance until he was sure Atlanta PD controlled the crime scene. Edgar and Trammell agreed grudgingly to stop Gannon from getting off the bloody gurney.

Glen. He groaned as Royce's voice boomed in his head. *What's going on? They won't allow me inside. Is Whitaker all right?*

A little worse for wear, but alive. Just be patient. Telling Royce to do that was like telling a fish not to swim.

Who did this?

Working on it. Edna took care of the major threat, but Tara's accomplice is still out there.

The next battle was with Whitaker and Edna. They insisted they were all right and didn't need to go to a hospital.

Delia planted her hands on her hips and glared at Edna. "You will go with these men to be checked out. Do you hear me?"

"We're leaving for England." Edna snapped. Her voice was muffled as she pushed the words past her swollen lips. Edna stretched out her withered hand, reaching for Whitaker's hand. "Where are they taking my rifle?"

"It's evidence, Edna," Delia huffed.

"It's mine, and I'm taking it to England."

"You fired this?" Deneen Trammell asked, astonishment in her tone.

"Who do you think killed the skank? I regret I didn't get her before she shot that sweet young detective."

Trammell glanced over her shoulder at Gannon. "Him?"

"Yeah, me." Gannon laughed as the medics maneuvered him down the steps.

"Well, he's younger than me," Edna replied. "May I have my rifle back?"

"No," Delia and Glen said in unison.

It was wrong to laugh, but bloody hell, Glen couldn't help it.

Edna glared up at him. "But it's mine." She tried to roll out her swollen bottom lip. "I was going to teach my new granddaughter how to fire it."

"We have an anti-aircraft gun you can teach Hope to fire," Percy assured her, causing Trammell to jerk her head toward him. "Delia," Percy continued. "I'll accompany them to the hospital and keep you informed." He nodded to the medic. "I'll ride with them."

"We'll be right behind you," Edgar added.

"Thank you." Delia threw herself at Percy, surprising him.

He hugged her back, bussing her cheek. "We'll take care of them, cuz." He winked, bringing a smile to Delia's face. "You have my word."

"Trammell, Marks," Edgar called. "If you need me, you'll know where to find me." He wrapped his arm around Fiona's waist as they followed Whitaker and Edna.

When Haynes spotted them, he demanded medical attention, insisting he was dying from a broken back, even if he stood and stomped his foot like a child. "I'm in pain. I had a dead woman fall on me." He stomped his foot again. "I will sue every last one of you for your lack of concern."

"Lack of concern," Delia repeated.

Bloody hell. Before Glen could pull her back, Delia stood toe to toe with Scott.

"Lack of concern, you egotistical, narcissistic asshole! Because of your constant lies and infidelity, you created that psychopath. Because of *you*—"

Glen slipped his arm around Delia's waist, pulling her away from Scott. They already had one dead body.

"I should sue you for slander. I had nothing to do with this," Scott sneered.

Delia jerked free. "Bull! Because of you, Buffy is dead, Katherine is a vegetable, and Amy has been missing for fifteen years. Their blood is on your hands. Add in what happened to Britney."

"I wasn't near Brit when she stupidly left the car running."

"You always have a damn alibi!" Tears streamed from Delia's face.

"Because I'm innocent. Someone's trying to frame *me*!"

Trammell stepped between Delia and Scott, shoving Scott back. "Someone get him out of here. He reeks of shit, and it's making me sick."

Marks pointed to two uniforms.

Cade shouted, stepping from the kitchen. "You guys need to see this."

"Hold up," Marks barked at the officers leading Scott out. "What do you have?"

Cade motioned toward the kitchen.

Glen tucked Delia against his side as they followed Cade. "You okay?"

"I'm good. Let's get this over with so we can find out how Edna and Whitaker are doing."

He knew Delia wasn't okay. He felt her pain and heartache colliding with today's revelations, tearing her apart from the inside out.

Cade clicked the mouse, bringing up a split-screen, one side showing Tara's approach while the other displayed the backyard. Whitaker opened the door as Edna came into frame. The other screen came on as a person wearing a black hoodie and skeleton mask hopped over the fence. He kicked in the kitchen door, rushing into the living room. Whitaker quickly reacted, striking the intruder and knocking off the mask. Cade froze the screen.

"I don't think Delia needs to see the rest. But as you can see, it's our dear friend Wally from the nightclub. Now, here's the real shocker." He clicked the mouse again, bringing up Wally's California Driver's license with the name of Walter Browning Haynes.

"I paid that bitch to get rid of it," Scott murmured from behind them.

Chapter Twenty-Eight

Exhaustion wore on Delia standing in the darkened room. She looked away as Percy stuck the needle into Edna's arm, glancing back as he hung a blood bag over a picture hook. "Six months ago, if someone told me supernatural beings existed, I'd think they were insane."

"I can understand," Percy replied. "You understand why I didn't argue when Father and Edna insisted on leaving the hospital. We couldn't very well heal them and not raise questions." Percy moved to the other side of the bed to examine his father. Whitaker rested against a pile of pillows. His cuts and contusions had already healed.

"Question." Delia stared at Edna, watching her bruises finally fade. "Why did she need a second blood bag before she healed when Whitaker only needed one bag and he had more severe injuries?" The man had several broken ribs.

Whitaker gently took Edna's hand in his. "I've received blood over the years from the family, whereas Edna only received it once." He reached over and brushed a strand of hair from her face. "She'll be right as rain by morning."

Nodding, Percy checked Edna's pulse. "Good. She's in the healing sleep. I'll check back in a few." He motioned toward the door. "For now, let's let her rest."

Whitaker glanced at Delia. "Now that I have my Eddie back." He pressed a kiss to Edna's temple. "I'll not let any harm come to her."

"She'll be fine." Percy gently squeezed Delia's shoulder. "Come along. You need to relax, too."

"You're right." She sighed.

"I'm always right." Percy winked.

Delia glanced back at Edna and Whitaker before following Percy from the room.

Glen pulled her into his arms as she entered the living room. "You're exhausted."

"Mentally. Physically. Pinch me, please, so I can wake up from this nightmare."

"The nightmare's over, love."

"No, it's not. Until Tara's accomplice is apprehended, it's not over." It would never truly be over as long as Scott hounded her and Amy remained missing.

Delia and Glen stood in view of everyone. Their expressions ranged from outrage to ones of pity, and she didn't give a damn.

"Do you want to crash here? There's a connecting door to the other apartment. Or do you want to go back to our place?"

"We've ordered takeaway," Percy announced. "You should eat something before you lie down."

Delia nodded. Her adrenaline rush from earlier was gone, leaving her bone-weary and numb. Food was the furthest thing from her mind. Sleep…She glanced up at Glen. "You know the answer."

"I do." He brushed a kiss on her forehead. "Do you think you can last long enough for Trammel to arrive? She's on her way with news about Wally."

"I thought someone was hunting him?" Delia sank down onto the overstuffed couch, allowing her body to be absorbed by the cushions. She exhaled, closing her eyes.

Soft male murmurs teased her mind. Lord Royce could speak mentally to everyone. Did he have to hold court? Yes, yes, he did. He was worried about her and Glen. Royce was a softie. Delia really should force her eyes open and join the conversation. She would. In a moment. Just a moment. All she wanted was a moment to shut out the world.

"Dilly," Edna's voice broke through Delia's foggy brain.

"I'm awake. Just closed my eyes for a second." Stretching, Delia opened her eyes and took in the strange room. "Hmm, guess I fell asleep."

"Honey, Percy said you were snoring so loud Glen had to carry you to bed so the guys could speak with Agent Trammel. Personally, I thought it was thunder I was hearing."

"I love you, too." Delia tossed back the covers and slid from the bed. "Let me get a good look at you." Edna didn't show any signs of injury. No swollen lip, black eyes, or even the slightest hint of bruising. "I can't get over how well you look." Maybe it was the room's lighting, but her wrinkles seemed fainter.

Edna's smile slipped. "Because of Whitty's and my fast recovery, we're flying out after breakfast. Royce doesn't want questions raised."

Staring at Edna, Delia saw Royce's reasoning. Her aunt looked a good ten years younger, if not more. "But what about your stuff?"

"They will ship everything not labeled to England, and I'll deal with it there."

"I see." Just because Delia understood didn't mean she liked it. What if she took her time to get dressed? No. She should be happy. It wasn't like they'd never see each other again. Glen had a private jet at his disposal. "Do you know what happened to my clothes?" Delia only wore one of Glen's button-downs.

"Glen asked Fiona and Edgar to swing by your place. I put your things in the bathroom. Now, hurry and get dressed."

"I'll hurry."

***

Why had she rushed? Delia stared at the sky, waving goodbye until she could no longer see Edna. As the plane carrying her away rose higher and higher into the clear blue sky, tears spilled from Delia's eyes. No longer able to see the jet through her tears, she leaned against Glen, tilting her face toward his. "As much as I fussed about Edna lately, I already miss her."

"I know you do." Glen slipped his arm around her waist, leading her back to the awaiting cars.

"Don't worry, love." Fiona handed her a tissue. "You'll see her soon enough."

"I know." Delia forced a smile as she dabbed her eyes.

"We'll follow you back to the office." Glen motioned to Cade, leaning against the massive SUV.

"Brilliant," Fiona exclaimed. "We can all head over to Francine's afterward."

Francine's sounded good, but sitting in Glen's office wouldn't distract Delia from her thoughts. Going through hoarder hell might. "Could you take me home but first swing by Edna's place? I want to grab a box she set aside for me."

"*Mo gràdh,* as long as Tara's accomplice is still out there, I don't want to leave your side."

"We don't have a lead on him yet," Edgar added.

She wouldn't be smothered by Glen, but now wasn't the time to argue. Later, however, she'd point out he couldn't be with her twenty-four-seven. "Fine, but I still want to go by and grab that box."

Glen exhaled, bringing her hand up to his lips. "Edna's place is still a crime scene. I doubt the police will allow you to remove anything."

"Speaking of which." Edgar pointed to a cloud of dust and flashing blue lights heading toward them. "I was wondering how long it would take them."

"Do you think they've found Wally?" Delia looked between Edgar and Glen. Judging from their serious expressions, probably not. "What's going on?" She peered up at Glen. The muscles in his jaw twitched, and his mind was a muddled mess.

"I'd say they've discovered Edna and Whitaker are no longer here," Edgar replied.

"But I thought you said you cleared them to leave."

Edgar shrugged. "I said it was fine with me if they left."

Trammel emerged from the passenger side. "Damn it, O'Brien."

"Give it a rest, Trammell," he bellowed. "This is above your pay grade and mine."

"I want to know where they are." Every degree of rage panned across her face.

"I would say getting ready to fly over international waters," Edgar shot back.

"On whose authority?" Marks demanded as he unfolded himself from the driver's side.

Edgar chuckled. "Now that's the million-dollar question."

"Cut the bullshit," Trammell stormed toward them. "I don't care if you are my superior, O'Brien. I want answers."

"Even if it means your badge? Fine. Douglas woke me at the ass crack of dawn. As to who contacted him…." Edgar shrugged again. "Possibly Livingston with Britain's SIS, or it could have been the Crown. I didn't ask who ordered it. I just did as I was told."

Trammell deflated, concentrating on Glen. "Who the hell were they?"

"They're just two people in love who deserve a chance to be together," Delia replied. "All my life, my aunt has mourned the loss of her love, whom she'd thought died in the war. They've just found each other."

"No." Trammell shook her head. "There's more to your aunt than that. I mean, her skills with a rifle are better than mine. Her pattern was tight. It was close range, but she was firing an antique."

"I'll explain it to you in the car," Edgar said. "You can ride with Fiona and me. Marks, you can follow."

Trammell arched her dark brow. "Where are we going?"

"Back to Daemon," Glen supplied. "Then out to eat. My treat."

On the way to Daemon Securities, Delia kept thinking about what Trammell said concerning Edna. There was more to her aunt than Trammell realized, just not how she thought.

Cade gave a shrill whistle as he pulled into the parking lot. "Please let me kill him as a mating gift."

The late-model black Mercedes taking up three parking spaces had Delia's shoulders knotting. Seeing Scott stop pacing and shoot a hateful glare at them flipped her bitch switch. She was out of the car before Cade had pulled to a complete stop.

"Didn't think I'd look for you here?" Scott shouted at her.

"What are you doing here, Snot?"

He curled his lip. "Suing you."

"For what now? Living my life?"

Glen snagged her upper arm. She jerked free, sparing him a glance and ignoring his glare. She'd allow him to yell at her later, but Scott was getting a piece of her mind, and she'd be damned if anybody would stop her. She'd spent the last fifteen years dealing with his childish temper tantrums. Hell or high water, it ended now.

Scott's eyes nearly bulged out of his head. "For my injuries when you dropped a dead body on me and for your lies getting me evicted from my home."

"We'll see you in court," Glen calmly replied, slipping his arm around her waist and gently tugging her to his side. "Mr. Haynes, you're trespassing. This is private property."

"It's a business," he snarled. "Not a home."

Car tires squealed as a vehicle jumped the curve and sped into the parking lot.

Glen pushed Delia behind him as if his body would protect her from a speeding car. His shoulders expanded, and the threads of his clothes popped, fighting to remain intact.

"Breathe." She smoothed her hand up his back. "It's probably a new client, don't want them to think they're meeting a daemon."

"The ass must think he's in Daytona." Cade chuckled, resting his hand on his sidearm.

"Hey," Scott screamed as the gray Honda blocked his car. "Move your piece of shit."

The Honda's door opened, and a familiar male sprang from it. Everything about him shouted danger. His expression was taut and decisive as he zeroed in on Scott.

"Well, well, looks like we don't have to hunt anymore," Trammell uttered.

Wally stormed toward Scott, wearing black jeans and an all too familiar black hoodie.

"Hands behind your head," Marks shouted.

"On the ground," Trammell ordered, drawing her sidearm.

Wally ignored them, coming nose to nose with Scott. "Hello, Daddy," Sarcasm dripped as he crossed his arms. A large medical bandage was wrapped around Wally's right hand. Delia hoped he'd received the injury from Whitaker.

"I'm not your daddy," Scott spat.

Tension pummeled Delia as the scene unfolded. She wasn't worried about her safety, but about Wally's reaction. Scott was an ass, a hothead, and so blind he couldn't see the pain-driven rage filling Wally. Delia slipped her finger through Glen's belt loop and took a step back, trying to tug him along with her, popping his belt loop.

Glen caught her hand, giving it a firm squeeze. "Get back with Fiona."

"You're right," Wally spat. "You're nothing but a sperm donor and a sorry one, at that."

"Hands behind your head," Marks ordered again, pulling his cuffs free.

Wally glanced at Marks. "Not until I'm done speaking with my *daddy*."

"Stop calling me that." Scott stomped his foot. "I'm not your daddy. I never wanted any brats. I told that talentless twit it was only sex."

"Scott," Glen warned, nudging Delia further from the confrontation.

"She was my mother." Wally's entire body trembled, but his tone was too calm.

"From the looks of you." Scott snorted. "Tara was as crappy a parent as she was an artist. I paid her to get rid of my mistake. For all I know, you're some other fool's—"

"You killed my mother," Wally screamed.

A bang, not as loud as yesterday, but still enormously jarring. Delia automatically looked at Glen, ensuring he'd not been shot. Satisfied, she peered around him and stared, speechless, as Scott gasped, stumbling back. A red spot slowly bloomed across his chest as he glanced down. His fingers touched his shirt before he found her gaze. "I'm the Scott..." He collapsed on the asphalt, his sightless eyes staring up.

"You're to blame, too," Wally shouted, training his bandaged hand on her. Staring at the blackened bandage, Delia knew her future with Glen was over.

Another bang.

Her screams were smothered against Glen's broad chest as he shielded her with his body.

Can't breathe. She tried to push against Glen's granite form.

"Sorry." He relaxed his hold, peering down at her, his red eyes slowly returning to their bright blue.

"Were you shot?"

"I'm good. Trammell got him. It's over, love."

She shouldn't look, but she had to see it was over. Drawing in a deep breath, Delia eased around Glen.

Edgar and Marks aimed their weapons at Wally, sprawled face down. She could see the blood soaking his back, even though he wore a black hoodie. Cade knelt, pinning Wally's bandaged arm as Trammell cut away the wrapping from his hand.

Wally's eyes slid open, and a smirk curved his lips. "I'm not a mistake. I fix mistakes. Been fixing Mommy's for years." His eyes slid closed, and he exhaled.

Trammell peeled back the bandages, revealing a small handgun. Carefully, she removed it from his slack grip.

Chapter Twenty-Nine

Glen tipped the brandy sniffer back, savoring the burn of the whiskey and the rich taste of blood. When he thought about how many times he could have lost Delia.... Did he deserve her? Didn't matter, Delia was his, and he'd kill to keep her. Bloody hell, maybe it was time to stop playing detective.

No, not until he had a head full of white hair and his eyesight was so bad, he needed a seeing-eye dog. Nope, he wasn't giving up. He'd just have to be more diligent.

"There you are." Delia's joyful voice was a soothing balm to his battered pride. "I've finished moving all my stuff into our room." She twisted her lips, staring at him. "Well, all the stuff I want to keep, anyway, and I've already called Freddie to come and get everything else. As for Gannon's gift, I placed Joe Friday in my studio. I can't believe he brought me a pet fish."

"Joe Friday? Is that what you named the Betta Gannon sent you?" Smiling, Glen held his hand out to his gorgeous mate. "I guess I'll have to start being nicer to him. Did you tell Fred what bedroom furniture you like?"

"I did, to both questions." Delia crawled onto his lap. She took the glass from him and set it on the table. "I see you're still sulking."

He wasn't sulking. He was contemplating. There *was* a difference. "How's Edna?"

"Wonderful. Whitaker took her to Edinburgh to visit some old friends. We talked briefly before she handed the phone off to your mother."

"My mum?"

Delia nodded. "She was pleased to finally speak with her new daughter, but slightly miffed you didn't ring her, telling her you're mated. She also expects us to visit for a time this summer.

Like from June through August and mentioned something about returning for the holidays."

"Let me guess, Saint Andrew's Day in November through Hogmanay." He brushed a loose strand of hair behind Delia's ear. "I'll call her later."

Delia rested her head against his shoulder. "Your mother also said for you to stop pouting."

"I'm not pouting, just trying to get my head around Tara and how she slipped under my radar. When I think how many times I nearly lost you."

"Stop it." Delia nipped his mate mark, sending a wave of pleasure coursing through him. "Tara fooled everyone all these years because of Scott." She made the sign of the cross. "I shouldn't speak ill of the dead, but he was the perfect suspect."

"Tis no' speaking ill if it's the truth." Glen claimed her lips, now needing her more than she needed him. He nipped, then sucked on her lower lip, begging for entrance.

Delia slid her delicate hands to his shoulders as she turned more fully toward him. She opened for him, drawing a moan as their tongues tangled. His daemon demanded to be a part of their passion. Apparently, his cock did as well. It throbbed, twitched, and thickened with every sigh Delia made.

He could fade them both to a more private place to worship her body. His cock and daemon thought it a brilliant idea.

A throat cleared behind them, and Delia jerked.

Slowly, Glen ended their kiss. No sense in alerting Paul to his demise. "What?"

"Trammell is here to see you."

"Bloody, friggin'—Show her in."

Delia scooted to move from him, but Glen tightened his hold, refusing to let her go. "Don't want Trammell to think I'm happy to see her." He twitched his cock, driving home his meaning.

His sexy mate laughed and slid from his lap. "Don't be rude."

"Yes, ma'am." He grinned and stood. "Good evening, Agent Trammell." He held out his hand.

Her firm grip didn't surprise him. The darkness oozing from her did. "The information I want to share…. I thought it best to drop by and tell you personally."

"Please sit." He motioned to where he'd been sitting and sat beside Delia on the settee. "Can we offer you something to drink?"

"No, thank you." Trammell's gaze briefly landed on his empty glass. Glen didn't need to read her mind to know she was composing her thoughts. Whatever she was about to reveal truly disturbed her.

Paul, would you bring a glass of rosé for Delia and a glass of whiskey for Trammell?

On my way.

Trammell straightened her back and exhaled. "I'm not sure where to begin. The last seventy-two have been intense. As you know, Walter made it out of surgery. Once he was coherent, he wanted to confess."

Paul strode out onto the porch carrying a tray with three glasses. "Agent Trammel." He held out a glass of whiskey.

She reached for it, pausing halfway. "If I take this," she met Glen's and Delia's gaze. "It's Deneen."

"Deneen, then." Glen nodded.

She took the glass, lifting it to her lips for a long sip. "Damn, this is the good stuff."

"Only the best," Delia assured her.

"As I was saying," Trammell continued. "Walter Haynes said he would only confess to Marks and me. We recorded his confession. He and his mother were responsible for thirty-two assaults, resulting in six murders over thirty years."

Delia gripped Glen's hand. "Six murders," she repeated.

Deneen nodded. "He described in detail what they did to anyone they saw as a hindrance to Tara getting back with Scott.

Apparently, she began stalking him in college. That's when he first started having relations with her.

"Walter told us where to find his and Tara's diaries. They're extremely detailed, including gruesome drawings. The diaries also listed the longitude and latitude of where they disposed of the bodies. We hope to close out several missing persons' cases."

Delia gasped. "Is one of them Amy?"

"We've given the detective in charge of her case the information. I'm sure it will give the family closure once her remains are recovered."

Glen had been down this same road before. Killers confess, offering bits and pieces of information to avoid a death sentence. "You seem confident he's telling the truth."

"I am." Trammell tossed back the last of her drink. She didn't even flinch from the burn. "According to the diaries, Tara was responsible for the explosion during the art show in Monterey. She also set the fire at the community center. Her first victims were her parents. They objected to her dating an older man. Everything she did was well scripted and planned. Dates, times, what her victims' last words were." Trammell grimaced.

"As for what happened in Atlanta, Tara saw on the news that some criminals wore black hoodies and Halloween masks when committing crimes to conceal their identities. She copied that idea."

Delia leaned forward, setting her glass on the table. "She was the one who pushed me, not Scott. Why come after me now?"

"Oh, your ex wasn't innocent. According to her diary entry, they ran into each other at a gallery. She returned with him to his hotel room. According to the date, it was the week before your attack."

"Figures." Delia took a sip of wine.

Mo gràdh?

I'm good. I need to hear this. We both do. "Let me guess," Delia continued. "Scott told Tara they could be together if he didn't have a baby on the way."

"I'm afraid so. Miss. Parsons—"

"Delia. If you're Deneen, I'm Delia." Her hand shook as she sat down her glass.

"Delia, then. It's my theory that you were no longer a target after your divorce until he moved back here and sued you. Whoever dated him, was involved in any legal issues, or gave him a bad review of his art, became her focus. The Oregon police are looking into the disappearance of a local art critic. Like I said, she and her son detailed everything." Trammell met Glen's eyes and exhaled. "The night he shot at you shouldn't have happened that way. According to the diaries, Wally was to pick a fight with you, then shoot you both in the parking lot."

"He would have been dead before firing the first round." Glen would have ripped the bastard's head off.

"I think he realized it once he found out you owned the place and your people provide security."

"Is that everything?" he asked, not wanting Delia upset anymore.

Trammell held up a finger. "One more thing."

Fuck.

Her attention darted between Delia and him. "You don't have to worry about Walter coming after you."

"Why is that?" Glen was hearing a big but and not liking it.

"During his transfer, he somehow got hold of a weapon and slit his own throat. Anyway, as far as your aunt goes, she doesn't need to return to the States." Trammell stood. "Good night. I'll see myself out."

"Deneen," Paul motioned toward the door. "Are you a dog or cat person?"

She laughed, following him. "Wouldn't you like to know?"

Delia exhaled. "Are they mates?"

"No, Cade and he have a bet about who can get the most information out of her." Glen stood, then swung Delia up into his arms.

"What are you doing?"

He carried her into the house and up the stairs. "Taking care of my mate." He continued to their room. His pace only slowed when he reached the closed bathroom door.

"Glen?"

"I'm going to prepare you a hot bath to relax." He pressed a rough kiss to her lips as he opened the door. "No argument."

It was a bloody good thing Rose had replaced the standard garden tub with a massive soaker tub. Now he had a decision to make, strip his mate, or prepare her a bath? This was about her. He slid Delia down his front until her feet touched the marble floor. "Why don't you get out of your clothes while I draw your bath?"

He leaned over the tub, twisting the knobs until water gushed from the faucet. Glen fought the urge to watch Delia strip. If he did, he'd take her against the bathroom wall or the cold marble floor like he had this morning. Instead, he checked the water temperature, not wanting it too hot. He added her favorite bath salts, lavender, and rosemary. Standing, he drew a deep breath and extended his hand to her. "Damn, you're beautiful."

"One of us has on too many clothes."

He shook his head, ignoring the need and desire burning in Delia's eyes as she stepped into the tub.

"Isn't sex supposed to be an affirmation of life? After what Trammel spewed, I need all the life-affirming sex you can give me."

"No." He kept his voice firm despite his daemon's growl. This was about Delia, not him.

She rolled out her bottom lip. "Fine, I'll get that box I wouldn't allow you to open. It contains a bunch of toys."

He let his daemon shred his clothes, then climbed into the tub. Delia laughed until he lifted her, then sank into the water, sloshing a good deal from the tub. He'd get it later. He had more important things to do than worry about a wet floor. With his back resting against the curve of the tub, he positioned Delia so she straddled him. "Do you want me, *mo gràdh?*"

"Always." She slid down his length, taking him fully inside her warmth.

"Then take me and give yourself to me."

She did. Several times.

When his bones were no longer jelly, he carried her to their bed and gently lowered her.

Delia caught his hand. "So, when are we leaving for Scotland?"

Epilogue

Delia took a deep, calming breath as she looked out over the crowd. This was unlike any unveiling she'd had before. This one was personal on so many levels. Smiling, Delia searched the group for her mate, her husband, the one person who'd promised to help, without finding him anywhere. *Glen, where are you?*

Trying to round up the kids.

"What has your knickers in a twist?" Edna asked. "This is a celebration, but you look like you're at a wake?"

"I was hoping Glen would be here to help me, Aunt Edna."

"He's trying to wrangle your bairns, though he'd have more success wrangling cats."

Angelique, Glen's mom, strode toward them. "Breathe, Delia. Everything will be fine. The children enjoy playing in the sun and getting to know one another, though Lachlan must learn he can't do everything he sees his cousins do. At least he hasn't taken a header from the battlement like George or hiked his kilt and whizzed on the roses like little Ian."

"Yet," Delia added with a laugh.

This was the first time the children had visited Scotland. She and Glen had talked about adoption. Then everything fell into place, and they'd been blessed with two highly energetic little ones. Lachlan ten and three-year-old Wren—" Where's Wren?"

"She's with the girls," Edna replied. "Angie, I think you spoke too soon."

Delia followed Edna's pointed finger to the castle's battlement, where Glen and Lachlan crouched in their Dhampiric forms with Ethan and Michael. "Oh, for the love of—*Glen*!"

Don't panic. Ethan and Michael dared Lachlan to attempt free-fading. We'll be there in a moment.

Use the stairs!

Mom! Lachlan's voice echoed through Delia's mind. *Dad said he'd do it with me.*

Lachlan!

He and Glen vanished, reappearing a second later, strolling toward her. Glen ruffled Lachlan's hair, laughing.

"Hey," she shouted, trying to keep the laughter from her voice. "Your skirt is hiked up."

"Tis a kilt, woman." Glen ran toward her, scooping her up in his arms and kissing her. "Good thing I'm wearing bike shorts," he whispered against her ear.

Ian, Glen's father, smacked him on the back, causing Glen to stumble. "Aye, that's for sure, lad."

"A little harder next time, Da." Glen set Delia on her feet, keeping his arm around her waist.
She leaned against him, soaking up his warmth.

"Mated life has made ye soft, lad." Ian chuckled.

"Mommy," Wren shouted, toddling toward them, carrying Tabatha. "Mommy, I want a pretty kitty."

Chase rolled to his feet in pursuit, waving a change of clothes, as his brother Cade laughed. Stacy, Chase's mate, sat on a blanket with Victoria, shaking their heads and laughing at the scene.

"Mommy." Wren shifted Tabatha to her shoulder. "Can I keep kitty?"

"Wren, set Tabby down so she can shift." Eighteen months ago, Delia would have never thought such a thing possible. Now shifting, fading, daemon, and flying were normal, as walking, talking, and eating. "Wren, I'll not tell you again."

"Hey, Lachlan, think fast." A soccer ball hurtled past Delia's head.

Lachlan bounced the ball, sending it flying back to Ethan.

Her daughter's plump bottom lip rolled out as her pale hazel eyes peered through thick lashes, an expression she'd quickly learned from Hope and Kimber.

The wind whipped Wren's unruly brown curls around her face as her hair bow dangled from Tabby's neck. "But kitty."

"Now," Delia warned.

"Fine." Wren huffed, setting Tabby on the ground.

Chase held out the tiny dress. "Young lady, time to put your clothes on."

The tiny mountain lion cub hissed and swatted at the dress.

"I'd say that was a no." Glen chuckled.

"I want to be a kitty." Wren tugged on Glen's kilt. "Make me a kitty."

"You no kitty," Tabby said, fighting her dad's attempt to dress her. "You flutter-fly."

"I flutter-fly!" Wren's wings unfolded as her horns erupted from her forehead, curling back over her head. She was air-born, giggling and chasing Tabby, who was back in her fur.

Chase once again pursued the girls.

Delia sighed and shook her head. As much as she wanted this unveiling to be perfect, watching her children laughing and playing with their cousins made it perfect.

"Sorry, *mo gràdh.*" Glen bussed her crown, tucking her under his arm.

Ian eyed the draped-covered statue Glen had commissioned over eighteen months ago. "Ye know lad, ye didna have ta do this."

Glen shrugged. "All I did was ask Delia. She's the one who sculpted it."

"Weel, I think tis time we all see what a fine piece she's made." Ian cupped his mouth and bellowed, "Ye all gather around, so says the MacPhee."

Everyone, the entire family, young and old alike, stopped what they were doing and gathered around. No one made a sound as they awaited Ian's ensuing words. Slipping his arm around Angelique's waist, he nodded to Glen.

Glen smiled, looking at his parents. "Eighteen months ago, dressed in a cheesy outfit, I found my true mate."

Chuckles and laughter filled the air.

"I can only pray that Delia and I have the same mating as my parents." Glen gripped the heavy drape.

Delia twisted her hands nervously behind her back, waiting in anticipation.

"Happy anniversary." Glen yanked, pulling the drape to the ground. "Even if it is a tad late," he muttered.

Ian gasped, and Angelique stood silent, her trembling hand coming to her lips as dark red tears spilled from her eyes.

Delia's anticipation quickly veered to panic. "I'm so—"

"It's beautiful," Angelique sobbed, reaching out to Delia. "When did you pick this memory?" She hugged Delia, stealing her breath.

The roar of cheers and applause nearly drowned out her voice.

"When you came to visit us in Atlanta the first time. Glen wanted something special, and when you told me how you and Ian met, I saw this image in your mind."

"It was the morning after our mating, the day of our handfast. I love it. I'd just told Ian as Dhampir I carried his bairn."

"Aye, tis a magnificent piece, especially the fine abs you gave me." Ian chuckled, wrapping Delia and Angelique in a bear hug. "I can no' believe the motion in it. I can nearly see us spinning and the wind in my lady's hair."

"Aye," Angelique agreed. She pulled from Ian's embrace and then ran her fingers over the fold of the statue's kilt. "I can no' believe the detail."

"Nor I." Ian nodded. "Delia, lass, you have the pattern of the MacPhee plaid perfect."

"Thank you." Never again. It'd taken her more hours to perfect the tartan plaid than it did the expressions on Ian's and Angelique's faces.

***

Delia watched Lachlan play soccer with the rest of the children as Wren slept with her head on Delia's lap. She tugged the wool blanket over Wren, protecting her from the chilly wind coming from the sea.

"Where's Dad?" Lachlan asked, dropping beside them. "He said he wanted me to see something."

Delia squeezed his hand and nodded toward the cliff. "He's piping down the sun."

"He's what?"

Standing on the cliff, Glen's silhouette was striking, dressed in his kilt with his bagpipes. The plaintive tune he played echoed over the sound of crashing waves as the sun set, signaling the end of a joyous day. However, this was only the beginning of their long lives together, filled with happiness, the family she'd always wanted, and a love to last the ages.

Other Books in the Crimson Series

Crimson Dreams

Crimson Hearts

Crimson Moon

Crimson Dawn

Crimson Haze

Crimson Shores

A Chaotic Crimson Christmas, a Novella

Crimson Nights

Coming Soon

Crimson Secrets

About the Author:

2019 winner of the Georgia Independent Author of the Year for Romance. Georgiana Fields was born in coastal North Carolina. She spent her summers along the Atlantic Coast, where she developed a love for the ocean, nature, and coastal ghost stories and legends. As a child, she enjoyed listening to her aunts tell and retell stories and myths surrounding New Bern, N.C., and other coastal towns.

Georgiana currently resides in North Georgia with her husband, two dogs, and two cats. While she loves nature, horseback riding, and scary movies, she spends most of her time writing paranormal romance and suspense, where strong women sometimes don't know their own strength.

Connect with Georgiana:

https://georgianafields.com/

https://www.facebook.com/AuthorGeorgianaFields/

https://www.instagram.com/fieldsgeorgiana/

https://twitter.com/georgianafields

https://www.goodreads.com/AuthorGeorgianaFields

If you'd like an autograph for your e-book purchase, contact me through Authorgraph! http://www.authorgraph.com

www.ingramcontent.com/pod-product-compliance
Lightning Source LLC
Chambersburg PA
CBHW030557180626
46816CB00005B/1584